THREE O'CLOCK DINNER

BY

JOSEPHINE PINCKNEY

The Viking Press, New York

1945

To Alice Huntington

Three o'Clock Dinner

Book I

JUDITH REDCLIFF floated up from the timeless and bottomless world of sleep, feeling its monstrous landscape swing away and fall before the yellow ray that pierced the eastern shutters. For a split moment she rejoiced to come out of those larger than life valleys into the safe habitations of her room and early morning; then the punctual dread hung there again above her healthy awakening. Grudgingly she allowed herself to recognize what shadow it was the dark wings cast, though heaven knew it should be instant as her own shadow by this time, for she had waked to its inexorable presence every morning since the death of Fen, her husband, two years ago. By now she should be used to grief as a bedfellow, she thought heavily, to that visceral sensation of impending ill that preceded her daily return to the half-living of widowhood.

Meanwhile her native earth in its passage was evenly spinning its own time which began to take her in its coils, and she rolled over and looked at her watch. A little after six. She rolled on her back again and stretched, burying her fingers in her sleep-tangled hair. She liked to wake early—there would be time to do some work in the garden before the sun climbed too high and Sarah, the cook, came and put on the coffee.

She got up and walked with a slight limp to the window that looked toward the back of the lot. As she rolled up the shade the sugarberry tree outside shone in her eyes like a lamp still burning. The window, facing west, stood in deep shadow, but the clotted young leaves beyond dipped into the stream of light gushing silently between her house and the next. It was the special morning effect of cities, she thought, her heart lifting again, these sharp golden clefts between dark perpendiculars. In the kitchen yard below, Rags, her terrier, snuffed the damp ground inch by inch.

with such singleness of enjoyment that Judith felt a stab of envy at his miraculous ability to come out each day to his narrow domain and find it fresh and delicious.

Beyond his barricade the garden posed like a period piece in such a stillness; about the grassplot the branches hung down in scallops and formed Gothic grottoes, ornaments of fabricated stone that aped the landscape of northern Europe. The terracotta bulges of the garden cushions, even the big earth-red jars at the four corners of the rectangle, looked overstuffed, absurd; and eager to stir this sleep-bound air, Judith turned back and hurried into her gardening sandals and an old blue linen dress. She grumbled over the job of combing and tying up her thick, unmanageable hair and half-resolved to whack it off, but though she didn't care much about clothes—for she considered herself plainer than she really was and consequently spent little time before the mirror—she knew short hair was not her style, which was tallish and inclined to be angular. When people told her, as they occasionally did, that she had a good figure, she didn't believe them, especially now that she was a little lame, so the compliment surprised her perpetually and left her tongue-tied.

She went down the steps into the hushed hall. The furniture still stood kneedeep in night and sleep, but at the opening of the front door the day rushed in; the mahogany table, the lamp, the silver cardtray sprang to life, and Rags, hearing her hand on the latch, began to claw and clamor at his prison gate. Judith sped to let him out before he should rouse the neighborhood, and they pawed at each other with a wholly uncritical enthusiasm. Presently she drew on her loose gloves and glanced about the garden, shaken to its corners now by doggish antics. How scraggly the annuals looked since the bloom was passing! She started down the border, angrily jerking out the yellow stalks and making her clippers fly. Her body dipped and rose in an easy rhythm, her thin brown fingers dealt confidently with plants as she herself did not with human kind; she pounced on the snails without ruth and trampled them in a sort of grisly dance.

"Well, how does your garden grow?" said a pleasant voice behind her, and she looked over her shoulder to see Bob Turner coming out of the servants' quarters at the back of her house, his baby son hanging on to his finger. After Fen's death she had turned the little brick building, whose steep slate roof shimmered sweetly now with pigeon colors, into a separate house for renting, partly because she needed the money and partly for company. And how lucky she had been to get the Turners, a likable couple near her own age, who had come South in search of a quiet place to write their short stories.

"Mary, I can see, is quite contrary this morning—"

She sat back on her heels. "The man who wrote that jingle was no gardener or he wouldn't have asked such an idiotic question. Look at that flowerbed; everything in it is blooming when it shouldn't. Did you ever see such a nasty combination of reds and pinks?" She pulled off her gloves and held out her arms to the child who ran to her. "I can't imagine," she hurried on to cover the greedy physical pleasure she had from holding the child in her arms, "what arrant sentimentalist started the story that flowers are sweet and innocent. They're the most rancorous, cantankerous, ungrateful creatures. And you writers spread the lie—"

"Come on, Bobby!" exclaimed Turner, seizing the boy's arm. "Let's clear out of this before our heads get snipped off and rolled out in the wheelbarrow. We writers have to make our stories pretty or people like you won't buy them." Under his banter, as if they carried on two conversations at once, he was offering her discernment and pity, so when he said, "Shall I leave Bobby with you for a little while?" she didn't know that he had changed the subject.

"Of course," she said, embarrassed to have exposed her infatuation, and hid her face in the child's fine-spun yellow topknot. Bob went off down the path declaiming (to cover her confusion), "The percolator just blew up and I have to help Manya, or the Turners will go without breakfast." No, airiness didn't sit naturally on him; he was too lanky to flap his arms like that.

Manya too understood her fervid envy of their child and was distrustful—not generous with him like Bob; so when Bobby began to wriggle in her clutch, Judith dropped her arms listlessly and let him go. He circled the grassplot in his yellow sunsuit, running in short spurts, making a tentative acquaintance with balance, gravity, and motion; he waved his plump arms and uttered seductive syllables. Watching his infant grace, Judith tried to shake off the reproach that dogs the childless woman. Her belligerence against the snails collapsed; she hunted about for her trowel under

[3]

the litter spread by her pruning, and knelt down by the herb bed. Pulling out the weeds, getting her fingers into the fresh-turned leafmold, brought her an inexplicable ease; the beebalm and dusty miller sent up a penetrating and curative aroma—no wonder the ancients had such faith in the healing power of herbs.

Pulling up the last tuft of grass from the bed, she rose and began to gather the stalks and lopped branches and pile them in the wheelbarrow. But Fen's death, she couldn't help thinking, had robbed her twice in leaving her no witness in flesh and blood that he had loved her. For Fen's falling in love with her had been a miracle, a constant source of astonishment to her and (she was aware) to their friends as well. With his good looks, confidence, his general ease and well-being, he was one of the gay ones of the earth and could have had his pick of the marriageable girls. And he had chosen Judith who was plain and shy, unready with her tongue, not popular in the social sense. In five years of marriage it had never become less miraculous.

To be beloved—and then to be denuded of love. How could the human constitution endure that violent change of climate? Judith stood aloof, lost from the garden, her head bent, her brain receiving no message from the pruned branch she held in her hand.

The new leaves of the loquat branch were pale green and plushy with fine silver hair. They grew in a tuft against the dark blue-green of old leaves which were coarsely cleft with veins, and at length their subtle form and contrast invaded her eye; she blinked at the branch as if rising from sleep, she saw it in her hand, and at the same time she saw the bubble-prison she lived in. I must learn to take pleasure again from the world, she thought, discouraged, to enjoy a leaf without making it serve my desire—for the moment she perceived the branch she had wanted to show it to Fen. Look, she had almost cried out, how beautifully loquat leaves grow, like a bouquet—compelling him to share her discovery. She looked hard at the branch, trying to admire it purely, when her self-discipline was interrupted by a voice: "Miss Judith, your breakfas' mos' ready." Above the kitchen fence Sarah's face hung like a bronze of Bacchus wreathed in vines.

Judith started and looked guiltily round for her charge. Bobby had jammed a stick in the lawnmower and managed to break a small but useful pin. "Bobby, you'll hurt yourself!" She rescued the child but was too late for the lawnmower which refused to budge. Judith bustled him toward the little house. Bob and Manya were sitting down to their orange juice when she opened the screen door and pushed him in. "Here—take your treasure; he's just wrecked my lawnmower, to say nothing of my nervous system. I really didn't mean to keep him so long, but when I get to weeding and pruning, my time sense just washes out."

"Good morning," said Manya coming forward and taking the child. She wore thin green silk pajamas and her black hair was sleek and close-cropped. "You're the most energetic woman, Judith, with your early gardening."

"If you slack off for a week in this climate, the jungle swallows you; I wish you could see the weeds." Under the empty trivialities with which human beings feel obliged to dissemble silence, Judith apprehended the picture before her—the parents receiving their child, the sun on the tablecloth and beflowered china owned in common. The air of the little room was warm, but less with summer, it seemed to Judith, than with the cheerful relaxation of people still trustful of life.

"I have to bustle along," she said, backing awkwardly out of the door. "I have to get a shower and breakfast and be at the office by nine." She crossed the back yard saying to herself, I have had the incredible happiness of being married to Fen; I mustn't repine because it couldn't last forever; I must be thankful that I had it.

Rags did his best to thwart her haste by planting himself in front of her feet while his nose made an enraptured inventory of the path. He was far from handsome; indeed, he had acquired his descriptive name from Judith's uncle-in-law, Lucian Redcliff, who teased her by saying he looked like the rag-tag and bobtail of all the breeds. But Rags had the gamin charm of the cur, and now his wholehearted sensuality began to affect her heavy spirit; half-unconsciously she drew a deep breath and gave heed to the testimony of her own nose, to the warm harbor water, to the whole complex of smells that was summer in Charleston—heavy salt, pluff mud, oleanders, and drains. Charlestonians harped on the pluff mud—"smells sort of like sulphur, you know"—and denied the drains, but at this season Judith was not exhibiting the town to tourists, so she acknowledged a whiff of drain as she turned toward the street on an impulse to savor more vividly this pungent and familiar medley before the day claimed her.

Judith's small house stood with its gable-end to the sidewalk. She went with Rags along the flagged side piazza which was shut off from the street by an enclosing façade. Through this the front door gave directly on the pavement, and Judith opened it and walked a little way to the beginning of High Battery, the sea wall that ran along the town's eastern boundary to the tip of the peninsula where the Ashley and Cooper Rivers met and, according to official sources, formed the Atlantic Ocean. Judith passed the last house and walked out on the sea wall. She stood by the railing and leaned out a little to meet the early wind that bathed her brown, sleep-walker's face like running water. The glow had faded from the eastern sky but the tiny-rippled harbor held a cast of violet in its sea-blue. The furled sailboats by the Yacht Club hung rapt on the tide in a late morning sleep; they hurt her because of Fen who had been almost a sea centaur . . . and now, as if the wind had changed, the harbor drifted off a little, became the backdrop of a lost rapture, a place where she and Fen had sailed together, she holding the tiller usually, while he ran about the small sailboat like a cat on his rubber soles, coiling the ropes and making every-thing shipshape. If only you'd take half as much trouble about the house, she used to say to him. But he never would, except when some carpentering job would strike his fancy and absorb him for a while. After his death Judith sold the *Skimmer*, and this necessity had closed to her a whole field of pleasures, of following seductive creeks and landing on new-found beaches.

The climbing sun blinded her; through half-shut eyes she saw the sky and water purple-darkened, the way they had looked that last time Fen came home. She locked her fingers round the iron balustrade as she felt herself slipping off in the current of fantasy. Below her the harbor lapped at the jagged stones that stuck out from the sea wall like the huge feet of the gods that stand at our backs, dealing out fate. But character is fate, the stone gods only carry out what we ourselves begin, she thought with sinking heart; revolving smoothly, they push acts that seem small in our near-sighted vision through to their monstrous conclusions.

Thus, Fen had been irritated with her that dreadful day. She saw —as if it had been another's and not her own heart's flesh that the

[6]

gods were beginning to grind—their room as it had been two years ago with its twin beds, though she was sleeping momentarily in the guest room because of Fen's cold. The cold had kept him in bed for two or three days, but that Friday he was up and about, expecting to go to the office next day. And having some time on his hands, he had decided to rearrange his chest of drawers, to sort the fish hooks and photographs from the shirts and shorts. He had pulled all the drawers open to shuffle his belongings more handily, and had gone for a moment into the next room to paste some loose photographs into his album, when Judith came blithely up from the garden with a vase of rain lilies for his bedside table. She saw the drawers open at different angles and thought, he's gone off and forgotten about them, and she slammed them all shut with a single exuberant shove. The clatter brought Fen to the door with the glue pot in his hand. "Hey, what the hell— What's the idea when I was just getting my stuff straight?"

"Oh, Fen—I didn't realize—"

"What have you got a head for? Did you think I'd opened these drawers to catch rainwater?"

"I'm terribly sorry, darling," she said, wanting to laugh and also wanting to cry because he could hurt her very easily.

"Well, for God's sake leave my chest of drawers alone!" He banged the glue pot down and stalked over to the chest; with ostentatious care he opened each drawer to the exact angle it had stood at before and tenderly replaced the contents. His narrow back was eloquent with outraged ownership.

All through the midday meal he was sulky while she waited for the tempest to blow over and tried to think what made the little incident so unaccountably annoying to him. The climax, perhaps, of a long string of small irritations running through their common life. Was she oblivious to his little interests? For even loving a person with your whole heart, you were often thoughtless of him. Or was it a male revolt against a woman's hands on his belongings for which he had his private plans? Or was it the simple physical reaction of his nerves to the fever and the aching bones?

Hopefully she grasped at this last explanation; and when after dinner he said he thought he'd go out on the boat for a while, she only said mildly, "Do you think you are well enough?" Of course he was, he answered testily; anyway he wouldn't stay long and the sun might help his cold. So the gods had started their grinding, and she, poor blind fool, had not seen, had not smelt the dire risk. Because she loved more than he did, she was loath to cross him; and perhaps the beautiful hot June weather would burn away his annoyance with her. The quarrel filled her mind when the good fear that warns of danger should have made her throw herself on him and say, "Don't go!" What folly, what timidity could have so dulled her instincts!

Fen called up Bob Turner, who was free to go with him, and presently they were setting off cheerfully in their duck pants. Fen took a look at the barometer as he went out. She had given it to him the first Christmas after they were married, and not knowing much then about barometers, she had casually ordered it from a Christmas catalogue. At first Fen had been polite, but by the next summer, when he was teaching her to sail, he had teased her about it, amiably enough, though he would thump it angrily when he wanted the weather to clear so he could go sailing. It was really just as good as the most expensive barometer, he would say, because if it read "wet" you could count on a fine day, and if it read "dry" you could expect a downpour and needn't water the grass. It was a typically female barometer, he would pronounce, grinning at her, while she felt foolish and tried not to get her feelings hurt.

So he had glanced at it that Friday as he went along the piazza and it was down from "dry," so he said "Nuts!" and gave it a passing thump. How little she had dreamed when she bought it that she was buying fate and should have mortgaged all she had to get the best! And so none of them had seen the shadow of the future racing forward like the long cone of an eclipse.

It must have been two hours later that the unnatural dusk in the room made her book suddenly hard to read. She jumped up and went out to look at the barometer which now said "stormy," and this time its word was supported by the dark green sky that pressed down on the rooftops. She walked out to the end of High Battery and searched the harbor. A few moth-like sails hung pallid against the far shore; the air around her was still, but in the middle distance broad wrinkled wedges scuffed the calm water. She went back to the house and called her father-in-law and told him that Fen was out in the *Skimmer*. He seemed startled. Though he said, "Oh,

[8]

they'll probably weather it all right," she knew he was alarmed. Next she called Manya (the Turners were living elsewhere then), but Manya was out. As she turned away from the telephone the squall broke on the town; the lashing rain and the wind in the torrential branches lifted her heart into her throat. Before their fury had abated, Mr. Redcliff and his brother Lucian came to take her to the Yacht Club, where Manya and one or two other wives were already gathering for news. Judith went out on the rainswept piazza of the club and stood by herself, her whole bodily mechanism paralyzed with dread. The ugly colored water filled the world with its collective menace to sailors' wives.

But Fen was not taken from her then. After a while Mr. Redcliff, who had been sweeping the harbor with a telescope, came up to her and said quietly, "There's a snipe boat coming along the Battery there to the right." Judith seized the telescope, but she was too tremulous to hold it steady, and it was the sharp-eyed Lucian who positively identified the *Skimmer*. She and Manya and the Redcliff brothers were at the head of the dock when it came up. Bob Turner was bailing; the torn sail flapped but still had enough spread to keep headway before the squally gusts. Fen stood on the afterdeck with the sheet in his hand; his open shirt flapped with the sail, his red hair, darkened by the rain, was plastered down except for a small crest that stood up unbowed. He guided the tiller with one bare foot and as he smiled up at Judith from the tossing deck, his face was flushed with secret joy in his brush with the elements.

Judith held on to the rail for strength under her insupportable gratitude. Even when he came up the ladder and threw his arms around her, she scarcely dared believe it; his wet cheek against her lips seemed to have kept the cold of the grudging seabottoms. She pulled herself together and bustled him home through the hubbub of greetings and questions. "The wind hit us off Quarantine. . . ." ". . . like bolt from the blue. . . ." "I never saw such a thing. . . ." "Come home, Fen, and get on some dry clothes— you can talk about it afterward." Mr. Redcliff, shaken but beaming, put an arm about each and pushed them along. "Get him to bed and give him a hot toddy. I'll stay here at the club until the other boats come in."

Judith rubbed Fen down and, in spite of his protests, called the doctor. He felt fine, he insisted. Judith needed a toddy herself, so she had one with him, sitting on the edge of his bed and feeling quite tight with happiness as, propped up against the pillows, he profanely described the storm. He slept quietly all night under the doctor's sedative, while she kept waking up with a sort of after-fright and listened in the darkness to his breathing. But it was regular, familiar as night itself and as much a part of her waking consciousness. . . .

The next day Fen felt logy and a little fretful; the tussle with death had tired him, apparently. Judith's memory never recaptured the details of the interval that followed; the next thing she remembered was the smell of disinfectant and the oxygen tent and the big gleaming tanks beside Fen's hospital bed. She remembered his smiling at her through the window in the tent; and later through that same window she had seen recognition fade from his face and heard the strange gasping that she couldn't connect somehow with that other, familiar breath. . . .

Even then her mind, unschooled by loss, had not grasped the oncoming event. She had never seen the faces of the stone gods, so she couldn't imagine that her happiness was about to be cut in two by a single stroke. She was still trustful and unprepared when Mr. Redcliff came into her room next to Fen's at the hospital, where she had gone to eat a little soup, and quietly told her it had happened while she was out of the room. Physical shock had obliterated also the details of this extreme hour and had left only, as if for a last insult, the memory of the pea soup she went on trying to swallow. . . .

Judith came back with a start to the sea wall and brushed away the spindrift that had fogged her eyes. She turned her back on the Atlantic with its dragging undercurrents and allowed the row of houses facing it to engage her with their homely associations; the sun shone gay and kind on the yellow and white façades, on classic porticoes next door to opulent bay windows, the linear spirit of Greece reproving the bulges of Victorian taste. The long-handled tufted shadows of the palmettoes along the sidewalk brushed them with dignified strokes, like resplendent feather dusters in a high public housekeeping. As Judith looked down the row she felt a shock of surprise; she seemed to be seeing the town for the first time in years. Was it the emptiness of the street, or the early light, crisp, real, domestic, that was thus opening the holden eyes of grief? For so long now the world had had the bleary white look of a country seen through a train window on coming out of a tunnel.

Half an hour later she sat on a shady corner of the piazza, severely combed and clean in a light brown chambray dress of the tailored kind she habitually wore. She dawdled over her breakfast, smoking as she finished her coffee and frowning at the *News and Courier*. The news from Europe was bad. Jaw-breaking Czech names filled the dispatches, a group of prominent Senators pled for peace and an end to this mad race for armaments. At home the campaign for state offices raged in the land. The candidates were stumping the county seats, putting on a show for the crossroads audience. Everybody was for economy and for the common man and for law and order, though at Mullins they bloodied each other's noses and three women fainted. . . .

The street door opened and slammed, and Judith looked up to see her father-in-law coming down the piazza, followed by his son, Tat.

Fenwick Redcliff was in his late fifties. Thinning hair and a fine skin drawn tightly over the bones of his face made his head look small on top of his tall, white-suited figure. Not clever, the family said about Wick, no intellectual giant, but a swell fellow—a pippin —a sweetie—or whatever their current catchword was for expressing enthusiasm. Judith said he was a perfect lamb, and doted on him.

"Hello, my dear," he said, sitting down beside her with his Panama in his hand. "Today is going to be a scorcher unless all signs fail."

"Good morning, Uncle Wick." Judith had long since adopted, to escape the formality of "Mr. Redcliff," the nickname given him by the children of the family connection. "Hello, Tat. Have some breakfast? Sarah will bring it in a minute."

"No thanks, Judy." Tat's round-arched eyebrows stamped his face with a look of perpetual slight surprise behind his spectacles, as if the world of appearances, breakfast, his sister-in-law, the sunny flagstones brought him unquenchable hope and expectancy. "As a matter of fact, I can't stay—I have to run along to the

[11]

filling station; lots of people will be out riding this kind of weather."

But he didn't move. He braced his shoulders against a pillar as if he liked its wooden solidity. His slight build gave an impression of softness except when it was tense with protest, which was most of the time, his being a generous and angry nature. He leaned back, looking uncertainly from his father to Judith, then he said, "My bus didn't come home with me last night, so I had to get a ride downtown with Dad." His smile was half sheepish, half challenging.

If he expected his father to rise to this bait he was disappointed. "I stopped in," Wick said to Judith, "to talk to you for a minute about business. You know you have a little money to be invested and we had better be thinking of what we'll do with it. What would you think of real estate?"

Judith frowned at the breakfast tray. She lazily preferred to leave the small competence Fen had left her to Mr. Redcliff's husbanding, but his question preserved a fiction that she should be consulted; so she frowned, and tried to look intelligent.

"That depends on what kind of real estate. Have you anything in mind?"

Mr. Redcliff's younger half-brother, Lucian, was in the real estate business, and it appeared he had one or two choice properties to suggest.

Judith said sagely, "In times like these real estate is probably the safest kind of investment because it can't run away."

Wick Redcliff smiled at her with one eyebrow lifted. "Sounds as if you had been listening to my pronunciamentoes. But I've recanted that one; if you're going to quote my fallacies at me you must at least keep up with the current lot. The late depression wiped out that valuable maxim of mine along with other overpriced holdings. Real estate can't run away, worse luck. But its value can, and leave you crawling around like a snail with a great house hooked to your back. We won't, however, buy you an unsalable, disintegrating hulk like ours, in an unfashionable part of town. We'll find something compact and modern—"

"Phoo!" Tat snorted. "You wouldn't sell our disintegrating hulk with its gen-u-wine Colonial atmosphere for a million bucks. Hey—what hit your lawnmower, Judith?"

"Bobby Turner. He broke it this morning. It needs one of those things—a cotter-pin, or something."

"Where's your tool kit?"

"In the tool shed," said Judith, hoping that it was, that she had remembered to put it back last time.

Tat ran across the grass to the small lean-to. His father stretched out his white linen legs and fanned himself amiably.

"Nobody with a million had better chance it. But after snapping up the million I'd probably go and buy myself another house just like ours. Most people, however, exhibit a depraved taste for small, shiny 'homes,' preferably below Broad Street, so we'll cater to their perversity in investing your money."

"Well, people like to live near their friends," Judith defended the modern age. "Everybody except for a few hard-shells like you has moved downtown to be near the water."

"Let them! That leaves more elbow room for me. One reason why I like living in the Borough—more elbow room. The Germans and the Irish and I get along quite happily in our native village—because the Borough is really still a village within a city, even if it isn't a political subdivision any more. Which gives it a fine, high reek of its own."

"A fine reek of slums and ward politics," Tat thrust in, coming back with the tool kit. He dragged the lawnmower to the edge of the piazza so he could keep his place in the talk which now had the smack of one of those family arguments that simmers perpetually like a soup kettle on the back of the stove. He emptied the box on the brick step and deftly sorted the tools.

"To be sure," his father answered. "Our politics are hot and rotten, we have the finest old houses and the most dilapidated shanties in town—and the pallid improvements of hygiene don't make up for flavor, in my opinion. So I'd miss all the life and incident in the Borough; it's a dull day when we don't have a murder, or at least a cutting scrape."

"We have murders downtown too," said Judith, "very fancy ones."

"That's true, but not as many as we do; you don't get the same choice. Take a look at the morning paper."

"I've been looking at it and I wish I knew a little more about this campaign. I don't hear much talk about politics now."

It's a half-world I live in, she thought, a woman's world, clean split as half an apple. The hour of the day when Fen came home from the Cooper River Drydock Company had been for her a corridor through which she passed into his hemisphere. For Fen was a direct creature, he poured out to her whatever his mind had gathered during the day, the progress of the ship they were building, the gossip that blew up and down Broad Street. . . .

She came back guiltily to Wick Redcliff's acid comments on the candidates and realized she had missed the answer to her question. But apparently it didn't matter. ". . . so local politics is a dispiriting game," he was saying. "There aren't any issues to fight for, there are only personalities."

"If we could just get a real live labor movement started here—" Tat abandoned the pliers, his body sprang to life—"then we'd have some issues worth talking about."

"That's assuming that the labor unions would take a more intelligent interest in government than the rank and file," his father said. "But after all, labor *is* the rank and file. Look here, son, hadn't you better be going along to your job? You're late already."

Judith had been watching Tat with a secret, maternal pride. He handled the tools smoothly, the lawnmower began to purr under his quick ministrations. Darling Tat; it was like old times to see him there doing odd jobs for her. He used not to be so quick—he wasn't by nature the kind that did things well with his hands, but his work at the filling station had trained him, or rather he had trained himself by a hard discipline, she perceived, to make edges fit, to make parts come together and stay put.

Feeling that he was being dismissed, Tat hitched his coat up on his shoulders and buttoned it with a touch of sulkiness. As his garment of flesh took shape from his spirit, his rumpled seersucker suit seemed to follow the curve of his revolt against the trivial convention of neatness—how complacent, his clothes were always saying, how idiotic to be groomed like a circus horse when the world is on fire with wars and famines, with cruelty and injustice. Suits that were always taking up arms for lost causes had no time to be dawdling in a pressing club.

He ran the lawnmower back and forth to test it and also, Judith thought, to let its mechanical racket make the loud retort he would have liked to give his father.

[14]

"Personally, I wish you'd stick around," she said hastily. "You're a wizard, Tat; you fixed that in no time. What I need in my life is a smart young mechanic to keep the place going."

"What you need in your life is some decent tools. God—if this isn't a typical female tool kit!"

But his gruffness was merely false whiskers. Besides he had borrowed it straight from Fen—that kind of remark in that very tone of voice. He had never quite shaken free of his youthful ambition to pattern himself on his older brother. The little revelation touched her.

"Well," he said, "I'll be toddling along. Oh . . . can I borrow your tango records, Judith? I have a little party on tonight and we need some more dance music."

"Help yourself. What kind of party?"

"Don't ask indiscreet questions," he said, delighted to have baited her into asking. "It might upset the family if I gave the particulars. My friends aren't registered Sacred Cows."

"Anybody that loves bull the way you do ought to like cows!" His father flapped the open fronts of his coat in irritable dismissal of the subject.

"Well, I don't. And they needn't parade their Sacred Heifers in the marriage market for my benefit—it just disgusts me."

"All men come to the marriage market, as to the grave. The women demand it—"

"I know some that don't! At least—" Tat came to a dead stop. Both men looked at Judith for a moment, hoping she would say something to fill the awkward pause.

"I'm not going to get into *this* family cutting scrape!" she exclaimed. "The records are in the living room, Tat. Take whatever you like. The Meyer Davis ones are good."

Tat disappeared indoors and came out in a moment with the black discs under his arm. "Thanks, Judith, these will be O.K. Well, so long. Don't waste too much time over that investment; the sharks will skin you anyway, going or coming." He gave them a quick, sharp grin and went off.

Wick looked thoughtfully after him for a minute and then came back to local politics. "I don't know how we came to such an unhealthy pass," he fretted. "Any issues would be welcome. But locally there's no death grapple between capitalism and so-

[15]

cialism, between free silver and sound money, we have neither radicals nor conservatives—"

"Aren't you overlooking Tat?" asked Judith, smiling. "He would certainly take exception to that remark."

"I suppose I am. As the Radical Party of South Carolina he is commonly overlooked, I'm afraid. Though actually he doesn't let me forget him for long, and to tell you the truth, I was hoping he'd leave so I could talk to you a little about him." He suddenly looked self-conscious and distressed, and Judith thought, this is what he really came here for, the investment was a pretext. "I hoped you could give me an idea of what he's up to."

"No," said Judith. "I don't see Tat very often, except when I run into him somewhere. He doesn't like my friends much."

Wick Redcliff looked off into the sun-soaked garden, holding his Panama up to shield his face from the glare, or perhaps from Judith's curious eyes. "Did he have our attractive neighbor with him when you ran into him?"

"Lorena Hessenwinkle? No, he didn't; but I know he goes with her a lot. Do you think he meant her—just now?" She paused, gathering up scattered details in her mind and trying to fit them around a picture of Lorena; but they were like snapshots, memories of the moment only, without depth or continuity. The Hessenwinkles were a noisy and numerous family in the Borough whose house stood back to back with the Redcliffs'. Judith, on her visits to her in-laws, had often passed Lorena walking on the Mall of a Sunday, a tall girl, usually smiling about her, smartly but rather loudly dressed. The Hessenwinkle children came over to the Redcliffs' on errands of one sort or another, and generally pervaded the sidewalk before the gate in their Indian suits and their red tin wagons.

There were those stories about Lorena. . . . She was supposed to have thrown water on the wife of Mr. Belchers, the department-store owner, when that lady came to remonstrate about the frequency of Lorena's telephone calls to her husband. And there on the front lawn was an expensive set of garden furniture with a row of wooden geese, right out of Belchers and Co.'s show window. And the other stories—Judith couldn't remember. But Tat always got furious when people gossiped about her; he said she had a right to sexual freedom, but the Belchers story just wasn't true—that she was really a swell girl, kindhearted and full of fun, the old cats were just jealous of her looks and independence; and knowing what claws gossip can unsheathe, Judith inclined to accept his view.

"I have an idea he's with her all the time these days," Wick Redcliff said. "Tat is so touchy about his privacy that he covers his tracks—that is, from his parents—even when they don't go anywhere; but he's very fond of you, and I thought perhaps you were permitted to know about his doings."

"No; I only run into them at the movies every now and then. But they've been going together for two years—or longer. I don't see anything to get excited about." She smiled at him—parents were ridiculous, they were always getting up foolish alarms about their children's conduct.

Wick's ready smile did not answer hers, and something in his expression reminded her of Fen. She remembered that serious look on Fen's face once when they had argued a little on this same subject. With growing curiosity she began to assemble the details in her mind . . . it was the first time she had ever seen Tat and Lorena together . . . that must have been the autumn after her illness and before Fen's death. She and Fen had met them coming out of the movies one night. They all stood under the glaring canopy chatting with conscious cordiality, and Tat suggested that they should go to The Hangover for a beer. But Fen said brusquely that it was too late; whereupon Tat made a defiant crack . . . she couldn't remember now what it was. "Oh, it isn't really late!" she said. "Come on, Fen, we have time for one glass"; for she could see that Tat's feelings were hurt, and besides, she was full of curiosity about them. There was nothing then for Fen to do but go, which he did with bad grace, grumbling about having to work tomorrow, and at the beer parlor the two brothers spat at each other across the red-checked tablecloth while she tried to be pleasant to Lorena. But her wifely attempts to cloak these family squabbles from the stranger ended in a disconcerting impression that Lorena understood the boys very well, that she spoke their language and, in a curious way, knew what this antagonism was all about. Judith seemed to be the outsider, which was ridiculous of course—for while Lorena had lived all her life in the same neighborhood, she knew Fen and Tat very casually.

[17]

As the beer went down in the tall glasses, Judith talked less and less; Lorena baffled her, her impression of the girl's personality became progressively confused. For one thing, she did not answer the remarks Judith made to her, or rather she answered them obliquely, as if she aimed them over her head toward the two men, and Judith found herself shut out of the conversation. Wisecracking away in her cheerful slipshod speech, her strongly provincial accent, Lorena seemed to be taking a private though acid enjoyment from the occasion.

On the way home Fen had been no help in clarifying the situation. In response to her eager speculations he only said, "Tat's a fool."

"Tat isn't a fool, Fen," said Judith. "He's awfully sensitive and you can hurt him more easily than anybody. That's because he adores you and at the same time resents your being so much more attractive than he is." Mollified, Fen told her she was as big a fool as Tat. But it was funny about Fen's attitude. She knew he loved Tat in a subterranean fashion that no fraternal exchange of insults could ripple; he watched over his younger brother and was always trying to steer him through his difficulties. Well, he certainly hadn't liked Tat's going with Lorena; Tat, he must have felt, wouldn't know how to handle himself with a girl who was older and as hardboiled as she seemed. Judith had puzzled over the incident for a while and then forgotten about it until Mr. Redcliff brought it up and made it significant. And somehow troubling. . . .

"I try not to concern myself unduly with the private affairs of my children," he was saying into the crown of his hat. "After all, Tat is twenty-nine and should know what he's about; but I'm not sure that he does in this case. You see, Tat looks on the conventions as targets in a shooting gallery—to be popped down for the fun of it; and that's all very well, except that in the field of sex you ought to make sure that your partner understands your line."

"Lorena certainly knows what it's all about."

"I wonder. Mind you, I like Lorena well enough; she's a handsome girl and good company. What worries me is that Tat's attentions may be misinterpreted there."

"I think you're taking it too seriously," Judith smiled at him again. "Lorena's no child; she's been married once and divorced —or was she? I never could get it straight."

"Neither could I exactly. She seems to go by her own name now. I used to see her walking on the Mall with her Marine, then she married him rather suddenly and went off to Cuba. I don't know just what happened there, whether she left him or he deserted her—it was several years ago—but I have an idea that when he died another wife bobbed up. At any rate, there was some kind of lawsuit."

Judith tried to think of a way to say that Lorena was cleverer than Tat without hurting Uncle Wick's feelings, and compromised on, "Well, she's old enough to know what she's doing —she's older than Tat."

"A little, yes—she and Fen were nearly the same age, as I remember, and she undoubtedly knows her onions. But it isn't exactly a question of age. When a man from the upper reaches of the social set goes after a woman who isn't 'in society,' there's a sort of seduction in it; the chances are she'll assume that the socially superior are also morally superior—which regrettably doesn't follow—and indulge in some wishful thinking about the future."

Judith's brown eyes fixed upon him with affectionate concern as she mulled over his idea. He had recovered his natural vein, his disarming smile was out again. He played with the little cowlick that stood up from his forehead like a handle and proceeded comfortably as if thinking aloud. "Take Lorena's father, for instance. I've known August Hessenwinkle for a great many years. His father was a baker in the Borough who baked so successfully he left each of his children a small inheritance, which August has used to go up in the world and become a wholesaler and commission merchant. He's a solid citizen, August, a good man to do business with, and I don't think Tat's revolt against the dictates of bourgeois morality will find much sympathy in his bosom. Well, perhaps you are right, perhaps I take it too seriously, but I have a pricking in my thumbs that tells me this affair is going to make trouble."

"Do you think they are really having an affair? I mean. . . ." There was a certain eagerness in Judith's voice.

Mr. Redcliff smiled confidentially. "Well, you know how it is in summer. Etta and I go to the mountains, Tat stays in the house alone, the town is dull, the weather is sultry, and when a siren lives just over the back wall . . . it's funny how walls, which are built to keep danger out, only make sirens more seductive."

"Do you mean she came over when Tat was there alone?" Judith couldn't help being shocked, seeing the back gate near the Hessenwinkles' house and Lorena slipping through the garden.

"It's mostly speculation. But we don't keep our doors locked, they can be entered very simply. And a man living in a big empty house—he's a vulnerable fortress too, my dear. Well, I must go along, I have a busy day ahead of me. The campaign you were asking about just now has stirred up the politicos to more nefarious activity, and I have to go forth and try to thwart them. Not that I'll succeed, but maybe I can fret them a little."

Judith withdrew her thoughts reluctantly from love and sin and asked, "Why don't decent people go into politics any more?"

Fenwick Redcliff spread his hands again in the deprecating gesture with which he met life's bafflements. "Selfishness and defeatism. Now you are looking at me with an accusing eye, as well you may. But I stick to fertilizer, which smells bad enough, but not so bad as politics."

"Still," said Judith, her brown face troubled, "our people ought to *do* something; they ought to try—"

"I agree—I agree. No two ways about it. But consider my grandfather who was in politics and his father before him. . . ." Uncle Wick was off again with a bone in his teeth, smiling and developing his theme with theatrical gestures. "They held the theory, the sound eighteenth-century theory, that the office should seek the man, not the man the office. But my grandfather held it too long. The Progressives of the nineteenth century knew no such doctrine, and the old man achieved the distinction of getting the smallest vote ever polled in this state by a candidate for governor. Well, I cling to the same dated theory, which is both a principle and an alibi with me."

They lighted fresh cigarettes and Judith silently prepared an excuse for being a little late at the office. "One trouble is," he went on, "that my generation in America has found the rewards of business juicier than the rewards of politics. Low pay and a little power through patronage—the prospect isn't enticing enough. I'm excluding, of course, the possibility of rewards through graft.

A man of moderate means like myself, for instance, with four children to raise and educate, has to have a powerful incentive to pass up the greater rate of rise offered by business. And local politics offer no issues worth dying for, or even being poor for."

He stood up to go; the deep shade of the piazza colored his high-shouldered figure a cool bluish white and muted the rosy cleanliness of his small face. (Lucian Redcliff once said that Wick's head looked like a china teapot stuck on a tall shelf, and while Judith had protested the gibe, she couldn't help laughing. Fine china, of course, Lucian had said—Chelsea or Spode. Lucian was outrageous, but his sarcasms had a way of being apt.) Wick's eyes were darting about now in the same quizzical way that Lucian's did; the half-brothers were much alike, she saw, but Wick's humor was kindlier and turned more frequently against himself. "For years I've been clamoring for an Opposition in the state, be it Republican, Socialist, or whatever," he was saying. "I've inveighed against the Solid South, against the folly of a one-party system—"

"Why don't you start a new party then?" She shot an accusing finger at the middle button of his shirt, playing up to his humor, but a literal note sounded in her voice. After seven years of exposure to the Redcliff idiom, the extravagant argument, the light touch, she still couldn't keep a natural tendency to literalness from coming through now and then.

"Me? Because I want to be a Democrat," he answered plaintively.

He sighed into his Panama and turned toward the door. Judith got up and walked along with him. "God made me a Southerner, an Episcopalian, and a Democrat," he went on, "and in a world of shifting truths these are the principles I like to stand on. Well, you have to have adversaries to keep your principles alive; no Opposition, no principles. But I didn't expect the challenger to crop out in my own family!"

They laughed over their shared pleasantries and he put his arm around her and squeezed her to him in a quick, casual parting. "Let me know if you uncover any fresh evidence," he said, "and I'll do the same."

"All right, we'll keep each other advised."

She waved good-by and turned back as the chimes rang quarter past nine. Snatching up her hat and bag, she ran for the garage.

As she followed her daily route to the office these trains of thought rattled in and out of her mind on separate levels. The traffic remotely engaged her attention, but as an irritant, an impediment to her haste. On another tier she heard her motor thrumming irregularly and she considered the question of turning the car in—it was probably time for it—yet she hated to. The *Formidable*, Fen had dubbed it, for Fen knew his Jane's *Fighting Ships* backward and forward, and was endlessly amused at the names the English chose for their naval vessels. So the *Glorious* had succeeded the *Courageous* and so on. Judith loved the *Formidable*; she had loved to see its pale canvas top anchored by the pavement when they came out of the house, and to set sail in it with Fen, never knowing what course he would take. Like the time they came home from the Simons' Christmas party with the top halfway back and reared up like a sail. Fen was in no mood to be thwarted by balky tops, nor by traffic signals, and when Judith insisted on his stopping for a red light, he revenged himself by standing up in the car and reciting "Whither, oh splendid ship, thy white sails crowding," and refusing to move on until he had said all of the poem he remembered, which luckily wasn't very much.

But topmost in her mind, above the honking of the present and the backward voice of remembrance, rattled the train of her astonished emotions at this new idea about Lorena and Tat. Judith was too humble-minded to be censorious . . . but sin in your own family is different, she thought. Its hot wings brushed her disturbingly. She couldn't help feeling shocked and also (she admitted with chagrin) a little admiring. Yet as she parked her car in front of the Fuel and Welfare Society and went toward the door, incredulity prevailed. Uncle Wick fretted too much about Tat's scrapes. He had gone off the deep end, she decided.

In the main office she managed to slide into the chair behind her desk unobserved by the presiding genius of the Society. Mrs. MacNab was a large, serious woman, a strict taskmistress, but today she appeared to be suffering from sharper irritants than Judith's lateness. Unpaid bills rasped her Scottish conscience; and the checks which should replenish the till had not come from the city treasurer—the way men conducted business passed Mrs. Mac-Nab's imagination.

The Fuel and Welfare Society was the hybrid its name implied because of her refusal to be fully absorbed into the city's social welfare program. Mrs. MacNab might be swallowed but she would never be digested while life endured, so she hardily stood off the forces bent on streamlining the city government, to the confounding of municipal auditors and accountants. Judith had tried to bring Tat and Mrs. MacNab together, thinking that two people so deeply concerned about the plight of the under-privileged would certainly be congenial; but for some reason it hadn't worked. Tat seemed to resent Mrs. MacNab and sounded off on the futility of private charity, upon which Mrs. MacNab scored centralized welfare work as soulless and wasteful, and it had ended by Tat's telling her she was a quack who put shin-plasters on a cancer.

Judith had apologized as best she could for her brother-in-law's rudeness, but actually the incident had left her less concerned about Mrs. MacNab than about Tat. He was so sweet, really, why did he have to be so extreme? Her thoughts spiraled around him like birds around a steeple. To escape from tribal loyalties and the profound attachments of place he flung over too far. He would say he had to do it, to free himself from the bonds to which he was subject like the rest of them. Yet Judith herself only half-comprehended this explanation, for her own attachment to the Redcliff clan, to her friends, seemed to her not a drag but strength, the stuff life was made of. She wanted urgently to help Tat find happiness and fulfillment . . . and from the very tribal loyalty he eschewed.

Above the humming of the electric fan, Mrs. MacNab aired her problems to the room at large. "Just what does the city treasurer expect us to operate on?" she was muttering, dealing the bills with angry resignation into a pile. "Does he think people just don't cook or eat when our funds are held up? Here's the Friendly Hearth Wood Yard now, sixteen hundred and eighty-five dollars, out-standing since the middle of last winter. O'Dell's reminders are getting pretty sharp—though I can't say I blame him. He's not really an unkind man, and he's been quite patient about this bill."

"He may have heard," suggested Mary Bonneau, the secretary,

"that we got an installment in the spring, and he's probably sore because none of it went his way."

"I couldn't help that," said Mrs. MacNab crisply. "We had such heavy bills after the flu epidemic. Yes, O'Dell may have got wind of that installment, and he may get nasty if he thinks we could have paid him and didn't. Perhaps if I had a talk with him and explained our situation . . . he's usually agreeable to deal with."

"As a matter of fact," said Mary, going back to her typewriter, "he hasn't complained personally so far; the letters have been signed by his secretary, Lorena Hessenwinkle. Maybe she wrote them without dictation."

"She might do the piping, but he'd call the tune," said Mrs. Mac-Nab.

"Is Lorena Hessenwinkle his secretary?" asked Judith in surprise. "Funny, I was just talking about her this morning."

"Yes . . . at least she's at the office of the wood yard off and on. She's his niece, you know, and she seems to have a job there when she wants it."

"Of course . . . I'd forgotten." Judith sat with pencil suspended, thinking how in a small community paths cross and re-cross, lives brush each other lightly, until one day they find themselves entangled (not perceiving how it happened) in some inextricable relationship. She tried to connect her picture of Lorena, which only today had become larger than life in her consciousness, with Harry O'Dell, whom she had heard described as a good businessman, an Irish politician, wonderful company, or a downright crook according to the predilections of the speaker. Certainly he was a man of varied enterprises, and in Judith's mind this flair for success provided a connection with Lorena who, she now recognized, had a similar one. Whether Lorena's poise came from the O'Dell inheritance or from her good looks and her sex appeal, Judith did not know. It was all mixed up in her mind; yet with this new element of the O'Dell connection, Lorena emerged a little more clearly from the disproportions in which Judith's memory and emotion had drawn her.

"You know Lorena, Judith. Doesn't Tat Redcliff go with her?" asked Mary.

Judith could see that the affair had bred discussion. "I saw them last night getting curb service in front of Murphy's Pharmacy," said one of the other girls. "They were drinking cokes."

"That seems harmless enough—" began Judith defensively, and instantly regretted the implication that it might have been otherwise. Mary caught it and smiled derisively.

"Before we tackle O'Dell," said Mrs. MacNab, "I think I'll make one more trip to City Hall and see if any money is forthcoming. I'll doubtless get the usual answers: the city is behind in its tax collections, the money simply isn't there, go home and have patience and we'll get it in time. . . . But at least it will strengthen our hand with O'Dell if he knows we have made every effort." Mrs. MacNab ordered the papers on her desk and rose. She went to the closet and took out her small peaked hat like a nurse's cap, a style of headdress which the winds of fashion had never dislodged from her head. The girls teased her about her toques—they couldn't imagine where she still found them. "I find them at the milliner's," said Mrs. MacNab imperturbably. "Milliner's!" crowed the office. "And where do you find a milliner?"

"There are still a lot of people like me," said Mrs. MacNab. Without self-consciousness she put the toque on top of her luxuriant wig and, nurse and protectress of all the world, went purposefully out of the door.

The office quickly filled with cases. Judith forgot hats and in-laws in her absorption with the dilemmas of Mrs. Discopoulos who wanted a larger allowance for food and brought five skinny, large-eyed children as evidence of her just claims. Miss Maybelle Johnson was suffering from bilious fever, and held the whole office in her thrall while she described with gluttonous realism the horrors of the disease. Mrs. Maguire wanted to save a doctor's bill by having the girls prescribe for her little cousin, who was off his feed; it must be the Old Boy got into him—she handed the fretful child to Mary Bonneau—and while they were figgering out what ailed him, she'd just run to the ten cent store a minute. He was good and fat, all right— In the middle of a phrase she vanished, leaving Mary trying to hand the child back to her.

Mary walked petulantly out on the piazza and dumped the little boy in the playpen kept for such contingencies. Judith meantime went on with the Negro applicants who demanded less; they mostly wanted a little kerosene oil or two pounds of sugar. To them and to all the clients the girls repeated the familiar formulas—yes, the allowances are small, we hope to have more funds later and we'll see what we can do. Meantime, if you'll spend less of your money on fatback, candy, and movies and more on stew-beef and greens. . . .

Tat is right, thought Judith. What we are doing for these people is dreadfully inadequate. But it wasn't only dollars the organization lacked, it was the wisdom people demanded in the touching expectation that "the Welfare" could give them everything the word implied. Her spirit wearied from the drag of their hope and their asking.

On her way out to dinner Judith found Mary Bonneau hanging over the playpen on the piazza. She went up and inspected Mrs. Maguire's young relative. "She says she's keeping him for her niece —a poor working girl, husband dead, etc. Sounds fishy to me. I suspect he's a little cuckoo in somebody's nest."

"You always suspect the worst," said Judith acidly, thinking of her dig about Tat.

"Well—there's something about the whole set-up . . . and you get suspicious in our line of work. This cuckoo is going to have rickets if he doesn't get better care. That's my diagnosis."

The child returned the girls' stares with grave blue eyes. "He's a funny little mutt," Mary went on, "and smart as a briar."

"Oh, he's not so funny-looking—" But he really was; his straight, sandy hair had already lost its baby silkiness and looked tough and scrubby. His stocky legs were undeniably bowed.

A look of sly merriment came over his plump face, as if, secretly, he too had his disparagements.

"Who does he look like?" Judith asked, teased by a flickering resemblance. "Somebody I know—"

"I don't see any likeness, except to some old man. All babies at the jowly stage look like Hoover or Churchill."

"Maybe that's it."

The child suddenly seized the side of the pen and shook it with a murderous rattle. Then he stood still and blinked at the two girls, as much as to say, "How do you like that?"

"You're a scream, fatty," said Mary. "But I must say you are cute."

"He's simply beguiling. Maybe he's a changeling . . . but I have to fly, it's after two."

Over her okra soup Judith thought a good deal about Lorena. How odd to cross her trail again so quickly. The coincidence touched with significance their tenuous relationship. Was Tat getting into a situation he wasn't equal to? A heady impulse seized her to pitch in and try to straighten things out. It was dangerous to meddle in other people's lives—dangerous but fascinating. If she could carry on for Fen, if she could do anything to help Tat or Uncle Wick. . . .

Back at the office she found Mrs. MacNab there before her, looking sourly on life. "It was just as I expected," she reported, "no prospect of funds for the present. Tax collections are down—because *men* are too timid politically to enforce them, if you ask me. But nobody did, so I'm back empty-handed. I suppose the next step is to see O'Dell."

Judith spoke up suddenly from her desk. "Let me go and talk to Lorena Hessenwinkle, Mrs. MacNab. I'll tell her about our troubles and maybe get a line on how serious O'Dell really is about the bill. Then, if it seems a good idea, I can tackle him too."

"Well, if you know the girl . . . will she talk to you? That is, are you on friendly terms with her?"

"I . . . I guess so. I hadn't thought about it before, but there's no reason why she shouldn't."

"Sending Judith after O'Dell is like sending a lamb after a lion," said Mary Bonneau. "She hasn't got a Chinaman's chance with that slick guy."

"Don't you be too sure about O'Dell," said Mrs. MacNab. "He may be a hard man to trade with but he's not mean; and Judith can talk back if she has to."

"Sure I can." Judith closed her desk. "I'll go now while we aren't so busy."

The *Formidable* stood by the sidewalk, wet and glistening from a thunder shower when Judith got in and turned east and then north toward the Borough, that amorphous district containing the Redcliff house at one end and the Friendly Hearth Wood Yard at the other. She followed a street along the river between a freight yard and a row of dwellings beached like arks by the ebb of fashion, their columns and cornices long strangers to paint. Between the street and the river the ground was low, the storm tides flooded it from time to time, and silt collected both physically and humanly speaking.

On the cobbled thoroughfare Judith picked her way between puddles on which the children were sailing boats of bark filched from the near-by wood yard. She supposed she ought to stop and tell them not to play in that dirty water, it was full of germs; but besides her unwillingness to spoil their ecstasy in their new-made lakes and rivers she knew that a more anthropomorphic bogey would have to be conjured up to scare them off; and shirking the obligations of social conscience she went on. Farther along a truck had stopped to sell watermelons and was being mobbed by the Negro residents. Discarded rinds littered the roadway with loud red and green untidiness all the way to the wood yard itself.

Judith shut off her motor by the high, rusty board fence that protected the cords of wood and the great bins of coal from the Borough's denizens, whose prehensile habits had not fallen into civilized desuetude to judge from the fenceposts sharpened against intruders. The office, a one-room building, stood outside, and was further set off from the wood yard proper by a coat of white paint and brash green and orange striped awnings.

As she went in at the door she saw Lorena Hessenwinkle sitting in the window looking toward the river. A narrow band of sun slipping between the awnings looped her head, tilted back against the jamb, in ruddy light. The gaudy effect was actually not deliberate—it was as if gaudiness had followed her even through the screen of canvas. But the leg braced along the window sill was perhaps a little fulsome in its own right. She was drinking a cocacola from the bottle, and her pose and opulent coloring, framed in the window, suggested the advertisements for that beverage.

"Hello, Lorena," said Judith, trying to down her shyness and speak naturally. There was a quick movement at the back of the room where Judith now saw O'Dell sitting in his shirtsleeves at his desk. Lorena started and swung her leg to the floor, but sat against the sill embarrassed at being caught off guard. O'Dell rose and came forward.

"Why, it's Mrs. Redcliff," he said in a pleasant, rich voice. "Come in—glad to see you."

"You have a nice cool place," said Judith, looking about. "It's the first time I've been here."

For an awkward moment Lorena sat with the bottle in her hand, obviously uncertain whether to offer Judith a coca-cola or to receive her on a strictly business footing. Then she crushed out her cigarette and, putting the bottle on the floor by her desk, she took her place behind the typewriter.

"Yes, we always have a breeze here," O'Dell was saying. "Have a chair." He moved one forward and Judith sat down thankfully. Smiling, he leaned on the desk and said, "What can I do for you?"

O'Dell, in his late forties, had kept a well-set-up figure; his green shirt, dark green tie, and tan trousers were carefully chosen for style and color. He had thick, straight eyebrows above slightly prominent gray eyes; his long nose, thick at the base, and the fleshy vertical lines about his mouth accentuated the length of a face molded by determination and close attention to the business of life. The face intimidated Judith, who was not businesslike and not very determined. But Harry O'Dell's thin lips smiled readily, the shrewd look could twinkle away with confusing speed.

Lorena looked like her uncle, Judith noticed, as the curiosity that had brought her here shot out feelers to measure this girl about whom her thoughts were obscure, excited, apprehensive without her volition. Her face would some day be like O'Dell's, when it lost the full curves of youth that gave it better proportions. The confident manner that had disturbed Judith came also from the O'Dell side of the family, it appeared, though she had a momentary perception, seeing them together, that it was not quite real, that it was a manner of meeting the world and hoping, rather than expecting, that the world would accept them at their own valuation. Lorena's coppery hair, which was also not quite real, curled thickly about her face; it in no way resembled O'Dell's thatch, nondescript in color and scrubby-looking for all his military brushes could do. Her eyebrows were plucked to a hairline and her full, mature body exhaled a warmth and richness at once human and disturbing.

"I came to see you about the Fuel and Welfare Society's bill, Mr. O'Dell. We realize that you've been kept waiting an unconscionable time—" She paused, feeling she had chosen the word badly; the others were weighing her statement and finding it stilted, as indeed it was. She tried again to conquer this shyness that made her stiff with people and continued. "Mrs. MacNab went again today to the Treasurer's office to stir him up about our money. You know, we get an annual appropriation and we set up our budget accordingly, but if tax collections fall behind—"

"Listen, lady, I know those birds at City Hall well," O'Dell interrupted. "Appropriating money is the best little thing they do. But when it comes to turning appropriations into hard cash, that's something else again. You can't tell me about those fellows. Now, I don't like to be put in the position of squeezing you ladies at the Welfare. I know you have a fine, loyal little outfit and do a lot of good. But I have to run my business—and it's a bad idea to mix it with charity. I take care of certain charities, of course: the Orphan House and the Catholic fund and forty other things, but I keep 'em separate from my business. Now, as to this account, we don't like to carry our coal and wood bills over the summer—you'd be surprised how people forget about the coal man when hot weather sets in."

"Uncle Harry's one of the biggest contributors to charity in this town," said Lorena, on the defensive. She smiled at her uncle, a smile that called on Judith to acknowledge his recognized liberality. "The Welfare bill is outstanding since February—"

"I know—I know," Judith reassured them hastily. "I've always heard that Mr. O'Dell was a great supporter of local institutions; I know he's awfully kind. And we really don't expect you to put us on your charity list. We are only asking you to wait a little longer—the money will be forthcoming—"

"Will it?" inquired O'Dell, smiling, but less genially. "Do you always have the dough in your hand at the end of the year that they appropriated so fast at the beginning?"

"Well, yes . . . that is, mostly." Judith braced herself to meet his challenge. "Now and then we run short and have to carry over; but take my word for it, Mr. O'Dell, we'll see that it gets paid."

"Well, now, of course if any of you ladies in the office wants to guarantee it personally—" O'Dell sat down and smiled with his special brand of impudence, which was somehow hard to reprove.

[3 0]

Judith didn't know whether he meant her to take him seriously or not. "I'm afraid none of us is in the position to do that," she said, stiffening again.

"You might ask your father-in-law." He clasped his long hands covered with dark hair about his knees and rocked slightly on his chair, half speculative and half mischievous. "Sixteen hundred and eighty-five dollars is a nice piece of change, but I'll wait a good while for it if Mr. Redcliff puts his name to it."

"At six per cent?" put in Lorena, quickly taking his facetious line. "You'd wait a million years at six per cent, I guess. Uncle Harry, you're a card."

O'Dell glanced at her with a little annoyance, Judith thought.

"Leave Mr. Redcliff out of it," she said, not smiling, a little annoyed herself.

This made a poor impression; they thought she was being high hat, she saw, and it united them against her. It began to seem almost a matter of hostile clans—the O'Dells against the Redcliffs. "He's so busy," she added, "I don't like to bother him," which, being untrue, sounded lame as she said it. "He doesn't know anything about the Welfare Society. He has other charities, like you, Mr. O'Dell."

The last words came out more naturally and O'Dell immediately met her half-way. "See here, Mrs. Redcliff, I don't mind so much waiting for the money—though I could use it now if I had it; but I doubt that old lady MacNab can wring it out of City Hall. She might if she was tough enough—you can sometimes pressure them to take a little from some other worthy purpose and give it to you. Now I know Butch Tracy down there, and Alderman Odenkirchen is a good friend of mine, and some of the other boys, and now and then they put things through for me, just as a favor, you know. But Mrs. MacNab don't have what it takes."

Judith saw how used he was to getting things done that way, by knowing useful people, by favors given and received, by the sales value of his warm personality. She also saw with a sudden widening of perception how Mrs. MacNab looked to the O'Dells —the Scotch Presbyterian lady, conscientious, dowdy, unaware of the possibilities that lay in making friendship a business. Judith sat silent for a moment, finding this a liberal education.

"Mr. O'Dell, it's a gent'man here to see you." A colored man, his clothes covered with sawdust, held the screen door open and spoke through the crack.

"O.K.," said O'Dell rising. "Excuse me, ma'am; I'll be right back."

"Hey, shut that door," Lorena called good-humoredly. "We got all the flies we need in here now." She gave a childlike giggle and looked at Judith. "He can't ever figure it out that he can talk through the screen."

Judith returned her smile eagerly and sat back in her chair. This was a break, this chance to be alone with Lorena. In a comprehensive glance she read the esoteric language of the other's clothes: Lorena's pink crepe blouse fastened, a little too low, with a row of gilt buttons; on a hook behind her hung a white beret and the blue crepe de Chine jacket that went with the short, tight skirt she wore. Her fingernails were lacquered blood red—but even as Judith made her mildly disapproving inventory, she thought enviously: it doesn't matter if you're as pretty as that. She saw that Lorena was making her own inventory and she began, disconcerted, to picture herself in the O'Dell frame: her shirtwaist dress, of a soft cocoa brown she had thought quite smart, her Panama hat, turned up in the back and down in the front, with its brown band—doubtless Lorena liked plain clothes no more than she liked fancy ones. Her bare arms suddenly felt all wrists and elbows and she folded them self-consciously, but the posture did nothing to soften their angles and she unfolded them again and clasped her hands behind her head.

This is ridiculous, she thought, and shaking off her ill-ease, she plunged at her subject. "Have you seen Tat lately?"

Lorena paused, leaned back and tucked her blouse into the belt of her skirt with elaborate care. "Yes," she said indifferently. She seemed to smile at someone behind Judith's head. "I see a lot of Tat."

"It's more than I do. He's so busy with the filling station and all his pet projects—" There was a pause; Lorena didn't help her but left the burden of conversation squarely on her lap, and she added to justify her pursuit of the subject, "I know you've known the boys a long time, living so near them."

"Sure, I've known them all my life." Lorena seemed to be taking up a challenge. "We all used to play together on the Mall when we were kids, and I used to go with Tat and Fen and my brothers when they built their rowboats on Town Creek. I never was much on playing with girls—the boys were always more fun." She smiled a sudden disarming smile, her natural magnetism made a flash appearance.

Like most shy people Judith responded instantly to friendliness, so she smiled back and said, "Fen used to talk a lot about those days—what was the name of the gang they all belonged to? The Black something or other."

"The Black Camorra—there was a big wop got it up; he lived here somewheres near the wood yard."

"They certainly were a bunch of toughs—" Judith stopped short in dismay, remembering Lorena's brothers and cursing her tactlessness.

To her incredulous relief, Lorena took it as a compliment. "They sure were. They used to steal bicycles and sell them, and shoot craps with the money in the railroad yard, and once they sneaked in and stole a locomotive. They were way the hell and gone up the track before the switchman caught them. Fen and Tat weren't as bad as the others," she added with a shade of condescension. "But Fen was kind of grown up even in those days—he always seemed older, somehow."

"But he was never as serious as Tat, though Tat's younger," said Judith, torn between her longing to hear of Fen's youth, to gather up every crumb about him, and her jealousy of Lorena who had been privileged to see his life in its precious unfolding.

"Oh, Fen wasn't serious; not him! Say—have a coke?"

"I'd love one. Thanks."

Lorena brought another glass and two bottles from the washbasin in the lavatory where they had been set in cold water. She moved with a sort of lazy sway that was agreeable and, somehow, included Judith for the first time in the sweep of her friendliness. Easing into her chair, she slouched sidewise and crossed her shapely legs.

"I never will forget the day Fen got his first job. He came out on the Mall with his chest stuck way out and said, 'Look at me —I'm a working man, Lorena—I got a job.' He was funny as a crutch, and we had a party, him and Tat and me. It was Prohibition, but Uncle Harry knew a man who sold near-beer with a stick in it, so I told Fen where to get it and he went off and came back with six bottles. It sure was powerful stuff—imagine us getting oiled on two bottles of beer apiece! Then we went to the State Fair—Fen just had to spend that dough. 'Course he hadn't gotten his pay envelope yet, so I don't know where the cash came from, but long as he was working for his father I don't guess he had any trouble drawing an advance."

"But Fen never worked for his father," said Judith. "He started in with the Drydock Company right after he finished college."

"No he didn't," said Lorena flatly. "He worked for his father awhile."

Judith felt this was her field of knowledge. "Fen started in at the Drydock Company." Contradictory temper gave an edge to her words. "At least that's what he always said. If he'd worked for his father I think he'd have mentioned it."

Lorena's face turned pink. "You can't tell me—he worked up at the plant for a couple of months before he went to the Drydock. I know because when he came home through the Mall in the evening his clothes smelt of fertilizer. I used to kid him about smelling like a dead fish." She swung around in the chair and ran her pencil through her reddish curls with elaborate nonchalance.

A wave of anger rose inside Judith and fell rasping on her pride, the more so as this evidence sounded uncomfortably circumstantial. She sat for a moment choked by the salty rush. The little incident challenged her rights in Fen, her husband; it struck at the happiness that alone enabled her to endure her loss. But how shameful to be quarreling like this. She couldn't trust herself to speak of Fen again so she changed the subject swiftly. "What was Tat like in those days?"

Her reproof disconcerted Lorena. "Tat?" She seemed to doubt if she had heard aright. "Just like he is now." After a pause she added, "Only more so, I guess; more serious. He takes things awful hard. Tat's a sweet boy and has plenty of brains, too." She shot a defensive glance in Judith's direction. "People seem to think that because Fen was brighter and quicker on the uptake he had more sense than Tat; but Tat's more brainy and independent than Fen ever was."

Judith guessed that this was less a slur on Fen than a thrust at her, but some force that she could resist no more than the pull of

[34]

gravity drew the contradiction from her lips. "That's not quite true. Fen had a good mind, and he was good at his job—even at college he did well while Tat flunked out; because Fen was better balanced, he didn't fly off the handle the way Tat does. Not that it matters. Tat is a fine person in his own way."

"That's big of you." Lorena's full red mouth had a curious little curve—of triumph? . . . hostility? . . . amusement? "See here," she said, "there's no need for you to come here tellin' me 'bout the Redcliffs. I know the boys all right; they been frien's of mine since I was knee-high." Long before they ever heard of you, the words implied.

Judith thought desperately, you're making this into a social matter which it isn't; it's a matter of husband and wife. . . . She said definitely, to end the discussion, "I don't question your knowing them—maybe you're closer to Tat than I am, I know you're his friend; but they're my family, I lived in their house for a while; and after all, Fen was my husband, so I ought to know more about them than an outsider—"

At her words Lorena's body drew up and flung forward, the hand hanging down by her chair mechanically grasped the neck of the bottle standing on the floor. She'd really hit me with it, thought Judith with amazement. She saw the curve the bottle would swing. But the fear she felt was not physical; it was the subtler sense of disadvantage in a war with this kind of uncomplicated rage. I couldn't crack people over the head with bottles . . . but she could, and maybe she's right . . . Judith pulled herself together and stared hard into Lorena's face, holding back the blow by the effort of her will. They hung for a moment equalized, the battle drawn; then utter disgust that she should be sitting there quarreling with a stranger about her family seized Judith and lifted her to her feet.

"This is idiotic—I only came in to see about the bill. I have to go now."

Perhaps Lorena took this as a sign of retreat. She threw the bottle over on the floor and it rolled away clattering. "O.K. We'll send our collector round in the morning."

"That won't be necessary—"

Neither heard the slam of the screen door.

"Well, now, what's this all about?" O'Dell's ingratiating voice

[35]

chided them, it appealed to their better selves, it poured oil on the screaming hinges of their argument. He came up and looked from one strained face to the other. "I don't like this talk about bill collectors—it don't sound friendly to me."

"It won't be necessary to send one, Mr. O'Dell. I'll see to it that the bill is paid at once."

"Now—now, Mrs. Redcliff, I don't want you to get the wrong idea." He went behind Lorena's chair and put his hands on her shoulders. "This is one of the most generous, warmhearted little girls in the world. Why, she'd give you the shirt off her back if you needed it, wouldn't you, Rena? She's just being loyal to my interests."

"I sure am." Lorena nodded positively. "God knows I don't grudge the fuel to poor people—I wouldn't want to see anybody go cold. But I say if it's going to be given away, Uncle Harry, you might as well be the one to give it, not those folks." She jerked her head sidewise toward Judith.

"We're not asking you to give the fuel," said Judith. "Please take my word for it, the bill will be paid within a few days."

She turned and went out, walking stiffly to disguise her limp from the eyes on her back.

O'Dell followed her to the car, expostulating that she mustn't take it that way, that she needn't worry about that business of the bill collector—Rena was just high-spirited, she didn't mean any harm. His face was furrowed, the patina of self-confidence had cracked, this direct female encounter had bested him; and warmed by his display of genuine feeling, she managed a wan smile.

"That's all right, Mr. O'Dell; it's perfectly natural that you should want the bill paid. I'm going to see that it is managed, somehow. . . ." As she swung the car round to drive out she had a last glimpse of O'Dell standing with his legs apart, his green shirt livid in the westering sun, bemusedly pulling his long upper lip as he gazed after her.

The late light gilded the cobblestones and transformed the shacks beside the roadway with glowing amber and velvety blue, but Judith's eyes might have been pebbles for all she saw of the Borough as she drove back to the main artery of traffic. Swinging toward the Redcliff house, she ran over the corner of the sidewalk and felt an angry satisfaction in the bump; the car rolled forward in quickening jerks, propelled by the inflammable essence in her mind. The more she thought over the conversation with Lorena the angrier she grew; she talked to herself, she snapped out sarcastic retorts—why hadn't she thought of that one while she was there? Thrice over she cursed her unready tongue.

Judith felt for the Redcliffs that mixture of affection and irritation, loyalty and identification of interest, that makes up the family tie, and since the death of her parents she had more and more taken shelter from loneliness among these people who had been Fen's own. In her deep disturbance she went at once to her father-in-law.

The square brick house swam in green shade behind the trees which the sun pierced with watery yellow. Its air of suspension in peace comforted her as she went through the gate and up one side of the double stone stair to the piazza. She tried the door, but it was latched, so she rang the bell. No answer. They must have gone out. She dropped on the bench by the door and slumped against the wall. Down the street to the east she could see a tug passing on the river; to the west the double line of trees fanned out into a lake of dark green where the street ended in the Mall, the ragged common where Lorena had sat and celebrated with Fen his turn into manhood. . . . She *must* see Uncle Wick and ask him about Fen's job.

Deliberate footsteps trod the garden walk. The piazza on which Judith sat was nearly a full story above the ground and in a moment she saw a disembodied head, wrapped in a white cloth and surmounted by a straw hat, pass along the level of the floor. It was the cook who lived in a small brick house at the back and who had come to spy out the disturber of the afternoon's peace.

"Oh, it's you, Miss Judith. How you feelin'?"

"Pretty well, Bekah. Anybody at home?"

"No, ma'am. Dey gone out in de cyar."

"Oh." Judith swallowed her disappointment. "Do you know when they'll be back?"

"I don' rightly know, ma'am. Dey gone to de beach to git a mouthful of fresh air. Dey tell Rosa she can go home; but if you want to come in an' wait, you welcome to."

The Redcliff summer supper never varied from cold shrimps, sliced tomatoes, and iced tea, which could be eaten at any hour;

so Judith sighed and said, "No, thank you, Bekah; if they let Rosa go, that means they'll be coming home late. I'd better go back and look after my own house." She went down the stone steps dispirited. "Of course Mr. Tat isn't in?"

Bekah came between the flowerbeds shaking her head, her mouth drawn up in a bunch of silent disapproval. "He don't never be in. He out all de time—all de time. . . ."

She seemed to nod slightly toward the back of the house which was also the direction of the Hessenwinkles—but perhaps it's just my imagination, Judith thought wearily.

"What's the matter, Miss Judith, you feel sick?"

Judith started—was it as bad as that? "No, Bekah, I'm just a little tired. It must be the heat."

"You sho' don' look good."

Judith smiled at her, touched by the concern folded within the words. "I'll be getting on home. Give the family my love—I'll call them up."

She drove away tingling still from the quarrel. Could it be that Fen had worked for his father before he went to the Cooper River Drydock Company? A small matter, she saw, as a shutter opened for a moment on her introspection—it was silly to take it so hard. But immediately the shutter closed again, for the trifling question mysteriously contained the whole threat of invasion which was building up in her mind, a threat to the love between herself and Fen and to their love and protection of Tat.

She talked stormily to herself, to Lorena: after all, Fen *was* my husband, his family is my family. Lorena's possessive manner had been insufferable about Fen, but actually they hadn't so much quarreled about Fen, who was safely dead and beyond the possessiveness of either; they had been quarreling about Tat—that was it, of course! Uncle Wick had been right about Tat and Lorena; their being lovers would explain her touchiness. But it didn't wholly explain it. Had the affair been on that time they all went to The Hangover after the movies? And if Fen had known about it that night, why hadn't he told her? It surely would have been natural to impart such a startling piece of news. . . .

At her own house she got out of the car and opened the gate, still wrapped in puzzlement. The place was deserted except for Rags, who welcomed her with bounding delight. The cook was off on Tuesdays, the Turners' house was dark, the long dusk of summer was beginning to settle in the corner by the wall and under the hydrangeas. She picked Rags up and held him against her face, grateful for his musky animal warmth in the purple emptiness of the garden.

Loath to go in to her solitary supper, Judith hung her purse and hat on the trellis and dragged out the heavy coils of the hose. She turned on the hydrant, and as the water began to babble coolly on the flowerbeds, the tension within her gave way a notch. The evening sky went about its gradual miracles, turned from purple to the submerged red of dried rose leaves, darkened to smoke color; and she stood still for a long time with the nozzle in her hand, feeling, like a breath on her skin, the increase of summer all around her. She had gone so wrapped in the cocoon of grief that she hadn't noticed the smooth rush from crinkled bud to leaves crowding out on the stem. Yet, impersonal as the swifts now darting among the chimney pots, the season had kept its flight, day and night had flown over her green hollow between the brick walls like the beat of wings.

Compunction seized her for her bondage to sorrow—but how to tear loose from its shadow-shape? At times she scarcely identified it with Fen's death, for it had come to have a faceless being of its own. She hadn't desired its presence, yet it crouched there under the surface of her thinking; her mind moved among her flowerbeds, directing the stream of water, but as it relaxed its preoccupation with the wet soil, the wet petals, and she came back to herself, there the shadow lay, sutured to her flesh. "You again!" she almost said, and all that was young and healthy in her beat about to escape the cruel fellowship.

It was full dark when she coiled the hose and went into the house. Her stormy anger of the afternoon had blown out and left her in a dispirited calm; she felt terribly tired and ashamed of the silly quarrel, of her failure to control her unwarranted and jealous emotions. Jealous of what? She couldn't remember. In the dining room a stuffy silence pressed against the ceiling and rang in her ears until she opened the windows; the single place set at the table hurt her with its mute statement. She went into the pantry and brought back the salad and iced tea which Sarah had left in the refrigerator for her. She ate the food without relish. The rise and fall of her fork gradually slowed and stopped, for the swollen tears that gathered inside pressed against her throat. Getting supper had been fun when Fen was there—she filled the kitchen with bustle, happy in their common life, in her right to feed and serve him.

She gave up trying to eat, put away the supper things and went upstairs. Her room with its one bed loomed empty, unlit, like the evening ahead of her. Well, this would be a good time to do a little work on a dress she was making; but even as she hunted about for the scissors, the buttons, the green linen, she began to ask herself an old question—had Fen really loved her? Not nearly as much as she loved him, of course. . . . She was unaware of the immemorial demand of women for more love, being too shy to discuss such matters with her friends, so she sat a while in blank suspension on the edge of the bed, going over the evidence. Fen's love-making was tender and ardent, she could ask no more there; but when afterward she lay adrift, deep-drowned in gratitude to life, when she wanted to keep him in her arms, feeling without thought the spiritual intimacy as yet unbroken by the return to their separate identities, he escaped her somehow. Love left her submerged and she tried to keep him submerged with her. But Fen was different. Passion released him, he rebounded from its yoke, he submitted to her clinging arms for a while but only to give her her desire, not because he shared her longing to spin out the sense of oneness. He became restless, he made an excuse to hunt for the matches, and presently he would be prowling about the room with a cigarette hanging from his mouth, having put passion behind him, talking about tomorrow's sail, or the Army and Navy game. She had to content herself with watching him from her pillow, drowsily aware of the easy swing of his movements, of his ruffled dark red hair like a jay's crest.

But he *did* love her, she thought with a rush of confidence; it was because he was not naturally articulate that he wouldn't reassure her all the time that he loved her. "Women always want words!" he would exclaim, pushing her amiably in the face when she importuned him about it. He was marvelously patient during her long siege of infantile paralysis, and he never complained once that she left him at home in the heat that summer while she stayed late in the mountains because of her eagerness to be done with invalidism before she came back to take up the exacting privilege of being Fen's wife. Fen had kept bachelor hall all that summer at his father's where Bekah could do for him, the older Redcliffs being also in the mountains. Tat was at home only spasmodically, so it must have been lonely for Fen who so liked to have people around. Had he sat out on the Mall in the evenings—had he found Lorena there, perhaps, talked with her?

The raw ache of jealousy rasped her again, bringing back the distress of the afternoon. But she couldn't go around being jealous of everybody who had talked to Fen, precious as every word and look of his short life seemed to her. She resolutely pushed the sensation down and began deliberately to remember the winter that followed that summer, the blissful interlude between her illness and Fen's. For Fen had been sweeter than ever before, more considerate and appreciative of her; and her happiness seemed too much for one body to contain, it flowed over and drenched the world about her.

One evening (she remembered) she had come home late. . . . The blustering wind of afternoon had fallen, the small winter-bound garden bloomed with silence. In the mesh of the bare thorn tree Jupiter nested like the Phoenix, supernaturally large and gold between the pointed black roofs, and her joy in her homecoming transformed the minerals and grasses—the planet seemed to tremble and almost spill from the sky with the very trembling of love. She crossed the dark grassplot, regretting the desire for warmth and comfort that drove her from this cold, pure moment in which she wanted to linger and steep her spirit.

The furnace man must have come, she thought with simple gratitude, as the warm breath of the house curled round her. Through the living-room door she saw Fen sitting sidewise in the big chair, his leg across the arm, reading the *Evening Post*. On her way to the sofa she leaned over and kissed him with uncontrollable enthusiasm, and he dropped the paper and lay back yawning and smiling.

"You stretch just like a cat by the fire," she said.

"Your nose is cold as a dog's from running around outside," he retorted. "Where in hell have you been?"

She threw herself down on the sofa and they exchanged news, immensely significant details—the furnace . . . the clogged

[41]

strainer . . . the cost of the repairs. . . . "I met your mother shopping on King Street, and she was in a tizzy; she'd been trying to buy a soup tureen and the salesgirl didn't even know what it was. I said she could have the soup brought in the plates, but my suggestion didn't go down very well. She said that was boarding-house style."

"If that's all she had to be in a tizzy about—"

"Well, it wasn't, as a matter of fact. She was on the warpath about some children who had come through the back gate to steal pecans and had trampled the flowerbeds. She suspects the Hessenwinkle children and says she's going to have the back gate nailed up. I told her she couldn't keep the Hessenwinkles out by nailing up the gate—not as long as she has pecan trees on her side of the wall. But that idea didn't go down either." Judith giggled and settled farther down into upholstered contentment. "Anyway the little Hessenwinkles are awfully cute, and a big garden like that needs children in it as much as it needs flowers."

Fen sat lost in thought for a while, then he came over to the sofa and threw himself down beside her. He buried his face in her neck, he sighed gustily into the warm hollow that she was a wonderful person . . . much too good for him . . . he didn't know why she should love him . . . she didn't know what she meant to him . . . Judith pressed her lips into his hair to keep them from crying out that she would lie down and die for him, schooling herself to accept this homage. Miraculous acknowledgment! Lying still in his hold, she tasted pure happiness.

Judith came to with a start on the edge of her narrow bed. She took a deep breath and shivered off her daydream. Fantasy, she warned herself, is the indigestible food the starved heart gnaws on. She gathered up her sewing things and went downstairs; but when she was settled in her chair by the living-room lamp, she found the dress dowdy, not worth finishing. The quick passage from the incandescent dream of Fen's arms to the glaucous substance of buttons had destroyed her balance. She threw the green linen on the floor and, getting up, walked restlessly about, hunting for a book to divert her from this obsession which her reason disapproved. But had the moralizings of the mind ever broken the spectral hold of grief and dreams? Maybe this wrestling with her private devil was the same struggle that tradition had preserved like a fly in amber in its tales of men possessed. And running her finger along the books standing straitlaced and dull on their shelves, she took comfort from the thought that it had usually required divine —supernatural—aid to cast the devils out. Where was that book Manya Turner had lent her? She hunted about the room and found it on the lacquer table Fen had given her for an anniversary present.

When she had settled in the armchair again she felt eased. The harbor wind poured in at the windows, lifting the organdy curtains, and gave coolness and movement to the room. The white parchment lampshade shed a realistic clarity on the familiar yellow and gray plumed chintz of the chair and sofa. She leafed rapidly through the first pages of the book, which Manya had said was good—quite out of the ordinary. It concerned some people traveling in Africa—that should take her well away from herself and all reminders of Fen; and she plunged willingly into a world of jungle trees, turbulent yellow rivers, and cat-footed beasts. After a few chapters she came on a paragraph:

In these swart glades the shapes of leaves faded out and thoughts not his rustled on the branches above his head. He kept on walking in an exaltation of weariness, and as he walked he felt drift down and pass through his body the immemorial wishes—that we could return and live the haunting moment over, unmake the blind mistake, and that the dead could come back to the familiar place. Love, he perceived amid this surge of sheer growth, is man's preeminent invention. To accept the brambly underbrush of desire and shape it to an artful pattern, this alone gives his little existence stature among these unconquerable trees.

Like arrows out of the jungle the words sped across land and sea and lodged in Judith's bosom. She wanted so poignantly to read them to Fen that she began to read them to him, recreating him there in his chair across the summer matting. She had seldom ventured to say this sort of thing because he would have thought it foolish; but here—she said silently to the presence in the chair— here is someone else who feels so, who speaks without shame of the burden and mystery of love. He shall speak for me. . . .

The present swarmed into the room again and shriveled the image that had sat there a moment ago in its full dimensions and colors. And if he had been there, she thought despondently, she probably wouldn't have read it to him. Fen had a good mind. What became of her hopeful plans to do lots of reading aloud with him? Selfishness had played its part in this scheme, to stay at home and read with Fen, and so had fear, fear of the pretty girls who liked him. For Fen took a naïve pleasure in the tributes from women's eyes; so he went with good appetite to the Yacht Club dances, while Judith always dreaded getting stuck. She had little small talk, little that caught the bulging, jaded eye of the stag line. Then her clothes never seemed quite right, an inadequacy that some-times disturbed Fen also. "Why don't you get something snappy?" he would say, looking sidewise at her old evening dress. Why hadn't she? Why hadn't she grasped the importance of dressing up to Fen? But she didn't care much about clothes actually, and looking chic was a business—it took time and thought and money that she saved for the new kitchen linoleum, a trip to New York, that bank account for the baby she had hoped to have. . . .

Judith nodded over her book. St. Michael's struck twelve dis-tantly, the bell notes caught in the white curtains, swelling and falling with the wind. Bedtime. . . . But she couldn't manage to rouse herself just yet from the slough of drowsiness and misery into which she had sunk. She twisted in the chair and buried her face in the gray plumes of the chintz. The natural warmth which a happy marriage had roused in her cried out for its satisfactions; desire and grief and longing constricted her body and mind in a coil of wretchedness. She sat thus for a long time between sleep and painful waking. . . .

A car door slammed sharply just outside the open window. Footsteps clapped on the sidewalk, and Judith's head came up with a start because they sounded suddenly like Fen's homecoming feet. Springy, mysterious in her ears, the steps padded closer; they hesitated at her gate. At the faint *tock* of the latch her heart bounded forward to run out and meet Fen as he opened it to drive in, an impulse-pattern her body had followed hundreds of times. But she did not move; she sat in the still room without breathing while a dreadful hope drenched her like a hot shower. Yet gooseflesh broke out on her body. The footsteps came in, went softly along the drive toward the back and died away. Judith sat rigid with agony while the silence coagulated round her, and in a minute or two the footsteps came tiptoe back. She got up and dragged to the door, for strongly as desire drove her forward, fear settled in her game leg and held her to a nightmare pace. Somehow she reached the piazza, but only in time to hear the gate-latch click again behind the visitant; and after a moment a quite corporeal car started and drove away.

Judith's trance burst round her like a bubble. She leaned against the door jamb, trying to hide her face in the unreceptive wood. Some friend of the Turners, no doubt, who had stopped in to speak to them and, finding the house dark, had gone away again with no suspicion what havoc his footfalls would play with her ravaged heart. She cried out for Fen's touch . . . if only he would come and help her, lift her out of the gulf of misery and delusion in which she was foundering. But Fen did not come back even as a ghost. He remained aloof in that unimaginable place to which he had gone; so she turned back and put out the lights on the gaping rooms and went to bed in the darkness, weeping.

Book II

ARLIER that evening Tat found the party getting dull and
began to wish it were over. For one thing, Lorena seemed
out of sorts, and he had come to depend on her for his enjoyment of places and people, on her verve, on her own capacity
for enjoyment. So did all the group, apparently—without her
special impudent humor, her energizing wit, the party was like a
motor trying to run without gas.

"What's the matter, honey—tired?"

"I guess so. What do you say we go home?"

"All right. It's kind of early, but we can leave in a little while."

"If we gonna go, we jus' as well go." Lorena got up and strolled
across the room. "Well—" she said smilingly to the group around
the radio fishing for a dance band, "we gonna blow the joint. So
long, you-all; had a fine time. We'll be seein' you."

Her announcement brought a storm of protests, gibes about late
dates, innuendoes that made Tat flush with discomfort. But teasing never fazed Lorena. Her superb self-confidence always bowled
him over. He gathered up Judith's records and followed in the
wake she left as she pushed through the crowd with unruffled calm.

They decided to drive around the Battery to cool off before
turning in. A line of cars stood along the waterside, the invisible
occupants seeking relief from the windless night. Tat pulled into
an empty space for a few minutes. He liked the sense of intimacy
a parked car gives, the sense of being in a group of people all enjoying together the lovely water and the privacy of their parked
cars.

Lorena said suddenly, "You seen Judith?"

Tat's round eyebrows arched a little higher. "Judith? No—
that is, yes—I saw her this a.m."

"Well, she came to my place this afternoon—and we went to the mat!"

"For God's sake! What was the matter?"

"Oh, everything, I guess. She gives me a pain. She thinks because she's Mrs. Fenwick Redcliff, Jr., she owns the lot."

"Nuts!" said Tat, astonished. "You've got her all wrong, Rena. She's just—well, a little bit shy, I guess."

"Shy—her? Don' make me laugh. She's cold as a fish, that's what."

"That's just her manner. Of course she goes round with a very reactionary crowd. I'm always telling her she ought to break away from them. If she went with some real people for a change she'd loosen up, because she's O.K. underneath."

"Don't make me laugh," said Lorena, not laughing. "She was lettin' on to me she jus' about owned the Redcliff family—"

"For crying out loud! You and Judy weren't fighting about *family?*"

Lorena took out a stick of chewing-gum and slowly unwrapped it. "No, I don't guess it *was* that. It was more—" she nibbled the stick and looked off toward the flashing buoy tossing majestically on the slow swell of the harbor. "I can't tell you exactly what it was."

"You've got Judy wrong," Tat said again. "You'd like her all right if you knew her better. She's really pretty liberal—she sees things the way we do; the only trouble is she tries to better social conditions with stop-gaps—she can't see yet you have to change the system. But she's not one of those people who are just complacent about unemployment and the rotten conditions in the jails."

"Maybe." Tat inferred that Judith's progressive qualifications budged Lorena not an inch. "I must say, Tat—" she turned to him with sudden warmth—"you're pretty remarkable, you haven't got a snobbish bone in your body. You're jus' as democratic as we are. I think you're swell."

"So you like me a little, eh?" Tat moved in and put his arm around her.

"You know damn well I do."

Tat had been teasing, and perhaps thinking wishfully, when he let his father and Judith believe that he had involved himself in a love affair with Lorena. That he hadn't was not his fault; all through the spring he had tried to waken in her a response to his growing fervor. He had set forth his ideas on love for hours on end as they drove around the Battery after the movies or sat drinking beer at The Hangover. But she refused to take him seriously, though he knew she liked him or she wouldn't have wasted time on him.

"Lorena—when are you going to break down and love me?" He moved closer on the front seat, trying to kindle her with the urgency of his body.

His raw passion and pleading stirred her, he thought, but after a moment she pushed him off gently. "Don't you ever figure on gettin' married?"

The question surprised him. "Why, you know how I feel about that, Rena. The trouble is marriage has been debased in our society by conventional morality; we've let it become commercial, barter and trade, a price set on love. The Russians are doing it better, they've put the relationship between men and women on a higher plane. What's really immoral is for people to go on living together after they've stopped loving each other. I love you terribly—there's nobody else for me, and if you could learn to love me, we'd live together with dignity, in a free relationship that would last because we'd want it to last."

Lorena hit him lightly with her white beret. "Well! I've had propositions in my time, but this one wins the custard pie."

Her coarseness offended Tat, even though he knew she put it on to tease him. "This isn't a proposition."

"Isn't it? Then where's the priest?"

"Haven't you gotten over that superstition? What have words got to do with it? We love each other or we don't. As if a little mumbled Latin could make it stick."

But with her frank brown eyes on him these considered opinions sounded not quite right. She had a disconcerting way of making him feel young whenever he tried to talk seriously with her. She wasn't much older really.

It was part of his enthrallment even while it baffled him.

She let up on him and relaxed for a moment. "I guess women jus' set more store by bein' married than men. An' it *sure* makes a lot of trouble. It's all well an' good for a man to be footloose, but a girl wants something she can lay aholt on. You wanta be free

[48]

to love me, sure—but you want the door open so you can walk out an' leave me, maybe with a parcel of little Redcliffs in the yard."

The mention of children, their children, made the blood beat thick in Tat's throat. The magic of a name brought them a step toward a sort of birth. "Lorena," he said, putting his arms around her and trying to master his voice. "What do you think—do you really think I'm the kind of guy who would walk out on a woman and leave her with my kids?"

Lorena kissed him maternally. "You're a sweet boy, Tat. I guess you'd never do anybody dirt."

"Not you, anyway, Lorena. You're the sweetest girl I ever knew. I'll never leave you as long as you'll have me around."

"Then what's your objection to gettin' married?"

Tat was silent. He couldn't give up his convictions like that.

She rubbed his cheek with her square, capable hand. "You're a romantic kind of guy, Tat, and I guess that's the difference between us. I don't expect too much romance—not like I used to, anyway. Eleck Thompson got me outa that idea. But what I say is, a rock on the fourth finger gives you something to build on."

"What good can a ring do?" Tat tried again. "Do you really think it can keep a man from leaving you?"

"It can't," she agreed, smiling and stretching, "but at least you got something you can hock."

Her good humor had suddenly come back. As they drove home along the sea wall she said, "Forget what I told you about Judith and me. I guess we're jus' a pair of dopes."

"I can't believe," said Tat, still puzzled, "that two sensible gals like you were fighting about family. As for Judith being stuck up about being a Redcliff, that's all so silly; and anyway her family is just as good as the Redcliffs—she has nothing to gain from us."

"Maybe we was jus' fightin' to be fightin'. You know how it is —sometimes you get started and can't stop. But she sure lets you know she's got the marriage certificate. Anyway, I didn't take a thing off her."

Tat gave it up and suggested a beer. "Swell idea—" and at the newsstand in The Hangover she bought the new issue of *Beauty and Health* and perused its lore with unquenchable feminine hope.

"You think if you eat yeast every day, you'd really look like that?" She showed him the picture of a houri printed in four colors.

"You look like that to me now."

"Well, I'm all diked up tonight for the party—and it sure was a waste, coming away early like we did. I even got a shampoo and brightener—cost me a dollar-seventy-five with the tip. Still, if you think I'm O.K.—" They exchanged smiles, assurances.

The Hessenwinkle house was in darkness when they went in. Lorena pressed the switch and the parlor sprang into being in the light of several high-powered bulbs. August Hessenwinkle was a man who liked plenty of light; he couldn't see the sense of groping around the house; candlelight was all right for the old days, they didn't have anything better, but there's no use in our ruining our eyes when we can get plenty of Mazdas.

The overstuffed chairs showed comfortable depressions, making immediate to Tat's senses the solid persons of August and his wife. He wanted to take Lorena away from all this tasteless stuff. His idea was for her to get a couple of rooms—it didn't matter how simple, as far away as possible from the Borough, where he could go to see her. They both had jobs, they were independent of each other and of their families, they could share the expenses. But this furniture, he realized, had to be reckoned with; the electrolier with the Tiffany glass stood proxy for Lorena's parents.

"What would your father say if you—if we—just set up housekeeping somewhere?"

Lorena laughed with an odd inflection and threw herself down on the sofa near the window. "He'd gripe about it at first; but after a while he'd settle down and get used to it."

"Your father's swell," said Tat, overlooking for the moment Mr. Hessenwinkle's bourgeois mentality. "I get along fine with him. But how about your mother? I don't think she likes me."

"Oh, she likes you all right," said Lorena. Her tone of voice required elucidation. "Momma don't think a whole lot of your job—she thinks there isn't much money in filling stations. I told her—I said, The filling station's just temporary, Momma; Tat's too big a person to stay there long. He's just got some ideas he's gotta work out."

Mrs. Hessenwinkle, like a lot of other people, said Tat, unconsciously falling into his father's oracular periods, would come to realize that the world was going to be different. In a mechanized civilization gasoline was an essential, and what people would be asking about a job was, is it essential? not, is there any money in it? There would be no more money in her real-estate operations than in filling stations in the socialized state that liberals like themselves were working for; government housing would bring rents down within reach of the poor (the projec's have undercut Momma already, Lorena put in—you ought to hear her on that business) well, that was tough, but everybody was going to have to make a readjustment. Mr. Hessenwinkle too; co-operatives, collective farming, etc., would cut out wholesalers and middlemen . . . look at these ratty tenements in the Borough . . . we've got to do away with all that . . . we've got to change the system. . . .

Lorena listened in silence and kneaded her gum. "You're sure the boy for ideas, honey." There was more admiration than acceptance in her voice, but he was content with this for the moment.

Actually, he liked the Hessenwinkle clan and had high hopes of winning them to his view—he even liked Mrs. Hessenwinkle, though she rented her tenements to Negroes at stiff rates. But he couldn't help being magnetized by her large good humor, her wonderful booming laugh when she was really amused, her pervading glandular fleshiness; and he was slowly working himself up to the point of confronting her some day with the unanswerable arguments of socialism. In the crowded, careless Hessenwinkle household he felt an ease that he never knew among his own kind; he went to the Schuetzenfest with August and the boys and drank beer and tried out the shooting galleries. The whole family accepted him quite simply at Lorena's valuation, they admired his brains and roared at his line . . . imagine an aristocrat who made fun of the St. Cecilia balls, who was all the time taking cracks at his folks—calls 'em the Sacred Cows! That was funny as a crutch.

Tat found this admiration curiously stimulating. He found he could be witty and sarcastic, and Lorena always liked him better that way. With her he was at his best, he could never talk that way when he was with Lucian, damn it; Lucian generally beat him to the draw. . . .

The bright parlor disturbed Tat increasingly. When would they bring good modern stuff down within reach of the lower income groups? He switched off the light, banishing the elder Hessenwinkles from the foreground, and went and sat by Lorena. She leaned against the back of the settee and they sat for a while in a pleasant silence. But in the dimness that replaced the too real parlor, another image materialized and disturbed the peace. His mother—how she would feel about his plans he well knew. He had a pang of wholly involuntary remorse at hurting her, for when he was away from her, his deep affection would well up unbidden. He was her favorite child, but her love shamed him and so he jerked away from her . . . along the cloudy backward track of his life that situation had taken form, had even pre-existed him, or thus it seemed. For what he had wanted as he scrambled among the monstrous uncertainties of growing up was not her female protectiveness but the male admiration of Fen and his father. Those two had always stood together in the family, with a kind of closeness Tat could never break into. It was partly because Fen was five years older, but it was partly something else.

Like that time he had rocked Rummy Mullins' greenhouse. He remembered his father fuming all summer about the city election which was a hot one even for Charleston. At the age of ten Tat didn't make much of it except that his father and Fen despised Rummy Mullins, who was a crook and a grafter.

"What's a grafter?" asked Tat, hating Rummy Mullins too and wanting to know why.

A grafter, it seemed, was a person who took money, decent people's, poor people's money, and spent it on himself. Look at that new house Rummy had built down the street—where'd he get money for all that swank? With a greenhouse, forsooth! He's getting it from you and me, Mr. Redcliff had answered his own question. We are paying for that greenhouse. . . .

Behind his spectacles Tat nearly burst with hate of Rummy who stole Redcliffs' and poor people's money; and on the way home from the ball-field that evening he went by Rummy's house to see the iniquity. There it stood, glistening in the dusk with newness and effrontery; the workmen had not yet removed the little pile of tools and bricks beside it. Nothing ever equaled the sensual pleasure Tat felt as he sent the bricks crashing through the boastful glass, smiting wickedness and making that gorgeous noise.

He ran home as fast as he could to tell his father and Fen. Look what I did for our side. I have taken a part in this man's war. But how incalculable the effects of righteousness can be. Rummy, it appeared, had recognized him as he sped away and had already telephoned his father. As shattering as bricks through glass was his father's anger . . . the way to sock a grafter was not to smash his property—he might put you in the cooler. Besides, the Redcliffs were now going to have to pay for the greenhouse the second time. "You big dope!" said Fen. His mother, a smasher of greenhouses in her own way, had taken his side and thus confirmed his folly.

It occurred to Tat for the first time that Fen might easily, at the age of ten, have rocked Rummy Mullins' greenhouse himself, and that his echoing the parental reproaches was merely his own attempt to seem adult, the impossible ambition youth so clumsily pursues. In any case, Fen's death had been a bewildering blow, and Tat thought now of their relationship in a mist of pain and regret. He wanted to tell Fen he was in love with Lorena. Warmth flowed through his body as it came to him that Fen would approve. For Fen and Lorena, he discovered, had something in common—a kind of success maybe. Fen had always liked Lorena and it was he, actually, who had directed Tat's attention to her—that is, as a personality, lifting her out of the group of shadowy-featured older girls who had grown up about him.

It was nearly three years ago now, that summer Fen had spent at the house in the Borough while Judith stayed in the mountains with the family, getting over infantile. Tat came home in September from a long cruise on a cattle-ship and at once sought Fen, who had gone out on the Mall, Bekah told him, to enjoy the evening cool. In the small public square Tat found him easily, sitting on a bench with Lorena; and hurrying over the offhand brotherly greetings, he sat down to tell them about his summer trip. He was eager to describe to Fen (and perhaps make him envious) the entrancing coasts he had sailed, the storms barely weathered, the sapphire Caribbean. But after a little of this his hearers' attention wandered, Fen and Lorena went back to the conversation they were having when he joined them—an argument about nothing in particular that Tat could see, just a sort of verbal thrust and parry as if they translated some private contest into a different language. As Tat sat excluded on his end of the bench, looking from one to the other for an opening to bring up his cruise again, he noticed on Fen's face a naïve male look of irrepressible interest in a woman who is close by and personally attractive. Surprised, Tat glanced at Lorena, and was even more surprised to see (as if he had changed seats with Fen) that she was, indeed, personable. He leaned forward on his elbow the better to scrutinize her abundant hair, dark at the roots but coppery on its outer waves, her teasing brown eyes, the cupid's bow of thick crimson superimposed on her mouth. Her pose against the back of the bench showed to advantage her full curves, and she met Fen's glance sidewise, as one used to bringing that look to men's faces.

Tat sat on his end of the bench, silent, bemused with this discovery, until it was time to go in for supper. He felt a little dashed to have missed something obvious that his older brother had characteristically caught. Later he broached the subject to Fen. "Lorena Hessenwinkle's got plenty of 'it.' " But Fen merely answered, "I'll say!" and went on mending his fishing tackle. Tat saw them talking together only once again that autumn.

But if Fen had forgotten his momentary interest, Tat hadn't. He took Lorena to the movies once or twice, and when she suddenly went off to Detroit, the Mall looked dull and drought-bitten. The following year she reappeared and he sought her there with new curiosity; she was so natural, so frank, and so democratic—she had no more use for the social crowd, he discovered, than he had. Later on he began to drop in at the Hessenwinkle house, where he talked politics with August, swapped gamey stories with Mrs. Hessenwinkle to hear her infectious laugh, and gazed his fill on Lorena whom he persuaded, as time went by, to go with him regularly.

Strange sequence of events, growing out of a passing look on Fen's face! Not that he wouldn't have fallen for her anyway—he couldn't imagine otherwise.

The gray room suffused with yellow drew round him again and he began to talk to Lorena, assuring her of the constancy of his feeling . . . it wasn't, of course, that he didn't want to marry *her*.

In the vague golden light coming in from the street lamps he felt her eyes searching him intently and with doubt. "Is that so?

[54]

I never thought about it much before; but since I saw Judith—well, it's got me kinda stirred up."

"Don't be silly, of course it's so. You know how I feel about you. You see, Rena, your trusting me would keep me yours as long as you want me—much longer than any piece of paper."

She thought this over for a while. "I believe you, Tat," she said at last. "You're a good egg. Yet still I can't figure it out. The kind of set-up you want is jus' harder on a woman than on a man. There's a lot of things . . . I guess that's what makes us feel different about it."

Tat paused in his turn. Was he being selfish about this? His readiness for self-accusation laid him open to horrid doubt. Was he asking more of her, his beautiful Lorena, than he realized? The world was not geared yet for the ideal relationship between men and women, people were stupid, mean and conventional, and women *were* more vulnerable than men.

Kissing reverently her full bare arms and round disturbing breasts, he found the idea of possessing them permanently did not revolt his sense of liberty.

Still, he wanted to fight stupidity. The only way to break down conventional morality was to break it down. And he wanted to get Lorena away from her family and their subservience to the Church; then he could make her see how all this stuff was just superstition . . . mankind *has* to go on to make a better morality. And having the unbounded faith of his kind in the promise and potency of argument, he kissed her good night and went home, marshaling his facts for the next time.

Book III

THE next morning came up clear. The sun, gathering power even by quarter to nine, intended to do its summer best, but there was an exhilaration in its golden stroke, or so Wick Redcliff thought as he stood for a moment on Broad Street between car and office. Fine cotton weather . . . he saw the blue-green fields checkering the state; if the rain would hold off for a while now the bolls could mature before the bollweevil got at them, the farmers would make good crops and pay for their fertilizer, his company would pay off part of its loan at the bank. He half-composed a prayer to the rain god to show a simple reticence that would make everybody happy. At this moment he wanted to have an altar, sweetly carved, in the garden behind his house, on which he could put the first figs or a pair of young pigeons (the damn creatures kept the piazza dirty, anyhow) and to importune the Deity—spare the crops, multiply the cattle, shower me and my children with blessings.

But we no longer have the conviction, he thought, going up the narrow dark staircase to his office. High or low pressure areas in Alaska had already decreed the weather for the next weeks, and he had no hope of undeserved benefits for his family. If they would just keep out of mischief, that was all he asked.

The morning mail engulfed him. The way people wasted paper! He treated his timberland conservatively, and to think of trees consumed by this stuff made him sick. He hurled a batch of advertisements into the scrap basket and startled his stenographer, but just as he began to lecture her on the South's waste of its natural resources, the feet of the first morning visitor sounded on the stair. He recognized the step, one heavy, one light, before Judith put her head in the door and said, "Uncle Wick, can I come in?" In the course of time that trochaic beat had ceased to connote a handicap and had become a part of her personality, of the gallantry with which she met her difficulties. His pink, clean face was puckered with a tenderness and pleasure that was almost a smile as he rose and went forward.

"Come in—why not? You 'modern' women amuse me. You think because you have a job that you're emancipated, but when you come down on Broad Street and beard the male in his last stronghold, you're as bashful as if you still wore chemises." He took her chin in his hand and scrutinized her with severe affection, thinking she looked pale and over-serious.

"But I *have* business," Judith protested, flushing under his teasing, "otherwise I'd be at my own office. I wanted to talk to you about that investment—and some other things." She rolled her eyes toward the stenographer clattering away at her desk.

"Well, come into my lair—" He led her back to a small room crowded with books, pamphlets, dusty cases full of bones, arrowheads, and sharks' teeth scooped up by the dredges in other days when his company had dug phosphate rock in the neighborhood of Charleston. Routed up from subsoil oblivion and strewn at his feet, the fossils touched some vein in his own composition; he kept them about him for their dry reminder of mortality.

"What's on your mind?" he asked when they were seated by the window, wedged between the golden oak revolving bookcase and his cumbersome walnut desk.

"I went to your house yesterday afternoon to tell you—I've seen Lorena."

His eyebrows went up, though less at her statement than at her curious distressed look. "You don't say! What sort of impression did you get?"

"Well—we—had a fight!"

He understood that she meant not a physical combat but an exchange of the shrill and naked epithets with which women settled their differences. "A fight? But my dear child, that hardly seems necessary."

Judith gave him a swift account of her reasons for going to see O'Dell. "Then he went off somewhere and I had a chance to ask her—tactfully, I thought—about Tat. At first she was quite friendly. The funny thing about Lorena is that sometimes she seems a simple soul, cheerful and wanting to be friends, and then you run onto a hardness that you can't explain. Well, before I knew it we were on the mat, about Tat, and the whole family. I'm sure there's something between Tat and herself!"

Her dark glance was so disturbed that he swung his swivel chair away from it and looked out of the window without speaking. He had been sure of it too, yet this new evidence disconcerted him; and at the same time his divided mind took his son's part (his own sporting days being not so far distant, after all). "My, my," he scoffed, addressing the view, "how censorious these advanced females get when their men infringe the moral code!" It really surprised him to find Judith taking the affair so seriously.

Before he could think this out she surprised him again. "Uncle Wick, Fen never worked for you, did he?"

"Fen? Well, yes, he did a short turn with us, the summer after he finished college. He wanted a job and I sent him up to the plant to learn the fertilizer business from the ground up." She was leaning forward on her elbows, her hands tightly entwined and he saw her bow her head so that the dipping brim of her hat would hide the dark red that rushed to the surface of her skin. Why in God's name—?

"What's the matter, my dear, don't you feel well?"

She ignored this and said in a dim voice quite unlike her own warm cadence, "I can't believe he wouldn't have mentioned it— sometime or other—just in the natural course of things."

"Didn't he ever? Yes, that does seem strange. But Fen was an active creature who lived in the present—and perhaps he didn't care to dwell on that episode, because he didn't do very well at the plant."

"He didn't?" She looked up, disbelieving.

"We fathers are a naïve race, Judith. We keep right on hoping that our sons will think our life's work important enough to carry on. Neither of mine did: one prefers to fill tanks with gasoline, the other found building tug-boats more to his taste. From the time he was a little boy Fen was besotted with boats and he couldn't put his mind on a grubby profession like digging up the ground for phosphate rock. I tried to interest him in my collections, but to Fen a buffalo bone was no good without the rest of the buffalo. As a part of the story of North American culture, it prophesied to him not at all. So he didn't attend to business very

[58]

closely and when a vacancy occurred at the Drydock Company, he shot off after it like a stranded fish that feels a wave under it again. If he didn't mention the plant to you, it was probably that he preferred to forget this discreditable episode in a ship-builder's career."

Judith seemed to have recovered herself a little, so he ventured to ask, "What has all this got to do with Tat and Lorena?"

"Oh . . . nothing."

"Well, tell me some more about your interview. What did she say about Tat that made you think the affair is serious?"

"Nothing very definite, it was more her manner. She was on the defensive about him, and talked as if she owned the Redcliff family. I must admit she made me furious, and everything I said seemed to enrage her. And yet I went there feeling perfectly friendly. I was curious, of course, but I went mostly about the bill . . . Uncle Wick, I want to take that money you spoke about yesterday and pay the Friendly Hearth Wood Yard. The Welfare can pay me back when the taxes come in."

Fenwick Redcliff shot a quick look at his daughter-in-law and the chiseled muscles about his mouth quivered as he thought how, yesterday, she had smiled at his concern over Tat and Lorena. But he couldn't fathom the profound pressure that tensed her long legs and her shapely brown hands as she sat there before him. "Aren't you taking the world pretty seriously today, Judith? After all, you have no personal responsibility for this bill."

"But I want it paid." This hard obstinate look was not becoming to her; it sharpened an angle of fanaticism in her face. "I promised them I would see to it; and I won't be subjected to a bill collector."

He took off his glasses, polished them with his handkerchief and put them on again, a nervous habit he had when honesty came in conflict with his natural politeness.

"I hardly think O'Dell will resort to a bill collector."

"But Lorena will."

"Oh, I see. This is an affair of honor among the ladies. Well, it would take a bold man to step between the carving knives."

His sarcasm brought a smile to her intent face, a relaxed, somewhat sheepish smile. She leaned over and took his hand. "Let me have my way this time, Uncle Wick," she coaxed. "You make any arrangement you like; I'll sign a note for the Welfare—or whatever you think."

He spoke with affectionate directness. "You can't afford to be taking quixotic stands about money, Judith. Signing notes is a bad habit—you won't find O'Dell doing that kind of thing. Suppose you let me think it over a bit. Perhaps I'll talk to O'Dell and see how the land lies."

"Promise you'll do something about it and not just shrug it off?"

"Yes, since you're so set on self-immolation."

She got up smiling and kissed him. "Uncle Wick, what a help you are—you're an angel without portfolio—I don't know what I'd do if you ever got really fed up with me. But I have to fly now; Mrs. MacNab's wig will be down on her nose by this time from telling the girls she *knew* Judith would be late again."

"What does Mrs. MacNab think of your offer to pay the bill?" he asked as he followed her through the outer office.

"She doesn't know about it yet. I'm going to talk to her this morning, though I won't go into the whole story, of course." The strain came back to her face as she stood for a moment against the white panel of the open door and said good-by.

"You look lovely, my dear, in your pink calico—or whatever it is." Wick had a helpful theory that if you told women they were beautiful they became so. Like a rose . . . like a picture, he would say; the banality of the terms didn't matter, so honest was his intent to please. Judith obliged him by flushing at his old-fashioned compliment, her ardent affections came up to him from the reservoir in which she confined them and played over her face like a ray reflected from water. Actually she had a special loveliness for him because he saw her touched with tragedy, her eyes dark and sorrowful with Fen's death, with her lameness, with other burdens he could not fathom. The slightly uneven step jarred along his nerves as she went down the outside stair.

He hung his light blue seersucker coat on the back of his chair, and while his spirit still held Judith, Fen, Tat, like bulbs wintering in a basement, he allowed the affairs of the office to take over the surface of his mind. He argued a matter of policy with James Courtonne, his partner; James was a sound businessman but infected of late with the modern fallacy that change is progress. But why modern? A fallacy as old as Eden; it was probably the desire for change *per se* that drove our forefathers out of the garden, a subtle heresy which the author of Genesis externalized, with sound literary instinct, as the serpent. . . .

He interrupted this congenial train of thought to war with himself awhile over whether he should go on the board of the Public Affairs Forum. Outwardly the war took the form of an argument with Miss Finch, his elderly stenographer, but in reality it was an engagement in the continuing battle between his better and his worse selves, or between the doer and the spectator in his make-up. Miss Finch had, alas, passed the peak of her usefulness; her typing was slower, she was absentminded and couldn't put her hand at once on the desired papers. But Wick couldn't make up his mind to replace her. Gratitude for her long service swayed him; then his argument with Courtonne that change was not necessarily progress somehow confused the issue; then too Miss Finch admired him extravagantly—and so one way and another he kept her on and offset her deficiencies as a stenographer by finding another use for her.

He called her to take a letter, remarking as he laid the Forum's communication on the desk that he supposed he should accept this invitation; forums were probably a good idea. Miss Finch was a lady, and within his private office they talked as compeers, so she replied that he should by all means accept . . . a valuable community enterprise . . . people like himself should take a stand. This being just the answer he expected from the Voice of Conscience, the role he forced Miss Finch all unwitting to play, he snatched his weapons from the wall. Speaking as a practical man he averred that most people had something of the busybody in them, that the only value of forums was that the busybodies blew themselves off in talk, that the more they talked the less they did, and thus kept out of mischief. Now if a man had anything of real importance to say about matters of public interest, he couldn't get it in edgewise amid the gabbling and honking and hissing that went on. If he got into one of these discussions, he would sooner or later lose his head and start telling the truth—that was the last thing anybody wanted.

"After all," said Miss Finch hardily, "there are some people who value honesty; after all—"

"Fiddlesticks!" Wick talked her down—against all his early training he couldn't help bullying the ladylike Miss Finch. "'There's not a grain of honesty to sweeten the face of the whole dungy earth!'"

At the impact of this robust pessimism Miss Finch's pompadour, which was excessively fine and straight, collapsed sidewise. Its fall brought Wick a sweet triumph. He dictated a short letter full of ironic formalities to the Public Affairs Forum and declined the honor they had thrust upon him on grounds of pressing business and his own unworthiness. Thin, silent, and resigned, Miss Finch wrote down the distasteful hieroglyphics.

Having watched the Voice of Conscience go with fallen crest out of the door, he felt well satisfied to have justified to himself once more his increasing taste for solitude. He scarcely went anywhere nowadays and luckily Etta, his wife, liked to stay at home too. For the past two years their being in mourning had served as an excuse, and while he thought she prolonged the period with a touch of the martyr's meek exhibitionism, he indulged her excess in this instance, since the passing of time had done little to ease the hurt of Fen's death.

He gave his chair a brisk half-twirl as he went back to thinking, not without malicious amusement, of Judith's encounter with Lorena. He wished he had witnessed it. It was true what Judith said about the girl; you felt in her a simple desire to please, and yet, she had a hard streak. Those stories about her—

But what promise did she see in Tat? She would surely be shrewd enough to know that Tat wasn't a money-maker. When he had failed in his examinations at Princeton he had gone angrily home and taken a job at a filling station, an act which Wick himself had approved. Regretfully he admitted that his younger son was not "college material." Tat had plenty of sense but he lacked stability, and a year or so of hard work, of standing on his own feet, would bring him closer to realities, and then they would see what could be found for him.

But Tat had remained at the filling station. He insisted he liked it, liked the cars driving up all day long with country men and their children, their crates of chickens and cabbages, the tourist trailers heading for Florida, Negroes from the sea islands in asthmatic model-T Fords, young fry with streaming hair setting off for the beaches. He hated the white chauffeurs of the Northern visitors. "But," his father remarked, "you relish your hates so much, you really enjoy that too." Then Tat had taken a legacy from Etta's brother and bought a share in the filling station, or rather, in the small chain of independent filling stations to which it belonged; for by that time he had identified his job with a crusade against the big oil companies. Lucian teased Tat about his excursion into cut-throat capitalism; he addressed Tat as "Mr. Rocks," or "the erl-king," and pretended that he was scheming to become the tycoon of his generation, but Tat ignored this and all of Lucian's gibes and persevered in his role of executive, station attendant, and street-corner orator against entrenched privilege.

The role was not lucrative, and Lorena must know this—or did she assume that the oil business meant money eventually? Wick decided to go and talk to Lucian about it. Lucian had a talent for knowing about people's affairs. Besides, Lucian, who was forty-five, bridged the generations and still spoke the language of the young, an idiom immeasurably subtle and difficult to the rusty tongue of fifty-nine.

The sun was blaring on the sidewalk like a brass band as he went out buttoning his coat. He crossed Broad Street in a long diagonal, walking with deliberation between the automobiles and the darting colored boys on bicycles, as a man walks who has confidence that his fellow-citizens all know him and would not willingly knock him down. On the shady side of the street he took his time, bowing and smiling on everyone, even on the leaden Indian before the tobacconist's, who sat on his bale of tobacco leaves and enjoyed the spectacle of men agitating themselves greatly about small matters.

Farther along, the sun struck fire from the great gold eagle spread above the classic yellow façade of the Bank; but while Wick had an abiding affection for the Indian sitting quietly there in the shade, the eagle merely entertained him as a naïve symbol of the folklore of finance. Almost in the shadow of its golden feathers, he saw James Courtonne talking on the street corner and vigorously exercising a palm-leaf fan. His own theories on gold and sound money were, he considered, irrefutable, and even if they weren't, he could always get James going in an argument. However, he resisted the temptation to stop and accelerate the flip-flap of the fan, and kept the straight path to Lucian's office.

His thoughts veered off like pigeons along the jig-saw roof lines that converged on the Old Exchange at the foot of the street. Most of these buildings had started out as dwellings, or shop-and-dwelling combinations, and had suffered periodic faceliftings. At the street level, plate glass and gold lettering spruced up the brokerage and insurance offices, striped awnings flapped over the drugstore and the bookstore (not yet amalgamated in these latitudes); the upper stories beetled with heavy cornices and other improvements of Victorian taste; and from the steep slate roofs the high dormers, small-paned, peered with old eyes at the anachronisms below. Of these last the stenographers were probably the most anachronistic, for this female invasion of the groves long sacred to man had come about within his recent memory. Young ladies, ungloved and unhatted, hurried with papers in their hands to the Bank, to the stationers, and their free stepping, their heads eloquent of the beauty parlor, altered the aspect of Broad Street more than the hand of any architect.

However the dormers might look upon the invaders, Wick warmed to them; he was not too old, thank God, to be disturbed now and then by a swinging skirt, the curve of a leg or a bosom. A peculiar disturbance, composed of sweetness, guilt, and nostalgia for certain flamboyant episodes of his youth. But he kept himself pretty well in hand, man being by nature born in sin. He had banked the fires of passion against the winter and he was happily married—or he supposed that the long train of collisions, shared adventures, annoyances, and physical satisfactions he had had with Etta added up to a happy marriage.

He approached an archway flanked by shops, above which a sign in bold Roman lettering said, LUCIAN QUINTILLIAN REDCLIFF—REAL ESTATE. In Lucian's youth this resounding patronymic had embarrassed him and he had tried to minimize it with modest type that read, "L. Q. Redcliff, Real Estate and Plantations." But he had come to recognize that it had distinction, a virtue he dearly cherished, and to like its evidence of classics-loving forebears whose taste he had inherited with the name.

Wick's blue seersucker took on a rich indigo as he entered the deep shade of the passageway. At the far end he crossed a court-yard paved with brown kitchen flagstones, to a small building with a columned portico. The reason for lavishing the frivolous formalities of the Greek Revival on a little house hidden in a back yard had perished with the builder, and the riddle, Wick thought, as he went up the outside staircase to the second floor, added salt and piquancy to this place that Lucian had nosed out and made into an office.

A tortoise-shell cat sat on the plinth of a column enjoying the breeze, and gave Wick an inhospitable glance as he came abreast. Through the open door he could see Lucian leaning on the window sill at the rear of the room and looking intently into the back yard of the adjoining house.

"Hello," he said, going in. "For all the fun you like to poke at animal-lovers, I believe you feed that cat on the sly to keep him away from his lawful owners."

Still leaning on his hands, Lucian turned his wary, intelligent face and peered over his shoulder as if from an ambush. "It's the people who go in for being dog- and cat-lovers that bore the pants off me," he said, "but I don't hold it against the animals themselves. It wouldn't be logical. Besides, Joseph is an exceptional cat."

"Oh. So you've baptized him already. The process of adoption is well advanced."

Lucian straightened up and faced about, smiling a little shame-facedly to be caught red-handed in an act of sentiment. "With that polychrome coat of his he couldn't escape the name," he said, glancing through the door at Joseph for justification as he went round his desk and sat down by his half-brother. He was shorter than Wick and his coloring was darker, but the same bones ran through them both. Lucian's skin also followed un-compromisingly the planes of his skull, indeed he barely escaped a too sculptured, almost a death's-head look, by the live move-ments of his gray-green eyes. His nose descended from his fore-head in a straight bridge, but at the tip it unexpectedly turned up and a little to one side, thereby spoiling the pure Greek line he would so have liked.

"What do you know about the social activities of your nephew Tat?" Wick began at once.

[65]

"Not much," Lucian parried, meaning he didn't intend to tell much until he knew what was up. "Been having parental worries about his indiscretions?"

"Etta put me up to it." Wick shamefully shifted the responsibility under Lucian's sarcastic smile. "You know Tat's the apple of her eye, and she's convinced he spends most of his time with Lorena Hessenwinkle, though she hasn't much to go on except intuition."

"Extraordinary faculty—this woman's intuition. It's unbelievable how it enables them to take a short cut to the truth, while we less gifted males are floundering among facts. Well, Lorena's a personable piece of—"

"Don't be so damned mysterious," said Wick, cutting short the anticipated ribaldry. This air of knowing more than he proposed to tell was one of Lucian's little vanities, and what made it irritating was that sometimes he did (his thirsty curiosity about his fellow-creatures was insatiable) and sometimes he didn't; you could never count on his knowing or not knowing. To Wick especially he liked to play omniscience, he teased him incessantly to disguise the affection tinged with a respect he had never quite been able to outgrow for his older brother. Wick well understood the familial origin of Lucian's gibes, and they had the same kind of sense of humor, so they seldom hurt each other. But today he had a worry on his mind and he found Lucian disobliging.

"I was talking to Judith about them yesterday," he went on, "and she took the same contrary attitude toward parents that you do. She thought I was making a mountain out of a molehill, until she saw Lorena herself. It seems the Fuel and Welfare Society owes O'Dell a fairly stiff bill and Judith went, ostensibly, to see about it, though I suspect curiosity about Lorena was at the bottom of it. At all events they had one of those feminine hair pullings—"

"Did they?" cried Lucian enthralled. Omniscience fell off him like a garment. "What about? I can't imagine Judith's really letting fly—but come to think of it, she's pretty intense, and full of queer loyalties. What did they quarrel over?"

"I couldn't quite make out. The payment of the bill had something to do with it, but Tat was the burning topic apparently. Judith is now convinced there's something between them."

"I could have told her there was 'something between them'; the question is—what? What are the terms? And what does Lorena get out of Tat? Of course her present residence in the crowded house of papa Hessenwinkle indicates that she has nothing more rewarding in sight. She used to have an apartment on Calhoun Street—you remember?—nicely fixed up, too. That was in her Belchers period. You know the story of her throwing slops on Mrs. Belchers."

"It was water when I heard about it," said Wick dryly. "Now it's progressed to slops."

"Clean water to slops is the natural progression—I never heard of its going the other way. But to get back to Lorena, sacred love seems to have triumphed over profane in that incident. Mrs. Belchers had society, which is even more dousing than slops, on her side, and she broke up the affair."

Wick sat frowning at the floor, his face doleful. He didn't like to think of Lorena with Belchers. She seemed so lively and attractive . . . perhaps it wasn't true . . . Tat would deny it . . . yet it had all the earmarks of the usual story. Belchers, businessman and good church member, fumbling for something his stodgy marriage failed to give him. And Lorena . . . well, Lorena—

"She must know Tat has no money," he said abruptly.

"She undoubtedly knows it. But she also knows Tat's old man is well fixed."

"You can't rule out the possibility that she may be genuinely fond of Tat."

At his brother's defensive tone Lucian's eyes changed. He dropped his teasing manner and spoke in a different voice. "I don't rule it out. Don't get me wrong, Wick; God forbid that I should be censorious about the Lorenas of the world. They have their necessities—and nature gave this one what it takes to go places. Why shouldn't she trade on the fatal gift of pulchritude? However, her admirable realism doesn't mean that she mightn't, like the rest of us, fall in love with the most unsuitable person; the tart isn't any safer from indiscretion than the virgin. Not that Lorena is either one or the other. But why are you in such a huff-snuff about it? I can't make out what you expect to do."

"I can't make out, either," Wick owned. "It's partly that I can't help worrying about Tat. Fen usually managed to get himself out of his scrapes, but Tat's actions always have the most unexpected consequences. To him, at least. I thought I'd talk to him and point out that Lorena's parents may take the view that he's trying to get something for nothing."

"Very likely they will," said Lucian reflectively, pushing the tip of his nose straight with his forefinger, a trick he had when preoccupied. "I'll venture that stalwart mama of hers is capable of meeting the situation forthrightly, with a shotgun if necessary. What I can't get the feel of is Lorena's attitude. She's got plenty of sense, and a sort of resilience—she takes life as it comes and gets a lot of fun out of it."

Wick observed with secret amusement Lucian's shift from skepticism to championship of Lorena. His irritation gone, he relaxed, smoked, and allowed his eye to travel about the office while Lucian spun out his analysis. Sunlight rippled on the cool undersea-green of the walls and on a large map of the town and adjacent waters in a narrow vermilion frame which covered the blank side of the room. Red-headed pins scattered over the map indicated properties in which Lucian had an interest, financial, historical, or sentimental. Bookcases filled the wall space between the windows, but the shelves were given over less to books than to junk—old locks and keys he collected in his dealings with houses, old pistols and clocks with their entrails indecently exposed beside them. Lucian was always taking things apart to see how they worked—his friends, his enemies, love, life itself; consequently he was surrounded by useless bits of mechanism. As for his own emotions, they lay strewn about him like fine powder from his incessant grindings and siftings. He still had the emotions; they sometimes blew up a gust against his own logic, so people found him inconsistent. But it was only that he was distributed, Wick thought; he was both the man of heart and the logician—you could never predict which character would come out on top.

"Going back to the fracas between Judith and Lorena," said Lucian, "what sort of hand did O'Dell play?"

"Don't know exactly, but no doubt he would like his bill paid. Judith has her head set on paying it; she's talking about taking some of her own money."

"Don't let her."

"I won't if I can help it. But Judith is a hard-headed piece when she's really roused."

"She and Lorena must have had *some* hair pulling!" cried Lucian enviously. "I can imagine Judith putting on one of her dedicated moods, and Lorena would be just the girl to take her apart. God, I'd like to have seen it!"

Wick laughed, noticing as he had before that Lucian was often a little nasty about Judith; it wasn't clear why, unless some obscure jealousy came into it, some envy because Judith had had happiness and fulfillment and even sorrow, a gamut of experience that Lucian himself had missed. For in spite of his sharp cracks he was devoted to Judith and saw a great deal of her—

"Which reminds me," Lucian was saying, "I was refereeing another battle of the Amazons when you came in. I wonder what's happened." He jumped up and ran to the back window with a quick, light step unexpectedly like Fen's on the deck of a sailboat. Wick rose and followed. The window looked on a row of back yards belonging to some Negro houses, a motley of umbrella trees, steaming wash-pots, children, roosters, cur-dogs, the piercing smell of mullet frying. The dark disputants had disappeared, though shrill words flew like plates and skillets from within doors. "They probably settled it with hatchets," said Lucian, "which is after all good sense. It finishes an argument with no loose ends."

"You waste the hell of a lot of time looking out of this window," Wick scolded, taking Lucian by the back of the neck as he used to do in their younger days. Aunt Quince (Wick's stepmother) always said he was the only person who could "manage" Lucian.

"I waste the hell of a lot of time," Lucian agreed. "But there's always something going on—this window is like a box seat at the season's best play, human nature in the raw. The patterns of behavior are horrifyingly clear down there, and you'd be surprised how they help in figuring out the patterns of the drawing room."

"Well, I've wasted enough time on *you* for one day," said Wick. "I'm going to see O'Dell about this disputed bill, and I'll try to sound him out about our family connection."

"I'll walk along with you," said Lucian, picking up his coat precipitately. His shirt was dry and clean in spite of the thermometer, his light suit unwrinkled. He followed Wick outside. "What becomes of Joseph when you lock up at night?"

As he went by Lucian tweaked the cat's yellow ear. "I give him a good breakfast, but at night he's on the town. Joseph is a bachelor like me, and if he can't find a hostess looking for an extra man, he's not the cat I take him for."

"A fine pair of scavengers," Wick grumbled as they fell into step going through the arch, for he knew Lucian was coming along out of sheer curiosity. He didn't, somehow, want Lucian there watching O'Dell and himself—it was going to be a delicate situation to discuss; so, emerging from the arch, he swung away abruptly, saying, "Well, I'll see you later. I have to stop at the Bank . . . see about some notes . . ." and darted in under the protective wings of the gold eagle.

Wick came out of the Bank and stood for a moment on the steps looking up and down the street. Lucian had disappeared, nor did he see any sign of O'Dell in the crowd. The affairs he had in mind were light yet important, and to seek O'Dell in his office would be too heavy-handed an approach. Besides, Wick preferred the street-corner method of doing business. From the small eminence of the steps he could see knots of people making deals, committees meeting in their shoes. Much better than stuffy conference rooms. Out of doors people were less twitchy, more amenable to common sense. He strolled toward the City Hall on a mild hunch that O'Dell might be there.

But the curved sweep of the marble steps showed no spoor of his quarry and he turned in through the scrolled iron gate of the park behind the building. It had a special appeal on a hot morning, this sequestered spot in the heart of the city, its quietude the more enclosed by the sound-truck blaring advertisements in the traffic outside. The children had drawn under the trees in clusters like sheep at noon, leaving their tricycles to bake in the sun; their black shepherdesses, with chain-store dresses and anti-kinked locks, sat against the boles talking and laughing in unrestrained falsettos. He would sit here for a minute, Wick thought, and get his ducks in a row before the interview, for O'Dell would show up sooner or later; everybody went down on Broad Street sometime during the morning, if only to find out what the talk was. The park was a small square, and he made for a bench that commanded the streets on three sides and enabled him to keep a casual vigil through the surrounding grille. He thought with a twinge of the letters Miss Finch would now be putting on his desk for signature, but these walks of rosy brick mottled with shade had a magic to shrink them in importance—indeed they were always unimportant to one of Wick's selves; and it was this amoral self that now came up from some under-stratum and sat on the bench, took off its Panama hat and crossed its legs comfortably.

"Breathes there a man with soul so dead. . . ." What is this love of country? he asked, for he could feel his affection for the park welling, flowing out through the gates, lapping on the sidewalk, and he thought he had better look into it. The bombast of Scott's lines explained nothing. Take the City Hall, for example, which the tide was now fluidly embracing: as an example of public architecture of the year 1801 he admired its proportions and restrained ornament; as the seat of government of his beloved city he owed it his devoir, in the fine old term; as the hatchery of city politics, American style, he was ready to put the axe to it. But though he inveighed against political abuses, though he cursed the stupid complacency of the citizenry, he continued most unreasonably to exude this genial sentiment which now flowed outward, embracing the bricks, the Court House, the Record Office, embracing even O'Dell who came twinkling past the palings of the iron fence and, as if in answer to his desire, turned in at the west gate and cut through the park.

At his hail O'Dell took the fork of the path to his bench. He surveyed Wick with a humorous smile that was wholly friendly.

"How're you, Mr. Redcliff? Taking the air?"

"I'm about to quit fertilizer for the park bench. I declare, it's delightful here this morning. Sit down; I've been wanting to have a talk with you."

He suddenly felt foolish about his lying in wait and began to cover himself with leaves of persiflage. "I don't know what the devil you're up to, but whatever it is it will probably turn out badly, or, at best, come to nothing; so you might as well sit down awhile and talk to me."

O'Dell was instantly willing. Not a bad fellow—who sat down so readily and talked.

[7 1]

"Is it hot enough for you? Phoo— Walking in the sun—"

"Nonsense. It's fine cotton weather, all a man could ask for. You should cultivate repose, like me. You know, I was sitting here thinking about this town—"

He would have liked to ask O'Dell if he, too, loved it absurdly, sentimentally; but you can't make such inquiries, it would be indecent, like asking a man right out if he believed in God. He went at it roundabout.

"Now over there in the churchyard," he nodded toward the high wall surrounding St. Michael's, its bricks purple as grapes against the sun, "repose the bones of the first of my people that came to this country, and here I am, the ninth or tenth generation, still on the site they cleared of trees and Indians. Why haven't I gone away where there are greater opportunities for making money and reputation? Because I don't want to go away. Why not? Blest if I can tell you. I lack the pioneer spirit—the idea of going away from a good place for ambition's sake has no appeal for me. Nor had it actually, I suspect, for the pioneers, who must have been damned uncomfortable at home to go bumping over the Appalachians in those springless wagons."

O'Dell's long upper lip puckered against the lower in a smile that was only half-suppressed; wrinkles gathered up the corners of his gray eyes. He got the drift, Wick saw; his limber, almost feminine intelligence, his unaffected desire to please, were quite disarming. They understood each other. Thus encouraged Wick took another flight.

"I rather like passing by the graves of the old people every day on my way to the office; it makes for continuity, which is the only way man, to my idea, with the stingy span of life allotted to him, can achieve anything. Now, those old people—the emigrants, as we call them here, to avoid the invidious *i*—"

"Now that's just the difference between us," said O'Dell, playing along easily in Wick's vein. "My grandparents were just immigrants. They came from Ireland after the potato famine."

"Eh? Well, they'll become emigrants in a generation or so," said Wick courteously. "I advise you to inaugurate the status right away. Ancestors are just like children, you can't begin training them too soon. Anyway, your children will make the change—it develops naturally."

"Maybe so, but bedam if I don't remember the old folks too well."

"Hmm. I have the advantage of you there. I'm free to imagine mine as fine-feathered as I like."

"I certainly do love to listen to you, Mr. Redcliff; you talk just like a book!" O'Dell gave him a half cheeky, half admiring grin. "I always remember my grandad with an old cap and a scarf knotted round his neck. He couldn't break himself in to a collar, though he made good money stevedoring—had a carriage and pair once. But it all went out the window in the War; he fought at Fort Sumter, you know, with the Irish Volunteers. Well, how'd we get to talking about our ancestors? People think we don't talk about anything else in Charleston."

"Why shouldn't we talk about them?" asked Wick. "It's damned affectation for a man to pretend he isn't interested in the forces that culminated so happily (as he supposes) in himself. But we can talk about our descendants just as handily. I had a visit from one of mine this morning, at least from a descendant by marriage. I refer to my daughter-in-law, Mrs. Fenwick Redcliff, Jr. She seemed to be in some distress about a bill which the Fuel and Welfare Society owes to your wood yard."

"Chicken feed," said O'Dell with a scattering sweep of his hand. "If that's all you wanted to talk about—don't take it seriously."

"Judith takes her job and all that goes with it pretty seriously," Wick persisted.

"Tell her not to worry about it. We had some differences at the office, but tell her to forget it; my bark is much worse than my bite."

"Hmm. My guess is it's the other way round."

O'Dell laughed appreciatively. "Hell, you and I aren't going to get in any argument over a little thing like a due bill."

"I gather that your niece doesn't think it's a little thing—at any rate the ladies seem to have had words on the subject."

With a sidelong flash of his gray eye O'Dell assured himself that Wick had been fully informed about the interview. "Phew!" he exclaimed, dashing it away with a flip of his wrist. "When women get to quarreling about money, it's time for us men to get from under. Cheesus!" They chuckled together, allied against the incredible, the silly, and dangerous sex. "I don't know what came over them. I went outside to see a man, everything was fine and dandy, but when I came back, they were cutting each other up small, and ready to start in on me. 'Look-a-here,' I said, 'you don't need to put me through the meat-chopper. *I* never said anything about a bill collector.' "

"Then you aren't really disturbed about the bill?"

"Not to speak of. The only thing is, sometimes at the end of the year the taxes run full and sometimes they run short, and the boys down there—you know how it is—pay off to the ones that have the inside track. Now old lady MacNab, she never had the inside track with anybody."

"Well, there was Mr. MacNab."

"I bet she never even had the inside track with him—God rest his soul. Anyway the Fuel and Welfare Society is nothing but a damn maverick; the county organization ought to take it over. I ought to keep behind them, but of course I wouldn't want to see your daughter-in-law lose her job."

Wick doubted if this motive carried much weight, but he recognized that O'Dell was making a generous gesture, so he accepted it as such. "That's very decent of you."

"Hell, we all have to live here, don't we, and do business together, so if you can do any little thing for a friend—molasses'll catch more flies than vinegar. Maybe we could get together on a proposition I have in mind. We could talk about it sometime. I may be in the market soon for a nice tract of timber."

"Well . . . sometime. But it's beyond me the way people will turn their land over to a timber company to be stripped. Nobody's going to do that to mine." Wick sat up, preparing to go. "I'm glad there's no real trouble about the Welfare bill, anyhow; and if the ladies back you into a corner again, send for me."

"They won't if I see them first! Apart they're mighty sweet, but together! One woman at a time is my motto."

"I wonder what was behind their disagreement." In his turn Wick looked sidelong at O'Dell.

O'Dell drew one foot up on the bench, his dark-fleeced hands embracing his knee. "It seems your son Tat had something to do with it—at least from what Rena said—" He retied his shoestring with nicety. "Rena's pretty fond of Tat, you know; she sees a lot of him."

[74]

A flight of pigeons landed before them and deployed on unsteady pink legs over the glowing brick, wading in rosiness. The breeze stirred the cowlick on Wick's high forehead. But he scarcely noticed; the park bench philosopher had drawn in like a snail and left a perplexed father, his tribe threatened, his pride on guard. In spite of his efforts self-consciousness creaked in his voice as he said, "I know Tat admires your niece very much."

"I mean to say! He camps around her like Grant around Richmond."

"But my daughter-in-law—Judith—is devoted to Tat. I can't imagine why they should quarrel about him."

"When women squabble it's about men or money, I always say." Some rising cloud had grayed O'Dell's sunny humor. "Well, I'll see you some more about that other business. I have my eye on some outside money I'd like mighty well to interest in coming here. Another party and myself are just looking around trying to locate a proposition that would appeal to them."

The idea ruffed Wick up, he didn't know just why. Some big timber company . . . he saw the heavy skidders dragging out the felled trees, destroying the young growth that should be husbanded for the future. He picked up his hat. "It's high time I thought about my neglected office, but I want to go back for a minute to my son. Tat's heart is in the right place and he's honest as the day is long, but he's young for his age and he has a lot of theories that life hasn't knocked out of him yet. Now, your niece is a very attractive, likable girl and I hope—or rather, I assume she is enough a woman of the world to understand Tat's attitude—"

"As to that, I couldn't say. Frankly, I think she's pretty stuck on him, and talk about heart—she's got all the heart in the world. People misunderstand Lorena because she's a little gay, you might say, and likes to have a good time—and why the hell shouldn't she? She's had tough breaks all around. She was as sweet a little girl as you could wish when she married Eleck Thompson, and he certainly treated her rough, leaving her high and dry in Cuba that way. Then he dies and another wife turns up and tries to claim the estate. Imagine how bad that made Rena feel."

The trouble with this story, Wick thought, was not that it seemed unlikely about Lorena, but that it sounded specious in O'Dell's mouth. He remained silent and O'Dell went on. "She's had a pretty tough time, all in all. You can't blame her for feeling sort of bitter."

"Is she bitter?"

"We-e-l-l, Tat's one of the upper crust. If he gives her a rush and then drops her—"

"He hasn't dropped her," said Wick shortly.

"Not yet. But you know what I mean."

Yes, thought Wick; it's just as I expected.

"Then," O'Dell pursued, "Miss Judith being high hat yesterday didn't help matters any."

"I can't imagine Judith's being high hat." Wick was genuinely astonished. He remembered her against the door of his office that morning looking defeated and unhappy.

"Rena seemed to think she was. Now, mind you, I like Miss Judith personally; she's a fine young lady and very game for being crippled like that. But she does have a manner; she holds herself kind of high, and if Rena takes a notion that the Redcliffs think they're too good for her—well, I wouldn't guarantee she won't shiver some crockery. Once she gets her Irish up—"

Wick swallowed his irritation and asked, "Does Tat's—er—hanging around worry Lorena's parents?"

"Naturally they don't want to see her get left. If I know August, he don't like it too much."

Wick twirled his hat and got up. "Well, there's no use putting up our umbrellas till it rains. Tat has good instincts and I'm sure he wouldn't want to hurt Lorena in any way. I think you are taking it all a little too seriously—but I have to be getting along. Coming my way?"

O'Dell remained seated, still clasping his ankle, and smiled up at Wick, but his gray eyes were shallow and no longer friendly.

"I don't mind telling you, August is going in with me on this timber proposition, if it comes off. You know August; he's a solid feller"—O'Dell's manner linked men of imagination like Wick and himself against the staid burgher—"and he likes damn well to see a net profit. I got a rough idea that if we can all get together and pull off something nice, it'll go a long way toward keeping him in a good humor about family troubles."

He rose, still smiling, and straightened his shoulders, throwing controversial matters behind him, and they walked along rapidly to cover the three blocks and be quit of each other. Small talk rattled between them: what could be done to bring new industries here . . . so many young men have to go away to make a living . . . this ought to be a great port . . . but the freight rates hold us back . . . well, we oughtn't to be talking like this—we ought to have faith in our home town.

" 'I have no faith, very little hope and only as much charity as I can afford.' " Quoting his Huxley put Wick in better humor, so when O'Dell said, "How about stopping in here for a coke?" he assented. "But make mine iced coffee; I'm not one of the Candler cult."

"Now take Asa B. Candler, there's a remarkable man. . . ." In the narrow café they lost themselves in the crowd and thus parted without farewell.

It was past noon, the café was full of conversation, the refreshing collision of ice particles, the drone of electric fans. Wick sat on for a while pondering his problem which loomed preternaturally large. So many incalculables . . . it's the unknown that makes you jumpy. The Hessenwinkle clan knew of Tat's infatuation, they were ready to resent it—that much at least was settled now that he had talked to O'Dell. And Lorena might "shiver some crockery." The idea of a noisy scandal disgusted him. He stirred his glass. "Coffee that makes the politician wise. . . ." He finished his, hoping there was more than mere poetry in the phrase.

Leaving the café he walked toward Lucian's office and was rewarded by the sight of his half-brother's rear protruding from the window of a car parked by the archway. The high-slung vehicle with its air of lumbering repose could belong to no one but Lucian's mother, to whom his invisible half was presumably talking. Wick approached and, pulling Lucian out of the aperture, he opened the door and greeted the plump little woman wedged in the corner of the seat, her morning's shopping piled about her.

"You came along just in time, Wick," she cried, tiny wrinkles of pleasure creasing her face that was as smooth as a cake of soap. "I was telling Lucian his posture was disgusting; imagine standing with your rump stuck out on a public thoroughfare! But he will hang in the window and talk to me about money."

"Trying to get some out of you, I suppose."

[77]

Lucian, still half leaning in the window of the open door, grinned self-consciously.

Mrs. Thomas Redcliff had received the family name of Quintillian as a middle name, and was known to her intimates as Quince. Wick often debated the question—do people take on the qualities of their names by a sort of fatality, or is it instinctive judgment that leads relatives to make now and then a miraculous choice of sobriquet? No one could be neutral about Aunt Quince; the entire connection lined up for or against her, depending on which half of her sour-sweet personality she faced toward them.

"How'd you make out with the eminent Hibernian?" Lucian asked.

"Oh, so-so. It was about as we expected." Wick gave him a significant look. "He came back with the suggestion that we might do business together."

"Hmm. Refined blackmail, in other words."

"Blackmail!" Mrs. Redcliff's eyes began to shoot sparks from the back seat.

How foolish to imagine that her sharp curiosity would let them exclude her from their conversation. Luckily Wick was endlessly amused by his stepmother, by the puckish forms her sense of humor took. In her early seventies she still had the wicked innocence of a child.

"I'll tell you all about it very soon, Aunt Quince," he said with a false air of taking her into his confidence. "But it's perishing hot on this pavement now."

"Why don't you come inside then, out of the sun?" She excavated a place for him among the vegetables and toys on the seat beside her. The ill-disposed said that the children of the family were just a pretext for Aunt Quince's extravagant buying of toys, she really wanted them for herself; someone even claimed to have surprised her once playing dolls all alone in her room. But Wick paid no attention to these jibes; besides, he would say, if it gives her any pleasure, in this world of illusory joys. . . . He climbed in by her and explained that he had just seen Harry O'Dell, who was a good fellow at heart, but sharp as a meat-axe.

"He's got hold of something, then, to blackmail you with."

Wick laughed. "You should be used to your son Lucian's extravagant talk by this time. No, I've committed no felonies lately.

But Tat's been going round a little with his niece, Lorena Hessen-winkle, and Lucian and I were wondering if it might make complications."

Mrs. Redcliff's thickly powdered face, turned toward him, shed these generalities. For a moment she sat fanning herself and him with kind impartiality, then she said, "So . . . Tat's picked up with that Hessenwinkle girl!"

Just what she'd expect, Wick interpreted. She kept up a polite but sleepless feud on Tat who countered her civil war with the ruder tactics of revolution. "Oh, come now; she's not a bad girl—" he paused and tripped over the adjective. By Aunt Quince's closely delimited standards Lorena was a bad girl, he supposed. Definitions change so with the generations. "The reign of Victoria has given place to the reign of Edward the Eighth, Aunt Quince, or what should have been his reign. As to Lorena, if you knew her, you'd be willing to make allowances." This, of course, was nonsense and sounded so. "After all, we're the product of our opportunities, our backgrounds, as you'd be the first to declare."

"Poor Wick, you do have awful pwoblems."

Learning to pronounce her r's had been a problem of Mrs. Redcliff's youth, and at moments her lifelong discipline in this regard broke down.

"Oh, it isn't as bad as all that."

"You do have awful pwoblems," she repeated and putting out her small, fat hand, pressed his with partisan fervor.

Wick laughed. "Well, I'll run along and attend to them. Can I do anything for you on Broad Street?"

"No, thank you, my dear. I must go along too. Lucian, remember what I said; please don't talk to me about money any more. It's a repugnant topic for ladies and gentlemen."

Wick got out and closed the door. "Well, good-by—"

As the chauffeur started the motor, she leaned forward and said through the window, "And I know that girl. So it's not a bit of use to tell me lies about her."

"Where did you ever know Lorena?" Lucian demanded.

"Never mind. In circumstances that might surprise you. Take my word for it, Wick, you'd better get Tat away from her right now." The old Cadillac pulled off with a long, lion snore.

Lucian and Wick stood on the curb and smiled after the car. "Now what in the devil does that mean?"

"God knows. You never can tell with Mother whether she knows more or less than she should."

"Hmm. Like mother, like son." Wick went on to give Lucian the details of his talk with O'Dell.

"It was a foregone conclusion they wouldn't like the heir of Redcliff's playing fast and loose with their pearl," Lucian commented. "Well, we might appoint Mother and O'Dell agents to settle all these claims. God, what a show it would be!" They parted chuckling.

After supper that evening Wick made up his mind to have his talk with Tat. But Tat didn't follow them out on the piazza, and presently Wick made an unostentatious survey of the house. Tat had vanished, presumably by the back door. Wick went to the back door and looked out—not that he expected to see Tat in the garden; it was too dark to see anything in the garden, except a few pin-points of bright light from the Hessenwinkle house across the back wall.

Thursday morning passed in comparative calm. Wick got home about two and found dinner not quite ready. Bekah, the cook, was slow-motioned and he suspected Etta of conniving with her about dinner, for in marrying Etta he had also married Bekah and the house with its set schedule. Wick was ready to compromise with modernity and have the midday meal at two o'clock, but while Etta acknowledged his masculine right to set the hour, she invariably added, "In Papa's time we dined at three," to underscore her concession, and somehow it was always nearer half past two when the soup came in.

He went through the French window to the piazza where it turned the corner of the house and settled down in a weather-beaten porch chair with the New York paper. The sky was lowering over Europe, violence in Austria had increased since the German occupation . . . could it be possible that man, who fondly called himself *Homo sapiens*, was tobogganing into another self-destructive war while the wounds of the last were still throbbing? He couldn't credit such folly, yet he seemed to feel across his breast the rumbling of the caissons. . . .

[8 o]

Presently these faint prophetic sounds began to be out-noised by a war closer at hand. Between the lines of print Tat's voice clashed with stranger voices, female and strident. Curiosity tugged at Wick; he went softly along the piazza toward the street and looked cautiously over the top of the *Times* which he still held spread out before him. The front of the house appeared to be under siege by Mrs. Manetti, wife of the neighborhood fruiterer, and a tribe of children. The heavy iron gate was ajar and Tat held the narrow breach; outside, Mrs. Manetti, flushed and angry, teetered on her high-heeled blond kid shoes, and they all shouted together. Seeing his son thus outnumbered, Wick came out from behind the editorial page and went down the steps.

"It's about the dog!" cried Mrs. Manetti, catching sight of him. "He stole our dog—a beautiful bulldog—"

"There must be some mistake," Wick began reasonably; and then he remembered the dog. He was so used to Tat's boarders, homeless cats, a rabbit with a broken leg, a mockingbird whose eyes had been put out by the Manettis or their compatriots to make it sing, that he had scarcely noticed the newest refugee about the yard, a brindled cur.

Tat half-turned toward his father but remained embattled in the aperture of the gate. His coat was off, his face damp with perspiration, and a desperate string of hair hung over his forehead.

"The Manettis all went off for the weekend and left the dog locked up in the back yard—"

"And while we were away somebody came and stole him!" cried the Manettis in outrage.

"I didn't steal him."

"Well, it's mighty funny how many times you been over to our place to tell us how to mind our own dog."

"I told you," said Tat with furious patience, "that it's cruel to keep a dog, a live animal, penned up day and night in a dark little corner of the yard. You have no business to keep pets if you aren't going to treat them decently."

"We haven' kep' him chained up . . ." "We got a right . . ." "It's our dog . . ." countered the Manettis, divided on the grounds for their defense. "We shut him up 'cause somebody might steal him, and somebody *did* steal him."

"Which shows it doesn't do any good to shut him up," Tat said.

But logic was no weapon for this battle, thought Wick. He stood a little behind Tat on the rectangle of tesselated marble between the gate and the house. The front steps curved up to a landing under which a passage ran through the basement to the back yard. A door, at Wick's back, closed off the passage at this end and he had been hearing, with a growing sense of guilt, snuffling sounds along the threshold. Now the high, self-pitying howl of a cur tore through the cracks and the key-hole. The dog had heard its owners' voices and desired to be reunited to them.

"Fido! Fido! That's him! What did I tell you! What a nerve—" With nimble footwork, Tat slammed the gate and held it against the assaults of soft pink flesh.

"I'm gonna send for the police," cried Mrs. Manetti, looking around at the passers-by who now swelled the crowd about her.

"If you do I'll send for the Animal Lovers' League and," Tat thrust his face through the iron bars to make his threat more fearsome, "you'll have to pay a *big fine* for cruelty to animals!"

Mrs. Manetti drew back, stunned into momentary silence. Following up his advantage, Tat dropped his bellicose manner and said persuasively, "Look here, Mrs. Manetti, I'll buy the dog from you. I don't want it, but I'll buy it and see that it has a good home with plenty of room to run."

"I don't know as I want to sell the dog." Mrs. Manetti folded her arms and looked Tat over with close appraisal. "Cost you ten dollars," she said.

"Ten dollars! It isn't worth fifty cents."

"It is so. It's a fine bulldog."

"It's about one-eighth bull and seven-eighths everything else."

"Its father is a bulldog what lives to the Argyll Hotel," said Mrs. Manetti crushingly. "I heard where a man got twenty dollars for a bulldog the other day."

"Well, this one isn't even a dog; she's a bitch."

"Shh!" said Mrs. Manetti, making a motion to stop her children's innocent ears. "She is so a dog." She looked over Tat's head at Wick. "Mr. Tat is a single gentleman, he don't understand these things."

"Crr-ipes!" exclaimed Tat. "I'll pay you two dollars for the dog, which is twice what she's worth."

"The dog is worth ten dollars," said Mrs. Manetti. "But I'll take three."

"O.K.," Tat put his hand in his pocket and fished up only some small change. "Father—" he appealed.

Wick took out his wallet. "How about settling for two and a half?" he suggested. "We'll pay you that for the one-eighth that's pure bull. That's at the same rate as twenty dollars for a full-blooded bull, eh?"

"O.K.," said the children, not following the arithmetic but seeing green money in Wick's hand. "O.K. Two-fifty."

Wick handed it over to Tat. "Better get a receipt. Wait a minute." He hunted through his inside pocket for a piece of paper and found a yellowed receipt left over from his old firm before its merger with the Stono Fertilizer Company. Scraps of paper were his pet economy; he never forgot that paper was once trees, so he used up old bill heads and stationery for his memoranda. He wrote rapidly on it and handed it to Tat. "Redcliff Fertilizers, Inc." ran the printed heading in refined script. And underneath, "Received of Tatten Redcliff for one octoroon bitch—$2.50."

Mrs. Manetti signed. When she looked up she was smiling, the air cleared, the sun shone. Courtesies were exchanged, the crowd passed on. The children, however, now grasped for the first time the net result. "But Fido, Momma, when can we have Fido back?"

"We done sold Fido, Son, to Mr. Tat."

"I want my dog," roared Son.

"Shut up your mouth," said Mrs. Manetti, bustling the troupe along with hand and foot. "I know where we can get another dog tomorrow, much better than Fido. An' we gonna keep him in the cellar where nobody can't steal 'im."

As they went up the front steps together Wick asked Tat, "How in the devil did you happen to—er—acquire the animal?"

"Climbed over the back fence and took him—her, at least. I heard her barking when I came home on Saturday afternoon and I knew exactly what had happened. Those Manettis don't know how to treat an animal; it's just greediness that makes them hang on to it. All Saturday night she barked and howled; it burned me so I couldn't sleep, so early Sunday morning I went down there and got her. I'd been there before and told them that if they kept her shut up in that dark little pen she'd probably go mad and bite them. Serve 'em right if she gave the whole family hydrophobia."

"Well, theft is a somewhat drastic form of righting wrongs," Wick began.

Tat pushed the hair out of his eyes and grinned sheepishly. "I meant to tell the Manettis I had the dog, but the whole bunch ambushed me when I came home today and I had to hold them off the best I could. I've been trying to get the A.L.L. to do something about it, but they wanted me to return the dog first. The usual mealy-mouthed attitude—I can't see leaving the dog to suffer while they quibble about the law."

"Quibbling about the law sometimes saves you a night in the hoosegow," said Wick. "I thought your threat to call in the Animal Lovers was brash, considering the bad blood between you."

"I guess there's nothing they'd like better than to see me get myself in a jam, but the Manettis don't know that, so my bluff worked."

"Come to dinner!" called Etta.

The dining-room shutters were bowed in against the midday heat, and the three Redcliffs sat down in the high-ceilinged gloom to their large plates of soup. The long white tablecloth, the polished floor, ran with a thin green stain from the leaves outside. Twelve damask tablecloths had been part of the dowry Wick had acquired with the hand of Henrietta Tatten, and while he had not allowed them, he often told her, to influence his choice unduly, food looked better, and therefore tasted better, and therefore digested better when served from a fresh, wholesome cloth than from the treacherously skidding bits of frippery they called mats. To this ratiocination Etta usually responded by advising him to pray for the continued good health of Dinah Washington, the only laundress left who knew how to "do up" damask, which caused Wick to wonder for the thousandth time how a mind as weak as hers in reasoning powers could sometimes go so directly to the point.

The Etta sitting at the other end of the rectangle did not seem to him very different from the girl who had come, damask in hand, to share his youthful fortunes. So imperceptible to us is our daily change for the worse. . . . A slight myopia prevented his seeing her features distinctly, and then, the eye of memory superimposed the image of the young, the beloved Etta on that of the woman sitting opposite. Her hair framed her face with the same lines—indeed it would have been hard to find any other way of doing straight hair like Etta's—at all events, it still drew back from her high forehead and lay against her ears like the sleek, brown wings of a bird. Lastly, she seemed the same because, whatever her faults, she was always, without apology, herself—a quality Wick prized even in those moments of controversy when he was wishing to God she'd be somebody else for the nonce.

Tat enlivened the soup course by giving his mother a spirited account of the brush with the Manettis. Etta laughed a great deal and applauded the direct action by which Tat had obtained the rescue of Fido; also, she took a naïve pride in the triumph of her clan. "But I hope you paid them well," she added. "Manetti's is the only good fruit store in the neighborhood. I'd hate to have our trade relations permanently disturbed. He's so obliging about sending things."

"There's no point in paying them a lot of money not to treat a dog badly," Tat objected. "If they're just too damn stupid—"

"People of that class treat their pets badly," said Etta.

Tat stopped in mid-flight and turned his steel-rimmed spectacles on her. "Class has nothing to do with it. Look at the way the so-called 'best people' go off all summer and leave their dogs on the plantations—"

"But they pay somebody to feed and exercise them."

"How do they know anybody feeds and exercises them when they stay North six, seven, eight months of the year? Besides, they only feed them to keep them in good condition for hunting; with people starving, they give them pounds and pounds of meat so they can go out and kill other animals."

"Choose your grounds and stick to them, Tat," said Wick. "Either they do feed the dogs or they don't; you can't have it both ways." Tat's habit of suddenly switching from an argument to its opposite never failed to annoy him.

But Tat and Etta ignored him; they didn't even see what he meant. They stared at each other across the corner of the table. Tat was almost pure Tatten, Wick thought, having inherited

[85]

nothing from the Redcliffs, apparently, but their near-sightedness. The spare figures of his wife and son were cast by the same intensity; their thin, obstinate features . . . but it infuriated Tat to be told he was like his mother; he thought of himself as an individualist who had shucked off both Tattens and Redcliffs. Yet, while their causes differed radically, they went at them the same way—no matter how trivial the argument, they were instantly ready to die for their own words.

Fenwick carved the chicken in silence while they wrangled, inwardly taking sides first against one and then against the other. How many American dinnertables, he wondered, were rent with the same contentions? It hadn't always been so; when his father had talked politics, the family had listened in respectful boredom. What had happened to the American father? Now Tat was doing most of the talking, words poured from him.

". . . don't try to sell me the idea that the 'best people' are big-hearted. If you ever took a walk through Crumble Alley and saw the over-crowding, the unsanitary conditions, the open privies . . ."

"Tat, remember you're at the dinner table . . ."

". . . and right near by people go on complacently living in their swell Georgian houses . . ."

"And very glad to have them . . . consider ourselves very lucky . . ."

"What this town needs is more smoke-stacks along the water-front and less crumbly Colonial. We need to eliminate poverty and unemployment . . ."

"The only unemployed I see are ones working for the government by leaning on their shovels . . ."

"You only listen to your rich friends—of course all the rich people are anti-labor . . ."

"Who are the rich people?" Wick put in ". . . hereabouts, I mean. I'm always trying to find them in my business, but I haven't got my hand on one yet . . ." Neither one answered him, and he didn't really expect it.

"That isn't true, Tat," Etta was saying. "It's the well-to-do people who take care of the poor and the sick. The Associated Charities and the churches . . ."

"Churches!" snorted Tat. "That's what burns me up—the good

[86]

Christians like you that dress up every Sunday and sit in the middle aisle professing Christianity and ignoring everything that Jesus taught. The truth is, the churches are social clubs where people go to have a good time in the name of the Father, Son, and Holy Ghost . . ."

At the sight of Etta's frozen face, the American father routed up suddenly. "That will do, Tat. If you can't be civil to your mother, keep quiet. There's no reason why our dinner should be ruined by your boorishness."

He thought he detected tears under Etta's eyelids. He didn't exactly share her attachment to her church, his own credo being simpler, but he respected her right to it. How was Tat going to get on in life with no sense of proportion?

Tat had relapsed into a silence as violent as his speech. Compunction, Wick guessed, was adding its stresses to the visible turmoil within him. His very attachment to his mother, from which he was always escaping, made him hit out savagely to hurt her. He slammed his knife and fork down on his plate with a clang that made Etta wince for her blue India china set.

They continued to eat for a while without conversation. Meals, when Tat was at home, often proceeded in an active silence, for few topics, it appeared, could be safely broached. The progress of the Spanish civil war, the day's news in Congress, a chance comment on a strike—and the fat was in the fire. In every country people were so deeply divided that the intelligent exchange of ideas about the problems bedeviling us had become impossible. How idiotic.

His reflections moved him to try to pull together the rent fabric of family harmony. "Everybody ought to have a religion," he opined airily. "It doesn't matter much what it is. A set of convictions is what a man needs to live by, even if they aren't 'right'; most of us haven't the wisdom or the backbone to get by without it. I happen to prefer the Episcopal Church, though I don't claim perfection for it; but I'm willing for the other fellow to be a Taoist if he likes, or a Mormon or even a Wash-foot Baptist. The important thing is that we all have the discipline of some sort of religion. Now you may say that religion makes for narrowness. But a little narrowness is a good thing—and for real bigotry, commend me to the atheist!"

Fortunately he rather liked talking to himself; it gave him a chance to develop his argument without interruptions.

Before the meal was finished Tat excused himself and dashed upstairs, and presently Wick and Etta went out on the side piazza to drink their coffee. He had intended, Wick remembered, to talk to Tat about Lorena, but he'd have to get rid of Etta somehow. He plotted vaguely behind the *Times*. Before he could hit on a plan, Tat reappeared. His small-featured, sensitive face was serious, but it had lost its frenetic look; he came and sat on the railing near them without speaking, as if wanting to make amends. Etta instantly accepted his intentions. It always defeated Wick the way they quarreled for nothing and made up for nothing, the insults forgotten.

"Will you be here for supper, darling? I'll have Bekah make you some clabber ice cream."

"No, I—I won't be here tonight." Tat wound his legs about the balusters of the railing and looked hard at his toes. He seemed embarrassed over his refusal. "Give me a rain-check on the ice cream—" He looked up and smiled at his mother.

As if summoned by the magic of her spoken name, Bekah materialized in the doorway.

"Oh, is that you, Bekah? I want to speak to you—" To Wick's relief Etta closed the *Atlantic Monthly* and went indoors.

Wick looked sidewise past his paper. Tat still gazed at his toes as if he saw in them the key to the mystery of life. As usual he wore sneakers and, as usual, they were not too clean. The line of his hair had crept down into his collar at the back.

"Is there anything in social justice that forbids your getting your hair cut once in a while?"

Tat didn't answer. He ran his fingers sulkily through his ruffled locks. That was a wrong beginning, Wick admitted, for the conversation he was leading up to—he should have left the haircut to another time, but confound it, it wasn't just hair; his irritation went back into Tat's childhood, it was part and parcel of the long struggle of adults to force the young animal to be kempt. Etta had done pretty well with the other children, but she had always indulged Tat; in the little world of the nursery, he had been the unsuccessful child, and she was always making it up to him. For this, Wick, in spite of his own fastidiousness, could have made allowances except for Tat's air of being above the minutiæ of neatness —an air that came easier than the habit of washing behind his ears.

He scanned his paper for a minute, allowing time for the breeze to dissipate his unfortunate start. Then he said with a show of casualness, "I had a talk with Harry O'Dell yesterday. He approached me about buying timber and in the course of putting the pressure on, he spoke of your attentions to his niece, Lorena. Have you any idea how her family feels about it?"

He saw Tat's legs tighten round the balusters. "What business is it of theirs?"

"Well—they want to protect her—"

"That's her business and mine, not theirs. Or yours."

"That's where you're wrong, Tat. It reaches out and touches us all. An affair like this—it becomes our business for all you can do. Are you sure Lorena understands?"

"She's not a half-wit. And she's not going to take any crabbing about her morals any more than I am."

Wick felt himself put in the wrong and couldn't seem to get back in the right. He had always had sympathy for the good-humored ladies, and now he was playing the part of lean caution. The process of growing up . . . of growing old. You were reckless for yourself but cautious for your son, for you had made a family between the two moralities, a slow, expensive, and precarious creation. And somehow the women he made love to had understood, thanks to the double standard, the limits of his involvement with them. Was Lorena of the old world or the new? He didn't know and suspected that Tat didn't either.

"Well, I'm in a hurry, Father—I'll be nipping along—"

"Hold your horses a minute; there's something I want to say."

He wanted so hard to make Tat see his point . . . damn it, why is it so impossible to communicate with your child, whose very cells have chipped off from your own? He tried again. "It isn't your morals I'm questioning. I just don't want you to overlook the fact that to the Hessenwinkles you represent a group—a group higher up the social ladder, and your conduct is going to be judged accordingly."

"The Hessenwinkles are very democratic. They accept me in spite of my class." Tat was pulling away now, impatient to end the paternal homily.

"That's handsome of them. But just don't forget that the Hessenwinkles also have a tradition—as tight as yours, or tighter."

"Tradition—hell. I'm sick of the past, sick of hearing about it." His face was hard as a nut.

"I didn't say anything about the past," said Wick mildly. "I don't believe in it, myself. There's no such monster. The past and the future are like a conveyor-belt—the past exists in you—" he looked at the sneakers, at the shaggy hair, but forbore to use the persistence of untidy habits as an illustration—"and it works in Lorena just as much as if she were in the *Almanach de Gotha*. Damn it all, you talk as if a man had only to ignore his ancestors to be rid of them. But everybody has ancestors, you know, Fido, ourselves, the Hessenwinkles, and they ride us whether we recognize them or not. It's important to choose your ancestors wisely."

He smiled at Tat but no answering smile came back. This was the sort of thing that really divided them—these little twists that Wick liked to give conversation didn't strike Tat as funny, they baffled and irritated him. Fen, on the other hand, always got his father's little jokes. . . .

"Well, they're not going to ride me," Tat was saying. "I'm not going on repeating the motions they made. It's the future we ought to think about. We can't choose our ancestors—that's the bunk—but we can choose our descendants, and I'm damn well going to!"

"Good God!" Fenwick exploded, glaring at his offspring. "Just try it and see what you get!"

Tat sprang off the railing and stood poised as if he were about to run out and beget three generations forthwith. Then he vanished through the door while Wick sat on in a fume that the breeze did not allay. What had he done to deserve an idiot for a son? A prodigal, a renegade he could have stood . . . you had a chance to deal with that type, but these tenderminded loons. . . . He had failed lamentably in his upbringing of Tat, he had not weaned the boy one little bit from the tribe of the tenderminded, those seekers after absolutes in a relative world who expected people to behave as they ought instead of as they did, the optimists who believed in free will and free love. Tat hadn't held forth about free love for some time, but Wick suspected he had outgrown only the term, not the principle, he probably committed

[90]

fornication with the highest motives. . . . Today he'd been more aggravating than usual, more nervous, for some reason.

Wick fidgeted and trampled the *Times* about his feet. He had a distinct picture, he told himself, of what the Hessenwinkles, the O'Dells would have to say about free love. Maybe they would teach Tat what his father had failed to; maybe the disease contained its own cure. There was no use to worry.

As he picked up his eviscerated newspaper he heard the front gate creak on its hinges. He stood up and looked along the piazza. Tat had come through the passage under the house and was throwing a suitcase into his car. He got in after it and drove off. For a moment Wick felt an absurd compunction, as if he had acted the stern parent and driven his erring child from home. But that was ridiculous, of course; Tat did not, unfortunately, fear his parents, and if he contemplated mischief, he would prefer to make it at home just to plague them.

Wick went indoors. Bekah stood in the pantry door talking to Etta with the family servant's precise admixture of respect and familiarity. They continued seriously discussing the Affairs of the House, and Wick waited a moment to be recognized, having been trained not to interrupt with matters of less import.

"Has Tat gone away?" he managed presently.

"Yes. He said he'd be off for three or four days. I think a little change will do him good."

"He didn't say where he was going, I suppose."

"Of course not. You know how he protects his privacy—I don't know who from," Etta concluded, tartness routing syntax.

" 'A dainty virtue, dearie, that fled when none pursued.' " Wick moved toward the hall.

Bekah spoke up from the pantry door. "He taken all his good underclo'es with him. He mus' be goin' somewhere very partic'lar."

"His best underclothes?"

"Yes, ma'am. He gone through my wash-kitchen like a harricane an' taken his bes' pieces an' stuffed 'em in his grip. It's a good thing I wind up with my ironin' on Thursdays or he'd had to take 'em rough dry. But Mr. Tat don't keer."

"Well, just so he brings them back," said Etta, "I don't care either." But her voice was full of curiosity. "That's all, Bekah."

She rose and followed Wick up the wide staircase. "I have an idea he's gone on some business he's been talking about. I think they're planning to open a filling station on that new highway to Florida." She went into the sewing room and Wick drifted after her into that jealous sanctuary. The house had been designed with a long drawing room on the second floor, but at some point a more prolific generation of Tattens had evidently been cramped for sleeping-quarters and had cut the drawing room into unequal parts, making the large bedroom which he occupied with Etta and, next to it, the high narrow apartment which she used as a sewing room. Umbrageous carving and ornamented moldings consorted oddly with the catch-all contents, the retired washstand, the sewing machine and Miss Jinny, the plush-bosomed dress form which Etta still used when the sewing woman came.

"I think it's a splendid idea," Etta was saying as she buttoned up the tucked yoke of the old white cambric nightgown that decently shrouded Miss Jinny's pronounced curves when she was off duty.

Miss Jinny made Wick suddenly think of Aunt Quince; the dress form had a queer, sharp personality, and was cut to the same pattern. Once he and Etta had come back from a summer in the mountains and found Miss Jinny attired in a ball-gown, as if she had gone like Cinderella to some fairy-tale dance and overstayed the stroke of twelve. Someone—they never found out who it was —had brought down from the attic Etta's old peach-blow satin that she used to wear to the St. Cecilia balls and rigged Miss Jinny out, with a scarf and a fan for verisimilitude. Once Etta said she believed it must have been Aunt Quince (Etta belonged, on Tat's account, to the Anti-Quince faction and liked to take a dig at the old lady), but she had nothing whatever to go on. Fen, who was living there that summer, said he didn't see a soul go into the sewing room.

Miss Jinny had never again escaped from reality, from the dusty nightgown she now wore. "I'm not sure," said Wick at random to Etta, "that the procreative purposes of nature weren't better served by a cover-all like that than by the bare-backed night-clothes you women affect now. There's a challenge in those long hems and sleeves, those high ruffled necks—it may not have been an accident that long nightgowns and big families were contemporaneous. . . ."

Etta's mind never strolled away frivolously, as his did, from a subject that engaged her profound interests. She snubbed him with a light glance and continued, "The new filling station, I mean. Tat's really doing awfully well in business. I'm quite proud of him." She gave this out impressively, as if they had never discussed it before, never tossed on their pillows worrying about their younger son.

Wick declined to answer. He went over to the north window and drank the cool draft, looking into the garden that lay somnolent in purple shade. Only the long kitchen building where Bekah lived glowed with the afternoon sun that baked the bricks to the hot, spicy color of gingerbread. At the back of the garden Wick could see the grass growing long under the fig trees against the north wall, and beyond the wall the Hessenwinkle house, painted a practical battleship gray with brown window-trim. He wondered if they knew anything over there that he didn't—that he would like to know. . . .

He turned back from the uncommunicative gray stucco and went into the next room, pondering Etta's idea that Tat had gone away on business. With her intuitive faculty, which made her so often and so irritatingly right, especially where Tat was concerned, she might have picked up a clue that his slow-footed reasoning had missed. The new route was obviously a good field if it wasn't already oversold. Tat would, of course, have to go and make a survey. . . .

The more Wick thought over the idea the better he liked it and the more he believed it. The extension of the chain of filling stations would increase Tat's responsibilities; and there was no specific for the rash of radicalism, in Wick's opinion, like a little material success. The company ran on a shoestring at present, and he wondered as he walked about the square, airy bedroom, how the boys intended to finance their expansion. He took a clean handkerchief from the top drawer and strolled over to the east window and looked down the street to where the river showed between the trees, its city tarnish overlaid now with the shallow blue of afternoon. Every morning since he had married and come here to live he had looked out of this window first thing to see how the weather stood, and more profoundly, to assure himself that the world, the street, the garden were still there, had not twitched away while he had been absent in sleep. But they never had; blue or muddy gray, the river slipped past the end of the street . . . how did Harry O'Dell make his money? (A little farther along, the river washed the pilings of the Friendly Hearth Wood Yard.) Not from that enterprise alone. From bringing in "outside money," doubtless. . . . The price of timber was improving last time Wick had checked it . . . if he sold to these people he'd have some ready cash. The phrase had a curious warmth in it, like the ugly but efficient trash-burner that stood on the hearth there in the early years: he had risen willingly in the cold to light it and warm up the room for Etta, the wife of his choice and his cherishing. Would the gesture have continued, the impulse persisted, or had furnaces been invented in the nick of time? . . . Well, if he had some ready cash he could help the boys out maybe. This would be an extra, he could afford to gamble some of it on Tat. But now he had put down his glasses and couldn't find them . . . he had a gift for depositing them in unlikely places. "Etta!" he shouted, to-ing and fro-ing in myopic agitation.

Etta knew what the thunder meant and came in from the sewing room. She had a complementary gift for finding things, indeed, her character complemented his in many little ways. Wick could never make up his mind whether this was accident or contrivance. Now she moved about the room tranquilly, her carriage straight and confident, her face half smiling, half sympathetic, and in a minute or two she handed him the glasses from the top of the chest of drawers where he had laid them when he took out his handkerchief. See, her gesture said, I have no brains; that's your province, but I do other things. You'd be lost without me.

Feeling foolish and grateful he polished the lenses, put them on his nose, and the room returned to its just proportions. "Well, I'm off to the office—anything you want me to do while I'm downtown?"

Would he stop at Manetti's and bring home some tomatoes for supper? In view of the late unpleasantness, Etta didn't like to ask them to send out such a small order. "Better not mention that Fido has again been abandoned for the weekend, this time by our humanitarian son."

Wick was still smiling when he reached the office. He continued to think about Tat and his journey, how he could get him some money to expand his business, and the salutary effects thereof. Presently the head of Miss Finch, with pompadour restored, materialized in the door of his inner office. "I forgot to say that Mr. Lucian Redcliff telephoned. He wanted you to call him when you came in."

Lucian wanted to know if Wick could let him have a little cash —he had over-extended himself temporarily on some property. . . . Wick said no he wouldn't; Lucian would have to learn sometime to curb his extravagance, he might as well start now. Then he said yes—but this was positively the last time. "By the way," he added, "I had a talk with Tat about the lady and got nowhere. He took it as a lecture on morals instead of on manners and told me to mind my business, which I might have expected. Then he packed his bag and went off without a hint of where he was going, except that Bekah reports he took his best clothes. As a matter of fact, I suspect he's only gone upstate on a business trip."

"Hmm. You don't usually take your best clothes upstate on a business trip," Lucian punctured his wishful thought. "It sounds more like a party to me."

"Well, business trips and parties are frequently combined, or so I'm told. Anyhow, there's no use worrying about Tat. We'll find out the truth, no doubt, in good time."

"No doubt," said Lucian and rang off.

Wick picked up the telephone again and called Judith's number, but before the call was completed, he changed his mind and put down the receiver. He would go to see her instead, to tell her about his talk with O'Dell; her nervousness that morning puzzled and disturbed him. He would try to find out what was eating her and get her to talk about it. For all his philosophy, his mild irony, Wick carried impounded within him a pool of rather simple emotion that stirred responsive to feeling in other people when his mind had no concept of their problems, and now as he got into his car and drove toward her house he felt the waters troubled by her obscure unhappiness about this incident which seemed to be overshadowing all their lives.

Absentmindedly he opened the street door without ringing the bell. He walked along the piazza and said, "Hello. Can I come in?" through the window screen, for he perceived by a movement inside that Judith was at home. No answer came back, but he went on into the living room. Her lifted face startled him as his quick entrance seemed to startle her, and their glances locked for a moment. Hers was distant, without personal recognition, except, he saw with distress, resentment against him for dragging her back to the threshold of reality.

"What are you up to?" he said crossing the room and sitting down by her on the sofa. He took her inert hand and gave it a sharp squeeze to wake her with the live current of his presence.

"Oh . . . I was just looking at some things . . ." She stirred and began sullenly to gather up photographs, scrap-books, a piece of faded blue cloth—the charms with which she induced her trance.

He opened one of the photograph albums, and a hundred little moments of his son's life came up from oblivion, and plunged him through. . . . Fen standing against the shining triangle of a sail . . . house parties on this or that plantation . . . Fen sitting cross-legged on top of a sand dune with a bunch of sea-oats between his teeth to make an absurd bushy mustache while the other pic-nickers lolled back in an abandon of laughter. . . . For an instant Wick was sucked into the whirlpool with Judith by this reminder of one of Fen's most endearing traits, his gift of mimicry. Judith was surreptitiously stuffing the blue object under a pillow.

"What's that?"

"Nothing—"

He pulled it out. An old shirt of Fen's. He held it up with the crawling, vivid sensation that personal belongings summon up. . . . Fen's shape and size hung there before him; the shirt was stretched to his beloved son's shoulders which it had outrageously survived. . . .

"It'll make a good dust-cloth," he said harshly, wrenching away from the brink, damming his pool of feeling with rough words against the drain she made on it. "Don't choke yourself up with widow's weeds, Judith. You're getting too damn morbid. You have much to give to the future—youth, energy, sweetness. . . ." He bundled up the albums and took them across the room away from her, harmful toys snatched from a child.

Judith sat supine against the cushions, her long legs stretched out starkly in front of her in a characteristic pose prompted, perhaps, by her lame muscles seeking their ease. He watched her sidelong—a young girl in a plain sports dress, who should be out playing tennis, doing things, not moping among cobwebs. But in her the sense of life was thwarted from two directions; she could surmount the handicap of illness if that were all—indeed she had tried to at first. He remembered her, with a sharp twist of his heart, learning to swim again after her recovery, paddling doggedly through the water while Fen held her chin up.

He sat down on the edge of a chair, polished his spectacles, flattened the cowlick on his forehead, as one girding for battle. "Let's get down to earth for a while. I came in to tell you that I had had a talk with O'Dell in the park this morning and, as I suspected, he's not losing much sleep over the Welfare's bill. So you needn't fret yourself about paying it immediately; if your office can't meet it in two or three months let me know and I'll help you straighten it out."

"But *I* lose a lot of sleep over it," she said slowly. "It would settle my mind to have it paid."

"You take this much too seriously, Judith." Her obduracy irritated him. "I assure you O'Dell doesn't; he has other fish to fry."

Putting on his glasses he saw how reluctant she was to be brought back to the reality of her quarrel which was somehow bound up with what she was trying to escape. Her mouth drooped like a sleeper's.

"What are you trying to do?" he asked very softly, as if coaxing her to talk in her sleep.

"I suppose I'm trying to reassure myself about Fen's loving me," she answered quite rationally. "If I keep reliving the times when he made love to me, it banishes my doubts—at least for a while."

"But why should you doubt Fen's love?" He was genuinely surprised.

"I don't know. For some reason I'm frightened about it. I always felt inadequate with him—why should he have loved me?"

"Don't be ridiculous; you're just indulging your inferiority complexes." He took advantage of her mood of revelation and pushed further. "And what has this got to do with that silly quarrel with Lorena?"

"Well—" she considered for a moment. "She's stirred up all my feeling of inadequacy. Uncle Wick, why did God have to make me so *plain!* If I just had *half* Lorena's looks! But she scares me, the truth is—"

"There are all kinds of 'looks,' " he said, "and Lorena's aren't the only kind. They aren't the kind you want."

"Aren't they!" she exclaimed, throwing herself forward with a face of reckless abandon. "She's attractive and sexy and bold about it—and I'd give my eyeteeth to be like her!"

"Why, Judith," Wick expostulated helplessly. "Why, you funny child!" He couldn't repress his amusement and nervous relief.

Judith continued to frown at her outstretched feet, but he divined his laughter had not offended her. "Well, after all," he said, taking off his glasses and wiping them again, "Fen married you; he didn't marry Lorena."

Her eyes came up and fixed him in surprise, as if she had overlooked this circumstance. "That's true . . . but there we are again—you nice men marry us but you can't help liking them, and that's what makes us afraid. It's that strong pull they have for you. You like Lorena yourself," she added accusingly.

"Well, yes . . . so I do. But I like you better." He put all the affection he had for her into his smile. "That's why I am so sure Fen liked you better, too. But in any case he married you and you had his love; there's no way Lorena can threaten that now."

"No . . . I suppose not . . ."

"You've exaggerated the girl's success. Come out with me, Judith," he said suddenly, inventing his therapy as he went along. He rose and taking her hands pulled her up from the evil softness of the upholstery. "I have to go uptown on an errand and I'd like to have company. In fact, I want to go to the Friendly Hearth Wood Yard, and we can interview the witch-woman—"

"Oh, I *couldn't*—" Judith jerked her hands out of his. She flung over to a table and made a business of lighting a cigarette but her hand shook and she upset the box.

He let her pick the cigarettes up from the floor to recover her ease. "Certainly you can. We'll talk about the bill again, and try to clear up the misunderstanding. You'll find her friendly and ready to meet you half way, I'll bet. You've sort of forgotten that she's just an ordinary girl who is sometimes nasty and sometimes

[98]

nice. You know, one of the surprising things about her is that she has devoted friends among the older women; she seems to take the trouble to make them like her. I was talking to one of them a while ago—do you know a funny little Mrs. Rupelle who lives tucked away somewhere near the bridge?"

"No," said Judith, cramming the cigarettes into the box.

He ignored the sullen monosyllable and went on. "I used to see her around in my youth, and she was rather a charming creature until she became a theosophist and went to live in a tree, which put her out of circulation, as it were. Of course she came down from the tree eventually, but she was always a little odd after that; too much intercourse with nature unfits us for human society, it would seem. Well, she was telling me in the Bank that Lorena was 'just lovely' to her—came to see her all the time and brought her food. Naturally she adores Lorena and wouldn't hear a word against her, said the stories about her were all slander. Now I doubt if Lorena shares her theosophical views, but with her warmhearted Irish side, she responds to the lonely old woman. Besides, I suspect she just likes to be liked—which is Irish again."

Judith had turned her head and was listening to him now with unstudied interest. "Come along with me," he pressed her. "I have to see O'Dell about some timber and I need to be entertained on the way with agreeable female society. Don't you think you owe it to my age and sex?"

This brought a smile to her lips. "Suppose Lorena doesn't trot out the warmheartedness? She was ready to brain me the other day."

"Then I'll twist her neck myself and never argue with you again."

"All right—if you swear you won't desert from my side to hers, I'll go. Wait till I powder my nose."

"Eureka!" he cried. "The patient is going to recover! I swear, I believe you could raise any woman from the dead by dangling a compact before her face."

The patient began to have a relapse. "I can't go, Uncle Wick, I really can't. I'm not dressed properly."

The pink calico, it was true, had deteriorated since he saw it in the office that morning.

"Run upstairs and nip into another dress," he urged. "I'll wait for you. And put on your best while you're at it. I want you to look smart and distinguished. You're going to find out that you don't really want to look like Lorena after all."

As she came down the steps he saw that she had taken his instructions in her usual literal way. A formal suit of heavy gray-blue silk, a little white cap with Mercury-wings, white bag and gloves —this simple and elegant ensemble was certain, he thought with a twinge of dismay, to intimidate Lorena and make her difficult. Psychotherapy was a more complex procedure than he had realized. Well, he had embarked on it now—and handing Judith into the car, he drove up the street, rambling along with his old-fashioned compliments while he wondered what in hell he would do when he got them together.

Wick headed straight for the Borough and the Friendly Hearth. Judith scolded him about this wild goose chase; still, he could see she was excited; color glowed in her cheeks. They jounced over the cobbled roadway toward the river, but even before they stopped at the white wooden box of an office, they saw that the windows were closed. Wick got out and tried the door just for luck; he looked through the window glass and saw a disordered desk with no Lorena behind it.

"Can you beat that?" he sputtered, returning to Judith. It astonished him to discover how much he had looked forward to the encounter.

"Well, well—all dressed up and no place to go. Is your face red!"

Getting back into his seat with sheepish mien, he thought it was all to the good that she could laugh so naturally; he had accomplished something anyway. But for the moment he felt too punctured to move, so he sat and glowered at the neat, successful white clapboards, the green and orange awnings. After all the effort he had made to get her here. When you had worked yourself up to an act of courage, of will, how life loved to let you down with a smack. He glanced about the place, but the sleeping beauty slept no more profoundly behind her high hedge than did the wood yard behind the rusty board fence. There was just no one about.

He began to grumble and blame O'Dell. "What the devil does he mean leaving his office like this with no one to tend it? With his keen nose for business, you'd think he'd have somebody here to take orders."

"Maybe he thinks Lorena is here; maybe she's playing hooky."

"Maybe so," he agreed uncomfortably, and his anxiety to know where Lorena had gone called up his anxiety to know where Tat had gone and became one with it.

"Well, can I take off the style now?" Judith asked. "It's hot as the hinges, style is." She slipped out of her blue jacket and fanned herself with the white wings of her hat. "As a matter of fact, I feel sort of deflated myself. I was quite looking forward to seeing you with Lorena, and how far your turning on charm would have got you. I'll bet you'd have been eating out of her hand before she finished with you."

"You sound like the uxorious shade of all wives. It's disgusting." He started the motor and headed back for the main street.

At the corner he turned away from the direction of Judith's house and drove with seeming aimlessness toward his own. They couldn't shake off at once their flat and foolish feeling. Suddenly Judith clutched his hand on the wheel. "Why are you turning into the Hessenwinkles' street, Uncle Wick? You don't for a minute think you're going to get me into their *house?*"

"All right—all right! You don't have to run us into the gutter! I just thought we'd drive by and see what we could see. No harm in looking."

She eyed him fiercely and as a diversion he offered, "Tat went off this afternoon on a business trip."

"Oh, then she may not be here either."

He had not mentioned, even to himself, that he was sort of hoping for a reassuring sight of a red head about the Hessenwinkle place.

The coasting of the car dribbled out in the shade of a sycamore by the curb. They both studied the house. Zinnias in row upon regular row filled the rectangle of the front yard, planted by a thorough hand. Off to the right red and yellow cannas surrounded a fountain, and from within the ring of fire a whitewashed swan, broad enough in the beam to have carried a Wagnerian tenor, reared its neck. No songless Elsa stood by, however. From the back of the lot came sleepy human sounds and the fat clucking of a hen.

"I know I've been horrid about Tat," Judith said with sudden compunction. "I really do try to think about this from his point of view; if he's crazy about Lorena, it's certainly no business of mine. But what always trips me up is: is she really what he wants? It's so queer for an idealist like Tat to fall for a girl like Lorena—even if she *does* make friends with old ladies."

"Well, we seldom know what we want ourselves, which makes it even harder for others to know. Tat wants a platform first; he has to have a row of fixed principles under him. The planks sometimes dissolve and let him fall through, but he scrambles up again and hammers at some new planks. He seems to have identified certain people with his platform—the Hessenwinkles, your friends the Turners, old Tony de Angelo's boys—and while I fancy he doesn't cotton to the older generation of Italians and Germans, the younger ones have mostly adopted the 'liberal' line. Their group leader is that young Sam Hartman who went away to Harvard and graduated as a labor organizer—*cum laude*, you might say. In fact, Tat gets on well with every kind of creature but his own family. He has to be in revolt against his background, apparently."

"I think Tat would be in revolt against any kind of background he happened to be born into."

"Yes, probably." They both stared at the gray house. The hot wind rustled the leaves of the sycamore above their heads in soporific gusts; and with the improbability of a dream, voices seemed to issue from the ground beside them. Lorena and August Hessenwinkle, coming down the cement path between the zinnias, were instantly upon them. At the gate they halted, transfixed to see the Redcliffs peering into their yard.

Surprise and guilt routed utterly whatever half-formulated plans Wick might have had for the meeting. "How d'y do—how d'y do—" he exclaimed heartily, "—just driving by—" and, unable to stem the impulse to flight, he gave the lie to his words by stepping on the starter. "Fine cotton weather, eh?"

The Hessenwinkles continued to gaze, bereft of speech, and thus having a moment to recover himself, Wick went on, "Fine for flowers too, it seems. We had just stopped in the shade for a minute to admire your display. You must have a green hand."

Lorena hung back in the gateway, but August came out to the car. "Fertilizer," he said with his slow engaging smile, "that's what does it. I pour the fertilizer to 'em; and plenty of water in the dry spells. You can call it a green hand." On his large face, fuller at the chin than at the forehead, pleasure had banished surprise.

"How are you today, Lorena?" Wick smiled invitingly, hoping she would follow her father out to the car. "Not at the wood yard this afternoon?"

"No, sir—at least I'm on my way back there now—" She seemed rattled for once. "Well, if you-all will excuse me, I'll be going. Uncle Harry will be tearing his shirt 'cause I been out so long."

"If I was your Uncle Harry I'd tear *your* shirt, leaving the office half the afternoon while you fool around the house." Her father spoke with rough affection.

"Well, good-by, sir; good-by, Poppa—see you this evening." Obviously anxious to be gone, she walked away with a slight swagger, a slight undulation of her rear in the tight yellow print dress. The strong sunlight seemed to bounce off the red curls, the shiny rayon, as she diminished down the street.

"We must be getting along too—as I said, we were just passing by . . . I saw O'Dell this morning, August. You and I must have a talk, I'll see you down on Broad Street some day."

August's blue eyes developed a sort of cast. "That's right," he said, "we could talk about different things. These promoters go off cock-a-hoop on all sorts of schemes." He smiled noncommittally. "Well, good day," he added formally as they rolled away and left him looking thoughtfully after them.

Rounding the corner, Judith and Wick collapsed with sheepish laughter. Caught peeping by the Hessenwinkles! Of all the childish performances! The shared escapade drew them closer. At her door they parted with no mention of introspective jags; his doctoring was pretty good after all, Wick thought with pride as he returned to the Borough.

On the way home he considered whether to talk over the matter of Tat and Lorena with Etta and decided not to; it would only distress her and she'd keep him all stirred up about it. Besides, when he added up all his evidence, there wasn't much to go on. So they ate their simple repast that evening in pleasant tranquillity after the squally weather of the dinner table. When he had finished the evening paper in the sitting room across the hall, Wick held a one-sided debate with himself as to whether he would go to the club for a while. He might pick up a little political gossip, besides which he always felt a trifle guilty about his hermitic tendencies.

But his old Morris chair gave a sweet support to his fundaments, he became conscious of all his bones. . . . The sitting room began to bind him with the tenuous web of use and wont. He liked its summer aspect, bare and airy without the red silk rep curtains, the festooned Brussels carpet with which Etta cluttered it up in winter. Now the chairs and sofa stood about in cool anonymity in their white summer covers; through the long windows leading to the front piazza the wind flowed along the floor and touched his ankles, the floor dark-shining from Bristol's attentions. Bristol was a rascal and, Wick suspected, stole his whisky, though he could never be quite sure . . . he hated locking things up . . . if Bristol weren't Bekah's husband, they wouldn't keep him on as butler. He had only one virtue. "Bristol is glorious to shine the brass," Bekah always reminded them when his shortcomings brought about one of those periodic crises of the pantry; and actually Wick's long bony hand lying on the table was reflected to perfection in the two columns of the student lamp beside him. The brass lamp with its twin green shades like dunce-caps had actually seen him through his student days, and when the house had passed, late and reluctant, from lamp-oil times to the age of the light-bulb, Etta had had the lamp wired for him.

"I heard from the girls today," Etta was telling him. "Marianna says they think out in California that we are going to have to fight Japan. But our navy is much better, they say, more modern and all. I've always hated those nasty little yellow men. I can't see any sense in sending them supplies to fight us with."

"I suppose we will have to fight them, some time or other." But he answered with his head only; sitting here on a fine summer night, he couldn't accept the improbable word "war." The table, the tall Hepplewhite secretary, the phonograph shattered by bombs. . . .

"Marianna wants us to come out to Long Beach for a visit."

"It's too damn far." Wick picked up the novel he was reading, and settling back, resisted even the notion of movement.

"You didn't think England was too far, when we could go there. We haven't had a trip in a long time, since things have been so bad abroad. We could go to California this fall instead of New York. We've never seen the West. They say it's rather pretty."

"You don't know whether you'll have enough money to go as far as Cool Blow this fall. No use getting delusions of grandeur."

He said this every summer in this queasy time when the crops, the weather, the fertilizer accounts all hung in the incalculable future. After the First World War when cotton was up, he and Etta had taken the girls and gone abroad two or three times. What nostalgia the word "abroad" bore on its back . . . he saw the ship's scrubbed deck with narrow black seams, and smelt the eleven o'clock chicken broth. The precious suspension between shore and shore . . . he used to lean on the rail for hours watching the long wave that curled steadily off the prow of the great ship and rolled up the everyday (the Borough, his life and Etta's) like a carpet stored for summer. England never seemed far . . . abroad meant England for him. Etta and the girls loved Paris, but give him the lake country, green and glowing with Wordsworth. Something far more deeply interfused . . . all England was deeply interfused for him with the subtle intoxicant of his reading. Nothing about London surprised him. "It's just the same," he had said, bemused, that first summer. "The same as when?" Etta had asked, for he had never set foot there before. But the streets, the houses might have been, and therefore became for him, the house where Dr. Johnson went to call (and no doubt to be odious), the lane down which Pepys walked home on a frosty night, it being a brave moonshine. . . .

He came back to the sitting room with a sense of anger and bereavement, of the infinite pleasures of the spirit destroyed for men everywhere by demoniac war. . . . "Well, shall I read awhile? We'll see about the trip when fall comes."

"Wait till I get my sewing." Etta went off on one of her daily hunts for the sewing basket, and he picked up *The Return of the Native* and found the place where they had left off last time. Actually, he admitted to himself while he waited, he usually managed to scrape up enough cash to go to New York each

November; it kept them from going seedy. They stayed at a good hotel, went to the theater and the Metropolitan Museum and bought shoes, good shoes being hard to get at home. They always left cards on a few friends, which seemed to surprise them unaccountably, though they hospitably responded by inviting Etta and himself to dine, which in turn surprised Etta who didn't expect Yankees to be hospitable. But the expensive scale of living intimidated them a little. Wick never knew how much to tip white servants, and he came home gladly to the simple life of the provincial, its known quantities.

Etta returned with the captured basket, sat down by her half of the student lamp and began to mend her damask napkins with fairy-small stitches. Wick glanced at her, ruffled by a twinge of guilt. Etta didn't really like Hardy much, but she listened evening after evening to his gloomy melodramas, or to Gibbon, or to the *Life of John Marshall*, because it kept her husband happy. Actually, she liked modern novels, especially the kind that made her cry, and this, Wick suspected, was one of the best kept secrets of their marriage, for neither ever acknowledged to the other that magazine serials were about her level.

Still, being a good wife, an adaptable companion, was her pride and satisfaction—so he might as well give her the pleasure of adapting, he rationalized, and was soon lost to conscience in the redundant periods of Hardy's prose.

He had been reading for some time when the faint creak of the gate, a footstep on the flagstones, began to nag at his attention. A visitor, who now came lightly up the steps outside. Wick glanced inquiringly at Etta. Her head had fallen against the bulge of the high-backed rocking chair, her active freckled hands lay still in the sewing basket in her lap. Some instinct warned him not to wake her; he put the book quietly down and went on tiptoe through the French window. In the black length of the piazza he couldn't see anything, so he went cautiously toward the stairs and almost fell over a man sitting on the top step. It was Lucian.

"God Almighty! You scared the liver and lights out of me."

"Sh-h-h," said Lucian. "I picked up another clue—a nice fat clue—and in the goodness of my heart I came by on the way home to share it with you." He got up. "Come on, unless you want to share it with Etta too."

"No . . . no . . . better not."

They gum-shoed down the steps and turned into the grassy semi-circle formed by the double flight. Wick fumbled and found the door to the passageway under the house. As he pushed it open the night-draft whished through and assaulted them with cellar smells of damp earth, leaf mold, the wood box. They stood in the black entrance and Lucian's voice, faceless and formless, said, "Lorena has gone away for the weekend, too."

"She has, eh? How do you know?"

"I found out. By the simple method of investigation. I called the Friendly Hearth two or three times this afternoon and got no answer."

"You could have called me and saved yourself some trouble. I would have told you she wasn't there."

"How did you know?" asked Lucian, crestfallen.

"Because I met her in front of her house. But she was on her way back to her office then."

"Hmnf. What time was that?"

"Oh, about four-thirty, I suppose."

"Well, I called her twice after that and there was still no answer. Now get this—"

A small disturbance spread through Wick's tissues—a prophecy of trouble, a resentment against the confusions of life and against his brother for his unconcealed relish of the predicament. Lucian went on. "This evening my lamentable curiosity overcame me and I called the *maison* Hessenwinkle. One of the brothers—it sounded like Fritz—answered and said Lorena had gone out, so I asked what time I could call her tomorrow. This seemed to upset him unnecessarily for so simple an inquiry, and he wanted to know who it was. Just an old friend, I told him, of the marine corps, passing through from Parris Island. I just wanted to see her and talk over old times. If I do say it, my voice was good—you could practically see the red stripe down my pants. Fritz said, 'Wait a minute,' and went off, and I could hear the family arguing about how to answer the untimely question. After a while he came back and said Lorena had gone away for three or four days, but if I called up the first of next week. . . . I regretted that my leave would be up then and rang off."

Wick felt for his cigarette case. In the tunnel the match flame made a sulphurous flare by which he could see Lucian's face, unnaturally large and orange, and his mountebank shadow capering along the ceiling. Wick dropped the match; the vision was blotted out as suddenly as it appeared. Good Lord, I'm getting as melodramatic as Lucian, he thought, and fell to wondering why he should take Tat's little excursion so seriously. This time he made no effort to bluff about it.

"So that's where she was going when she left us! I wonder August didn't put his foot down."

"What in the hell could he do? After all, Lorena's above the age of consent."

"Still, August is a conservative fellow." Wick moved to the entrance of the passage and stood looking into the leaves, faintly luminous from a distant street-lamp; the oleanders rustled and shook down a dry sweetness like powdered sugar. He couldn't get over the idea that August would dislike Lorena's going off this way with Tat . . . he would mind it more than the Belchers affair . . . Belchers was married and well-to-do . . . it was perfectly clear what Lorena could expect of her relationship with him and what she could not. She could take the offer or leave it. But Tat was unmarried and impecunious, which made everything obscure. Being free to marry Lorena made his not marrying her the more invidious; his notions that love should be free would not make anything clearer to August's mind. Couldn't Tat see that he was heading straight into the position of slighting them? He, Wick, would have to convey to August somehow that this love affair had developed without his knowledge or approval. Yet one couldn't say these things actually, even to the clear-cut August. He would have to find a roundabout way . . . O'Dell's suggestion in the park came into his mind as being unkind but shrewd, a successful timber deal might soften the slight.

"Confound Tat, he would choose this moment to play into O'Dell's hand." Wick frowned into the rustling garden, feeling snared.

Lucian came up beside him. "It seems to be on the cards for you to be obliging to them," he said in a different voice. He had stowed the mountebank in the tunnel like a costume in a wardrobe. Lucian had two distinct voices; the high timbre with which he twanged out his cynicisms made his own, his natural voice, sound deeper and pleasanter. Marveling at his half-brother's dexterity, Wick started up the steps.

"Come in and have a drink before you go home."

"All right," said Lucian, "I guess we need a drink. But don't take the thing too seriously—we usually get by with our indiscretions somehow, and Tat will learn from his just as I did, and just as you did, if I remember correctly, though I was pretty young at the time. But I seem to have done a lot of reprehensible listening at keyholes while you had it out with the old man. The only trouble with Tat is he's all Tatten; he hasn't any Redcliff in him to get him out of scrapes."

"That's so," said Wick, diverted. "He's his mother's own child for all their squabbling; he's given to the same incontinent decisions and defends them with the same heat and turbulence." But Etta's emotionalism entertained him, it seemed to him wholly feminine, the proper foil for the balanced, the reasonable male she made him feel; while Tat's was a handicap to a man with a job to do.

"Here's Lucian, Etta," he said raising his voice as they went into the hall. "We were just saying, as among Redcliffs, that we mustn't be too hard on your son Tat because he's the victim of inheritance. It's not his fault that something went wrong with the genes and he came out all Tatten."

"From the remarks he lets fall, I gather Tat doesn't regard the Redcliffs with such admiring complacence as you and Lucian do. Maybe he bears his misfortune with more fortitude than you think."

Etta answered lightly, but on an acid note. She did not like her brother-in-law, and she was congenitally incapable of dissembling her feelings for more than a few moments. Lucian was "too critical," she said, besides he was a smart aleck about religion. Lucian ought to get married. A wife would take the "sass" out of him. Wick tried to explain that Lucian was critical of the town, of the family, because he couldn't get them out of his hair, so he lashed out when they disappointed him. But these well-meant explanations merely showered off the umbrella of Etta's protective opinions. Lucian for his part admired Etta's directness, her being all of a piece. "I get on with Etta much better than I do with Tat," he told Wick once in a burst of frankness, "though that isn't saying

[109]

much." But he couldn't resist a crack at her now and then, and he had an uncanny aim for her funny-bone.

Wick began to tell Lucian about the abduction of Fido and Tat's battle with the Manettis. It was the sort of story he enjoyed telling and he gave it his best in the deft selection of words. In a few minutes they were all in stitches and Wick had to take off his glasses two or three times to wipe his eyes. When he had finished Etta said, "By the way, Wick, Tat didn't basely abandon the octoroon after all. Bekah says he made her promise to feed her until he came back."

"Tat's gone away?" Lucian cocked one eyebrow mischievously.

"Yes, he's gone to the Upcountry on business—he's done awfully well with the filling station, you know, and they're planning to expand their chain—"

"It's time for that drink," Wick interposed hastily, and taking Lucian by the arm, he propelled him across the hall into the dining room out of temptation's way. "Let sleeping dogs lie," he muttered beneath the fluty gurgle of the decanter, and in a natural voice he began to ask Lucian again about the price timberland was bringing these days.

"Actually it might be a good time to sell," he went on, "but somehow I hate to think of those trees going. I suppose it's asinine, but I can't help feeling it's a sort of betrayal to sell them out to this 'outside money' of O'Dell's."

"I don't think you ought to sell out to the O'Dells," said Etta from the next room. "There are too many of them and too few of us. I think we ought to hold on to whatever advantages we have."

"My dear sister, your hearing and your instincts are both acute." Lucian strolled back into the sitting room, glass in hand and sat on the arm of the sofa, keeping his weight, however, on the ball of one foot to be ready to leap in any direction. Wick followed him nervously.

"I don't believe any good comes of compromises," said Etta. "In life, you start to do business with people like the O'Dells and before you know it, one thing leads to another."

"How right you are, Etta—how right you are!" cried Lucian,

his green eyes sparkling. "Apparently there's something very leading about the O'Dell blood, something hard for our kind to resist, especially when it's mixed with Hessenwinkle."

"What *are* you talking about?"

"He talks too damn much, and about nothing!" His back toward Etta, Wick turned upon Lucian as ferocious a scowl as his neat, pink face could contrive.

Lucian looked up at his tall brother with undisguised relish. The temptation to set off a small bomb in Etta's lap and send the table-napkins flying was more, his eyes said, than flesh and blood could withstand. His free leg hanging over the arm of the sofa begin to swing faster and faster. Wick waited to see him leap into the air, shouting, but instead, the leg stopped abruptly and Lucian stood up, both feet on the solid floor.

"O.K.," he said bowing slightly to his brother. "I'll take myself and my talk home. Well, here's to our side; we'll hold the pass together." He drained his glass, and set it on the table. Putting his hands in his coat pockets he walked over to his sister-in-law and looked down at her curiously as if his glance, by its very fixity, could pierce her garment of flesh and show him the perdurable essence within.

"I'm with you and Wick—you can count on me—whatever may betide," he said. Unexpected feeling sounded in his own, his deeper voice, as if a volunteer instrument had joined the orchestra.

Etta flushed under his close gaze and began to fold up her sewing elaborately. She was by habit so braced to ward off his thrusts that this sudden tender of loyalty unhorsed her. For a moment they all stood rapt in awkward silence, then Lucian swung round and started for the long window. "Well, good night," he said, still subdued; and to Wick, "Let me know of any developments." Against the black rectangle he turned and looked back at them, at the room, as if he were about to be severed from it for long. Or so it seemed to Wick; though perhaps he only imagined that look of humorous detachment touched with pity on Lucian's distinguished, cadaverous face. Like the Cheshire cat's grin, the look seemed to hang there between the light and the dark after Lucian had gone.

"I declare, Lucian is the most curious creature," said Etta, beginning to straighten the room for the night. "You never know what he's going to say next." She closed the book, returned the high rocker to the corner of the hearth, and plucked at the white sofa cover where Lucian's galloping leg had pulled it awry.

Wick refrained from saying that Lucian would cease to disconcert her if she would only realize that under his sardonic crust he was as emotional as any other human; like Old Faithful, his feelings could be counted on to spout at intervals. But Etta would never know Lucian as long as she lived, and still seeing his brother's disembodied smile, he murmured, "I thought he looked rather thin."

"Thin? I didn't think so. Lucian's the skinny kind." Having brought him down with this flat pronouncement, she started up to bed.

Wick snorted. "My God, you Tattens have a literal eye." Her retreating feet on the uncarpeted stair put a period to the argument. He took off his coat, and went about bolting in the bowed shutters; at the last French window he went out on the piazza for his nightly glance at the weather.

The deep sky was thick sown with brilliant points of light; the fine cotton weather was holding. He walked up and down the colonnade, cooling off his thoughts before going to bed. Etta . . . what a woman. But the truth was he had a natural taste for family life, the Sunday dinners, the clan funerals (but not the weddings) . . . a diversity of people brought together by some kinship hidden in the blood. Not that their kin were all likable, far from it. The Catesbys, for instance. Etta's niece, Janie Catesby, had been born a Tatten and was a caricature of that sufficiently remarkable tribe. But Etta usually invited her to Sunday dinner, and even while he suffered, Wick approved. For they all swung together in a common fate, a common confusion; from the eminence of his high piazza he saw them small and clear, struggling alike to find their level in the quagmire of human society.

Life in small cities is still settled . . . families have stayed on in the same place and grown up together . . . you headstrong "moderns" (he silently addressed Tat) like to think you are individuals, but actually we are all composites and here we see each other so, because we not only know a man, we know his parents, his children, the peculiar old uncle he "takes after," and they all keep cropping out in him. Though perhaps that settled phase is over now . . . the age of transportation is rolling over us too, at last, and bringing a new Babylonish dispersion.

For the big houses were being abandoned more and more. Tat wouldn't be able to afford this one, wouldn't want to. Fen might have, if he had lived, and had children . . . the image of Judith sunken in her slothful cushions came up to him painfully clear in the dark piazza. What a waste of warmth and sweetness that should have been fertile, that promised the Redcliffs a worthy continuance! Her illness and Fen's death—both insensate accidents. Would she right herself, marry again? He doubted it, somehow. She was fine-grained, with a serious sweetness that made a strong appeal to him personally, but what she had said this afternoon was true; she had none of the female resourcefulness of the highly sexed, of the Lorena Hessenwinkles, for example. Indeed, Judith's ultimate tragedy, he thought, was not the illness and the widowhood but the plight of a fine girl who demands quality in men, but in whom nature has scanted the color and scent that should draw variety to her choosing. And this drove her back on her ingrowing passion for Fen.

Fen would have been a help in a crisis like this. Tat wanted what he wanted so hard . . . the early years came up and overlaid the grown stature of his younger son; by a sort of transference, he saw Tat as a child, the round solemn spectacles that were always getting broken (or lost like his father's). . . . At the corner of the piazza, Wick reached out an arm and leaned against a fluted pillar, and the warm wood under his palm brought him back to the house with a sinking sense of loss. For it was a pleasure to his eye, a retreat from a world he found strident, a home place of which the mere wood and plaster were impregnated with the events of his married life and with memories held in the profound unconscious; and it hurt his reasonable pride that it might become a derelict like so many others about the town, paintless and tenantless. He stared out into the black leaves that closely encompassed the porch; the night wind suddenly drew through the branches with a silky sound like a unison of violins and made him shiver. They were left behind amid the husks of old years, he and Etta and the house. He

[1 1 3]

missed his girls, flown away on their own seekings, and above all he missed Fen. Children were promises, and three of his had gone, taking expectancy with them. There was still Tat; but what to expect of Tat, Wick couldn't imagine.

The next day was still hot and clear, and Wick awoke in a more cheerful mood. His distressful family problems were, he told himself, no more than the common fate. On the way to the office he recited, "The Assyrian came down like the wolf on the fold," for no other reason than that its galloping dactyls suited his vein.

The day's business brought a welcome respite from the per-fervid atmosphere into which his family had plunged him—against his will, he considered. When he had attended to the mail he went into the back office and sat still for a while and stared at the dusty cases about him while he made a decision. He listened for a shaking among the bones, the sharks' teeth, the arrowheads . . . his feeling about the trees was sentiment, perhaps, but intrinsic to himself. . . . Yet he dreaded an unpleasant ruckus for Tat, and for himself and Etta. But again (he flung the other way) Etta's contempt for compromise was sound. Ezekiel too thundered against it . . . well, what was life but compromise? A deep breath from the four winds came through the open window and blew over the dry bones, but if it lent them life, Wick's ears were too dull to register a speech so fine and grave. He pulled a sheet of paper toward him and wrote O'Dell a note saying he would be glad to meet August and him and discuss the timber deal. Yet the real sin, he acknowl-edged as he affixed his signature, lay in the appeasement to August's moral conscience. It cheapened them all. But then—

At two o'clock he went home, stopping by Tat's filling station on the way, ostensibly for gasoline. Tat's partner had already gone home to dinner, so he gathered no clues about the mysterious journey.

As he drew up before his gate he saw Etta's large faded garden-ing hat bobbing among the little brick-bordered diamonds and crescents beside the house. At the warning cry of the hinges she looked up and forestalled his question. She was afraid dinner wasn't quite ready—the butcher had been late sending the lamb; it was very trying, they really should buy somewhere else, but they had been dealing with the Borough Market for so long, let's see—three generations. . . .

Wick left her talking and made himself ready for dinner. When he came out on the piazza again, Etta was going into the passage under the house to put away her tools. He walked idly down the steps, inspecting the shrubs while he awaited Bekah's pleasure. The weather was favorable for roses also, he observed. The banksia climbing over the staircase rail had shot out predatory arms that angled for passing sleeves and hats. He stopped in the curve of steps and bent them back, weaving them between the iron spindles of the handrail. Gradually his annoyance about dinner oozed away in the subtle satisfaction of puttering about his place, for when he had married Etta she had insisted on making the title of this house over to him; she at once set about making him feel that it was his, and her scheme had worked well. He recognized that this was in part wifely tact and in part a female device to anchor him, to secure her future and her children's; but this possessiveness amused him as her other characteristics amused him: her irrational views, her extreme and unpredictable actions. The only trait he thoroughly disliked in her was her complacency about her family and her surroundings, and even this he had learned not to notice through the merciful anaesthesia of conjugal habit.

As if to remind him that after all he was not born to his suzerainty of the house, a fierce shoot of the banksia sprang back and clawed him.

Wick cursed softly. As he stood sucking the row of red gouts along the back of his hand he heard the cheery nasal music of a jew's-harp on the street. A Western Union boy rolled up tootling, and tipped his bicycle against the gate. He removed his cap, took out a telegram, and replaced the cap on his thick-sprouted yellow hair. It was Fritz Hessenwinkle and Wick went down the steps to meet him.

"Hello, Fritz," he said taking the envelope. "How are you getting along?"

"Pretty good, sir; pretty fair. Only the hours aren't so good. I can't get to baseball like I used to." Standing astride his bicycle, he gave Wick a disarming grin and added politely, "I certainly do thank you, though, for getting me the job with the Company. It's O.K."

"Glad to hear it. How's all the family?" Wick went on, working round to the topic that was on his mind, but Etta, coming out of the passageway, interrupted his plan.

"What's that—a telegram?" she exclaimed, fussily alarmed. Etta belonged to the generation that indulged in telegrams only in case of accident or death.

"Yes, here—it's addressed to both of us, which means it's for you. An advertisement probably; people waste a lot of paper these days on advertising by telegram." He handed her the envelope and she went up the steps with it to read the ill tidings away from Fritz's eyes.

"And they sure keep us on the jump," said Fritz. "Uncle Harry sent out a thousand last Christmas: 'The Friendly Hearth Wood Yard sends Warmest wishes for a Cozy Christmas.' "

"Your Uncle Harry did?" exclaimed Wick, seizing this lead. "And by the way, how's Lorena? Is she still at the wood yard?"

"Sure, she's still working for Uncle Harry. She's on a vacation now, but she'll be back there next week—or at least—I guess she will." He looked down and twiddled the pedal of his bicycle.

"Vacation, eh? Where's she gone?"

"I don't know exactly. Momma said she might go to see Aunt Mary Maguire over in Christ Church Parish. I wasn't home when she left. Well, I have to be getting along, I have some more deliveries. Good day, sir." Suddenly formal, he mounted his bicycle and rolled away. It wasn't until he had passed the corner that the lilt of the jew's-harp threaded the air again.

Fritz was embarrassed . . . he knows something . . . I'm sure I didn't imagine it. Perhaps I had better talk this over with Etta. After all it's her son, and I can't go on protecting her forever. She'll go up in the air, of course, but perhaps that's my fault, too. I've treated her too much like a child and that's kept her so in some respects—

"Fenwick!" cried Etta; the voice that came down from the deep shade of the piazza was wholly adult and sharp with fear and pain.

Book IV

LUCIAN was lying on the sofa that had belonged to his maternal grandfather, the late Lucian Quintillian Jones, when his half-brother's call came. It was a pudgy sofa of tufted black leather, now laced with brownish cracks, but subtly curved to rest the head and back, so he left it on reluctant feet to answer the telephone. Damn modern inventions anyway. Telephones let the public in on you; any fool could waste your time with his quacking when you preferred to be communicating with a book or an idea. He had taken *The Greek Anthology* from the shelves with which the room was lined and it wooed his palate with its crude sweet savor like a cherry pie.

"Lucian, will you come over right away? There's something I want to talk to you about." The constraint in Wick's throat added a full paragraph to the meager words.

"Sure—I'll be right over. Any news?"

"Yes. Plenty."

Whew, bad news, thought Lucian, putting down the receiver. He went back to the den where he had been reading and put his head in the door. "I'm going out for a few minutes, Mother. Don't wait dinner for me. I'll get something to eat when I come in."

Mrs. Redcliff looked up from her big wicker armchair whose latticed side pockets bulged with the sea haul her wide net gathered in. It was a hoarder's chair but also a giver's, keeping books, toys, scraps of cloth and ribbon, letters, biscuits handy until the appointed moment when she brought them out and bestowed them on the children of the connection, on her less fortunate relations, or merely on some surprised caller. Lucian was aware of the jibes current in the family that this habit of his mother's sprang less from generosity of nature than from an unquenchable hope of finding some blithe spirit who loved kickshaws as she did, who might even be beguiled into playing with them, but he scoffed at such romantic inventions. In his own opinion of his mother, her dignity and authority loomed large, and her naïveté was a device for getting her own way. If she gave any evidence of juvenescence, he had managed to overlook it.

"Must you go out just before dinner?" she inquired. "Well, at least put your book away first." *The Greek Anthology* lay open and face down on the sofa where he had left it.

The reproof, he understood, went for both irregularities. "Good grief, you have an eye for detail!" The idea of her trying to tell him how to treat books.

Secure in the rightness of her position, Mrs. Redcliff sat silent in the high-backed chair. The sprigged muslin skirt of her house-wrapper billowed on the floor; her short round body, full face, and little bun of gray hair drawn up on top looked, Lucian thought, like a pyramid of pincushions. But one discipline she had succeeded in imposing on him was "manners," so he merely rolled the impertinence under his tongue as he crossed the room, closed the book and put it on the table.

"Well, see you later." He went out jingling his keys and jumped into the well-kept black and chromium coupé standing by the curb.

Curiosity sped him toward the Borough while his nose for drama smelt out the possibilities behind his brother's summons. Tat would get himself into some sort of jam; no man was more the victim of his good qualities than Tat. Take this business of his hanging around Lorena Hessenwinkle. He considered it showed his independence, but Lucian's guess was that love of democracy had less to do with it than had his dubious success with his own social level. For the young men and girls of his crowd grew bored with being lectured about their social consciences, or lack of them; they didn't like his moral earnestness nor the way his socks hung down. On the Hessenwinkle level, though, Tat might feel at ease, might even feel superior; it could be that he sought them for this reason.

But what had happened now—had O'Dell pulled something nasty? Because O'Dell could be nasty. Hessenwinkle would not; he would be dignified, heavy, practical. And Lorena? The situation looked threatening from any angle. She was capable, Lucian guessed, of doing Tat physical violence. . . . He stepped on the accelerator, ran through a red light and drew up soon in front of Wick's gate.

The house showed no sign of turmoil within its summer shade; the gingerbread bricks, overcast with violet, stood course above course in stout Flemish bond. The brass finials on the iron fence twinkled from the regular ministrations of Bristol. Lucian had half-expected to see corpses strewn about.

He ran up the steps and went through the long window into the sitting room. The half-darkness from the bowed shutters and the silence in which his brother and sister-in-law were sitting made a little chill on his skin. Wick got up and came forward.

"We've had a great shock, Lucian. Tat and Lorena Hessen-winkle were married this morning."

"Good God!" Lucian stared from one to the other. "I never expected *that!*"

Wick handed him Tat's telegram which said merely that they had been married at Myrtle Beach and would get home on Satur-day evening. It seemed scarcely possible that the stark words could contain the explosive reality.

Etta had not spoken since Lucian came in. She sat in a straight chair self-banished from their conversation. Now she stirred and said, "Without giving us so much as a hint that he was going to—" Her voice was as strange and raw as a sea bird's.

Lucian's imagination recreated so vividly her deep-wounded love for her son that he felt the blade between his ribs, and he went over and took her hand. "Etta, my dear, this is tough for you." His own voice sounded raw, unused to such runaway emotions.

Her prejudices wiped out in the moment of tribal assault, she wound her intense fingers around Lucian's and looked at him with an appeal that unnerved him. "We've got to do something quickly. Think, Lucian. What can we do to stop them?"

"Have you any idea where they are?"

"No," said Wick, walking back and forth between the sitting room and the hall, "they didn't give any address. I telephoned the filling station, but Jim Bland says he doesn't know anything ex-cept that Tat supposedly went to study traffic conditions as far up as Myrtle Beach."

"Well, we can catch them in Myrtle Beach," said Etta en-

[119]

ergetically. "The police can find them. You can telephone the police, Wick."

Lucian gently extricated his fingers from her blind grasp. "What then?" he asked a little timidly. "Calling the police is pretty drastic." He began to follow Wick's inconsequential ramblings.

"They can be separated if we can find them in time. Tat will come to his senses, I know he will, and realize what he's done. We can't let him ruin his life like this. These boys—they don't know what marriage is."

"Luckily for the human race," Lucian muttered to Wick, as they crossed.

"There's certainly not much chance for happiness for either of them," said Wick with profound sadness. His clear-skinned face looked small and helpless on his high shoulders. "But what's to be done? Divorce?" He sighed, took off his coat and resumed his to-ing and fro-ing.

"Divorce or anything!" Etta exclaimed. "I know he didn't mean to do it."

"Divorce would be easier," Lucian remarked, "if they had had the consideration to cross the state line and get married in North Carolina instead of at Myrtle Beach. But you South Carolina women, Etta, have the inestimable benefit of living under a law that says when a man marries you, he's married for keeps."

"It's a perfectly outrageous law. There must be some provision for cases like this."

"Dear me, how quickly Episcopalian morality buckles under stress," Lucian murmured, passing Wick on the starboard tack.

"Don't be ridiculous!" cried Etta. "This is entirely different."

"Maybe so, but even if the Episcopal conscience is compliant in such cases, you've got something else to reckon with—the Catholic Church."

"Great God!" said Wick. "I'd forgotten that. Do you suppose they were married by a priest?"

"I don't know, but I'll bet a hat they were. And that's going to be harder to crack."

Momentarily thrown back, Etta drew a sharp breath, then she steadied herself. "No, it isn't," she said crisply, "that may make it easier. The Catholics allow annulments if the man and woman haven't . . . that is . . . if nothing has happened."

"How do you know nothing's happened?" Lucian modestly addressed this question to Wick.

"Well, they were just married this morning—" Etta snatched up the telegram and reread it to confirm this point. "That's why we have to find them at once. We ought to get a lawyer, Wick. Call up George Wilkins and ask him to come over as quickly as he can. And see if you can get Dr. Styles too. I think we ought to ask his advice."

"A very good idea," said Wick. Outward bound toward the hall he passed Lucian on the return trip and mumbled, "Maybe they can handle her."

While Wick summoned the Law and the Church to their aid, Etta renewed her appeal to Lucian. "You must think of some way, Lucian; you're always so clever. Tat would never have gone off and gotten married of his own accord without telling us—that girl talked him into it—"

But this time Lucian did not respond. He was off on the fascinating search for the human motive behind the human act. Why did Lorena want to marry Tat? He paused a moment by the window, pushing the recalcitrant tip of his nose straight. He was chagrined to have been mistaken about Lorena. Had he misjudged the strength of her feeling for Tat or the strength of her desire to belong—to enter the Redcliff circle? She seemed too sensible for either; but then who could estimate properly either passion or snobbery? . . . Etta, sitting upright in the gloom, gave up trying to reach him and shrouded herself in her own plans and her own necessities.

"I couldn't find George Wilkins," said Wick, coming in from the hall, "but Dr. Styles was at home and will come right over."

"How long will it take to drive to Myrtle Beach?" Etta asked.

"Four or five hours, the way we travel."

"We'll have to drive faster. I'll pack while we are waiting for Dr. Styles."

Wick resumed his march. "Etta, my dear, there's something you must face. We can't do a thing about this without Tat's cooperation, and we have no way of knowing that he wants to get out of it. After all he's twenty-nine years old."

"But he's still a baby," exclaimed Etta. "And he's so generous

[1 2 1]

and warmhearted, he's just the kind to get caught by an older woman."

"W-e-ll, Lorena can't be more than thirty-five."

"Don't be idiotic—she's years older than he is in experience. And why do you just keep saying we can't do anything? Of course we can do something—we can at least try!" Etta jumped up and drove down on the Redcliff brothers with such force that they scattered involuntarily and sat down at the periphery of the room with their backs against the wall. She took up their nervous pacing as words poured from her. " . . . and you just sit there like a bump on a log and let an adventuress ruin your son's life . . . don't think I haven't seen her lying in wait for the boys out there on the Mall . . . first, Fen—and when she didn't get him, then Tat. . . ."

"Come now," Wick protested, "she's not as bad as that," but Lucian considered Etta's words attentively; females understood each other's predatory instincts better than men who were loath to see the sweet creatures too clearly.

Wick's reasonableness was the last straw to Etta. "You men make me sick!" she cried. "You're no help—you've never been any help. Oh my God—I can't fight this all alone—" and covering her face with her hands she sank on the sofa behind her, her bones gone brittle, crushed down by deep, defeated sobs.

The snapping of her self-control shocked Wick and Lucian to their feet.

"Etta . . . Etta . . . don't do that, don't." Wick went over and sat down by her, trying to steady her convulsive shoulders.

Lucian fled on tiptoe into the dining room, leaving them alone. Might as well try to pat an earthquake. He mopped his face and went outdoors a minute to pull himself together, to recover from the damage her naked grief did him. He leaned against the piazza rail and fanned himself; he looked at his watch. Nearly three o'clock. He was ravenously hungry.

He walked round to the back door of the kitchen and went inside. Bekah was standing over the big coal range stirring some Circean mixture, her head wrapped in a cone of brown paper. She turned as he came in, and he saw at once that she had been told of the marriage. She gave Lucian a long silent look that said: What a time! The son of the house . . . but we see eye to eye on this . . . no words are needed.

[122]

Right, thought Lucian, so he said, "Hello, Bekah; anything cooking in this house today?"

"Yes, Mr. Lucian, it's mos' ready. You stay an' take dinner here; *dey* gonna be need'n' you—" the stately cone inclined in the direction of the sitting room. "I'm gonna call Bristol an' sen' it right in."

Returning to the dining room, Lucian heard the argument still going across the hall. "But we can't possibly get to Myrtle Beach now until night, and then it may be hours before we find them—if we do find them—" Wick's voice creaked with unwonted exasperation.

"But if we were there we could do something if we could." Etta's urgency carried through her incoherence. "You never do anything but argue."

"What do you expect me to do—break into their room and drag them out of bed? You are quite capable of that, I know, but frankly, I'm not."

"Oh, you're impossible—"

Poor souls, they're hungry and don't know it, thought Lucian compassionately. He went to the dining-room door. "How about some dinner? You can think better on a full belly, poets and saints to the contrary."

"Bless my soul," said Wick, pulling out his watch, "it *is* late. Take a little soup, my dear; it will make you feel stronger."

"Soup!" Etta's stinging contempt made it sound like gunpowder. "Just go away and leave me alone, will you? That's all I ask."

"Just as you say." Wick sighed and made for the sideboard and the decanter.

Bristol brought in the tureen and the Redcliff brothers being of grosser appetite wolfed the hot soup and rice without apology or indeed conversation of any sort. As their tension relaxed, Lucian's mind began to function again.

"By the way, I wonder if the Hessenwinkles know anything about it? Do you suppose they got a telegram too?"

"I wonder. Maybe they'll know where Tat and Lorena are." Wick looked at Lucian, a little dismayed by this contingency.

"That's so. Or maybe they don't know anything. If they don't they won't believe it." The telegram suddenly seemed too fantastic to be true.

"We'd better find out right away." Wick put his napkin on the table.

"Why don't you let me go?" Lucian began, but his brother glanced at him distrustfully as he put on his coat.

"No, it's better for me to deal with the Hessenwinkles. You stay here in case anybody should come in or telephone. She's in no condition to speak to anybody—you'll have to get rid of them somehow. Don't let anyone in but Dr. Styles."

Lucian was tempted to ask if he should keep a list of the floral offerings but he contented himself with saying, "I'll be glad to do anything I can," in his best pall-bearing voice.

After Wick had gone down the back steps and through the garden, Lucian sat on in the dining room to finish his coffee. Now and again he glanced unhappily through the open doors toward the room opposite from whose twilit recesses came an occasional tingling sob. At one point he jumped up as if to go to his sister-in-law; then he paused, and doubling up his napkin, hurled it down on the disordered dinner table. Damn it all! Rachel mourning for her children would not be comforted by the admirable realism he had to offer. And realism suffered in the encounter. He strolled along the walls of the room, straightening the Audubon prints which hung a little crooked as if shaken by spiritual earthquake.

His futile motions betrayed a sort of guilt. Maybe Etta was right —maybe she showed a sound instinct in wanting to rush off to Myrtle Beach and do something about the situation. Etta was a doer, in contrast to Wick and himself who were thinkers (or so they liked to call it), and her pride and passion, her headlong protest against defeat had won his profound sympathy against his own grain. In the convulsions of social change their little upset was only a pin-point, but to Etta, Tat's happiness loomed enormous, and who was to say which scale was true? If he had met the losses and defeats of his own life with such hardihood, perhaps he wouldn't be a philosopher now. He certainly wouldn't be a bachelor, he might even be married to Amy, that ambiguous and charming girl. But could he have *done* anything more than he did; in the fell clutch of circumstance, could a man be unconquerable by the mere power of the will? Because in the end it had been her corruption that thwarted them, and brandishing his fists could have done no good . . . or he might have married her, and now wished himself quit of his reward. . . .

But here he was sliding off into rationalization again, and he fingered his nose, thinking that with Wick and himself realism might be less a hardy acceptance of things as they are than a hedge against failure. He prowled about the room with increasing nervousness. What in the devil was keeping the Reverend Styles? He was supposed to be able to handle the devil, wasn't he? The minutes went by on insufferably halting feet.

When the musical cry of the gate announced a visitor, Lucian, unused though he was to leaning on the Church, rushed out to the steps and cast himself penitentially on the grave and handsome Dr. Styles. After a hasty résumé of the situation he led him tiptoe into the sitting room, and having placed the problem squarely in the lap of the clergy, he went tiptoe out again and soundlessly closed the folding doors on them. Then he went down the back steps into the garden where an old wistaria vine proffered a shady seat among its coils, and wriggling himself into a comfortable position, he took a short nap.

He dreamed briefly of Joseph, the cat, with his one black and one yellow ear. The mismatch was involved somehow with Lorena and the duality by which she was both a good sort and a bad sort; shadowy figures in the background seemed to be similarly equipped though he couldn't quite see . . . perhaps we all have a black and a yellow ear . . . and swimming up to consciousness, he seized the analogy and made off with it. For Tat was likewise a good sort and a damn fool; Wick and himself were reasoners but they must also have something of the doer in them or they wouldn't feel guilty about the life of reason. . . . If we all turn out to be twins it's going to be damn confusing, he thought, sitting up and shaking the waters of sleep out of his head.

What had really waked him was the sound of Wick's returning feet on the brick walk. From afar Lucian saw that he walked with resignation. "It's true," Wick said coming up, "they've had a telegram from Lorena. She gave no address either, which is probably just as well."

"I suppose it would have to be true. How are they taking it?"

"They are confused just as we are, and at present very much on the defensive, which is only natural. That damn mother of Lorena's was a little inclined to gloat, I thought, but Hessenwinkle is a level-headed fellow and knows it isn't going to be plain sailing for any of us, especially for his daughter. He said his family had made the place they have in this country by their own efforts, which I took to be his way of telling me he disapproves of marriage as a means of social advancement. Well, I respect August Hessenwinkle and we've all got to be careful of his feelings."

"What did the telegram say?"

"Just the same as ours did except for one addition. Lorena's wound up: 'Don't worry, I've got the certificate.'"

They both laughed with good relaxing laughter.

"By the way," said Lucian, "Dr. Styles is in there with her."

"Oh, I must go in then; I want to talk to him myself."

Wick went up the back steps and Lucian followed at a little distance. It took all his fortitude not to put his ear to the sitting-room door when it closed behind Wick, but he had really outgrown that habit, so he went upstairs to surmount temptation and incidentally to wash his hands. In the company bathroom he noted a lapse in Etta's housekeeping, for the wide marble top of the old-fashioned basin was covered with a thin layer of dust. On a purely regressive infantile impulse he drew two hearts on the marble with his forefinger, put a T in one and an L in the other, linked them with the shaft of an arrow and went out leaving them for Etta to find.

The company room breathed out a ponderous quiet as he entered it. The high mahogany bureau, the wardrobe, the double bed, seemed to inquire of him what all this rumor below stairs meant for them. Don't ask me, he told them silently, and fell to thinking of another time of change when he and they had been here together and the answer had seemed easy. How glibly the future promises and then forswears itself. He had come upstairs after Sunday dinner that time, and Judith and Fen had called him into the room, where they were staying while their own house, which they had only leased at first, was being remodeled for them. Wedding presents, boxes, and samples of chintz were piled everywhere.

Fen had sat there in the window seat, his arm around Judith, and they regarded their loot with fatuous delight. Judith, Lucian remembered, had looked really quite pretty; her skin, which latterly seemed sallow, glowed with a sort of brown flush, like a delicate stain from her eyes and hair. Lucian approached them with that mixture of tenderness and jealousy we feel toward people who are wholly happy.

"Listen," Fen said, direct and intense as usual. "Judith and I have been talking about buying that house of ours instead of renting it. I believe they'll sell it, and we want to ask your advice— do you think it's a good buy?"

"I don't see why not. It's solidly built, in a good location."

"Don't say anything about it," said Judith. "We haven't told the family yet that we're thinking of it. Mrs. Redcliff wants us to come back here to live after a while—when we've sown our wild oats, she says. Fen likes the idea of the other house because it's near the Yacht Club where he keeps his boat; but if we're going to have this house some day, it seems to me better to rent and not tie ourselves up."

To rent or to buy—how serious the decision had seemed. "I doubt if we'll ever have money enough to swing this joint," Fen said, scanning the walls, the ceiling, as if testing their solidity. "I'm for buying the other place while we can."

"Why don't you go live on the boat?" Lucian suggested. "That would solve everything."

"Oh, *Lucian—*" said Judith, half laughing, but half taking him seriously.

"Don't be a dope," Fen told her. But Judith was being literal, Lucian guessed, because at bottom she wanted to live here.

"As to not having money to keep this place up," he said, sitting down judicially on the edge of the bed, "what's the matter with living here in fallen grandeur?"

"That's all right if you don't have the upkeep on the ruin; but if you had to sweep and paint and mend the plumbing—"

"Oh, there's something timid and materialistic about this cult the cottage people go in for now. The life of man circumscribed by the reach of a broom. Dining nooks and kitchenettes. We accept the limitations of poverty too easily. Have a heart for high ceilings, I say. What if there are cobwebs? Are you going to let a cobweb change your whole way of life?"

He had waxed rather eloquent on that theme, Lucian now remembered with pride, and while he had given the wrong answer, as it turned out, about not buying the little house, he still agreed with himself about fallen grandeur. He couldn't recall the rest of the conversation very clearly; Judith had made him look at the yellow material with the gray, plumy pattern she had chosen for the living room; the glint of the fresh chintz and the wedding presents had made this room, its massive furniture, its good but faded cretonne with the pink cabbage roses, look more than ever outmoded. Then Fen must have gone out because he remembered that he and Judith had giggled together over the Tatten taste and the Tatten furniture, and Judith confessed she was itching to do the house over, it would be such fun if we had the money . . . she stood absorbed, with a candlestick in each hand, looking about her.

"Stop undressing this house in your mind," Lucian had said, "it's indecent."

"Lucian! Don't be common." Judith put the candlesticks down and ran to the window. How well she had moved in those days, her long legs and straight back smoothly co-ordinated. After a while she said that this would be a marvelous garden to bring up a family in. He saw the garden peopled with little Redcliffs, a sand pile, a rocking horse, Etta's flower beds trampled. . . .

Well, they had bought the smaller house in the end and it was a good thing; Judith wouldn't have this one now, wouldn't want it without Fen and the lost children . . . it gave him a queer feeling to think of them.

A door creaked below and voices came up the stair-well. Lucian stirred, shaking the thin ash of the past from his clothes, and went toward the stairs thinking he hadn't actually liked Judith much in those days. With her female instinct satisfied, for a man, a home, security, she had seemed a little complacent—and we seldom go out, he thought, to satisfied people. Besides, there's no place for us in their lives. He hadn't realized then when he had made little cracks about the shameless complacency of married women, how brief hers was to be. Since Fen's death he had felt much closer to her, seen her more often, bound up her wound all he could with the balm of understanding. But was his irritation exaggerated . . . was it perhaps self-protection? He still felt it at times; he turned the scalpel on himself and cut away a layer of his feeling about Judith. She had had with Fen a completion, a wholeness he himself had never achieved, and he resented it—absurdly, in a man of reason.

As he came down the steps Wick and Dr. Styles were going toward the front door. "Mrs. Redcliff will be all right," Dr. Styles was saying, "just give her a little time. She'll see that Tat has assumed a responsibility that he must stand up to. . . ."

Poor Etta, thought Lucian; the men have ganged up on her. What might she have accomplished if they'd let her alone. He joined Wick as he returned from seeing Dr. Styles out.

The sitting-room door being open to traffic once more, they went in and sat down near the window, smoking and talking in low tones. Etta lay on the sofa in a trance, as if the forces of love and grief, pride and despair had quit her to join battle more freely somewhere above her body. Wick had taken off his coat, his shirt stuck to his flanks. Poor devil, he looks like wet wash, thought Lucian. I feel as if I had been through the wringer myself.

Presently Etta stirred on the sofa. She gathered herself together and sat up abruptly. Their talk fell away; they looked at her with breath indrawn, at her features thickened, estranged by weeping. "What time is it?" she said. "I'm horribly thirsty—and hungry too, I think. Tell Bekah to bring some coffee, Wick, while I go wash my face." She got up and went unsteadily out of the room.

When she came back her appearance was ordered and the wings of dark hair were folded again. Bekah brooded over her with a tray. "I'll have it right here." Etta went to her accustomed rocking chair and Lucian brought a little table for the tray. She ate with relish the hot soup and cornbread Bekah had provided, and they all three drank coffee and talked with the excessive affability of people released from strain. In the midst of the trivialities Etta said suddenly, "When do you think they'll get home?"

"Who?" asked Wick, taken aback.

"Tat and Lorena, of course."

"Oh. They said tomorrow evening."

"That will give Bekah and me a chance to fix the company room for them. Tat keeps his such a sight."

"They may not expect to come here," Wick parried. "They may prefer to stay at a hotel. I would if I were in their shoes." It was plain that this was a hope as much as a wish.

"I should think they would naturally come here," said Etta.

"His parents' house is the proper place for Tat to bring his wife."

"Dear me," said Wick recovering, "how we do fall back on the forms in times of crisis. That's all right, my dear," he added hastily. "Thank God for the forms; without them you fall on your backside. By all means get the room ready in case they do come. But maybe they'll go to the Hessenwinkles."

"There probably isn't room there."

"Oh, they can always move a few little Hessenwinkles on to the floor and make an extra bed that way," Lucian suggested.

Etta shuddered slightly and said, "We'll send a note for them to the Hessenwinkles and say we expect them here."

"Aren't you moving a little fast?" Wick asked.

"There's nothing for us to do but accept the marriage, is there?"

Oho, thought Lucian, glancing shrewdly at his brother, your eloquent persuasions have done a job! Well—

"Nothing, nothing," said Wick gustily. "If Tat must stand by his act we must stand by him. Confound the boy, if he had to marry her why couldn't he have done it in the usual way? Why couldn't he have let us know, given us a chance to discuss it with him, or at least to make up our minds to it gradually? It's the utter disregard of anybody else's feelings that makes me so damned sore." Fatigue was fraying his nerves thin.

"Tat isn't selfish, Wick." Immediately Etta took up arms. "He makes awful mistakes," her voice shook a little, "but they are mistakes of heart. When he gets into trouble, it's always because his feelings are involved. Tat never makes the mistakes of head some people do." Her glance flicked from Wick to Lucian like cut sapphire.

"I didn't say anything," said Lucian.

"You didn't say anything, but I know what you're thinking."

Wick nipped off the argument. "I went over to the Hessenwinkles' while Dr. Styles was here." He gave Etta an account of his visit and added, "August sizes up the situation pretty well; he wanted to know, as well he might, how Tat is going to support a wife. He would have liked some assurance from me, I think, that I am going to help them out, but I refused to make any commitments today that I can put off till tomorrow. As I was saying to Lucian, however, I respect Hessenwinkle, and we've got to be careful of his feelings."

"Of course we're going to be careful of his feelings," said Etta, putting down her coffee cup with decision. "To begin with, we owe it to ourselves, and then we have Tat's feelings to think of."

"Considering that Tat hasn't been exactly mindful of our feelings," Lucian began, but Etta cut him short.

"Since we've decided to accept this marriage, Lucian, that means we also accept Lorena and her family who are now Tat's in-laws."

"O.K.," said Lucian. "Certainly I've no intention of being rude to the Hessenwinkles. They aren't any more responsible for being linked to us in the bonds of matrimony than we are. I only wanted to say I'm going to be polite on their account, and not on Tat's. Well, I think I'll be trotting along. Are you going to release the news right away? I'm afraid you've got to expect that it will stir up quite a huff-snuff in our little circle—in fact, some people are going to get an unholy pleasure out of it."

They were all silent for a moment while their minds took stock of public opinion, of the wave of talk running over town, below Broad Street, up Legare Street, over the Borough, lapping the doorsteps of the O'Dells, the Manettis.

"Yes, there's something in the misfortunes of our best friends—" Wick smiled a little acidly. "In any case you must tell Aunt Quince. I wonder how she'll swallow the H.'s as in-laws?"

"I take no responsibility for my mother's actions," Lucian disclaimed hastily. "I'll just give her the message."

"She'll have to accept the Hessenwinkles as we will." A fanatical wrinkle grooved Etta's brow.

"Well, I hope to be there when the introductions are made," said Lucian.

"That reminds me," said Etta, "Tat and Lorena will be here for Sunday dinner, won't they? I think we should invite the family to come and meet them."

"Not this Sunday!" said Wick incredulously.

"Why not this Sunday? We have most of the family for Sunday dinner anyway and I think we should present Tat's wife formally to them. And I think we should invite Mr. and Mrs. Hessenwinkle."

"For God's sake, Etta, we don't have to break our necks about this. Give us time! Let's see how things stand!" Wick batted the air helplessly with his spread hands.

"We know how things stand and you've been saying for the last

[1 3 1]

three hours that we have to accept them. Well, I've accepted them . . . so what's to be gained by waiting? Let's show Tat that we do accept his wife."

Jesus, how women love revenge, thought Lucian, walking away and leaving Wick and his protests. She's going to rub everybody's nose in it. And yet it wasn't only that, he recognized; back of this and of all her intransigent stands lay her capacity for emotional directness. She protested the marriage violently, but being forced to swallow it, she swallowed violently and set out to act upon the new situation. He began to regret her admirable singleness of character. If she were only a twin, now, you could appeal to her other side. But Etta had no other side, she was like Deity, one and indivisible. . . .

He strolled about the dining room straightening the Audubons to an even finer hair line, giving Wick time to blow off steam and arrive at the realization that he was already defeated. Then he returned to the sitting room and said, "How many of the Hessenwinkles do you propose to take on for this function? They're a pretty numerous tribe, and combined with the Redcliffs—will the forks and spoons go round?"

"We have plenty of spoons," said Etta. She considered the social aspects of the problem for a moment and then said, "We'll just ask Mr. and Mrs. Hessenwinkle—that will do, I think." She went to her desk and got out a pencil and paper. "Let's see, the Hessenwinkles, Tat and Lorena, Aunt Quince and ourselves. Then there's Judith, and Janie Catesby—"

"Can't we skip Janie?" said Lucian. "She won't enjoy her new relations-in-law one little bit."

Etta winced but wrote Janie down. "The Tatten connection ought to be represented. We always have Edward and Janie and the children to Sunday dinner. I'll write a few notes and invite them."

"You haven't much time; this is Friday."

"Well, you can't give out invitations of this kind on the telephone. I think the invitations should be written and sent out by hand. Bristol can carry them out this afternoon."

"My car's at the door," said Lucian. "I'll be glad to take them as I go downtown."

"I believe that's the best idea," Wick agreed. "The family will want to know all the circumstances and if Lucian tells them, that will save us a lot."

"Very well," said Etta, rising and going to her desk. She stood for a moment shuffling the papers and said without looking round, "It won't be necessary, will it, Lucian, to say he went off like that without telling us he was going to be married? You can say it was a sudden decision . . . on the road . . . because I'm sure it was."

"You are probably quite right," Lucian assured her. "Leave it to me. I'll tell them all a good story."

She turned round, her features compact and practical again. "Shall we say three o'clock, Wick? That seems more formal, somehow—more suitable for an occasion like this."

"Why not say half past two? Remember, lots of people dine at two nowadays; some people even eat at half past one. They'll be ravenous by three."

"If they take a glass of iced tea and a biscuit after church they won't be ravenous."

"The Hessenwinkles probably eat at twelve-thirty," Lucian offered. "They'll either be ravenous or have their dinner already inside them."

Etta's face hardened. "We'll have dinner at three because that is when we have dinner. The Hessenwinkles can come full or empty as they choose."

Wick and Lucian went to brace themselves with another toddy while Etta wrote her notes. When she joined them in the dining room her face had lost some of its strained look, as if action had relieved the internal pressure. "There are only four," she said, handing Lucian the envelopes. "It's awfully good of you, Lucian, to take them. And I want you to know that it means a lot to Wick and me to have your help and support at a time like this."

Lucian rose and lifted his glass. "Here's to our side again. You know, when I left this house last night, I had a funny feeling it was going to be different next time I saw it. I must be getting psychic—though God knows no table tappings prepared me for just this. Well, it's after five. I'll run along now with these little hand grenades and if anything else turns up, let me know."

"All right," said Wick. "I think we might go out for a drive, eh, Etta? It'll do us both good."

Lucian went and got his hat from the hall table, and passing the dining-room door on his way out he made Wick and Etta a bow that was both mocking and tender. But as he ran down the front steps and jumped into his coupé his green eyes had begun to flicker, his spare sardonic face was alight with irrepressible relish at the task ahead of him.

Lucian drove slowly down the street while he planned his Grand Tour. The households he would visit floated before him in their innocence; his felicity welled up at the prospect of carrying the news. The Hessenwinkles would be the first stop geographically, but they already knew about the marriage, and his interest centered on Judith and how she would take it. In the light of her quarrel with Lorena, that quarrel which had more in it than met the eye—

He stopped by the Greek's at the corner and went in and telephoned Judith's house. No, Miss Judith wasn't home, Sarah answered, she had gone to take Rags for a walk, but she ought to be back after a while. The store was full of the clack of shopping and social interchange and it came over Lucian with a wry surprise that these people had a legitimate interest in the story he carried under his hat—their neighbor August Hessenwinkle's girl marrying Mr. Redcliff's son . . . well, well . . . wha'd' you know! But he forewent the dubious enjoyment of tossing the story into their midst like a bunch of firecrackers and went back to his car. At the head of the Mall he turned right and on the next street doubled back toward the Hessenwinkles'; the wind was rising, the million-leaved oaks hissed softly in a dark green flowing, great gold and gray thunderheads cut across the sky above the roughened river as if the empyrean too was bustled by this seismic event. . . . Against the Brydale day, which is not long: Sweete Themmes! runne softly till I end my Song. . . . No knowing how this song would end.

Before the bride's house the zinnias marched like attendant maidens, their festive heads bobbing in the wind. The observant Lucian, going up the cement walk to the front door, noted that the steed of Lohengrin in the fountain needed a new washer, for a little dribble of water ran out of its bill and made a long green

[1 3 4]

stain down its plump bosom. He had to ring twice to make his summons heard above the hearty racket of family living, then the younger children came to the door and let him in.

In the front hall a bicycle with a Western Union cap hanging from the handle bars indicated that Fritz was taking time off in honor of the nuptials. The children clattered over the brown linoleum, and following them down the hall, Lucian came to the dining room where August Hessenwinkle and his wife were sitting. Ledgers and papers covered the dinner table on which Mrs. Hessenwinkle leaned, her forearms flattened out by her weight. But her obesity had nothing of softness about it; indeed her straight black hair, drawn up in a topknot and stuck through with the yellow shaft of a pencil, gave Lucian an impression of squaw-like directness as her glance fell on him.

"Who's 'at? Oh . . . walk in, Mr. Redcliff." She looked at him down the length of the table with ready hostility. "You'll have to excuse us, finding us like this. It's the first of the month, you know, and I got my accounts to get in shape. We weren't dressed for company so early."

The radio which had been going suddenly dropped its voice and Lucian now perceived that August Hessenwinkle was sitting beside it in a rocking chair where the sun, slanting through the thick lace curtains, had mottled him with the protective coloring of their coarse pattern. "Good day, Mr. Redcliff," he said somberly. He and his wife both rose but did not come forward. Lucian was conscious of excited whisperings from the room beyond, of faces peeping in and whisking away.

He savored with his fingers the note in his pocket and held it back. "Howd'y do, Mrs. Hessenwinkle; howd'y do, sir." He went toward them, smiling heartily. "Well, I understand we've all got congratulations coming to us. Your daughter and my nephew certainly pulled a surprise on us—took me all of a heap, I may say. But I don't hold that against them, and I hope they're going to be mighty happy."

"My, yes—quite a surprise," said Mrs. Hessenwinkle uncertainly. She seemed to find the heartiness overdone. "I guess we were all quite surprised. Take a seat, Mr. Redcliff." She came from behind the table, slow-motioned, conceding nothing, and they both sat down. August remained silent, his blue eyes steady, his large face smooth and reserved.

"When do you expect the bride and groom back?" Lucian stepped up the affability in his voice. "They said they were coming home Saturday evening, didn't they?"

"That's right—Saturday evening. I sure will be glad to see them. Your nephew's got a fine girl, Mr. Redcliff. Our Rena's a fine girl."

Her tone touched Lucian; he found himself liking the Hessenwinkles and their pride. "I know it," he said, dropping his goodfellow part for a moment. "Lorena's got plenty of spirit, and I must say I like spirit. Besides, being a susceptible male, I'm on the side of good-looking girls. I only hope Tat's got what it takes to make her happy."

Mrs. Hessenwinkle's shrewd glance sized up the sincerity in his words; two quite unexpected dimples showed in her full cheeks. She sat back comfortably and her abundant rear upholstered the spindled arms of the chair with a row of little bulges. "I think you and Rena gonna get along fine, Mr. Redcliff," she said, with a gleam of elation. "She's always straight, Rena is, and talk about spirit, you'd split your sides to hear her sassing the boys back! There was a feller hung round her a while ago—Buster—what's 'is name?—anyway he come up here one evening and tried to get rough—I guess he wanted money, or something. Well, I'm tellin' you, August didn't have to lift his finger; Rena took that bum by the collar and rushed him to the door 'fore he knew what hit him and threw him out on the walk. And he *laughed!* He didn't hold it against her." Her own guffaw gave the incident an irresistible funriness.

"Lucky for her," said August. He smoked, aloof and dignified, not elated about Rena's good match.

"Mr. Hessenwinkle," said Lucian, "I'm not going to have any trouble liking Lorena; in fact I like her already. To be perfectly frank, the only thing that buffaloes me is, why she took a notion to marry Tat."

August smiled for the first time and lifted his arms in a wide shrug. "As to that, I can't say. I always told my girls they could marry any man who had an honest reputation and didn't drink.

Outside of that—well, love is a funny thing, and you have to give 'em rope. Tat is an honest young feller and has a fine education. Rena isn't so educated, but she appreciates him. I've tried to bring all my children up to appreciate education."

Lucian lighted a cigarette, taking his time. He addressed Mrs. Hessenwinkle, as man to man.

"How's real estate up this way? My stuff's moving pretty slowly now—it's the slack season, of course; it looks as if in summertime people would rather buy a car or a radio than a house."

"Ain't it the truth? Some type of people never think about a rainy day. But I'm right optimistic about real estate; rents are bound to go up. Anyway that's what my cards say. He don't think anything"—she nodded toward August—"of my cards, but he's gotta admit they've steered me pretty good, eh, Poppa?"

August chuckled. "With all the foolishness of females, Mr. Redcliff, they've got a funny knack of hitting the bull's eye now and then. Vinny's 'way tougher than I am as a business proposition; she takes chances 'd turn my hair white."

"Oh, Poppa's too easy-going," said Vinny. "But he hasn't done so bad." She smiled on him fondly. "He's raised a big family and they never lacked for nothing."

Stretched out at ease on his chair, ankles crossed, hands in pockets, Lucian glanced appraisingly at the expensive overstuffed sofa, the shiny dining room suite. Through the kitchen door he saw great white cubes of chromium and enamel. "Looks to me as if he'd had damn good pickings."

August's thick-lipped, harmless mouth smiled benignly. "I like to spend money, but I like to make it even better," he owned. "It gives a man a kind of balance to know he can make money. Yessir, this town's been good to me and my family; all you need is to work hard—"

"Is that right?" said Lucian, interested. "People are all the time saying there are no business opportunities here."

"Fiddlesticks! Plenty of opportunities for anybody who's looking for them. Take my father now; he was born here, but they sent him back when he was fourteen to my uncle in Westphalia to learn the baking business. While he apprenticed there he had to get up at four every morning to tend to his bread. The trouble with people in this country is they don't want to fool with apprenticeships; they want to make money right off. But my dad learned baking from the ground up."

"Show Mr. Redcliff Poppa Hessenwinkle's diploma wreath," Vinny suggested.

"Well—" said August, scarcely reluctant. He got up and Lucian followed him to the opposite wall where he took down a faded photograph. "All the apprentices had to bake a piece for their diplomas. Poppa baked a sweet-dough wreath of oak leaves with cinnamon drops—see there? Every leaf perfec'."

Lucian exclaimed over the perfect leaves, the cinnamon drops which some pious hand had painted their natural red. August hung the photograph back on the wall with simple reverence while Lucian's eye made quick excursions hither and yon, gathering clues, fitting Lorena into this background. On the mantel between the alarm clock and the vase of paper roses he noticed a folded flag. "What's this—a Confederate flag?" he said. "Raising your children right, huh?"

"That? Well now, that's kind of interesting." August unfolded the little flag and took out a rusty horseshoe. "My dad got back to this country just about in time to go off to the War, and in the first battle of Bull Run the captain's horse stepped on him and broke his leg, so he got captured and sat out the rest of the War in a Yankee prison. Before they picked him up, he got ahold of this—the horse was shot by that time—the very shoe that broke his leg. He had a kind of feeling for it, and brought it home as a souvenir. Yessir, I keep it where my children can see it. 'Don't you forget,' I tell 'em, 'that your grandfather did his military service for this country.' But the young people nowadays don't care anything about military service, they don't want to *give* any time to their country; and my kids aren't any better than the rest." He mournfully rewrapped the ineffectual horseshoe in the ineffectual flag and returned them to the mantel.

Lucian couldn't see the Confederacy bulking large in Lorena's life, but his limber imagination easily reconstructed the running battle that growing up in this crowded house must have been, between the abrading forces of August's phlegmatic realism on one hand, and the sharpness, the secret firm purpose of Vinny on the other. Not that the young Lorena would have had to fight for

[1 3 8]

the essentials of life. She would have had the department-store chairs, the artificial flowers; and the ample shapes of her parents bore silent testimony to the table they kept. Still, growing up here must have been a scrap. It occurred to Lucian that the girls' quarrel might have had some such simple origin as Lorena's acquired readiness to fight about little things or about nothing at all. But he didn't care for this explanation; he preferred to think that a female rivalry, springing in caverns measureless to man, had erupted at the clash of their personalities, and he wondered what light August and Vinny could shed on the mystery. He tried to imagine Judith in this milieu and decided she wouldn't survive long—darling Judith with her lame leg, her heart bearing the deep cut life had dealt her, and her too-humble estimate of herself. No, she would be no match for Lorena. Maybe if she had been brought up in a rough-and-tumble like this, nourished on blood-puddings and applestrudel, she would have developed a crust and wide hips. . . .

But he had to abandon the fascinating idea of an exchange of environment because Vinny was saying, "Whew! it's hot in here. Le's go outdoors, Poppa. We sit out under the shed a lot in summer, Mr. Redcliff, where it's cooler." She heaved out of her chair, mopping her neck and arms in a futile race with the rivulets that ran from between the fleshy creases, and started toward the door leading to the back yard. "Annie! Fritz!" she shouted ahead in a sudden, fine baritone. "Fix a chair for Mr. Redcliff. And you children scram, now; we got a visitor and we don't want no little pitchers hangin' round."

Outside assorted rocking chairs stood in a circle on the concrete floor under the shed, and as the grown-ups appeared the younger Hessenwinkle children scattered out of them and burrowed from sight among the rabbit-hutches, chicken-coops, and pens which cluttered the back yard. Fritz and two older girls looked at Lucian self-consciously but held their ground.

"You know my girls, Lou and Annie," said Vinny. "Move over, Annie, and make room for Mr. Redcliff's chair where he kin get the breeze." Annie, Lucian knew, was married to Big Bill Hahn who ran the city abattoir; she had her mother's build, the smooth oval face and straight black hair, but she seemed to have inherited none of the O'Dell animation. She looked stupid and a little sly as she stared up at him without moving. It took a second admonition from her mother before she hitched her chair to make room for his.

Lucian would have liked in some tactful way to get the Hessenwinkle angle on the quarrel, but the conversation now became general, and he hesitated to expose Judith to unbridled discussion. He shaded his eyes with his hand and looked over the cluttered yard, wondering if Lorena had pets. Feeding rabbits didn't fit with her. Most of the cages were loosely knocked together, but in one, elaborately built of cedar-posts in rustic style, he saw a gleam of gold feathers.

"What's that—a gamecock?"

"That's mine," said Fritz eagerly, and gave him the answer to his other question. "Uncle Harry gave him to Rena, but before she went off she gave him to me, so he's mine now. You like to see him, Mr. Redcliff? He's sure some fighter."

"No, Mr. Redcliff don't want to see it," said August flatly. "You can tell he's no chicken man; he don't have time for such tripe. You better get your Uncle Harry to give you a hen, boy; a cock looks mighty pretty, but he's wasting his time without a hen, eh, Mr. Redcliff?" He winked at Lucian with heavy amiability.

"Do you ever go to a cock-main?" Lucian asked curiously.

"Me? No, I don't fool with that stuff. Vinny and Rena go once in a long while with Harry O'Dell, but they don't really like it. They just go to be sporting, 'stead of staying at home and tending to their business. It's a lot of fool nonsense."

"You don't know anything about it," said Vinny imperturbably. "It's like he's always running me about politics, Mr. Redcliff; he says I'm the politician of the family because I get out around election time and do a little work for the party; but lemme tell you, when things start cooking at Murphy's Drugstore, he's right there with the boys."

Lucian chuckled. He could well imagine the substantial August taking his common-sense part in the drugstore primaries where the ward politicians sat out in the alley in summer, their chairs tilted against the wall, and settled matters not dreamed of by starched voters going through the motions of dropping a piece of paper in a ballot-box.

"Well, I expect you pull your weight when it comes to politics," he said eying Vinny, feeling in his finger tips the quiet power of her great bulk.

"Oh, I just kind of keep the boys in order and do odd jobs. Outside of that, I'm generally on the telephone around primary time."

"I should think you'd be ashamed to say so before Mr. Redcliff," said August.

"I ain't ashamed of nothing. Mr. Redcliff's got sense—he knows how things are run. Now don't get me wrong, Mr. Redcliff; all I do is telephone a list and find out if the people are sick or dead or gone away—you know, so they can't get to the polls—and then I give the names to the secretary. Well, if the boys go on and vote the graveyard, I don't know anything about that. It's none of my business. I ain't done anything crooked."

Her guilelessness charmed Lucian. "Oh, politics is no teaparty," he reassured her, as one of the boys. "How about Lorena, has she got the family taste?"

"Lorena don't care much, she's got her mind on other things. But now that she's married and settled down, I might get her to help me some. She'd do all right in politics; she knows how to handle the boys, and she don't take nothing off them."

That would be a turn of fortune's wheel, thought Lucian, a thin smile rippling his tight-stretched skin; the Redcliffs, once a power in politics, might be on their way in again—by the Hessenwinkle strain . . . "Lorena Redcliff's on the telephone this election" . . . Sweete Themmes, runne softly till I end my Song. . . . He must tell Wick about this. Among the advantages of exogamy to our tribe, he would begin, may be a return to political influence . . .

August cut in on his search for the ironic phrase. "We've sure let the privilege we've got here of voting for the government we want come to a sad pass. Not that I don't blame it on myself, too, but you can't be too dainty as long as party politics is like it is. You got to fight the devil with fire, especially when you got bastards to handle like Rummy Mullins and his gang."

"Oh, Rummy ain't so bad," said Vinny. "Rummy's got to get his cut, but outside of that he's O.K."

"You can't blame it all on Rummy," the girls chimed in.

August looked at his females with distaste. "You Irish always

[141]

hang together," he said. "Long as Rummy goes to Sacred Heart and crosses himself you'll stand up for him." The bleak, defeated look on his plump, fair face betrayed his lonely hand in his Catholic family. He loved them, Lucian divined, in a large engulfing fashion, without having much sympathy for them as individuals.

Embarrassed by this revelation, Lucian inquired hastily, "By the way, do you know where the wedding took place—I mean, were Tat and Lorena married by a priest, do you suppose?"

They took this so for granted that his question astounded them. "Oh, sure, I guess so."

"She wouldn't make sure she'd got him otherwise," said August.

"Wish we could of been there," said Annie, and they all fell to talking of what they really wanted to talk about . . . what did Rena wear at the wedding, she took her good flowered silk with her, where have they gone on their honeymoon, where will they live when they come back? "I guess they'll stay here with us awhile," said Vinny.

"I think my brother and his wife would be glad to have them there," Lucian offered. "You may be sort of crowded here."

"We've always got room for our children," said August tranquilly. "They ought to take plenty of time to look for a place to live. With the little money they've got—by the way, how much does Tat make out of that filling station?"

Lucian had a general idea of Tat's earnings but he instinctively parried the inquiry. "Oh, I don't know. Tat doesn't take me into his confidence." But August, he realized at once, didn't intend to pry; he was merely expressing forthrightly his legitimate interest in the financial status his daughter had assumed.

"You should of seen Rena at her last wedding," said Annie. "It was a beautiful wedding—she sure made a beautiful bride."

"I got a lovely picture of her," said Vinny. "Fritz, run upstairs and get sister's wedding picture out of the wash-stand drawer."

Lucian had almost forgotten about the first husband, and while Fritz was gone he asked a few tactful questions. Eleck Thompson was a handsome feller, Vinny said; Rena met him at a dance at the Isle of Palms pavilion while he was up from the Marine Base at Parris Island on liberty. But he turned out to be no 'count. He took Rena off to Cuba, and when he got his orders to go some place else, he left her with only six dollars and a quarter in her pocket-book. She waited and waited for him to send her some more, but nothing ever came, and she had to write August for money to come home. Then a while afterward he died—his appendix burst on some island. . . .

Fritz returned with the picture. "See?" said Vinny, holding it up. Lucian took it and looked at it with unfeigned interest. The harsh lights and shadows of the cheap photograph showed a young Lorena, bedizened in white, smiling out with dimpled satisfaction at life, at the joyous state of being a bride. Her hair, dark brown in those days, was crimped under the veil, her face thinner than now and not indicating by even a faint tracery that life had shown her its ugly aspect. Yet, fighting for survival in these strident surroundings, sharing a bedroom with one or more of the others, seeing her brothers through the sexual excursions of adolescence, she must have acquired early the knowledge of good and evil. But good and evil bounced off some people without making much impression—even Lorena's maturer face was almost a blank page. The untouchable youth of the face in the photograph moved him to the quick; he sat speechless, with the Hessenwinkle eyes fixed on him, waiting for suitable tributes to their beautiful Rena. Their naïve expectancy, their surprise and dawning disappointment, made speech more and more difficult.

At last he managed a sort of croak. "She sure is a looker." But he had missed his lines as a good fellow, his attempt to talk their language fell flatter than flat. This was not what they expected —from Mr. Lucian Redcliff they looked for phrases more eloquent and refined. Fritz rescued him from one embarrassment by confronting him with another, a photograph of Lorena's former husband. There was really not much to say about the strapping young man in the Marine uniform; he didn't look like a bad sort, but the Hessenwinkles had declared that he was, so "What an elegant uniform," seemed the only way out.

"She sure was nuts about that bozo," said Fritz, regarding the uniform covetously.

"Rena was nuts about having a good time," said August. "You're all nuts about having a good time. That's all you think of."

"Don't talk against your own child, August," said Vinny.

"I'm not talking against her. She's always been a big help in the house. I'll miss my girl when she leaves us. Being our eldest, Mr.

Redcliff, Rena's done her time taking care of the younger ones, helping to bring them up, and she's pretty strict with 'em too, eh, Fritz? She ought to have had a dozen or so children of her own, that would have settled her down."

"Don't talk like that!" Vinny's voice rose; she would have shouted, Lucian thought, eying her with curiosity, if he hadn't been there. What was bothering her? Not propriety, he felt sure; her language could unquestionably take the skin off your ear if she really cut loose, and he wished she would. Good Lord, he thought, suddenly putting his hand in his pocket; in his enthrallment with the habits and customs of the Hessenwinkles he had utterly forgotten the purpose of his visit.

"I've got to be shoving," he said getting up, "and I almost went off without leaving you this." He handed Mrs. Hessenwinkle the square envelope of thick creamy paper that, in this milieu, seemed startlingly Etta. Quality without swank—it had almost the unctuous texture of a wedding invitation. "My brother and sister-in-law hope that Tat and Lorena will stay there when they come back," he said, somersaulting from the colloquial to the formal, from the role of good fellow to the role of court chamberlain. "They are inviting the family for Sunday dinner to meet the bride and we all hope you and Mr. Hessenwinkle will join us." If he had had a chamberlain's gold chain he would have toyed with it.

Mrs. Hessenwinkle took the envelope in her hand and turned it slowly as if unequal to the effort of opening it. "My, my," she said slowly, "that's mighty kind of Mis' Redcliff to do that for our little girl." Suddenly her face sharpened with the spiny glint it had worn when he first came in. "They ain't gonna be mean to Rena now—they ain't gonna get her there to make her feel bad? I won't stand for anybody being mean to her."

"Mrs. Hessenwinkle," Lucian said, making her a bow, "I assure you my brother and sister-in-law are incapable of asking anybody to their house to be rude to them. They are old-fashioned folk, and whatever their faults may be, they won't violate the laws of hospitality. If you will come to the dinner you will see for yourself that your daughter will be received like the best."

Either the honesty of his intent or the length of his words impressed Vinny. The glint vanished; "Jus' as you say." Without further ado she took the pencil out of her topknot and opened the envelope.

August, who had remained silent about the invitation, now said, "I think we'd best leave the thing work out by itself without any fuss."

"I couldn't agree with you more," said Lucian. "But Mrs. Redcliff seems to want Tat and Lorena to know that they accept the marriage; she wants to do the right thing by them. Anyhow, there's the invitation; you can do as you think best about it."

"She says her and Mr. Redcliff hope very much we will come, August." Vinny looked up expectantly from her perusal. "I think it's mighty nice of her to ask us—real kind and friendly—"

"I thank Mrs. Redcliff kindly, but we'd best eat our dinner at home, Momma. You write and tell her."

"Well, I've enjoyed this visit more than I can say," said Lucian with slightly barbed sincerity. "Most interesting to see you all here. . . ." The good-bys were cordial all round as he bowed himself out.

August went with him through the garden to the front gate. As they passed the swan, Lucian saw between the cannas that the pool was built of artificial rock bedded in cement to give an effect of rustic elegance.

". . . a swan lake in a ring of fire . . ." he found himself murmuring.

"How's that?" said August.

"Nothing," said Lucian; "it ought to be a quotation but it isn't. I like the way you carry on the Wagnerian tradition. That's a magnificent bird you've got there, but it would take a derrick to get him off the ground."

August chuckled with pleased proprietorship. "Well, I'll never have to buy another, then. I got him from the old Exposition grounds when they were being dismantled, and the boys and I built the fountain Saturday afternoons. Well," he sighed ponderously as they reached the gate, "I guess it will all turn out for the best—this wedding, I mean—I just hope Rena isn't looking for something Tat hasn't got. She used to be sort of sweet on Fen a long time ago, you know."

"You don't say!" Lucian's eyebrows went up.

[145]

"Oh, she was just a pullet then and always had her head full of boys. But I remember she cut his graduation picture out of the paper and kep' it stuck in the mirror over her dresser. It didn't last, of course, and she fell in love with Eleck and married him. I always thought they'd have suited each other fine if he'd been a settled feller instead of traipsing all over the world with his outfit. Well—" he sighed again as if his children were too much for him. "I just sort of wondered if she was thinking about Fen, because Tat isn't Fen, not by a jugful."

"Oh, I don't believe so," said Lucian. "Anybody could see with half an eye how different those boys were, and Lorena has more than the usual number of eyes for sizing up the menfolks."

"That's right," said August, smiling broadly. "I guess I'm just being fanciful."

The adjective applied to the honest, earthy August enchanted Lucian. He shook hands with him in a rush of genuine liking.

This was Lucian's favorite season of the year. Let the tourists rage amongst the azaleas— He loved his city in the high dress of early summer, when the oleanders foamed over the walls in red and white and pink excess, and the golden thorns cropped out in cockatoo-blooms along their green-feathered limbs. The light on the streets was changeful all day from the abundant clouds sculling through the deep sky. As he sped toward Judith's house, his sensory antennae, running free before his mind, swept up a motley of colors, smells, and images.

Suddenly a barren spot struck his feelers, a hot blast, arid and metallic. He was passing a trailer-camp crowded into an empty lot between mean houses. But through the vague distress it spread, a shaft of color stopped him; he jammed on his brakes and pulled the coupé over to the curb. A herd of elephantine shapes browsed in the sun; alongside the nearest monster, petunias and geraniums bubbled out of a row of tin cans, which their owner, a lumpish young woman, was beginning to move to the shady side. Bending with difficulty, she took the sweltering rays full on her back as she lifted the painted tins two by two and lugged them round the trailer.

Lucian opened the door and put a foot on the running board on an impulse to speak to her, but she trudged back and forth ab-

[146]

sorbed in her task with no suspicion that to the skinny gentleman sitting half in and half out of his automobile she was symbolizing the quenchless optimism of the human spirit. He wanted to urge her to settle here . . . you're the kind of settler we could use, with your tough determination to make a garden in spite of the devil . . . but he rejected this as too florid an opening and said instead, "Do you move them back to the west side every morning?"

"Yes, sir; the morning sun's mighty hot too." She straightened up and answered him naturally. "But my petunias did fine, anyhow. You shoulda' seen them last week, they're going by now. The roots dry out so quick in these tin cans. I could have a nice flower garden if we had some good dirt here and some shade." She looked without rancor at the cindery ground and the spots of oil sludge. "But we're going to get us a piece of land sometime and plant a flower garden."

"That's the thing," said Lucian heartily; "there's nothing like having a patch of ground. Why don't you think about settling down here? This is a good climate for flowers and you can find a little place easily. I'll be glad to help you if you want me to—"

But this was really going too far; he drew back slightly, feeling foolish. The fat girl seemed to think so, too. She said distantly, "I don' know; we goin' to settle down someplace."

"Well, keep your flowerpots blooming in the meantime; they make a mighty pretty show. And lots of fine big gardens have flowers in pots. In Spain, you know, they go in for potted plants in a big way. They learned that from the Moors. The Moors were travelers, like you, and they had to keep their gardens in pots so they could pack them up handily and move to the next place." He gave her a friendly, impish smile. "I bet you never thought of that."

"Moors?" she repeated wonderingly.

What the word connoted to her mind Lucian didn't know, but apparently nothing good. "Good-by," she said with hard finality and clambered up the steps into the trailer.

Grinning, Lucian drew his foot in and slammed the door. There you were; people were always misunderstanding his kindly impulses. A good thing she didn't know he was in the real estate business, no telling what she'd have made of his offer to find her a flower garden. He bowled down the street whistling.

He'd swing round by High Battery, he thought, and see if he could pick up Judith and Rags on their promenade. He tried to picture how she would take the news he bore. She'd have that peculiar female jealousy toward another Mrs. Redcliff—coming right after the quarrel, Lorena's usurpation of the name would burn her up.

As he came to the end of the street and turned toward the water, the wind buffeted his car in soft gusts—the warm, damp wind from the Caribbean with rain in its web. The dry spell was over, he guessed. As if in support of his prophecy a black and white liner came smartly up the harbor with a low-slung freighter splashing along in her wake, and fanning out behind, the shrimp trawlers like sturdy Portuguese Salomes veiled in their spread nets.

All along High Battery people were taking the air; the clatter of foreign languages came down from the walk above his head. A group of dark, animated women, turbaned (by the dime-store) and crocheting incessantly, stopped at the stair by his parking place. They screamed to their swarthy progeny in a staccato Mediterranean tongue, scanned the harbor, tasted the wind and, as if blown before it, they streamed down the steps and piled, about ten of them, into a big shiny new car and drove off uptown.

There were no signs of Judith so Lucian went on to her house. He opened the front door and walked along the flagged piazza toward the back from whence voices came. She had come in, then, but she was not alone, to his chagrin. Manya Turner lolled in a deckchair while Bob, with the long-handled clippers, helped Judith with her pruning. They called to him to come out and join them.

He crossed the small rectangle littered with shorn branches. "Well, this is a work of piety," he said turning over one of the big terra cotta pots and seating himself upon it. "I like my gardens formal, and I've been itching to get my hands on this one for a long time and lop off some of its extravagances."

"I don't," said Manya. "I like a garden to be natural, informal —especially a small garden."

"Contrariwise," said Lucian argumentatively, "with a small garden you have to be formal more than ever. You can't compete with a big garden in excess, in room to mass color, so the only thing you can do is to make a more intricate pattern."

[148]

But while he debated classic versus romantic with Manya, he followed Judith with his eye, trying to catch her attention. Happily absorbed in cutting back the flowering pomegranate which had half-blocked the garage, she wouldn't glance his way. Lucian admired Judith's looks, holding, as he did, the ugly and distinguished in higher esteem than the merely pretty. Not that Judith was ugly; today she looked quite handsome with her hair tied up with a green ribbon, and her face seemed to have lost a look of strain which he noticed chiefly in its absence.

At this moment she came over to bring him a branch thick-studded with vermilion flowers. "Look, aren't they heavenly?"

"What a clear, watery red," he said, taking the branch and turning it so the light struck through the thin petals. "No wonder the Greeks thought the pomegranate sprang from the blood of Dionysus."

"Lucian, you always know the oddest things."

He warmed himself at the ready admiration in her voice as at a chimney-place. He liked to play the man of letters to Judith, to sound philosophical, witty, profound, and in a measure he was all of these because she accepted him as such. Through his waspishness about her ran this desire to gain her attention. But now he had other things on his mind. "I have a message for you," he muttered. "Can't you get away for a few minutes, follow me indoors?"

"Yes," she answered under her breath. An awkward pause followed, then he said aloud, "May I go in the house a minute and use the telephone?"

"Of course," said Judith. "I'll . . . I'll come and help you."

"I don't exactly need help . . ." What a bad liar Judith was. "But I could use some advice, maybe. Excuse us, Manya?"

Manya said she had to go and put her child to bed anyway, and Lucian followed Judith into the living room with mounting excitement. "Well, my cabbage, guess what's happened now?"

"What?" His tone stopped her in her tracks.

"Brace yourself . . ." He prolonged the sweet suspense. "Hold on to a chair . . . this is really the pay-off . . ."

"What on earth . . . ?"

He paused for a full moment, then said with exaggerated calm, "Tat and Lorena were married this morning."

She looked at him without breathing. "It can't be true . . ."

and breaking away from his stare, she took a few steps, the lightness gone out of her gait.

"All too true."

"I don't believe it." She turned on him angrily. "This is one of your jokes—"

"My jokes are in better taste, usually. I assure you they were married this morning at Myrtle Beach. I read the telegram."

"Myrtle Beach? But I saw her yesterday afternoon."

"So I hear. Well, she was on her way to the altar then. You evidently missed the bridal signs. They must have gotten to Myrtle Beach late last evening and spent the night there—to what purpose we can only guess—and were married this morning by a priest."

"How *could* Tat do such a thing!" she exclaimed, her face crimson. "How can he spoil our lives like this!"

Lucian looked at her dumbfounded; he had expected his mother to take on about the marriage but not Judith. "Come, now," he said, nettled, "a man has a right to please himself in the matter of a wife. And Lorena's not unpleasing to the male sex, I assure you. She's good company and has plenty of hard sense under that luscious exterior—" He modeled abundant curves out of air with caressing hands. "In fact, I'd have a lot of sympathy for my nephew if I thought he was marrying her for what she was instead of for some fuzzy notion of being democratic. Lorena, the Handsome Gangstress. She holds men up with her sex appeal, to be sure, but why else was she so plentifully endowed? We all use the weapons God gives us to get along in the world."

"I suppose so—" She pulled herself together with a violent effort. "I don't know why I feel she's trying to take you all away from me, even Fen—"

"For God's sake, Judith! Look here, what in the world did you two quarrel about to make you hysterical like this?"

At his stinging tone she covered her face. After a moment she dropped her hands and said, her head still bowed, "I know I'm being an idiot. I try to fight it, I really do, but I feel like the frog in the well; every day I climb up one foot and fall back two. You're infuriatingly coolheaded; doesn't it ever happen to you—to see that your feelings are base without being able to stop them?"

Ignoring Lucian's mystified look she went over to the window and sat down by it, talking in a low voice as if to herself. "As to

[150]

the quarrel, I don't know how it started, how I got into all this. I don't want to quarrel with Lorena, all I want is for her to let me alone; but she keeps creeping up on me and getting into my hair. Now here she is in the family and I'll never get away from her again; we'll have to have dinner together at Uncle Wick's every Sunday and it will be awful."

"Sometimes an excuse to get out of Sunday dinner in the Borough might come in very handy. Redcliffs are at their worst in bunches."

"But I don't want to get out of it. I don't want to be pushed out of the family; they're all I have left."

"Well, if family dinner is what you want, you're going to have a chance to get your stomach full on Sunday. Etta is hell-bent to give a blow-out for the newlyweds—a very exclusive function of Redcliffs and Hessenwinkles. Admission is by invitation only." He drew Judith's from his pocket. "Here's yours."

While she slowly read it he sat back smoking and looked at her silhouette against the window and wondered for the hundredth time how Fen had happened to marry her; Fen's tastes in girls had been so different from his own. Despite the dissimilarity he had always been fond of Fen, his fondness tinged with both envy and condescension because Fen had never been crossed in love. With Fen Fate had pulled its punches and then delivered them all in one knockout, whereas Judith and himself Fate buffeted from day to day, thwarted their desires, taught them the briny taste of failure.

He pursed his mouth, speculating for a moment on what kind of bedfellow Judith would make and decided she would be satisfactory. It must have been Fen's best instincts that made him discern the warmth and sweetness that lay behind the classic angularity of her façade. But had they been enough, the warmth and sweetness? Fen was attractive to women and followed his instincts, his bad ones, no doubt, as well as his good. . . .

Judith bowed her head over Etta's note and said in a buried voice, "I couldn't possibly go—I couldn't face it."

Suddenly the man of heart in Lucian took over, the unquenchable residuary who was always jerking the props from under the cynic and the mountebank. He remembered how besotted Judith had been with Fen, how vulnerable it made her, and he was filled with remorse at having come there to tease her, at having spoken crossly to her, even for having thought of her just now in a manner unbecoming an uncle-in-law and a gentleman. He went over to the window and took her hand.

"Don't pay any attention to my crabbing, Judith; you know how I like to air my head. And nobody's going to push you out of the family. It was a lucky day for the Redcliffs when we got you, and we're not going to let you out again. Now cheer up. Why don't you run up the street tomorrow and get a new hair-do? It'll make another woman of you."

She smiled and pressed his hand, inarticulate. "It's hot in here," she said in a moment. "Let's go outside."

Clouds had covered the sun, the piazza was gusty and cool. "I have some nice rum," she said tentatively.

"Good. I could use a drink. It's going to rain like the devil in a little while."

They pulled up the awnings and settled themselves comfortably while Sarah came tinkling from the pantry with the ice and limes. "You mix them, Lucian. I never know how much to pour for a man. I'm being simply odious about this marriage," she went on while he busied himself at the tray. "As if it mattered what I feel about it when it's really Tat we ought to be thinking of."

"It's too late to be thinking of Tat. He'll have to do his own thinking from now on, and plenty of it."

"I hate being cut off from him. I don't suppose I'll see anything of him now."

"A minute ago you were moaning because you were going to *have* to see them," Lucian couldn't help pointing out.

Judith laughed and flushed. "That's true, but what I mean is that I'll be cut off from any of the nice friendly talks Tat and I had for a while. You know, after Fen's death he used to drop in here all the time—he minded about Fen much more than he ever let on. He used to just sit on the edge of the piazza there and talk about the old days and what a wonderful person Fen was; and every now and then he'd ask me how I thought Fen got that way—how he managed to do things well and be liked by everybody. He sort of hoped I had discovered the secret and could tell him."

"Damn!" said Lucian fervently. "What you say is roweling me," he offered by way of explanation, "and I don't like to be roweled. Tat, poor devil, did have rotten luck to be born Fen's younger brother. If he'd been the only boy-child in a large family of girls, for instance, he'd probably have been a successful stock broker by now."

"Oh, he wouldn't, Lucian. You're too hard on Tat. He's sweet, really—if you'd seen him the way he was then it would have cracked your heart. I used to go upstairs and cry after he'd been here—as much over Tat as over Fen."

"Don't be so damn literal," said Lucian fidgeting. "It's cracking my heart now. That's the hell of this business of consanguinity. If Tat and I could pour out our Redcliff blood we could just dislike each other and let it go, but because we're kin, we snap at each other, we can't forgive each other for being different. And a sort of loyalty neither of us specially wants makes us suffer for each other. I'll tell you something else, Judith; Fen's ease and balance gave me a slight complex, too, so I understand Tat better than you think."

"Why Lucian! How extraordinary—I never dreamed—you always seem so—so—"

"Cocksure," Lucian supplied with his cadaverous grin. "Well, things are not what they seem; all is not gold that glitters; life is a dream. Et cetera. Of course, Fen didn't buffalo me the way you say he buffaloed Tat. I've known all along," he added hastily, "that romanticizing Fen was part of Tat's trouble; what you say just makes the pieces slip into place."

"It's one of the things that makes Tat's falling for Lorena so surprising," said Judith. "In spite of our quarrel, I could accept Tat's being crazy about her and feel that he may be happy with her, if she's what he wants. But I have a funny feeling that she isn't, probably because she wasn't at all the type Fen liked."

"Is that so? I'd have thought she and Fen would get along swimmingly."

"Well, he never liked Tat's going with her," she said a little defensively. "At least, he told me so."

"That does tangle the skein," Lucian agreed, looking thoughtful. "Maybe Tat's just being independent; maybe he's decided he has to stop trying to be Fen and be himself. Which makes it all the more tragic, when you think of it." He looked at Judith, his green eyes still and sad for the moment.

A cheerful voice broke in on their probing. "Why so exclusive, you two? Come on over to our place and have a drink." Bob Turner, looking aggressively bathed and sunburned in white trousers and shirt open at the collar, came along the piazza from the back. "Oh—you've got a head start on us, I see. Well, never mind, our liquor's just as good."

Lucian and Judith looked at each other in silent dismay.

"Say, am I interrupting something?" Bob backed off, lanky and abashed.

"No," said Judith, "but have a drink with us instead. Call Manya and tell her to come over here, as long as we've already started."

"I don't want to barge in on anything—"

"You aren't barging in. Lucian has just given me a big surprise, but I guess it's public property by now. Tat got married this morning."

"Tat? Why, the old fox—who'd he marry?"

"Lorena Hessenwinkle."

"For God's sake!" Bob couldn't dissemble his astonishment. "Well, well—isn't that *something!* Why, the old so and so."

Lucian rescued him from his predicament of not knowing whether the occasion called for congratulations or condolences. "It would seem that a health to the happy pair is in order. Go fetch your spouse and let's get down to drinking. I have a couple more errands before dark catches me."

While Bob was gone Lucian gave Judith a highly colored account of his visits to the Redcliffs and the Hessenwinkles. He was pleased to observe that she was taking the affair more sensibly, laughing at his impudent characterizations. In a little while Bob returned followed by Manya, crisp and handsome in a pajama suit of thick Chinese silk.

"Bob told me the news," she said directly, "and I think it's simply swell. I've only seen Lorena once, but I thought she was grand fun."

"We met her with Tat one night during the Azalea Festival," said Bob, "and we all did the street carnival together. We liked her lots, she's a real person."

"How do you mean 'a real person'?" Lucian raised one eyebrow and frowned with the other.

"Well—just that," said Manya. "She's a real person. She works for a living, for one thing; and I'll bet she's good at her job."

"Though only stuffed with sawdust, most of Tat's family work for a living, too," Lucian cut in, but Manya ignored him and went on, smiling at Judith: "I love Tat—he's so sincere; I love him when he gets going on the state of the world, with his hair getting wild, his shirt riding up, his arms waving—"

"And knocking over the drinks," Lucian mimicked her tone.

"Well, what of it? The point is, Tat has the courage of his convictions, as this marriage proves, and I think it's swell."

"That's true," said Judith, looking from one to the other, her loyalties divided. "We all talk about juvenile delinquency and slum clearance, but we're too busy or lazy or something to get at them."

"Exactly," Manya agreed. "Tat really tries to do something about conditions."

"So he does," said Lucian; "all the wrong things. I couldn't wish a worse fate for a pet crusade than to have Tat take it up. He's guaranteed to raise everybody's hackles before he gets through."

"I say we drink the health of the bride and groom," Bob interposed. "Long life to them, happiness et cetera . . ."

"I wish them health with all my heart," said Lucian rising and bowing. "They're going to need it—to wear through the next few years."

They all laughed and drank and chatted for a while, then Manya returned to attack. "You must admit, Lucian, that it takes guts for Tat to heave up out of his background the way he's done and thumb his nose at the old guard. I don't mean the Redcliffs particularly, I just mean—well—" she opened her arms in a wide gesture—"the social background. You'll admit, won't you, that they're pretty reactionary as a group; they've never had a new idea because they've never been anywhere—nowhere else is good enough. It's small town stuff, and Tat's just too big for it."

"This isn't a small town," Lucian objected, "it's a small city, and that's very different. You cosmopolites don't understand the nature of true provincialism; you call us names because we don't immediately give up our fundamentalisms for the gospel according to St. Marx; but why should you give up your own idea for somebody else's? There's no virtue in that, that I can see. The trouble with the cosmopolite is that he passes himself round from hand to hand, from Frenchman to Russian, from Turk to infidel until he's like a slick dime—he has no superscription of his own. As to never going anywhere, we get around pretty liberally. Until traveling abroad got so unhealthy, you'd find us in all the nicer *pensions* of Europe; all the smaller ocean liners carried their quota of sea-going Carolinians."

"Is that so?" said Manya, sipping her drink. "You wouldn't think travel could do so little good."

"Oh, skip it," groaned Bob. "You'll be fighting the Civil War next and I want to hear about Tat and Lorena—"

A clap of thunder cut him short and, as if called from the prompter's box, Lucian jumped up, went behind his chair and addressed them in a sort of recitative. "Before I depart I'd like to say just one thing. I'll go with Manya as far as she likes in one respect: the top row in Charleston—in this country, in fact—doesn't live up to its pretensions; we claim a superiority we can't deliver. I have a whole speech on this subject which I'll be glad to come round and make for you if you're interested. But I disagree that the sort of thing Tat's doing is the remedy. . . ."

He went to the edge of the piazza and scanned the sky as if he feared the curtain would come down before he finished. "Last year," he went on, hurrying back and taking the lapels of his coat in either hand, "a friend of ours, Benny Lamotte, got married, and at a pre-nuptial party at the Country Club he got drunk and erroneously imagined he was a canary and tried to fly out of the window. Thanks to the zeal of the Confederates, who threw up the earthworks the club is built on, the window was quite high from the ground, and Benny spent the next month, when he should have been wedded and bedded, in the single strictness of a hospital room. Well, the story ran all round town, and though it has its elements of humor, the little people weren't amused; you could have heard disapproving clucks all up and down the Borough. They don't particularly resent entrenched privilege; what they resent is being made suckers of by the privileged. And I resent it too—that the younger crowd doesn't give a damn for its responsibilities, that they make goats of themselves before the public. Not that a man can't get drunk occasionally (and if I'd been marrying that

[156]

fish-mouthed Fitzgerald girl I'd have pretended I was a canary too, and tried to fly away); but he should have some sense of fitness —he ought to know the difference between an escapade and a scandal."

Manya had been getting restless. "But you talk as if Tat had committed a scandal. After all he married the girl; I can't see why that should be a crime."

"I think if you could go through the Borough tonight like the angel of death and pause at each lintel you'd find that Tat's marrying her had caused much more of a scandal than if he'd merely had a whirl at adultery."

"Well, it defeats me. I just can't figure this place out."

"Which was obvious from the first," said Lucian. "At last we've agreed on something. Well— 'Come, my coach; good night, ladies . . . good night, sweet ladies . . .'" He went delicately toward the door, and having closed it behind him, he broke and ran for his coupé as the first big drops began to fall.

Lucian had overstayed his curtain after all, for the thunderstorm drove him into the shelter of the nearest filling station where he sat for its brief duration in full harmony with the crackling and sputtering of the universe. Damn these crop-headed females in floppy pants . . . maybe I am complacent (he addressed her angrily) but for true smugness give me the cosmopolite visiting the provinces. . . . The downspouts gushed over the sidewalks and Lucian let his exasperation gush with them. But why in hell did she get under his skin like this? Judith's friends liked the Turners; they said Manya was unusual . . . awfully bright . . . very attractive. But Lucian considered her superficial . . . so why did he let her acidities get his goat? Well, his feeling about the place was as contrary as any other passion, he supposed. The swampy area on which he had been born, had lived, and hoped to die was probably in no way superior to similar acreages . . . but no . . . that was hardly true . . . some special lucence bathed this plot of ground, he insisted . . . this precious stone set in a slightly muddy sea. For people loved it with extravagance . . . in spite of its absurdities, its gross failures. Perhaps because of them (and this would always defeat Manya). For life was richest when it was dappled, paradoxical, in flavorsome layers running counter to each other. August Hessenwinkle had pleased Lucian's palate mightily today. Take the old German families he represented . . . they had managed to preserve their viewpoint, their taste in food, their *Schuetzenfests*, and he cherished them for it. He even liked the O'Dells for their gaiety and impudence (and the hard materialism underneath it) and for the high fluted columns of the Hibernian Hall. He liked his mother (quite apart from filial affection) for her invincible provincialism; the little group of low-country plantation families that bounded her horizon entertained and exasperated him immeasurably . . . their tight code and the superb scandals they made when they burst out of it. And those hard-headed Huguenots . . . Lucian, who had a Welsh streak, was always tangling with them . . . no later than Sunday he had locked bumpers with one in front of the Huguenot Church after service, and they had tied up the traffic in Church Street for more than an hour while they battled it out on a point of precedence. The Irish cop, far from unjamming them, had merely added a third intransigent element.

And take the Negroes, the earth-color, the ocher and umber in the canvas; the high unbridled laughter and the cutting scrapes, the art with which they elevated the commonplace, translating shrimp and mullet into food for Neptune's table as they cried it through the rivery streets. Take the streets themselves . . . the dark crooked streets he still remembered in his legs because he used to run past them as a small boy coming home on winter evenings, and the wide streets with the garden gates . . . one gate he never passed even now without stopping to peer in, hoping to catch the inscrutable, the unheard of, walking in the thickety shade.

Take old de Angelo, the chain-store magnate . . . a valued client, unctuous as olive oil . . . the last time Lucian sold him a new fruit store he had gleefully recalled that he got his start "wit' da monk." "God gave us and the Ark two of every kind of critter," Lucian loved to say, "lunatics and murderers walking at large, scholars and geniuses, cranks and saints and bores—my God, what bores—in that, at least, we are superlative." And this wilful love—of the town, each other and ourselves—stubbornly survives even the bores, and the greasy breath of the dirty little cafés along the sidewalk, and the ugly demand of the white man that his sense of superiority be bolstered by servility from the Negro.

His mind veered down the street toward Manya again . . . the perspective of houses, spouting rain like so many waterfalls, closed ranks to the sidewalk and kept their piazzas, their gardens sequestered from passers-by who, they assumed, would be strangers, not neighbors . . . Well, we do have a God's plenty of strangers walking up and down, and damn glad to have them. We'd bore ourselves stiff if the new people didn't come in and joggle us with their ultra-mural ideas. Mostly bad ideas, of course, but no matter, they stir up our livers. Even the Turners, he thought, as the rain slackened and cooled his susceptible blood, he was even damn glad for the Turners, for had they not come here on their own behoof, seeking, they didn't know what, but some strand in the complex of the place . . . after all, they weren't born with the burden of love for this tongue of land between two rivers, with the illogical, unshakable burden that so galled the thinker, the rationalist that he had to sit for half an hour in a sopping downpour trying to explain it.

Something quite uncomplex moved Lucian to turn on his motor —the simple pang of hunger returning. The storm dripped itself out, the thunder growled around the far horizon, vexed to find the roofs and steeples unbowed by its chastisement. He drove slowly down the street, not all unregenerate. He felt light from his self-shriving, or from excitement and weariness, perhaps, and floating thus he came to the corner of a street which was the shortest way home from Judith's house to his. For ten years he had avoided it, he had always gone the long way round. But now the narrow aperture pulled at him again, it dragged at his fluid will like an open sluice; he swung his car into it so abruptly that he almost overset a lone passer-by trying to cross.

It was a short street, boxed in with close-set gables and a white wall along one side with a small blind gate in it; the little sidewalk was narrow as a tape. He had a momentary sensation of slipping on a canal through the heart of some foreign city; rainwater gushed silently along the gutters, the asphalt mirrored precisely the clear pallor of the wall and its tassels and swags of creepers. The dark cloudy trees in the garden beyond swayed in the ravelings of the storm-wind and blurred their images in the glassy street.

Opposite the door in the wall Lucian stopped and stared at it with furious surprise that it still stood there, blank and blind, after all these years. Something exclusive about the door said, I've kept the secrets long and well of the family I serve; you and your little intrusion were as nothing in the welter of our lives. . . . It was a side door into the garden, and Lucian wondered without much interest what secrets they now concealed, the door and the steep roof with the sky-shimmer flowing over its wet slates— since old Mrs. Matthewson was dead and Dan Matthewson kept his wilful privacy there.

Amy, her husband James Matthewson, and their two children had lived there with old Mrs. Matthewson. Singular that Amy should have failed entirely to pass on to another generation her strange stillness, the Proserpine quality that had so bewitched Lucian. . . . Pale beyond porch and portal, crowned with calm leaves she stands. . . . Half of her breathed the sun-soaked earthiness of the plains of Enna (this he had known as her lover) and half of her turned away toward the dubious descent. He had never made out what she was or what she felt within her when she went among the shades, nor did anyone else know, he surmised; doubtless she seemed to most people a young woman with dark bangs, pretty and composed, who loved her children and went every day with her shopping list to the A & P.

Funny that he couldn't remember now when his admiration for her and the reserved sympathy that sprang up between them had turned into love. At first he had done all the talking while she watched him with an ambiguous smile, the perfect listener. Then one day, after a quarrel with her husband, the ice jam had broken; she poured out to Lucian her cold resentment against the situation in that house. Her mother-in-law was an invalid . . . but only a semi-invalid, Amy said, who used her ill health to keep them there, to bully James and everybody else. She sometimes felt she would fly apart if she lived there much longer; she begged James to move, she craved privacy, she told him, a house that was hers, where she could be alone when she wanted. But James only said, I can't leave Mother, she's ill; and as their tempers flared he told her she was egotistical, that she never thought of anybody but herself, and she asked him if he thought any woman could love a man once she knew him to be utterly spineless.

Lucian, with his passion for the human predicament, had never got her out of his mind after that. The drama and its lovely heroine engrossed his thoughts. He could see from where his car was parked the top of the sycamore under which they had sat the first time he had gone through the door in the wall. He had gone at a call from Amy. Mrs. Matthewson was in the hospital for a few days for treatment and James had gone to sit with her—he wouldn't come home for hours, not if she knew Mrs. Matthewson. Would Lucian like to come around? Her telling him to use the side door betrayed the atmosphere of suspicion in which she lived; it also acknowledged a definite stage in their relationship . . . but even so, when she looked at him remotely out of her garden chair on his second visit and told him that she loved him, her declaration nearly knocked him over.

They managed to meet often after that—a difficult matter in a place where they both knew everybody. Zest, guilt, and sweetness beyond imagining, the fear of discovery and the bold hand in dealing with it—these experiences intoxicated Lucian. Intoxicated was the word, else the realist in him, that good guardian, would have wondered at his power to stir this calm girl's passions.

But for once Lucian had been quite wholehearted. He began immediately to persuade her to divorce her husband and marry him. He had no compunctions about that poor fish, James; but there was her duty to the children. They argued it back and forth for the better part of a year. He still couldn't unravel her feeling about them, except that it belonged to her sunward aspect. But in the end the children had defeated him; he had no convincing answer to maternal duty. He had seen one of them back in town not long ago, and it astounded him to think that he had been despoiled of happiness by that gangling boy with the buck teeth.

It was during that year that Lucian became conscious of another inmate of the house, an occasional one. Dan Matthewson was a nephew of James' father, years older than James, and good-for-nothing, people said—at least, he had enough money to do as he pleased, and did. He traveled about the world, appearing in town from time to time to stay with his uncle's widow. That year his heavy, attractive, dissipated face was seen about oftener than usual. Lucian admitted that handsome Dan's make-up was faultless for his part.

It had been Wick who, all unwitting, dealt the first blow. There was a lot of whispering, he remarked to Lucian, about Amy and Mr. Matthewson's nephew—the family had quarreled unpleasantly about it. "If I were James Matthewson, I'd take my wife out of that man's reach."

Lucian hadn't been able to see Amy immediately, but after a maddening delay, he got a chance to ask her about it. She took a half turn away from the window as if to veil her humiliation. Dan, she admitted, had been importunate. "I didn't want to tell you because I knew how you would hate it for me. I saw this coming long ago and I warned James that we had better get out; but he wouldn't face it—he said I exaggerated. He didn't want to be forced into a show-down with his mother."

"God damn his soul!" Lucian cried. She put her cool hand over his mouth, but he shook it off. "What—happened?"

"Well—he—made advances to me . . . and I begged him to go away. But he refused, of course, so I told James he would have to ask Dan to leave. James spoke to his mother about it and she immediately sent for Dan."

"Well—"

"Lucian, it's too awful. They wouldn't ask him to go. Mrs. Matthewson said her husband's nephew would always have a place in her house. Then—"

"For God's sake, go on!"

"Well, they took the attitude—from Dan, I suppose—that I had encouraged him, that it was my fault. Mrs. Matthewson's afraid of being left alone and she won't believe anything that gives us an excuse to leave."

Lucian raved and cursed about the room. Then he pulled himself up and said, "You must come away at once. You can go to Reno or Florida. I'll look into the divorce laws and see which is better for you."

"Yes," she had said. But he saw now that the word had fallen from her like a dry leaf with no weight of meaning. She couldn't move out immediately, she said. She would have to make arrangements about the children and prepare them for the shock. But she agreed to come to Lucian's office in two days to make final plans.

For two furious days Lucian prepared every detail; he sought legal advice, he sold some property at a sacrifice to have ready cash for Amy. But in two days she didn't come, nor in three, nor did she send any word. She had forbidden him to call the house. Mrs. Matthewson kept a telephone by her bed and listened in on every call. He didn't dare write, and Amy didn't appear at any of the usual places. Frantic, he lay in wait on the fourth morning— in this very spot—watching for her to come out, and was at last rewarded by seeing her slip out of the side door and go hurriedly up the street. He started his car and caught up with her as she went into the corner grocery.

Following her in, he stalked her between the rows of cracker-boxes with the glass windows. She made no attempt to avoid him. "What's the matter, Amy?"

"Lucian—we must never see each other again."

With painful intensity he searched her face in the leprous glare of the neon light. "Do you still love me?"

"Yes—oh, yes—but that doesn't matter; or so it seems. James—" A long silence in which she picked vegetables out of the bins and put them into her basket. "James went away on business and left us there together . . ."

In the second it took him to grasp the import of the words she slipped past him and swung the basket between them.

"Amy, you *must* come with me—now."

"It's too late." Her face swam before his eyes, already far beyond his reach. "You understand?"

"That animal!" he cried, "I'll kill him—"

"Sh!" The hand she put out was quick with fear. "There's no use to kill Dan. He—I—it isn't entirely his fault. I love you, Lucian, but I'm not strong enough for love; there's something in Dan that has a drag for me I can't pull against. So leave me alone, I beg of you. Think of me as lost. . . ." She turned and traversed the store with her usual composure and went out.

The grocer, so far as Lucian knew, was never paid for the vegetables; indeed, the triviality, the final humiliation of the scene didn't escape him . . . Passion, the love I waited my whole life for, slain among the onions. His eyes stung painfully as if from their sharp juice.

Lucian came back with a shock from having gone again with Amy to the gates of hell. Chaste water-drops plopped quietly about him as evening drew the gradual dusky veil over the street. Would he have killed Dan Matthewson, he wondered? He hoped so. He doubted if now he could fire the shot; conscience, fear, rationalization, the knowledge that things are seldom what they seem, would stay his hand. But then he had been young and surprisingly naïve. He hoped he would have shot him. Of course, he would have got short shrift with a jury, he acknowledged for the first time. An outraged husband might get off lightly, but an outraged lover—no; especially since the husband declined to be outraged. Gooseflesh broke out on him to think that he wouldn't be sitting here now. . . . And he would have deserved the chair for killing the wrong person. Or was Dan the wrong person? There had been times when Lucian believed that Amy had only said it was her fault to save him from murder and punishment. But the Matthewsons had all gone on living together behind the vine-clad wall, and he didn't know how the *ménage à trois*—or *à quatre*, if you counted in the wicked old woman—had worked, for he set the whole mess aside in his mind like one of those burial urns in which people used to seal the entrails of the deceased.

After a while James' office had moved to Atlanta. It was during the depression when jobs were scarce, so James and Amy had to go with it, and Dan had settled down to live with the old lady. When Mrs. Matthewson died she left Dan the house; apparently his charm had worked on her, too.

Lucian rolled away from the gate, uneasily aware of the passage of the years since it had closed in his face, and of his long hesitancy to expose himself again to love with its hazards and denials. At the corner the sharp green and red of the traffic light slashed across the legend of Amy and dimmed its colors; the whole affair began to seem overdone, melodramatic, in dubious taste. But what was it in a man that compelled passion and devotion? Fen, he thought with a pang, had begotten them in Judith, while he hadn't been able to hold his love even against a lug like Dan Matthewson.

He wondered if, after all, it was Judith he envied . . . had she been unjustly the victim of his acidities? Perhaps it was really Fen he was jealous of, on some profounder level than his scalpel had yet exposed—of the ease with which he had taken a woman's heart. . . .

Because of the short cut through this street Lucian reached home quickly. He parked his car beside a fat turret crowned with a lacy cast iron diadem; from the lower windows the lamplight shone out on the wet leaves, and he found his own house greatly inviting. However widely it might be regarded as a Victorian horror, Lucian delighted in its lush perversity. He let himself in and hung his straw hat meticulously on the hatrack; through the dining-room door he could see his mother finishing her solitary supper in the ring of brightness from the red-fringed light that hung over the center of the table.

"Is that you?" she called as the door clicked behind him. "I had given you up. William, set a place for Mr. Lucian."

"Give me five minutes to get a shower," said Lucian, sagging against the door-jamb. "I've had the hell of an afternoon—" He looked down with loathing at his now crumpled and sweaty suit. Besides he just didn't feel equal to his active-minded parent yet. Turning away, he went mildewedly upstairs.

When he came down again in a clean silk seersucker his step had briskened. He sat down to his supper with relish, and Mrs. Redcliff sat beside him and fanned him with the palm-leaf fan which was seldom out of her hand summer or winter.

"You look tired, dear. What have you been doing all day?"

Soothed by her solicitude, Lucian decided to hold his news for a little, so he parried her question. "Emulating the psalmist. I ran about through the city and grinned like a dog, after my incorrigible habit."

To encourage him to eat she took over the conversation, telling him of the small domestic events of her day, her little grand-nieces had come to see her and said some extraordinarily clever things. ". . . and the evening paper is full of conflicting reports. Some say there's bound to be a war; others think we'll keep out whatever happens. It really puzzles me why those Germans should be led around by a *paper-hanger*. . . ."

Lucian half listened, half looked about him in a sort of surprise to find domestic comfort still surrounding him, what with the news in the paper and the news in his pocket which, it must be confessed, seemed more explosive to him at the moment. Beyond the circle of the ceiling light, Abbotsford looked as pastoral as ever in the big engraving over the mantel, the mounted stag antlers bristled above the sideboard, persistently recording the golden age of Mr. Thomas Redcliff, Lucian's father, and his plantation deer-hunts. Then, as the bountiful meal his mother had provided assuaged his ravening, he began to perk up again, to think about thunderbolts and the Jovian sport of letting them fly.

"Well, I have a piece of news in my pocket that is almost as good as a war, Mother; so if you have tears to shed, prepare to shed them now."

His mother's quick glance clashed with his and it was plain whence he had inherited his sharp curiosity. She wouldn't, however, give him the satisfaction of asking a question, and for a few moments it appeared that they might both spend the evening deprived of the power of speech. But Lucian knew he wouldn't have the strength to keep this story long, so he prepared to give in, rambling purposely, fighting a delaying action.

"When I left here at dinnertime I went to Wick's and found our revered relatives in a lamentable state. Etta, by the way, is a fascinating character study—when she goes on the rampage she's something else! It took the combined efforts of Wick and me and the Church to handle her." He watched sidewise for some hint of impatience but her lucid gaze didn't waver from his face as she said, "Must you say 'handle'? Such a disagweeable word."

Lucian scowled at his parent; it made him furious to have her correct his English, especially when she was right. He snatched the envelope from his pocket and put it down before her with a snap of the crisp paper. "Handle that," he said sulkily, "and see if the word's disagreeable enough." He tilted his chair back from the table by way of reprisal.

She took up her spectacles from the table and read the address. Then giving him a glance of rooted suspicion she opened the envelope. Lucian lolled in Delphic repose, drawing clouds of smoke from his cigarette.

Mrs. Redcliff read the note through carefully, then she looked at Lucian. "So he's married her, eh? A very suitable match." She tore the note across. "It's cooler in the den; shall we sit in there?"

For a moment her perfect performance took Lucian in; he brought his chair down and looked after her dumpy back in unconcealed surprise. Then he rose and followed her, meditating revenge for being cheated of his sensation.

Mrs. Redcliff had already established herself in the tall wicker chair, exhumed her mending from the basket-arm and was burying a box of biscuits and *The Little Episcopalian*, with which, Lucian judged, she had been entertaining the grandnieces.

"I'm delighted we agree," he said adopting her casual voice, "on the possibilities in a Redcliff-Hessenwinkle alliance. Some of the family seem to lack vision about it. The old girl—Mrs. Vinny O'Dell Hessenwinkle—is quite a power, you know, in the upper wards, and it came to me when I went there this afternoon that Lorena might put the Redcliffs back into politics. If she gets busy like her mother and votes enough dead men in enough elections, the Hessenwinkles might put us over with the Democratic machine. So I hope great things from the collaboration. The trouble is I can't think what the compensations are for the Hessenwinkles; the advantage seems to be all on our side."

Mrs. Redcliff threaded her needle and ignored this nonsense. "Every family has its renegades," she said. "The Redcliffs have had them before and weathered them. We can weather Tat. And the Hessenwinkles."

"Renegade's a hard word."

"Perhaps. But it's a hard thing, to go back on your blood. If Tat chooses to do so, he's a man and can make his own life. But he's lost to our kind and we might as well accept it."

"Hell!" said Lucian. He threw himself down on the black leather couch and bounced on its deep springs, his feet flying up, like a child in a tantrum. "You talk as if the Hessenwinkle blood was pure poison. I like August Hessenwinkle—he's quite a fellow. And as you justly remarked the Joneses and the Redcliffs have produced some prime stinkers in their generations."

His mother meekly abode his rudeness to her, knowing, as he also was aware, that compunction would follow in time. Besides, she had her own methods of chastising him. "And that female politician," she inquired, "are you fond of her too?"

"Well—in a way—" The question threw Lucian off a little. "To tell you the truth I could spare Vinny from the family tree."

"I don't deny that the Redcliff stock needs bettering, but do you pretend that that girl is going to improve it?"

[167]

"I doubt it," he admitted, lying on his back and blowing umbrella-shaped puffs of smoke over his head. Alone with his mother, Lucian regressed easily to the spoiled child who had plagued her in years gone by. But remorse was beginning to stir faintly within him, so he let the argument drop and squinted out of the turret in which the couch stood to see what the weather was doing.

The wind still sighed through the garden and stirred up a banana tree growing beside the turret to batter the window screen with wide-sleeved arms, as if a blackamoor concealed below fanned a sultan in his pleasance. The conceit pleased Lucian; he would have liked to be a sultan and was not ashamed of this childish fancy. It was childish only because it was unattainable, and the unattainable, he would argue, is the noblest aspiration of man. He felt less and less inclined to leave his private breeze and go out again to see Janie Catesby, of all people, so he procrastinated, his mind fiddled about amid the flotsam that surrounded him. The den, into which his turret pleasance opened, was paneled with bookshelves painted to simulate oak; along the top shelf a clutter of Joneses and Redcliffs paraded, for a kindly tact forbade Mrs. Redcliff to retire a single photograph given her by a member of the connection. Clasping his arms behind his head, Lucian eyed them afresh: what in hell would Lorena make of them, he wondered—of these apple-faced babies, of the pompadours and hips and refluent trains, of the mustachios and horse-collars, the World War uniforms already beginning to look naïvely stiff. On the topmost shelf a bust of that elder statesman, the first Lucian Quintillian Jones, peered down on the ranks he had fathered with a sort of bleary surprise, or perhaps it was only the dust on his eyelids that lent him that baffled expression, since his exalted position placed him beyond the ordinary range of the feather-duster. The Holy-Joneses, as Lucian hyphenated them (with a teasing eye on his mother), to distinguish them from others of that name, were not much on looks; the Redcliffs were handsomer and, on the whole, more honest; but the round pugnacious Jones face reappeared among the photographs with an astonishing persistence that augured well for their chances of surviving whatever dilutions might be in store for the strain. Still, Lorena wouldn't have to battle the Jones genes, since they were only step-relatives of the Redcliff genes. Now, in this tussle between the Redcliff and the Hessenwinkle genes—well, in Lucian's opinion it was going to be a near thing. . . . On either side of the mantel perpendicular rows of yellowing photographs recorded his parents' travels—the Colosseum by moonlight, Holyrood Palace, the Arc de Triomphe. . . . Manya was right, he thought, secretly observing his mother's compact person; the capitals of Europe had availed little against her robust provincialism. She went a Charlestonian and came back a Charlestonian. But after all (he defended her to Manya) what else should she have come back? If she had returned with French clothes and an English accent and international ideas what, I ask you, would have been my early environment? Why, she might have wrecked my nervous system.

But possibly Manya would reply that this was a calamity she could bear with fortitude. A smart minx, and right attractive, he had to admit—which was why she had got under his skin and started him off scrutinizing his house, his mother, his tribe, like this. You have to remember, he explained to her further, that Mother grew up after the War when the family had tough going under the abrasive of poverty, and she's battled all her life to keep them up to a certain standard. That's why she runs us all ragged about our grammar . . . and that's why she'll never forgive Tat; he's dealt her long effort a resounding blow.

He was feeling quite fond of his mother again as he warmed to her defense; his remorse grew for having been impudent just now. Whatever her peculiarities were she never bored him, and for that he gave her due reverence and affection.

"I had left Tat the Meissen teapot that came from the Redcliffs," she said presently, "but I'll have to change my will. Remind me to see Mr. Burnett about it in the morning."

Lucian didn't reply immediately because his first reaction to this was frankly selfish. The teapot was decorated with a fat Chinese astronomer climbing a perspectiveless stair to look at infinitude through a telescope mounted on a curious twisted column, and the bulge in the teapot's side elevated his brocaded rear with an unpremeditated vulgarity dear to Lucian's heart. Not wishing to be avaricious, he refrained from offering himself as a suitable legatee, but said mildly, "Aren't you being rather precipitate?"

"You have to be precipitate at my age. And I don't intend your grandmother Redcliff's teapot to fall into the hands of a—demimondaine."

Lucian guffawed. His mother's choice of words was a constant refreshment to him. "It's all very well for you to laugh," she said, "but modern life is dreadfully confusing—so many new and puzzling things to deal with. I'll be glad to die before vitamins and divorce and democracy undermine my family. The only way to live in this fearful confusion, at least that I can see, is to stick to your kind. People change their opinions over night, and their politics, but blood doesn't change."

"Well, blood can produce queerer bedfellows sometimes than politics. Look at Tat. And don't be too tough on Lorena—she's quite a gal; and after all she's the victim of circumstances in many respects. You know, it's a funny thing, but if she—or you—had a different name, you might like her a lot. She's honest and direct, and you both have a sort of—" he fished around for another word for unscrupulousness that would combine truth with filial respect and failed to find it—"well, you share certain qualities that are both admirable and reprehensible, if you know what I mean."

She knew he meant to tease her so she didn't rise. Thus far, he was aware, she hadn't asked him a single question about the circumstances of the wedding or how the family had received it. He suddenly wanted to describe his adventures, as he had always wanted to describe to her his trips to a circus, a Sunday-school picnic. Her curiosity and interest in people were so vivid they were in a way creative; he could always tell a good story to her. Then his fond, his forgiving mood inclined him to give her the pleasure.

He sat up on the sofa and abruptly launched forth on the story of his tour, mimicking the Redcliffs, the Hessenwinkles, and even Judith. His mother dropped her sewing and drank the excitement of his tale like an intoxicant. She was often at loggerheads with Etta so, though she sat quite still, her round eyes danced at the thought of her step-daughter-in-law's discomfiture by her over-indulged younger son. To Lucian's account of the Hessenwinkle household she lent the same enraptured ear as to a traveler's tale of foreign lands. Judith, however, was a great favorite of hers, and during this chapter she interrupted the narrative flow with clucks and murmurs of unabashed partisanship.

"Poor darling Judith, she's had such a hard time. What a tragedy she has no children. And now more than ever, eh? She's not looking well."

"I don't know, I thought she looked quite handsome today, with a green ribbon in her hair. But then I like Judith's looks—and you never have."

His mother pursed her lips into a small button that made her every contour a curve and shook her head regretfully. "Too many angles. Poor darling Judith."

"But good angles. Like archaic sculpture. You have no eye for line, Mother; you're hipped on curves, for obvious reasons."

"What an atrocious pun."

"On the contrary, it's surprisingly good, considering that all puns are awful."

"Well, I must say I like softly rounded arms and cheeks and a womanly figure."

"Well, you'll simply love your new step-granddaughter-in-law then. Mmmm—" He rolled his eyes lasciviously.

His mother gave him a look of odium. Then she spoke apparently at random. "Fen was a charming boy, but selfish I'm afraid."

"Only reasonably selfish, I should think. There are all kinds of selfishness. Fen was never mean—in fact he was right generous. But he was a contented creature and enjoyed living in the world, and he couldn't understand why other people think it is a cess-pool."

"He was selfish, I'm afraid," she repeated obdurately. "There was a side to Fen that was like that—girl; something that made them congenial."

"Who—Lorena? You're all wet, Mother. Why Judith was saying only today that Fen didn't like Lorena, though I can't see why."

"Did she say that? Well—it's just as well. I'm old-fashioned and not at all clever, but I see more than you think I do. I saw Fen and the girl together once—"

Lucian's feet thumped on the matting with surprise, for she made the statement quite simply, and he knew her simplicities.

"When did you ever see them together? Oh, that's what you meant when you told Wick you knew her!"

She blinked, darted him a look of malice and triumph and buttoned her lips.

So, it was her turn to hold out, was it? Well, he could wait too—he could wait all night. He sat and glared at her while the long minutes passed, and the silence between them ached like a stretched sinew. Give her time . . . she'd break down . . . the desire to tell all, to impart the startling news, would overcome the desire to punish him for his impudences.

But she sat, small and stout, like an oaken peg. Lucian thought, She'll crack—maybe, but I'll crack first.

"You're making it up," he said heavily. "You're an incorrigible scandal-monger."

"On the contrary, I never speak ill of the dead." She folded her sewing and interred it deep in the arm of her chair, as if it were the secret of the Redcliffs. "It's ten o'clock," she said rising; "old people's bedtime. Will you lock up, dear? You'd better come to bed too; you look fwayed out."

Who frayed me? Lucian wanted to ask, but he was really too tired; he ached in every muscle. "I have to take Etta's note to that damn Janie Catesby," he groaned.

"Janie Catesby? She'll be in bed, I should think. She's that way again, you know—the vinegar voyage."

"Very obviously, I should say," said Lucian. "But it will give me pleasure to rout her out. I promised Etta I'd deliver those notes. Don't forget to answer yours."

"I don't think Etta can expect us to take up the Hessenwinkle family. Let her have them to dinner. They're her problem. Tat's her son."

"I've always believed in my innocence that he was also my brother's son," said Lucian, following her to the hall door. "Are you casting doubt on the honor of his bed?"

Such lewd talk, said Mrs. Redcliff's glance, was beneath contempt. Holding up her skirt before her in two great handfuls, she went swiftly and silently upstairs.

As he drove down the street Lucian worried the idea his mother had thrown out about Fen and Lorena. What in the devil had she seen? Or had she seen anything? She was mischievous enough to be exaggerating some chance encounter between the two just to annoy him. Fen had been a likable cuss. They had lots in common, including a frankly collegiate taste for bathroom humor . . . their fishing trips, an occasional drinking bout, summers abroad together whirred at cinematic speed through his mind.

Judith had said today that Fen didn't like Lorena. Suddenly Lucian didn't believe it. It wasn't in character. He took both hands off the steering wheel and ran them through his hair. So Fen and Lorena! Fen's reason for the fib became obvious. Judith—poor darling Judith! But what she didn't know couldn't hurt her . . . no falsehood was ever more justified. At once he felt an unworthy exultance that the wonderful Fen hadn't given her the whole, the perfect love of her imagining. And an unworthier pang that she could never be told this. Her illusion would have to be preserved, fable must outwit truth, the figments we live with dispossess the living; and he least of all men could destroy hers, for the nature of his jealousy was now clear to him.

These disturbing revelations were cut short by his arrival at the house Edward and Janie Catesby had built in a new part of town. As Mrs. Redcliff had predicted, the lower floor was dark, but by the bright light that streamed from the windows above, Lucian could see the insistent red of new brick and the white colonialoid trim. He crossed the front porch between the inappropriate columns and rang the doorbell.

"Who's that?" asked a cautious voice from above.

"A Greek bearing gifts of a very dubious nature."

"Oh, Lucian? Edward's away," Janie apologized, "and I don't like to answer the door late at night when I'm here alone with the children." Framed in the lighted window her figure, beginning to fill out with her fifth child, looked the very symbol of motherhood and fertility, and Lucian's conscience pricked him gently for his carping at her. Janie meant so well. Nevertheless he kept right on disliking her.

"I have a note for you, from your Aunt Etta; and late as it is I thought you'd like to hear some news that concerns the family."

"Sh. . . ." she glanced into the room behind her and added in a low voice, "You'll wake the children."

"Damn the children," Lucian responded in a penetrating stage

[173]

whisper. "I thought you'd like to know that your cousin Tat also is adding to the family. He's taken himself a wife."

"Tat?" she exclaimed, forgetting to whisper. "Why how *exciting!* When did it happen? And who is it?"

"This morning—though I can hardly believe it, it seems years ago. And it's Lorena Hessenwinkle."

"Oh—" There was a long pause, in which Lucian imagined he could feel Janie sorting her confused emotions and trying to come out in the right. "Well," she said presently, "if they really love each other, that's fine. They have a right to get married, and if Lorena really loves him . . . being in love can change a person entirely . . ."

"I really can't contend with this sort of thing," Lucian muttered into the shrubbery.

"What?"

"I said I think it will be fine too," he shot back in a whispered roar, "if love makes a Redcliff of Lorena. But suppose it makes a Hessenwinkle of Tat—had you thought of that possibility? Well, in any case, a little red blood will do the family good, both the Tattens and the Redcliffs. I'll put Etta's note in the letter-box. She's giving a blowout on Sunday and wants all of you there to meet your new cousin. Dinner at three."

"You mean day after tomorrow?" Janie paused again. Lucian filled in from memory the outline of her calm, pure face. Janie didn't use make-up, on the theory, he supposed, that good wine needs no bush and a Tatten needs no embellishment. "I don't believe I can go," she said formally, as though he were the host. "Edward is in Sewanee at his class reunion and—I usually take the older children to Aunt Etta's on Sunday, but they'll need time to get adjusted to such a new situation. I'll have to explain things a little."

"I'd love to hear your explanation, but I really can't wait till tomorrow. Just let Etta know so she won't put your names in the pot. Good night, and sweet dreams."

So Etta wasn't going to get her feast of self-immolation after all. The guests would have none of it; he had worn himself out on a sleeveless errand. Damn! He hadn't realized how much he had been looking forward to that banquet. Sort of tough on Etta and Wick, too, to leave them alone to face the bride and groom. But perhaps the bride and groom wouldn't go either; nobody seemed to have thought of that contingency. Perhaps they'd prefer to dine with the Hessenwinkles. Or just with each other.

Well, he had done his part; he had carried the news of the marriage to the family, he had wrangled with everybody, and now he was left alone with his own feeling about it. The rain had stopped but the clouds had clamped down like a lid on a stewkettle, beneath which the town steamed. He drove aimlessly along under dark dripping trees, hoping to meet a cool breath before he turned in, and trying to unthink the contrary opinions he had scattered about and discover his own thought. Lorena wasn't a bad sort— she had a hearty directness and simplicity he rather envied; yet he had plumped for her mostly because the pack was against her.

He found it hard to concentrate. From a window on the street a metallic voice exhorted: ". . . try this delicious drink, serve it to your family . . ." and beat down the still small voice within seeking the ultimate verity. "And now from our Chicago studios . . ." the next window took up the story. It was the hour for a popular music program and house after house crooned the same refrain. It was a relief to come abreast of the Baptist Church where evening service was just ending and where the bare white interior, glare-white from an overload of electric bulbs, echoed with high and holy hymning.

. . . Furthermore, he considered that Lorena was following a sound instinct in wanting to find a better hole for herself—for what would become of the human race otherwise? Obviously she would agree with him that this step was a step up; neither would pretend about that. In spite of the Redcliff peculiarities they were a pretty decent sort . . . taking us by and large, he addressed the new recruit, we're honorable, reasonably intelligent, not disagreeable to live with and some have a sense of humor. He fancied he heard Lorena acceding that she might do worse.

For the moment he wouldn't think of Judith. His feeling about her was too newly revealed, too unsettling in its implications. He thought of Tat instead—did he suspect anything? Lucian guessed not. But Tat probably knew that Fen had liked Lorena. This fitted in better with his dream of being like Fen. Jeepers, what a family for complications! Did Lorena, for all her admirable realism, know why she was marrying Tat? Had she looked into the gulfs between them of habits, tastes, inherited mores, so hard to disestablish? He wished he knew more about her . . . he must ask around. . . .

His coupé had carried him, almost inadvertently, past a street that still held for him the faint pungency of forbidden fruit despite the disenchantments of age and experience. He stopped, backed his car and parked it at the corner. He would go and see Lillian, he decided, and have a nightcap before turning in. Lucian never got himself involved with nice women; they were always mistaking love-making for love and producing awkward situations. Of all the lost treasures of antiquity he most lamented the hetaera; that was what a man needed in this life, a woman, agreeable, sophisticated, who understood the male without wanting to get something (marriage, for instance) out of him, who stimulated the desires of the mind and the desires of the flesh to enhance each other. His rounds of the houses were in part a never quite hopeless search for such a paragon. Sometimes he found a girl with a flicker of imagination whom he endowed with the character he sought, but he couldn't keep up the pretense for long; he could get only a limited fun from talking to them, from exploring their points of view. For even these human interest stories showed a lamentable sameness—the dears were always supporting an aged parent or putting a kid brother through college. People thought Lucian was a libertine, and he encouraged the idea because he wasn't. Most of the time he just liked to talk with the girls and buy them drinks. They regarded him as a swell who was free with his money, and he liked that too.

He walked along the ill-paved street to a big brick edifice of some age—appropriately for the oldest profession. It was hot inside with the shades down; the electric fans only mixed the humid air and made a fretful racket. Lillian was luckily free; he sought her out in a well-lighted parlor. She was sitting by the radio catching up on her crocheting; "Oh, hush, little baby, do-on't you cry . . ." sang the universal voice from the ubiquitous box.

" 'Lo, Lillian, how's tricks?"

"Oh, sort of slow on account of the storm, I guess. It looks like the boys are 'fraid of getting their feet wet." She made a place for him on the settee and offered him a cushion. Across the room another girl was talking to a sailor.

Lucian rejected the cushion with a gesture. The bright print on its cover he ascribed to Lillian's taste. It showed a young man holding a flag, with God Bless America coming out of his mouth in a balloon. Lillian had a mind of her own; she was a staunch isolationist and drew heavily on the patriotic motif to support her stand. Lucian had frequently taken issue with her on this subject, pointing out with incontrovertible logic that America couldn't possibly keep aloof from foreign wars. But to no avail; she remained unalterably opposed to sending the Army and Navy out of the country.

They wise-cracked amiably for a while over their whisky sours and Lucian marveled again that Lillian's life had not dampened the spontaneity that illumined her conversation and somehow denatured its coarseness. The sailor and his girl began to whisper in their corner, and Lucian took advantage of their preoccupation to speak of his own private concerns.

"Listen, Lil, you know a girl named Lorena Hessenwinkle?"

"I know who she is."

"Don't you ever see her round?"

Lillian pursed her lips and shook her head. "She don't go round with any of us girls."

"I didn't think she did. Still, they do say. . . ." He watched her from the corner of his eye.

"I guess she isn't too good to be true, or anything like that. In fact, Mr. Youknowwho paid for that flat she used to have. But I guess she calls that being a good woman."

In her acid undertone Lucian thought he smelt professional jealousy. Lorena took business away from Lillian's kind. Still, he was glad to have this tribute of a sort to his new niece's moral character.

"I don't blame anybody," Lillian went on in a slightly aggrieved voice, "if they don't want to do this kind of work; but if she wants to settle down, why don't she? Why don't she get married?"

"And get out of circulation, eh? Well, she has. She's just married my nephew, Tatten Redcliff."

"God sakes! Did she, honest? Well, what do you know!" The aggrieved note changed to one of frank envy. "So she's all fixed up, hey? I swear some people get all the breaks."

Other girls began to come in, interrupting their confidences. Lillian dropped a hint to Lucian—she was a working woman, she didn't have a whole lot of time for talk. . . .

"You've got time for another drink, haven't you?" said Lucian. "Order a round on me, then I'm going home."

He listened through a haze of fatigue to the laughter that fizzed above the highballs. He had been running about all day, he thought, like a strolling trouper, taking all sorts of parts; he had played the cynic, the good fellow, the fractious child, the champion of the underdog. But this was a house where truth was made too clear for play-acting. He put away his props, returned the costumes to the wardrobe, removed the grease-paint . . . he couldn't even pretend that Lillian was a great courtesan. He eyed her listlessly. She was prettier than the others, but he still didn't want what she had, so he got up and said good night. Or maybe she didn't have what he wanted . . . he couldn't straighten this out because he really didn't know what he wanted, except sleep.

Book V

AFTER midnight it settled down to rain in earnest. The chimney-pots, the crowns of trees, the sharp, dark roofs rumbled with the onslaughts of water. By morning the gutters were in spate, the pavements awash in the low-lying sections, people scuttled to work between downpours. Wick couldn't put his mind on the office and went home early. He walked the piazza, anxiously scanning the hurly-burly in the sky; he kept telephoning the weather bureau in spite of its distasteful reports; the rain was moving upstate. He saw it gouging red gullies, washing the young cotton plants out of the ground, the sprouting corn waterlogged in the soggy fields. It fretted him for Tat, though he feared no actual danger—this was one of those tropical rainstorms without much wind—but he couldn't shake off a foolish feeling that it was a bad omen for his boy. . . . Etta got her feet soaked buying the dinner for Sunday, but she trudged from shop to shop to find the food Tat liked, and with twelve expected at table, she had her morning cut out. The complexities of housekeeping served as an anodyne for all the hopes she had given up; the rain was merely part of the discipline. . . . In the afternoon the sun almost pushed through and for a moment the roofs floated in silver mist. All that part of the Borough by the Friendly Hearth was under water; the boys got out their rowboats and paddled them in the streets with incredulous cries. O'Dell, stopped on the foreshore of the muddy lake covering marsh and cobblestones, dickered with an urchin to row him over to the wood yard; two bits for the round trip with a bonus *if* they got back dry. After making sure the property was taking no harm, he put the watchman in charge and declared a holiday; Rena had pulled it off, and that seemed to call for a celebration. The Hessenwinkles asked to dine at the Fenwick Redcliffs! Sitting in the stern, muffled in his raincoat, he floated on an unreal lake in an unreal world, and yet through his astonishment, his elation, ran an obscure strand of regret, as if he saw some bright citadel tarnished. . . . Then the rain came down harder; it drenched Judith running from the *Formidable* to Miss Parson's Beauty Shoppe to get a new hair-do, but she took a savage pleasure in this purge of water, it would wash old slates clean, it would make it easier for her, she thought, to start over, to come out of morbid fantasies and live in the hard, clean world. The memory of her conversation with Lucian embarrassed her. How could she have been so petty? And why had she got herself into such a stew about Tat and Lorena? The reason escaped her. But she had returned to her senses now; the pounding of the drops invigorated her will; she thrust her childish moping behind her. . . . Where did all the water come from? It held up the bride and groom on the road so they didn't get in until three in the morning. Lorena was scared stiff of the torrential ditches and brimming creeks. She clung to Tat and buried her head in his shoulder when it thundered. The storm filled Tat with elation for he saw that Lorena's fright was genuine; as a husband and as a man used to squalls at sea he soothed and supported her. Besides, they would get home so late that facing his mother could be deferred until tomorrow. During a letup in the rain Lorena telephoned her family. They were fine about the marriage, said they'd fix a bed for them, leave the door on the latch. The thought of the Hessenwinkle welcome and approval warmed some interior chill. . . . Then the wind rose again; it tore at the filigree limbs of the thorn trees and paved the sidewalks with scales of hammered gold, it stripped the shrubs and vines and humbled the pride of the horticulturalists—all except the fat young woman who moved her garden under the trailer out of harm's way. . . . It blew in a window in Aunt Quince's boudoir in the second story of the turret and soaked her as she was "resting her eyes" on the box-lounge. . . . A downpour caught August and Vinny on King Street when he went to get a haircut; the pervasive wetness got into the wiring of his car and made a short-circuit. He beat on the horn-button and cursed it in angry gutturals. While he dived under the hood to try to stop the maddening noise (and got wet to the skin in the process), Vinny managed to slip into a shop for a pink kid bag she had long had her eye on and only waited for a good excuse to buy. . . .

Lucian also cursed the wind and the rain as they splashed his clean shoes and trouser-legs in the late afternoon when he went by Wick's house to see what was up. As if the Lord hadn't let enough devilment loose on the earth this weekend without drowning everybody. The tesselated walk was a cloudy pool that took some acrobatics to skirt, but he managed to hop, skip, and pirouette his way to the steps. The gray and white marble square seemed to shift eerily under the water, and he twitted Wick and Etta about the discomforts of living in sea-lost Lyonesse, and pretended he saw fish swimming in and out of the windows.

Wick didn't respond as usual to his brother's sallies. He sagged in a rocking chair, his coat off, his face bleak on his high shoulders It was all too much for him. Etta, on the other hand, showed an unexpected fortitude. She and Lucian exchanged tales of automobiles stalled, friends marooned, the Borough's chickens roosting on the second-story banisters. Lucian vowed he saw fat old Mr. Popplemann swimming to work on Broad Street with a brief case in his mouth.

"How's your dinner coming along?" he ventured, after a decent interval.

"Everything is arranged for," said Etta with a touch of housekeeperly complacence. "There'll be twelve with Janie's children, so we can all get at the big table."

Lucian blinked. "Twelve, eh? Have you heard from everybody?"

"Yes, I think everybody is accounted for." She indicated with a nod some opened envelopes on a silver tray.

"May I see them?"

"Certainly—" She pushed the tray toward him.

Lucian picked up the top letter, on tan paper with a brown border. It began "Mr. Hessenwinkle and me—" but this had been half erased and "I and Mr. Hessenwinkle" substituted . . . in any case they were very pleased to accept Mrs. Redcliff's kind invitation; it would make them very proud to see their darling daughter so happily married, and she was Etta's truly, V. O'D. Hessenwinkle. Etiquette seemed to have drawn Vinny's teeth, her pungent personality and conversation had been rendered harmless by the awesome exigencies of the written word. Lucian could imagine August grumbling and protesting, but being beaten down in the end by the determination that ran like bone through Vinny's soft flesh.

His mother's fine, small, regular writing caught his eye. With many underscorings she assured her dear Etta that she deeply sympathized with the position Tat had put them in, but that since he had taken the irrevocable step she would, as the eldest of the family, be with them in their hour of crisis; she was always devotedly, "Aunt Quince."

So—she had decided to hold her nose and come. She hadn't told Lucian of her change of mind, perhaps for the pleasure of springing this very surprise on him; or perhaps she had talked it over with the others—the Redcliff network of telephones had been hot all day—and arrived at a more temperate viewpoint. But no, he doubted if the democratic method of free discussion would alter her opinions one jot. She just couldn't bear not to be in on it.

Judith, Etta said with a shade of disapproval, had answered by telephone. In the morning she had called and said she felt badly and didn't think she would be well enough tomorrow—"though how she knew she was still going to feel badly tomorrow, I can't imagine." Etta, he saw, had decided to make acceptance of the invitation a test of family loyalty; any member who refused to drink the cup would be her enemy until death and beyond if that were possible, so he was relieved for more than one reason to hear that Judith had called again in the afternoon to say she felt much better, and if her place hadn't been filled. . . .

Janie Catesby, Lucian deduced, had written the really right note. In a large, immature hand she opined that Aunt Etta had been *wonderful*, and the family would stand by Tat to the end. She hoped he would be very happy—and who knew, perhaps all would turn out for the best. Of course she would be there with the children as usual on Sunday.

Lord, what a family, Lucian thought for the twentieth time. He might have known they'd come trooping, for all their acting up. "The funny part is," he said plaintively, "that nobody's ever thought to invite me to the party, and I'm the only one that knew from the start I wouldn't miss it for a farm and lot."

"Why, Lucian," Etta expostulated, "of course you're expected —of course we counted you in—we assumed you'd be with us."

"By God, it's raining again," said Wick. He went over and sat down by the window and stared morbidly out.

Etta stood up and looked over his head for a moment. Suddenly tears started in her eyes. "Why did he have to go out in this storm," she said tightly, "why did he have to go away?"

Her voice made Lucian shiver. Its anguish had nothing to do, he recognized, with Lorena; he was hearing the primitive cry of the female in the pangs of the second birth. Her youngest was tearing loose from her to go out into the world.

"Don't worry about Tat," he said with an embarrassed smile. "He'll get wet, but it won't hurt him."

Etta didn't answer. Lucian wanted to go on in a light vein; he thought of mentioning that the rain fell alike on the just and the unjust, thereby shirking our moral dilemma of deciding who was which. But he supposed Etta wouldn't think his jest appropriate, so he sat in silence and let the rain fill the room with its vacuous drumming.

Book VI

To Aunt Quince the Sunday morning service offered a variety of satisfactions. Deep in the recesses of her heart she knew she was a sinner; her unscrupulous acts haunted her in the night season, and she found a genuine relief in going to her church every seven days and pouring herself out in repentance, silent confession, and appeals for divine aid in her always hopeful but usually unavailing battle. Kneeling on her red-covered footstool, she felt small and pure, after her honest confession, with the empty purity of the young. The beautiful prayers of the church service were, from long association, like songs without words; they spoke, chiming to her spirit without an intermediate mental process, for which Aunt Quince had no great use anyway.

On the morning after the storm she had more of thankfulness than repentance to send up from her red cushion. The town had been spared the blows of hurricane or tornado; through the open windows she could see still leaves on lilac-damp air as the soaked earth and overcast sky breathed in gentle convalescence. Her family had suffered misadventure, it was true; but with serene confidence that effects follow causes, she had always predicted that Tat would come to no good end, spoiled as he was by her step-daughter, and now faith had been justified by works. She looked forward with relish to dinner and the spectacle of Etta's discomfiture; whatever mischief her tongue might be tempted to make was still in the future and didn't require penitence yet awhile.

After a decent interval she glanced about to see who was at church. Ever since her arrival in her pew she had been resisting a pull to look round for Wick and Etta; her neck being excessively short, she couldn't manage this without a movement in the nature of a revolution. Presently she decided to grant herself the indulgence of one full turn, so while Dr. Styles was giving out the hymn, she gyrated on her small feet and had a long rewarding stare before seemliness, like a stretched elastic, pulled her round again.

So—Tat had come with them. There he stood, big as life, between his father and mother. A little late for repentance, forsooth. Did he imagine all his wild talk against religion hadn't been heard in heaven? Well, he hadn't brought the adulteress with him at any rate.

Lorena just didn't seem a Redcliff to Aunt Quince. I don't accept her as part of the family. She really isn't. Perhaps she'll run off with somebody else. Perhaps her real husband will turn up and claim her. . . . This possibility, so lush with drama, dazzled her for a few minutes like a vision of the last judgment. Then she came back to reality and thought about dinner with increasing appetite, not only for Etta's celebrated cuisine, but for the chance of getting in a few thrusts at that girl, and giving her a good scare. Doubtless they thought—Fen and the girl—that afternoon three summers ago, that she was an old fool who wouldn't suspect what they were up to. The arrogance of the young, who seemed to imagine sin was their own invention! They probably thought that she had gone to the sewing room looking for them instead of for Miss Jinny.

The image of Miss Jinny, coming into her mind, flooded her with a warm, thoughtless pleasure. Miss Jinny was like a wonderful big doll—more human than the little puppets she gave her grandnieces, more congenial, more reckless than the adults who tiresomely expected old ladies to corset their minds as well as their middles. In the conversations they had managed to have when the house was empty in the summer, Miss Jinny always gave the right answers. . . . But Fen had come in quietly—for good reason!—that time with the girl. Their presence had prevented her returning the ball dress to the attic, so Etta had found it when she came home. No such incident, however, could discolor the luscious remembrance of Miss Jinny in the peach-blow satin beaded with gray pearls. She was like an ideal Aunt Quince had known in an old dream that had never been dreamed out. . . .

Dr. Styles, having concluded the sermon with a fine peroration, descended from the pulpit and began to give out the notices. There would be a church supper in the parish building in connection with the membership drive . . . a moving picture would be shown . . . all were urged to be present. Aunt Quince resented these devices to increase church attendance. Church suppers bored her and she disapproved any attempt to make religion democratic. God was to be worshiped, not fraternized with; he was unique, therefore exclusive, superiority was of His essence, and those who from shallow egotism tried to make Him folksy should join the Holy Rollers and leave the Episcopal Church to those who were willing to adore Him.

But at last the service was over, the congregation began to flow at a glacier's pace down the aisles. Without pushing, Aunt Quince managed to take ruthless advantage of every opening and gain on the main body, thus arriving at the church door almost as soon as the Redcliffs. They had halted in the vestibule and, backed up against the baptismal font, they presented a united front to the world. The news of Tat's marriage had traveled apace and they were meeting for the first time the onslaughts of friends. What a surprise . . . I had no *idea* . . . how naughty of you to run away and get married . . . how romantic. . . . The voices shrilled with excitement and curiosity.

Aunt Quince kissed Tat remotely on the forehead, as if he had been away on a long journey and hadn't quite got back. Scorning the platitudes rattling round them, she made no verbal allusion to his change of state. She couldn't honestly think of Lorena as his wife, and the words she found applicable to that personage she couldn't use with propriety in a consecrated building; but without more ado, she ranged herself beside them, indeed her protuberant front pushed the glacier slightly out of its course.

The bridegroom, standing between his parents, said little except, "Thank you," "That's mighty nice of you," and left to the other three any extended remarks on his conduct. He looked ready to jump out of the window or into the font, and Aunt Quince divined that this public appearance was his mother's idea. She closed ranks more firmly; she had no idea of running away or of letting him do so. Here was her friend Bessie Brailsford almost at the end of the line. "How are you, Bessie? Always behind, I see, like the cow's tail. . . ." Offense was the best defense, and she could tell that Bessie was going to give her trouble about this marriage, that the misadventure of the Redcliffs had filled her with unchristian joy. She'd be rubbing the Hessenwinkles in to the end of time. Aunt Quince darted a lightning glance at the cause of it all, pressing a crumpled handkerchief against his forehead. He was no longer able to relax, between well-wishers, the plaster cast of his smile.

Bessie, rocked back momentarily on her heels, managed to recover her center of gravity and proceed down the line with passable though disconnected phrases of congratulation, and presently they all drifted out into the churchyard. Etta was thanking Dr. Styles warmly for coming to her with good counsel in her time of distress, and Aunt Quince made a mental note to find out somehow about that interview. "Can we take you home, Aunt Quince?" Wick asked, pressing her arm in grateful recognition of her loyalty, but Bessie Brailsford came back to say, "Do come for a little drive with me, Quince; my car is here and there's so *much* I want to talk to you about. . . ."

Aunt Quince gave Wick's hand a returning pressure and said, "No, thank you, my dear. I'll see you presently." Bessie was a nettle and had to be grasped firmly. "So much obliged, Bessie; shall we go along?" She couldn't think, immediately, what she would say, for the harsh realities of the family predicament couldn't be denied. But she'd manage somehow; she had on occasion downfaced Bessie with the power of a look, her black eyes dominating Bessie's faded blue ones by sheer intensity of pigment.

She nodded good-by to the little clusters of friends. Tat was not in a cluster. He stood in the path, his face tuckered down, drawing on the gravel with the toe of his shoe. The storm had gathered and rushed on, leaving him, its center, forgotten in the wake. To Aunt Quince's noticing eye he was shaken by more than the mere diffidence of a bridegroom. The muscles of his face were tight, he drew his cabalistic signs wth fanatical concentration. Youth—overwrought, extreme, defensive, trying to keep its feet in the strong gust of public opinion. . . .

If there was one thing Aunt Quince hated it was having a well-considered dislike undermined by compassion, so she stood for a few minutes and scrutinized her step-grandson with a frown as concentrated as his own. Perhaps she was hard on Tat . . . he was going to pay for what he was, when it was really Etta's fault. She turned and trudged heavily down the path under her burden of tolerance, a vice to which she, like any other, was liable at times.

The Fenwick Redcliffs drove home from church, and after putting the car in the garage, Wick broke for his porch chair like a fox going to earth. Their house, he and Etta always said, was the coolest in town; if there was any breeze they got it on their piazza. But even in this blest spot scarcely a breath stirred, the storm had lessened the heat, but the earth spewed forth its surfeit of water at such a rate that the elements lost their separateness in the simmer of light mist. The three Redcliffs sat in a languid ring and drank the iced tea and ate the biscuits Bristol brought them.

"Very trying weather . . . God knows what we'll look like by the time the guests arrive," Wick said ruefully. His linen suit, the pale gray shirt and gray silk tie in which he was wont to meet gala occasions, wouldn't hold up long between the moisture without and within. Etta's white tucked crepe de Chine stood the gaff better; it still looked clean—and just like all her other dresses, he thought, a shade critically; but Etta cared little about style and less for what people thought about her clothes. Her tribute to the occasion was manifested not in her person but by the dinner, the centerpiece, the flowers on the mantels, the *brouhaha* in which they had lived for the past two days. Tat, he observed, amused and touched, had yielded to the pressure to dress up for the function. His ready-made white suit was new; he had actually had his hair cut and had slicked it down with pomade, his fresh blue shirt became him, he must even have conceded garters because his socks stretched smoothly over his well-shaped ankles. Three pairs of unctuously whitened shoes in a little circle before them revealed their common anxiety to please.

Presently Etta went off to coach the swarm of Bekah's relatives brought to help in the kitchen and left father and son together. The three had got by their first meeting somehow or other; when Tat came over from the Hessenwinkles' after breakfast they had had a few minutes of painfully flustered talk during which they had looked about for suitable words—out of the window, on the ceiling, under the furniture—everywhere but at each other. Tat had seemed anxious to justify the abandonment of his principles.

"I guess it will take a long time to change the moral code," he admitted; "my ideas weren't very practical, at least, not for the present. I suddenly realized that you were right, Father, when you said out on the porch the other day that I was making it hard for Lorena, that her family was only trying to protect her, and that made me decide to go ahead and get married. . . ."

"But I didn't expect—I didn't mean—" Wick began and suddenly walked away to escape the high, thin laughter he thought he heard cascading from the upper air. Then Etta and Tat had gone up to her room, and what the nature of that interview had been was not revealed to a mere father and never would be, but they had come down peaceably enough afterward, and Etta told him with a gleam of triumph that Tat had consented to go to church with them, since Lorena was going to the Sacred Heart with her family.

Now, Wick sat looking hard at the thin, serious, idealistic face of his son; he smoothed his cowlick tenderly, his own face twitched as the naked emotions in his heart strove for utterance. But how to clothe in words such perishables as love, marriage, the absurd tenderness of a father's heart! His mind fiddled about, temporized by fixing itself on a grasshopper that crawled with nightmare slowness out of a spiderweb only to fall back entangled each time it reached the top . . . he supposed he had been at fault with Tat in being irritated by what were after all differences of temperament. His attempts at training Tat to be other than he was had only made the boy more so. But could he have concealed in the realistic medium of family life, could he have dissembled day in and day out his natural preference for Fen's type? He knew people had said how hard that the able and successful son had been the one to die . . . he knew it because the thought lay like a pebble in the bottom of his mind.

The unfairness of this feeling shocked him, he threw it off with a vehemence that made his wicker chair squeak. Of Tat's good instincts and genuine desire to make a better world he had no doubt; he must school himself to accept the boy as he was. . . . Now that Fen no longer stood between them, they could come closer to each other, perhaps. . . .

Tat was also watching the insect which, propelled by a terrible

[189]

urgency to live out its inconsiderable grasshopper day, was making its twentieth climb up the spiderweb. Wick couldn't think of any way to plunge into conversation except to plunge.

"What about your plans for opening up some new filling stations, son? Tell me what you have in mind."

The splash startled Tat for a moment, but he at once turned to his father, eager to establish good relations. He and Jim Bland had feelers out for a property near Aiken on route 215; it was just above the crossroads where Standard Oil had that big station; they hoped to get the Florida-bound traffic and especially to raid Standard's clientele. Tat grinned engagingly; the mere thought of a brush with Mr. Rockefeller brightened his circulation.

Wick had no prejudices in favor of Mr. Rockefeller so he encouraged the rivalry, and they talked harmoniously about ways and means of enlarging Tat's chain. Presently Wick said he might be able to lay his hands on a little money to help with the financing.

It struck Wick full in the face that Tat's marriage had removed one complication: it would no longer be necessary to placate the parental anxieties of the O'Dells and the Hessenwinkles. All that debate . . . he had sold his conscience and, practically sold his timber, to no purpose! Was there *anything* about this whole damned affair he had done right? If so it must have been an accident. Well, well—this left the timber deal merely a matter of business. Orienting his mind to the new situation, he decided to consult Tat.

"Until we hear the reports from over the state on the crop-damage from this storm, I won't know where we stand at the office, but I may have another chance to pick up a little cash . . . remember my telling you that Harry O'Dell had approached me about some timber?" He outlined the pros and cons, blinking with the effort to be fair to everybody.

"Well, seems to me you might as well sell the timber; we could use the money all right, to build up Independent's chain. Anyway, I don't think we ought to own that much land. . . . If it was Harry's idea though . . ." Tat paused, finding the problem not simple, which was unusual for him. He skirted his new family loyalty by adding, "It sounds to me like a typical business proposition with profits at the bottom of it."

[190]

Wick nodded solemnly. "Self-interest seems to be the motive of all concerned. We might as well keep that clearly in mind." This wasn't the thing to say if he wanted Tat to accept his help, but habit pushed him into it.

"Well, I'll have to think it over. The last scheme Harry promoted took the land we needed for a government housing project —with the crying need there is for more housing and recreation facilities. Do you know that this town is thirty-five per cent deficient in playgrounds per population? Honestly, Father, we ought to get busy on that situation."

"We do need more playgrounds; you're perfectly right. Well, I'll think over your proposition while you are thinking over mine, and we'll talk about it again, eh?" He smiled at Tat with hope and appeal.

Tat smiled back and rewarded him with a burst of confidence. "To tell you the truth, I don't trust any scheme out of Harry's slick brain. I don't want to get hooked up in some cut-throat deal to make profits for a lot of business men."

Wick swallowed, then he said mildly, "You are certainly hard on us business men. I don't think anybody could accuse me of cut-throat methods; the truth is I'm the other way—lazy and not ambitious enough, and since the depression 'profits' haven't exactly fattened any of us. But you need a new filling station, this house needs painting, your mother wants to go to California to see Marianna. . . ."

"I can't get excited about the poor downtrodden business man."

"I'm not asking you to get excited. I'm only suggesting that you're a little—ungenerous in your judgments."

"Well, I'd like to see people more generous to the lower income groups."

"It isn't so rare to find people generous to the poor, but to be generous to the rich, to the man who's better off than you are, that takes spiritual breadth." He smiled at Tat again. "I'm not speaking only of money, of course, but of an attitude of mind."

Tat took a quick breath, the muscles round his thin lips quivered with determination to keep back offending words. Less practiced than his father in the vocabulary of conciliation, he had to resort to silence to maintain the new pact of friendship; he threw his leg over the arm of his rocking chair and buried his chin in his cupped palm. They both returned to a studious scrutiny of the grasshopper.

The spiderweb slanted up from the edge of the piazza to the overhanging branch of a shrub growing close by, and now the spider came out from between the leaves to watch and wait for the moment when, by the laws of a bountiful nature which taught it to make its miraculous tough web, the grasshopper would wear itself out and fall a prey to its smaller and wittier enemy. The grasshopper might have escaped by moving horizontally toward what appeared to be an opening at the side, but a terrible single-mindedness urged it upward to the point where its entangled legs could pull no more and it fell back exhausted into the center of the web, bouncing like an acrobat.

Both men watched it fascinated. Suddenly Tat muttered. "I can't stand this any longer—" and jumping up he reached between the balusters for a small stick.

"Take care how you meddle with balance of nature," said Wick smiling. "Spiders are among the saviors of man . . . remember the grasshopper plagues in the West a while ago?"

But Tat lashed at the web with his twig. "You and your cold-blooded rationalizations—" He freed the grasshopper which fell on the piazza floor too far gone to comprehend its good fortune.

"I'm not cold-blooded; I'm sorry as hell for the creature. I only accept an order of things I can't change, and I know it's lucky for the farmers that you Don Quixotes can't go about rescuing all the grasshoppers caught in spiderwebs. It looks as if your rescue might be in vain anyhow; the creature's about done for."

"If you saw a house full of people burning down, I suppose you'd light a cigarette and start debating whether fires weren't a natural check on overpopulation."

The rasp in Tat's voice was sharper than the incident warranted. The old tension between them drew out again fine and taut as the pearly web. He continued to squat by the banisters watching the beneficiary of his humane action.

The grasshopper moved one leg and finding that it worked, cautiously moved the other. "It's going to be perfectly O.K.— see there?"

The grasshopper continued to massage its legs; it crawled experimentally over the boards for a few inches. Then it gave a startling bound back into the spiderweb.

Irresistibly Tat looked round at his father. Their glances met, hung balanced for an instant, then the tension snapped and they both rocked with laughter. Tat tore the web in shreds and flipped the grasshopper out into the garden.

The first guests arrived at the gate.

As Bristol let them in Wick rose and went forward. While they were still concealed on the lower reaches of the steps he heard Lucian's stage whisper: "This is going to be like a family funeral, only better."

"*Lucian!* Behave yourself . . ." Aunt Quince's little black beetle of a hat with two feelers out in front rose above the floor level. Lucian had her by the arm and Judith followed them. On the top step Aunt Quince stopped and gave a little snort by way of comment on the steepness of the Redcliffs' stairs. "Well, here we are," she said with bright anticipation.

Wick took her arm from Lucian and escorted her to the side porch. As he turned round he saw Tat at the front railing looking down the street. "Where in the devil do you suppose Lorena is?" he muttered as Wick passed, then Judith and Lucian came up and engulfed him in congratulations.

"I expect she'll be here before long," Wick told his son soothingly. "It isn't three yet."

"Only twenty minutes of," said Lucian, pulling out a thin gold watch. "We came early so as not to miss anything."

When Wick had seated Aunt Quince as head of the family in the largest rocking chair, he turned to Judith. She looked gay and flushed in her sheer white dress, but the arm she slipped round him when he kissed her clutched him overanxiously. He held her off and made a smiling inventory of her appearance. "Ruffles. White wings and flowers and flounces. How cool and crisp you look. And such pretty pink cheeks."

At his last words she turned her face away with agonized self-consciousness. His light game . . . apparently he had overdone it in speaking of the pink cheeks which she couldn't yet carry off; he had put his foot in it and he hurriedly gave up his idea of mentioning her hair. Actually they didn't suit her, these beauty-salon waves; they spoiled something straightforward and unpretentious that was essentially Judith.

She broke away from him and sat down, looking at her shoulder knot of yellow roses. "Yes, aren't my flowers lovely?" She smiled across the grass rug at Lucian.

Good boy, thought Wick, shooting his brother a grateful glance. It was like him to divine that this would be a hard day for Judith and bolster her morale with flowers. Women, with such a badge of popularity, could face any ordeal, whether by fire or water.

The squeak of the gate announced new arrivals and Tat hurried to the railing, but it was only Janie Catesby and the children. She approached the group with her long, dignified step, looking slightly like a kangaroo, Wick thought, in her beige crepe with the draped front. "Why, Tat, you sly boots! Why didn't you let us know?" She kissed her cousin enthusiastically. "Congratulations. I think it's simply wonderful."

Wick couldn't help admiring the way Janie went the whole hog. "Where's the bride?" she was saying. "I'm dying to meet her. I know we're all going to love her."

"Thanks," said Tat, wriggling out of her long grasp. "The question is, will she love us?"

"Why, *Tat*—"

The others broke this up with howd'y do's and a general shifting of chairs to make room for Janie. "Well, he certainly sprung it on us, didn't he?" she said, looking around for a chair that would support her back. Everybody sat down again and said it was quite a surprise.

Tat passed by his father's chair and murmured, "I think I'll go over next door and see what's happened."

"So the bridegroom's nervous, eh? Don't fash yourself, son; you've just begun waiting round for women."

"I think I'll go anyway." A peal at the bell diverted him and he went off like an arrow to the front door.

Wick was half in and half out of a conversation with Judith and Lucian about the Bob Turners. Manya was writing a novel and had let Judith read several chapters. "It's really awfully good . . . Manya is certainly a smart gal," Judith sighed enviously.

"It's a stark, moving story about little people, isn't it?" said Lucian.

"Well, yes—how did you know?"

"The occult." Lucian assumed a thaumaturgical solemnity. "And it's written in the simple, homely, unaffected style that's the great affectation of our period. I could do a prospectus for the publishers now if they'd ask me."

"Don't let Lucian rag you, Judith—" Before Wick could finish Tat came round the corner with Mr. and Mrs. Hessenwinkle.

Wick sprang forward with such cordiality that he tripped over Aunt Quince's chair and nearly measured his length. But he couldn't stop to decide whether her leaning forward and tipping up the rockers at that moment had been accident or design. He pumped the newcomers' hands enthusiastically. "Howd'y do, Mrs. Hessenwinkle; howd'y do, August; *delighted* to see you. . . ."

The Hessenwinkles had slowed down involuntarily at the sight of the group on the piazza, and stood close together with unexpectant faces, much as the early Christians might have tried not to believe in the lions. Wick seized their hands and drew them along; childishly he wanted Etta to come . . . where in the devil was she? But he guessed she was staying indoors to meet her daughter-in-law for the first time without the inspection of curious eyes.

He performed the introductions with flourishes. "Aunt Quince . . . the mother of the bride! My stepmother, Mrs. Redcliff, senior . . ." The Redcliffs, even Aunt Quince, rose with a unanimous roar of chairs over the floor-boards. "How do you do . . . so glad to see you . . . take a chair . . . do sit over here. . . ." Above the hubbub Wick went on waving his arms voicelessly like a cheer leader.

The Hessenwinkles seemed stunned by the volume of the welcome. They allowed themselves to be plumped down, snatched up, resettled, murmuring the while in subdued voices, "Thank you, ma'am . . . pleased to meet you." Then the noise died down as suddenly as it rose and for a long moment the group sat conversationally becalmed.

"My, it's warm today, ain't it?" said Vinny, feeling the eyes on her. "Quite a storm we had yesterday. I hear the Manettis sold their fruit store to a chain and gonna move to New York." This exhausted her repertoire and she fell to fanning herself with one expansive hand.

"Do have my fan." Aunt Quince held out that nearly inseparable member. The extent to which this was a sacrifice, an olive branch, was lost on Vinny, but she was grateful for the attention from old Mrs. Redcliff. Judith brought more palm leaves and doled them out. The corner of the piazza fluttered with pale yellow moons.

"What have you done with the bride?" Wick asked.

"Isn't she here yet?" August fussed. "I thought she was coming early."

"Martha O'Dell didn't get out to church this morning—she didn't feel good—so Rena went off after mass to see her," Vinny explained. "Harry said he'd shoffer her round, and I guess they stopped by to see friends—when those two start out visiting, I never can get them home."

"I expect she'll be here soon." Wick smiled reassuringly at Tat. "Were you out in the storm yesterday?" He threw the topic into the middle of the group and they snapped it up gratefully; everybody, it appeared, had seen the funniest sight. . . . A drink all round—that would help break the ice—but could you begin to drink without the hostess and the guest of honor? Where in the name of a kind God was that girl? In desperation, he dumped etiquette overboard. "I think we need a little liquid refreshment. Son, tell Bristol to bring out the juleps."

The talk was going now with great amiability and laughter, but it seemed to him that he had been at it for an age when the bell at the gate made a sweet tinkle. "There she is!" He and Tat rushed for the front.

Thus it was that he stood on the high top step and saw with a pleasure and relief he had little dreamed his daughter-in-law come through the iron gates. Escorted by O'Dell, she crossed the rectangle to the steps, smiling up expectantly at the house. Her pink and green plaid dress made, immediately, a new, a bizarre pattern against the checkered marble pavement. As she came briskly forward one high heel wabbled awkwardly for a moment, but the uneven old tiles merely slowed without halting her confident approach.

Tat ran down the steps saying, "Where in the hell have you

been, Rena? I thought you'd sneaked out on me. . . ." They threw their arms around each other and rocked back and forth, frankly delighting in the sense of physical support at this moment.

"Me sneak out?" Lorena exclaimed, pulling away and laughing. "You don' know me very well yet—I'm not the gum-shoe kind. Lemme tell you something, honey—if I ever leave you, the whole neighborhood'll know about it."

Wick came down to the lowest step and took Lorena's hand. He bowed over it, looking down on her with eyes that misted. "Welcome, my dear—welcome to this house. . . ." His voice creaked and stopped; simple sentiment, never far from the surface with him, closed his throat. The new wife on the threshold . . . the young husband shouldering a man's responsibilities. . . .

His display of feeling threw Lorena out of her stride. "Oh— thank *you*—it's mighty nice of you to say so. . . ." Her smile became forced, her thickly reddened lip trembled a little.

Tat, in a flutter of pride and delight, said, "Well, let's don't cry about it." Tucking Lorena's arm under his he led her up the stairs.

Wick held out his hand to O'Dell. "Good morning to you. We were beginning to think you had lost the guest of honor somewhere."

"Gee, I'm sorry if we kept you all waiting. We went up home for a while to see my wife, then we dropped in on some other folks and it seemed to get late too soon, if you know what I mean."

"I do indeed. Won't you come in?"

"I guess I better be moseying. . . ." But he glanced up at the corner of the house from which the sound of revelry came in hearty bursts and a wistful look softened his long, shrewd face. This unexpected guilelessness touched Wick.

"Oh, come in, come in! You have time to have a drink with us anyway; it's not too late or too soon for that." They went up the steps assuring each other that this, like every other, was just the right time for a drink.

They overtook the bridal pair at the door of the house. "Tat, take Lorena in to see your mother. And tell her the guests are all waiting. We'll go this way—" He took O'Dell's arm and steered

[197]

him away from the door and along the piazza. As they rounded the corner Bristol was just bringing out the big silver waiter with its garden of frosty green.

"I have another customer, he's just in time. This is Lorena's uncle, Mr. O'Dell. . . ." But he found that O'Dell knew everybody, one way or another, "Howdy do . . . howdy . . ." he said, doffing to each in turn his brown straw with the fold of Persian silk. "Is it hot enough for you?" He found himself a chair without assistance.

While Bristol passed the mint juleps Wick sat down by Mrs. Hessenwinkle and surveyed the guests. . . . Etta needn't have worried about their not taking her banquet seriously. They had turned the mahogany wardrobes inside out; they all exuded style, affability, and perspiration. Vinny was got up regardless in a tiger lily print, and fondled a pink kid bag of grand proportions. August looked neat as a pin in a pepper and salt mixture; a very recent haircut ringed his round head with a pale halo. The boxy cut of his coat did nothing to minimize his girth, though it thinned Lucian, sitting beside him, to a straw. Lucian's raw silk suit was like thick cream. . . . I wonder how much he paid for it, the damn extravagant creature, or *if* he's paid for it. His green tie, or his natural malice, made his eyes as green as gooseberries.

"We were just talking about summer plans," Aunt Quince was saying to Mrs. Hessenwinkle. "Mine are to stay on my own piazza. At my age you like to have your own way; and you can do that better at home."

"We don't have any summer plans; we generally stay home too. An' our house is mighty nice an' cool." Vinny gave Aunt Quince a dimpled glance. "We got too many children over there to go to a hotel."

"Very sensible." They rocked and nodded in mutual approbation.

Wick thought of a promising topic. "By the way, Mrs. Hessenwinkle, weren't you related to Sergeant Nolan? That was a remarkable thing, his inheriting that fortune."

"Cousin Ignatius? I'll say! Seventy-eight thousand, nine hundred and sixty-three dollars! And from a' old lady we never so much as heard of. Could you beat that?"

O'Dell, on the other side of the group, leaned forward with his elbows on his knees to get in on this. "You ever know Cousin Ignatius?" he asked.

"I knew him very well," said Wick, exaggerating. "He was a fine fellow—the old-school police sergeant. They don't make 'em like that any more."

"Too bad he didn't live to enjoy it longer." Vinny made a cheerful sucking noise in her julep glass. "We buried Cousin Ignatius last spring. And the fortune was all broke up among his different relations. We ought to had a share of it."

"The other relations' lawyers were just better than ours," O'Dell averred smiling.

"Well," Vinny admitted, "it's kind of hard to prove; we don't know exactly *how* we were related to Cousin Ignatius."

"Do you even know if you *were* related to him?" August tossed this out from his place of retirement.

"You hush, August—'course we were!" But the sparks Vinny shot in his direction caused not a flicker on his smiling, pear-shaped face.

O'Dell laughed good-naturedly. "Well, it's a wonderful thing how the chink of money will jog your memory—"

The family argument was cut short by the entrance of the bride.

The long window opening out from the dining room enclosed Etta and Lorena in a strange embrace. Lorena's gay plaids and brilliant make-up made Etta look pale and dry; those forthcoming curves were cruel to the straight folds of the older woman's figure. Scales of use and wont fell from Wick's eyes, as an accident sometimes restores lost sight . . . the Hessenwinkles, a crashing accident here on his piazza, so jolted the myopia of marriage that he saw his wife with unseemly clarity, saw her as she moved from day to day among intense and limited interests—her family, her household, her many charities in the neighborhood—in clothes of good material that hung too long and too full on her spare frame. "Like a cross between a crow and a curate," Lucian had described her in her mourning black. Damn it, there's such a thing as being too highhanded with clothes. Yet he perceived that in defeat Etta took an unconscious revenge on her opponent; her unapologetic plainness struck back and gave Lorena's red hair and redder mouth, gave even her youth, a spurious look.

Again the chairs roared over the floor, everybody shouted at

[199]

the bride. Vinny rose with the others and waved the pink bag to encourage the demonstration. This time Aunt Quince sat firm and so did August; this is a little overdone, their steadfastness seemed to say. When Lorena was brought up and presented, however, Aunt Quince gave her a welcoming smile.

Wick came out of his trance and took Lorena's hand. "Come and sit over here—I'll get you a julep—" He drew her through the group that pressed round her smiling and shaking hands, toward an empty chair on the other side of the circle. Judith, pushing in from the periphery, stopped in front of them.

"I want to wish you every kind of luck, Lorena," she said, holding out her hand. "You've got a swell guy. Tat's as fine as they come—and I hope you're both going to be very happy." She smiled at Lorena with tremulous friendliness.

Good! Wick thought. My cure's working. He slipped an arm round her and brought the two girls closer. But Lorena looked back at Judith, on guard, yielding nothing of the new ground she had gained. "Thanks, pal," she drawled, managing to make her handshake ironical. "But I'm pretty happy right now." She dropped Judith's hand and took Wick's again.

Damn . . . Well, Lorena was too Irish to give up a good quarrel so quickly: and of course she knew nothing of Judith's change of heart. It would take time to smooth these kinks out. . . . Turning sidewise, she brushed past Judith, drawing Wick along now in her wake. As he let go of Judith he turned back and murmured, "Good girl!" They left her standing alone in the middle of the ring.

When they had sat down Wick became conscious that Lorena was still holding his hand tightly. It was becoming a shade embarrassing. She was excited, of course. He perceived now that she was more than excited; under her smiling front she was scared. He pressed her hand encouragingly and offered his general purpose formula. "You're looking pretty as a picture, my dear, in your bridal finery. A goodly Babylonish garment as ever I saw. . . ."

Lorena, grasping his honest intent to please, flushed all round the edges of her make-up; for a moment Wick thought her highly enameled surface was going to crack. "Say, you're mighty sweet. I didn't have time to get me any new clothes." She recovered her equipoise and said literally, "This is my best dress, but I haven't hardly worn it at all. It's taffeta." Unctuously she rolled a fold of the skirt between her thumb and forefinger. "Good goods," she boasted, smiling. "Feel. . . ."

He took the fold she held up, and the silken crunching of the material sent an electric impulse up his arm. "Delicious," he murmured. "I like these feminine styles, these gay colors." It was not the formula he was repeating now; the pink and green plaid trimmed with tiny black velvet bows, the flowered green straw sailor riding at a rakish angle, crowded his senses somehow and suffused him with nostalgia for the light loves of his youth, brightening as they took their flight. The sweet crispness of the silk as he went on rolling it between his fingers troubled that half-story of the mind where erotic memories live on in astonishing health and vigor.

He was remembering Lucille Carter now . . . it wasn't that Lorena looked like her, for Lucille had been petite and dark (and damn it all, he remembered her partly because she had cost him the hell of a lot of money); but this pinched-in jacket beside him . . . the pertness of its short tail. . . . Though the fine points of women's styles eluded him, there was a cut to Lorena's turnout that he recognized, a something beneath the pastel plaids, and subject to neither fashion nor fading. . . . He dropped the skirt in a painful confusion of sentiment; dismay for his son's future, and a creeping sense of guilt that made him look hastily round to see if anyone had observed the little byplay between Lorena and himself, which hadn't, perhaps, been ingenuous on either side.

But, in the strings of speech loosened by the juleps, the company was in full cry. Etta, her arm around Tat, was talking to Vinny; O'Dell was laying himself out to be agreeable to Aunt Quince, the names of important people tripped from his tongue. He seemed to feel Wick's eyes on the back of his head for he spun round and raised his glass.

"Congratulations on the juleps! A drink for the gods."

"Give Bristol the credit; he's the best damn julep maker in the Borough."

"Well, whoever mixed it, it's super, and fit for such an auspicious occasion. How about a little health to the bride?" O'Dell rose and looking about, commanded attention with the practiced art of the toastmaster of the Hibernian Society. "My friends, I want to propose a health to the beautiful bride over there. Long life and happiness to the lucky pair!" Amid the laughter and waving of glasses, he drained his julep, set the glass down, clasped his hands and shook them toward Lorena in a mock handshake.

Wick slowly washed down his irritation. A childish irritation . . . but toasting the bride was his, the host's, province, and even now three dusty bottles stood on the sideboard, the last of some old Madeira saved for weddings and christenings. He had even planned, while shaving that morning, the speech he would make. Now it would all have to be changed. He rattled the inescapable banalities about in his mind, despondently searching once more for the not-too-fulsome phrase.

They settled down noisily and the fans fluttered again. In the change-kitchen-furniture that had been going on, Judith found herself next to August Hessenwinkle. She turned toward him with anxious cordiality, but the plaguing question, what shall I talk about? drove every thought from her head. They smiled at each other uncertainly for a moment, then both launched forth at once. Both stopped as suddenly.

"Oh, do go on!" Judith cried. "What were you going to say? I didn't have anything special. . . ."

"Neither did I." With a quizzical grin, August took the morning paper from a near-by table. "Have you seen about Andy Gump today? He's liable to go into bankruptcy any minute." His full face puckered. "And poor old Uncle Bim, he's sick and can't help him out. . . ." He shook his head over the threatening outlook.

Judith welcomed this promising topic, selected with the utmost good will as pleasing to her age and tastes. "I haven't read the paper yet," she apologized, "I didn't have time this morning." She didn't add that she had actually spent the whole morning getting groomed for the dinner, polishing her shoes and her fingernails, doing her hair over five times with as desperate anxiety as if she had been the bride. "Do tell me what I missed."

"Ella Cinders is in a bad fix too. She fell out the airplane, Friday, remember? Well, today the boys are going after her; but it says she's beyond aid. You don't have to worry much, though," he added to console the tearful sex. "If she died the strip would be finished, and those fellows make too much money to kill off a good thing. I guess she'll live forever."

Folding the paper into a compact rectangle he went on, impassioned, to the next strip, while Judith sat back thankfully and tried once more to cope with her private misery. For yesterday she had thrown off her morbidness, had snapped out of it for good, she thought, and had come here today resolved to be sensible, to permit herself no futile jealousies. . . . But she hadn't counted on the vivid reminders this setting brought up of that other dinner nearly seven years ago when she had come to meet Fen's family. Uncle Wick had been adorable. She had sat on his right and he had teased her and flattered her, he had shown his unaffected delight at Fen's choice of a wife . . . she had scarcely been able to eat for thinking of her incredible fortune, and for watching Fen there on his mother's right. She had never doubted that they would live happily ever after. . . .

All the Redcliffs had looked beautiful and intelligent to her that day—an opinion that she had since revised. Etta was always taking ridiculous stands on unimportant matters; furthermore, she was slightly jealous of Fen's wife and yet, in her irrational way, was also jealous of Fen for Tat, whom she spoiled ridiculously. Still, among the crosscurrents a drift of affection and loyalty ran between them.

As for Uncle Wick, their mutual devotion had become an established vine and thickened in these seven years. He alone felt Fen's death as she did—or almost—and his unashamed emotionalism had been alms to her necessitous heart. And that was why it had hurt so awhile ago when he had brushed by in Lorena's train, when he had sat by Lorena with that intent and fascinated regard. It was perfectly natural, of course, that as host and father-in-law he should give Lorena his attention on this day which was rightfully hers; but somehow. . . .

A nervous movement from August made her realize that her unseeing eyes were fixed on his square-cut hands. He surveyed the backs, glinting with gold hair, and his wide wedding ring, to see what she found amiss. An anxious wrinkle grooved his smooth forehead; he took out his penknife and began unostentatiously to clean his fingernails. Judith looked guiltily away and saw that Aunt Quince on the other side of her was watching the operation over the edge of her fan.

"He'll cut himself," she murmured behind the flimsy windbreak. "I wish he'd put that knife up; he makes me vewy nervous!"

"Ssh! Do allow him a little privacy."

At the reproof Aunt Quince's mouth drew into a button. She opened the large woven basket she carried as a handbag and took out a roll of gauze bandage which she kept in readiness for a world full of cut fingers. Assuming her special air of antic innocence she held it out across Judith. "Do let me offer you—"

With a snap of her middle finger Judith flipped the roll out of the advancing hand. It described an arc, bounced on the sloping floor and rolled off the edge of the piazza.

Aunt Quince stared at her in outrage. Tat gave a joyful chortle, others saw the flying white roll and laughed. "Judith! What on earth . . . ?" But the diversion thus created obscured Aunt Quince's malice. It brought Lucian over to investigate.

"What sort of game are you two playing?" He sat down on the arm of Judith's chair. August put up his knife, unconscious of the mischief that had been deflected from him.

"I'm just trying to keep Aunt Quince on her good behavior."

"For Pete's sake, do. So far Etta's lustral rites are going great guns. Everybody's so affable they're fit to bust a rib. If the Redcliffs go any more democratic and the Hessenwinkles go any more refined we'll whizz past each other. Then we'll just have the situation in reverse."

"They'll never learn refinement from you, that's one sure thing," said his mother, trying to be offended but unable to repress her naïve enjoyment of the play. "You might at least curb your vulgarity before strangers."

"All right—all right. You know, it occurred to me as I was observing this happy family all together that the Redcliff men have shown an admirable catholicity of taste in wives. Take the four Mrs. Redcliffs assembled here—" He eyed Judith and his mother with joyful malice.

"Considering that you've been a conspicuous failure in acquiring any sort of wife—" Aunt Quince began energetically.

"I never could find anybody preposterous enough to complete the gallery. If I wanted to maintain our standard I'd have to choose among the Copts or the Manxwomen."

"I wouldn't put it past you," said Judith and looked across at Lorena with whom she found herself thus bracketed. What wouldn't she give for just a little of that Irish mettle. Somehow her new hair-do, her white dress with its hand-made look and its little ruffles of fine lace, hadn't stood up against the plaid taffeta. A small annoyance invaded her that her effort to make up with Lorena had been brushed off. Of course she was furious with me because I was critical of Tat . . . maybe they were planning to get married then, and she wouldn't like my saying he was spoiled and all that. But I tried to make her understand that I really love Tat, I said nice things about him. And Lorena had brushed her off. "Thanks, I'm pretty happy right now . . ." as much as to say, "I don't need your silly wishes." Well, it wasn't a very original remark . . . but then neither is getting married original . . . Judith wished she had thought of saying that to Lorena instead of just standing there all aback at being brushed off. . . . The misery she had kept impounded all day pressed up within her like a head of water, her will was helpless to push it back. . . . How childish, how idiotic! she railed at herself, to give way to this jealous grief! But there it was in her heart and lungs, thrumming in her ears—dense and separate from her person and no more to be put to flight by wishing than the solid person of Aunt Quince.

Luckily Aunt Quince and Lucian were meshed in one of their imbroglios and Judith closed her eyes; she called up from above and around her the immediate sensory memories of Fen with which this house was hung and laid them like leaves on her bruises. . . . Her bridal dinner here, and the first breathless weeks of her married life . . . the stumbling, joyous progress she and Fen had made toward the passionate discovery of each other . . . these pictures colored the walls and carved the cornices with enrichments not dreamed of by the classic designers of the house. Why should she doubt that Fen loved her? "He married you," Uncle Wick had said, "and you had his love; there's no way Lorena can threaten that now."

She opened her eyes and shot a brave glance into the dazzle of blue-white light with that puppet in plaid at the center. I won't let her make me doubt it ever again.

Bristol announced dinner.

The company rose with alacrity, for it was now half past three, and milled about disposing of empty glasses. The last to get up was O'Dell. He had one of the Catesby children on each knee and was telling them some tale that made their eyes bulge. Etta and Wick exchanged looks.

"Stay and take dinner with us, O'Dell; we're about to go in—"

O'Dell looked up in great surprise. "Say, is it that late? You must think I stick around like a burr in a mule-tail. I meant to be on my way long before this. But you can't blame me for liking such nice folks, now can you? This certainly is one lovely party. Still, I guess you've got your table all set, Mrs. Redcliff—"

"We have plenty of room." The words plopped from Etta's lips like smooth little pebbles. "We'll be glad to have you stay."

The pebbles showered harmlessly off O'Dell's light blue Sunday suit. "Well, thanks. I'd certainly hate to pass up this good company, and your good dinner. I'm having a wonderful time!"

The obvious sincerity of this statement was disarming. "Come along, then," said Wick, beginning to herd them toward the dining room. "I expect everybody's hungry." He gave his arm to the bride.

"I'll say!" exclaimed Lorena exuberantly. "I'll eat anything don't bite me first!"

"I better go 'phone the ball and chain," said O'Dell. "Can I use your 'phone, ma'am?"

"Certainly," said Etta. "Children, show Mr. O'Dell where the telephone is." Then with only a moment's pause she added, "Won't you ask Mrs. O'Dell to come and join us?"

"Oh no, thank you—you're mighty kind—" He appeared to think that enough was enough. "She wasn't feeling good this morning; nothing much, just a sort of bilious attack." He went off with the little Catesbys.

They streamed toward the long window into the dining room. Judith had one foot on the low step when she heard Uncle Wick and Lorena just behind her and drew back to let the bride go first. Her short leg threw her off balance a little, and she caught at the shutter awkwardly.

"Hey there, what's the matter?" said Lorena, with sudden expansiveness. "The juleps haven' got you, have they? Go ahead in."

"No, no; you go first—"

"Oh, go ahead—we got all the time in the world." Riding on the crest of the wave, she seized Judith's arm and boosted her over the threshold.

The gesture was full of the kindness of the perfectly healthy being for the handicapped one and it made Judith conspicuous. She felt on some sensitive epithelium a scorching, small but intense, like the flame of a match. Wincing, she pulled away from Lorena's excited grasp and rearranged her rumpled sleeve.

Etta came quickly in through the other French window and had Bristol set a place for O'Dell. The dining-room table was extended to its full length and she appraised it swiftly, with a satisfaction that relaxed her pale, tight face a little. The big gold and white Sèvres epergne had come down from the garret whither it went in summer when windows were open and rude winds blew; with its load of white gladioli and long trails of asparagus fern it gave a monumental festiveness to the table. Banished was the blue Canton china of every day and the company set filled each place with a pool of beflowered green porcelain. The empty glasses like little lamps held up sparkles of light.

"Lorena, will you sit on Mr. Redcliff's right . . . Mrs. Hessenwinkle on his other side . . . Mr. Hessenwinkle, come by me, please . . . the groom sits on my right . . ." Etta held out her arm toward Tat, her formality buckling in a rush of emotion both fatuous and noble. Tat came to his place and gave her an answering smile, his devout nature kindled by hers. "Judith, you sit next. . . ."

In the general sorting and sifting Judith moved inconspicuously round the table and took her place between Tat and O'Dell. She could feel Tat simmering with defiance and boyish pride; she linked her arm in his and squeezed it to her. Uncle Wick drummed on the table for silence with the handle of his knife and said grace.

The antistrophe of amens died away, the gentlemen in unison stepped behind the ladies' chairs and pushed them in a sort of religious schottische. All but Vinny, who stood up like a church steeple. A few minutes of confusion followed while Wick, still holding the back of her chair, tried to discover what was amiss. But Vinny, not budging, fixed her eye on the hostess.

"I don't know if you noticed, Mis' Redcliff, I don't know if you counted heads. It's thirteen at the table."

"Oh," said Etta and glanced briefly at the cause of it all. O'Dell was oblivious; half turned toward Aunt Quince, he listened with flattering attention to what she was saying.

"Well, I expect we'll just have to overlook that," said Etta, "and hope the fates will be kind. We can't take these things too seriously, can we?"

If Vinny sensed the reproof, it died among the tiger lilies on her sleek slopes. "This is a wedding party; we can't take any chances. I wouldn't risk my little girl's happiness for the world. . . ." She looked ardently at Lorena.

A buzz of talk broke out, in the midst of which Tat said sharply, "You needn't worry, Mrs. Hessenwinkle; we'll take the chance, won't we, Rena?"

Lorena nodded doubtfully with a propitiatory look at her mother, and Wick tried to undermine Vinny's resolution by pressing the edge of the chair against the backs of her knees. But the stoutness of those members matched the heart they carried about. "Harry," she boomed in her sudden baritone, "you gotta go home."

In the dead silence that followed, O'Dell turned round, his long face full of innocent amaze. "Well! What have I done to get picked on?"

A murmur, half laughing, half protesting went up from the table and, quickly gauging the drift of public opinion to his side, he added, "I haven't got smallpox or anything—there's not a thing wrong with me excep' my wife says I snore, and that isn't catching. Now, Mrs. Redcliff and I are getting on just fine, and if you think I'm going to pass up this chance to talk to one of the most entertaining ladies in this town—"

Aunt Quince leaned forward and said nakedly to Vinny, "Of course he's not going home. He's telling me a delightful story and I want to hear the end. Do sit down."

The smell of acute danger made Wick resourceful. "Can't we put the children at the side table, Etta? That would solve the difficulty, I think."

"Yes, of course," said Etta. "Bristol—"

The children, sitting on either side of Janie, looked into her face for their cue and, finding maternal chagrin there, opened their mouths and roared a protest as unabashed as Vinny's.

"Oh, dear—never mind, darling, a lovely little table just for you, won't that be nice?" The wails redoubled. "I'm so sorry, Aunt Etta, of course they've been looking forward so to this party, naturally they're disappointed—" Further conversation being impossible, Janie rose with martyred calm and led the inconsolables out into the hall.

As soon as they had left the table Vinny sat down. She leaned forward and sent a barbed glance toward Aunt Quince, then she smiled all round the table, she showed her dimples engagingly. "No use taking chances when you don't have to, that's what I say. I know a woman and her mother asked thirteen people to her baptism, and that night a rat gnawed her face so bad she's been real plain ever since."

While everybody shivered over the awful consequences of flouting the Parcae, Bristol and Bekah brought in the soup. Etta's shrimp soup was the result of long and artful collaboration between Bekah and herself, and it went to the spot; tempers eased, Aunt Quince and O'Dell, now in close alliance, bandied pleasantries with congenial infantilism. "Why, he's simply delightful!" she said to Judith, leaning behind his back, making a play at muffling the confidence with her fan. "Why, he's perfectly outwageous!" More fan play, an art she had not lost when others of her generation had. Her hands were very small—too small, now that her flesh overbalanced her small bones; with their short fingers and square nails they gave almost the effect of a freak's little hands, as if she hadn't grown up evenly.

But in spite of the famous soup, in spite of Aunt Quince's wholly unexpected fancy for Harry O'Dell, the number thirteen seemed to have cast its shadow on the table in passing by. The front of good will showed soft spots here and there. Judith sat withdrawn in her private discipline; Lorena, at the other end, talked too much in a high, nervous pitch; and Wick laughed a little too loudly at her sallies. The removal of the children to the side table left Janie in gloomy isolation between August and Lucian, neither of whom she knew how to talk to. Besides, Lucian had embarked on an argument with Tat cater-cornered across from him.

". . . so the haves," he was saying, craning round the garlands

[209]

of fern, "are trying to hold on to what they have—and some of them are damned unattractive the way they do it—and the have-nots are trying to take what the haves have away from them and get it themselves, which is not a pretty sight either. The point is they both show a healthy interest in material benefits."

Tat met sarcasm with sarcasm. "Of course, you won't believe this—" craning in his turn—"I don't expect you to understand this, but there are people who believe in liberalism, who want the wealth of the rich distributed even if they don't get a cent of it themselves."

Aunt Quince's fan ceased to beat for a moment. "Oh. Is that what you call liberalism? We used to call it dog in the manger. So many new words nowadays. We never used to talk about liberalism. . . ." The fan flapped again as she looked about the table for enlightenment.

"Good Christ! I guess you didn't—in the times of the dodo. It's a wonder you learned to talk at all."

"Tat!" Etta's hand came down on his. "Remember whom you're speaking to! Remember you're in your own house—"

Tat's breath escaped his lungs in a long blast. He began to eat his soup furiously . . . the compulsion to be polite to Aunt Quince was a social injustice he could scarcely stomach.

Aunt Quince looked at her step-grandson as if she hadn't finished with him, then she turned and studied Lorena for a while across the table. The moving fan scratched against her black and white voile dress with the sound of sandpaper.

Vinny, having triumphed single-handed over the Redcliff clan, was in fine fettle. Still . . . she didn't want these folks to get the wrong idea about her. "I'm not superstitious," she assured Wick. "I don't fool with a lot of fortune-tellers and stuff. Those people are just fakers; and the worst part is, they give science a bad name. I think everybody ought to learn to depend on science."

This ringing assertion seemed to astonish Mr. Redcliff. He murmured, Of course; while science didn't have all the answers by any means, it had the only ones there were—though he sometimes thought scientists indulged in a little mumbo-jumbo, too—

"Not if you get ahold of the right kind," Vinny insisted. "I use science a lot in my business. It's a big help. You know Mr. de la Marr?"

"Mr. de la Marr?"

"He's a real scientific man, none of this tea-leaves stuff about him. He figures things out by sidereal time and ascensions and declinations. . . ." A man of Mr. Redcliff's brains should be impressed by the mere words, as she was. "You ought to go see him, you'd be surprised what he'll tell you."

"I probably would. What is he, an astrologer?"

"A scientific astrologer. He has all the Tables of Houses down cold. He's good on personal matters, too, of course, but what I like about him is he handles business problems like he was a business man. He might put you in the way of making a lot of money."

But he only laughed that funny way and said, "Well, I don't know—what you say confirms my suspicions about science. And as for making a lot of money, the truth is, making a lot of money seems to take a lot of time, and I need time more than I need money, especially now that my own declination has set in. You have to decide which you'd rather have to spend—time or money."

From under the wide brim of her hat, Vinny gave him a sharp look. You talk too much, she thought. For a smart man you haven't done so well. If I'd a had your start. . . . Well, now Rena would. Across the table Rena, all life and color, was kidding Mr. Lucian Redcliff like she owned the shop. And so she did, miraculous Rena. Vinny cast about for the right thing to say, to show she also belonged.

"My, you've got some beautiful old antiques here."

But Mr. Redcliff didn't answer because he was all eyes for Rena, who was kidding him now. And he liked it—glory be to God! She had him eating right out of her hand.

Actually, she didn't mind being left out of the conversation; it gave her a chance to get a good look at the inside of this house that, standing so close to hers, held for her the fabricated mystery of the unknown. Her first reaction was disappointment—the Redcliffs weren't somehow as stylish as she'd expected. The rooms she looked into from her side of the table were handsome with their high ceilings and shining floors, but those plain white summer covers made the furniture stand up kind of ghostly . . . if I had

[2 1 1]

all that money I'd get me some snappy cree-tonne. And mixed in with the antiques was a lot of old stuff like you see in anybody's house, a black wicker settee with the paint bumped off and a Morris chair with mashed down cushions by the fireplace. . . . Husbands must be alike (Vinny gave a startled glance from Wick to August) both high and low . . . there was always some old chair they thought they had to sit their bottoms in.

Mr. Redcliff, much diminished by the common touch, was serving chicken fricassee from a great silver platter. Vinny accepted her heaped plate with reservations. A suspicion stirred that Etta hadn't taken the trouble to have party food for them. Macaroni and sweet potatoes and guinea-squash—anybody could have those. They could at least have had a jellied salad on a side plate. . . . The lack of it began to seem significant.

"Cheer up, Momma, you look like this was a club meeting in ward seven." Rena's smile broke up the clouds of doubt. Vinny gave a resounding chuckle, full of her deep favoritism for her first-born. The Hessenwinkle family considered each successive baby that blessed their home the cutest ever; no matter how many might arrive, their chirpings and toddlings were miraculously new and uniquely adorable. Vinny herself was a slave in all her great hulk to those tiny creatures, naked and dependent in her hands. But she didn't like babies, she always said, when they got big and mean, so her adoration passed on easily to the next, leaving Rena to bring up the dethroned godlings. Rena was the bright exception. Vinny never flagged in her love for Rena, who was beautiful and smart and had a genius for success. Rena didn't deserve all that bad luck she had had—something must have gone wrong in the sky when she was born. But in spite of weak signs and afflicted planets she had kept going and had come out now on top. Where she ought to be.

Because nobody knew about their trouble except Rena and herself, not even August. It was a sin, all right—though she, who had had nine children like the Church said, couldn't feel it was such a big sin. But Lorena had done enough penances, she hoped, and as long as nobody had found out. . . . Vinny brooded above the table with the irrepressible superiority that comes of knowing something of which everyone else is fatuously ignorant. She wouldn't have them looking down on Rena, saying she wasn't respectable. Anyway, she was married now—none of them could change that.

From the ambush of her hat brim, Vinny tried to get the feel of these people. She and Aunt Quince made no pretense of talking to each other; by tacit consent they had abandoned the front of good will. Vinny felt a slight contempt for old lady Redcliff because she hadn't had but one child, and he was sort of puny looking. Etta she secretly admired; in spite of the house not having much style, Etta, somehow, had style. Vinny watched her closely for the key to this mystery, observed how she ate and the way she talked. Suddenly Etta looked up, as if she felt something prickly on her neck, and caught her staring. Vinny's squaw glance fell away, intimidated.

But not for long. "My, you have some beautiful old antiques," she brought out again, since nobody had heard it the time before.

Etta seemed at a loss for the right thing to say back. "Well . . . yes . . . that's very kind of you, Mrs. Hessenwinkle. I don't exactly think of them as antiques . . . we. . . ."

"Oh, but they are," Vinny assured her. "I can tell they are real fine old pieces. I'll bet Schuler's Antique Shop would pay good money for them."

"Well, I hope I'll never have to sell them. I grew up with most of them."

Again Vinny felt a faint reproof, like a cool draft round her ankles. She was only trying to be helpful. "You never can tell what'll happen, and you might as well know what your assets are." She could see Mrs. Redcliff had no head for business. And there was something else she could see: Mrs. Redcliff was all tore up about Tat. It was plain as plain. . . . I wouldn't be surprised if she broke down crying. Tat was the apple of her eye . . . Fritz went around a lot with those dagoes over in ward nine and that was all right, but if he tried to bring one home to live, he'd hear from Vinny. So she knew just how Etta felt . . . and the extent of her own triumph over her.

These thoughts lay deep-swallowed within her, while in the upper reaches she was able to think quite opposite thoughts. Thus she wouldn't of course admit even to August that the O'Dells weren't as good as anybody. . . . She could hear August at the other end of the table smacking his mouth over the fricassee; this was just the type food August liked, he was eating with a moony look on his face, a kind of thoughtless enjoyment. Vinny never enjoyed anything thoughtlessly, but she was glad he was having a good time, after he kicked up such a ruckus about coming.

"We haven't got any call to go eating with the Redcliffs," he had said about the invitation. "Leave them eat their dinner with their friends and we'll eat home with our own family."

"We've got a right to go," Vinny had answered. "I can't figure you out, August; you haven't got any ambition. Our daughter's a Redcliff now, ain't she?"

"Yes, but—"

"Well, she's just as good as they are, ain't she?"

"Sure—sure, but—"

"Well, we're just as good as she is, ain't we? So who you running down?"

That had fixed August. Logic. Here August was, and from the noises he was making, damn glad he'd come . . . before they went to bed that night, she'd make him eat crow. Vinny settled herself on her monumental base with such a weight of rightness that the Hepplewhite chair gave a threatening croak. Holy Mother of God! she sat for a moment not breathing. But the chair held, the honest work of some cabinet-maker long dead saved her. She'd have to take those pills more regular the doctor gave her . . . some kind of gland stuff. But she couldn't get excited over pills to make you thin; she who had been stout ten years and got along better than most. . . .

Her eye was taken by a man hanging over the mantelpiece in a beautiful gold frame. Must be somebody important, though what for he wanted to have his picture painted in that outfit. His hair looked just like a wig. . . . She felt a pair of eyes on her and dropped hers quickly to find Mr. Lucian Redcliff giving her the once over.

"That's an early version of a Redcliff," he said in that way he talked, half sharp, half frivolous. Vinny had to admit she hadn't been able to get the feel of Mr. Lucian yet. "Done in his judicial robes. But between ourselves there was some nasty talk about his having come to this country as a pirate; though that, of course, was before he was made a judge; afterward, all such rumors became libelous. . . ."

[214]

"Is that right?" exclaimed Vinny, shocked. "A pirate? Well, the O'Dells were stevedores . . . for three generations they've made a' honest living stevedoring, and worked up a dandy business. . . ." Snatching the topic of ancestors right out of Lucian's mouth, she set off on a long description of the prowess, physical and financial, of her father and grandfather. But as she talked she kept thinking with surprise that the Redcliffs didn't stick together. They said bad things about their own family. The O'Dells always stuck together, Vinny would never run down her family or her church to strangers. How did the Redcliffs expect to get ahead? That Mrs. Catesby across the table, they just left her alone like she was trash, old lady Redcliff was all the time picking on Tat, and Tat talked mighty sassy about the whole kit and caboodle of them. Vinny heartily enjoyed hearing the wonderful Redcliffs held up to ridicule, but underneath her laughter she disapproved of Tat's talking his folks down.

Mrs. Catesby, she saw, was islanded with no one to talk to. Vinny caught her eye and gave a sympathetic nod. She leaned forward and said significantly, making a little tunnel of communication under the hubbub, "How you gettin' along—all right?" But her only return was a dumb stare from a pair of large, light eyes. "I guess you mind the hot weather, eh? Well, I always say the first months are the hardest, though none of it bothers me much, to tell you the truth."

The eyes slid right and left nervously to see if this had been overheard. "I . . . feel quite well, thanks," their owner murmured inconspicuously.

Vinny obligingly lowered her voice. "When you expecting?" This was pure "manners," because her accurate eye could tell to a day.

Mrs. Catesby asked August loudly across the gap between them if he thought there'd be a war.

Could you beat that! She didn't want to mention she was having a baby, like it was a disgrace. Did she think nobody could see? This kind of finickiness was beyond Vinny, so she wrote Mrs. Catesby off and joined the general conversation. August was saying he hoped we'd keep out of war somehow.

"But if England gets involved," Etta began.

"We'll just be suckers enough to let her drag us in again," said

Tat. "A lot of people will fall for the same old propaganda."

"That's right," said Harry. "We think we're smart people, but every time we mix with the British, a lot of money seems to change hands and always in a' out-going direction. We don't know nothin' when it comes to dealing with those birds."

Harry was fine . . . Vinny and Lorena both laughed and looked up and down the table to see if his brains were being appreciated.

"You've come to the wrong person, if you're talking to me," said Etta. "I'm as pro-English as I can be."

"You're awfully prejudiced, Mother—"

"Certainly I'm prejudiced. There are good reasons for admiring the English too, but if you like people you don't have to hunt about for reasons."

"Well, you can go fight for them then; but I tell you right now nobody's going to drag me into a war to save the British Empire." Tat shook his forelock and fell upon his salad.

Vinny's feeling about Tat had been changing ever since the telegram came announcing the marriage. She wouldn't have picked Tat, but he was of her tribe now, and on their side in the curiously sharpening line-up that threatened to rend the damask expanse of the tablecloth. She ranged herself beside him. "Well, I never liked the English. They're all snobs with their royalty, and all. I wouldn't give two cents for a duke."

"I don't imagine you'll be called on—" old Mrs. Redcliff began, but Vinny rode her down. "I can't stand a snob. I wouldn't go bowing and scraping to any lords and ladies—not me."

"Come now, Mrs. Hessenwinkle." Those gimlet eyes of Mr. Lucian's were on her again. "Suppose you had a lot of people bowing and saying 'my lady' to you—that might put a different face on it, eh?"

Vinny had never thought of this contingency of aristocracy and it threw her back for a moment. Her repeated, "I can't stand a snob," was less ringing. Also, she was beginning to get the feel of Lucian. He had acted very democratic and all that at her house Friday, but she knew now she distrusted him. All that palaver. How much did he net in the real estate business?—that's what she'd like to know.

She was perspiring freely and the pink handbag kept slipping down the facile descent of her rayon lap. But her rule was never to let her bag out of her hand in anybody's house but her own, so she switched it stickily from one damp arm to the other. Then she floundered out of the argument like a giant turtle from the sea. "Well, I guess we're all good Americans anyhow, aren't we?"

"To be sure," said August with hearty relief. He had been following the argument with growing nervousness. "America's a great country; it gives a man a chance to work and thrive. You can't ask any more than that, can you?"

But these Redcliffs . . . Vinny couldn't figure them out. They never seemed to give the right answers to even the simplest questions. "Yes . . . I suppose so . . ." Mr. Redcliff said, fooling with his tumbler, "though the adjective 'good' sort of stops me. *Am* I a good American? It's a startling question, actually." He caught Mr. Lucian's eye and they smiled at each other like they were embarrassed; and Mr. Lucian said, "It's like suddenly being asked if you're a good biped. You don't know the answer offhand—"

"Name of God! Don't you even know if you're an American?" Vinny's resonant pitch made all the glasses ring faintly together.

"Well, he don't look like a Chinee, does he, Momma? You gotta take something for granted."

Rena's imperturbable good humor made them all laugh and dropped the tension. Down the table Tat was saying, ". . . there isn't any such thing as a necessary war. All wars are destructive; nobody wins anything except poverty, famine, and disease. We can do more for democracy by keeping out of imperialistic wars and building up a real program of social betterment in this country."

Tat was O.K., Vinny thought. Even if he was no great shakes as a provider. But had he not already provided Rena with a place, a starting-point from which to scoop up with both hands the good things she had a right to? And some day they'd have his daddy's money (which hope plumped up in Vinny's mind to a figure larger than life). Tat was a sweet boy—you couldn't help liking him, even when he talked that socialistic stuff—he was so sincere. And this morning at breakfast she and August had nearly split their sides to see him with Rena. A young husband was the funniest thing on two legs, and Tat beat any they had ever laid eyes on; he was so pleased to have himself a wife, and to have gotten Rena, of all people. "I bet you never thought I'd make the grade," he had boasted to Vinny with his chest stuck out a mile. Sitting there at the table with his arm around her and drinking out of her coffee cup . . . men were curious creatures, to Vinny's idea—they could run around nights like tomcats, but when they got married they seemed to think they'd really done something. Of course, you could see Tat was no night prowler, he just knew his luck in getting a swell girl, and for that Vinny forgave him almost everything.

How Rena felt about Tat, beyond the obvious advantages of the match, Vinny was not quite sure yet, but she seemed gay as a lark across the table there. She sure looked good in that taffeta dress. But then Vinny had never been able to fathom Rena entirely, which was one reason why she admired her eldest so much. Take that business with Fen . . . he was a handsome young feller, but he was married and didn't have much money. Vinny herself had married young, and between the regular procession of babies and real estate ventures she had no time for skylarking. She had pointed out to Rena that she was wasting her time with Fen, she'd better satisfy her mind with somebody less fancy and get married. But though Rena couldn't explain why she was so foolish, she had said no . . . and Vinny had to admit now she had shown good sense, she had saved herself for this.

Vinny grappled the bag again and thought of all the trouble she'd been through with Rena. That poor little baby was on her mind, it wasn't right to raise him away from his own people. She loved that little cuss, so cute and so helpless, even though he was getting kind of big now. A vast relief flowed through her that that trouble was all over and past, it looked now like everything would work out. . . . She was lost in amaze at the inscrutable ways of heaven. Suddenly it struck her as very queer that Mr. de la Marr hadn't forecast this remarkable marriage. If he had dropped a hint, if he had even said "a great social change is ahead," it would have given them a steer in those tough days, it would sure have helped. Could it have been there all the time, in the sky, and he just plain missed it? Or could the stars have held out on them!

Speared on this choice of heresies, Vinny felt the galaxy swinging off its course: the earth shook under her shifting weight

[218]

A low groan escaped the Hepplewhite chair, it folded in its dainty legs and bearing Vinny still upright upon it, sank to the floor.

For a moment Vinny's slow occultation congealed Lorena's veins. Suckled on miracles, religious and astrological, she accepted with simple credence the possibility that the earth might be opening to swallow her beloved parent. But when the smooth oval face came harmlessly to rest with its chin on the edge of the table, and even the wide black hat was not thrown out of plumb, the gaping floor-boards closed up again. Recovering herself first, Vinny let out a great booming laugh so spontaneous it fairly lifted the company off its feet. They all shouted with her, carried along on the current of her invincible naturalness. Lorena made a wide swing from horror, she shrieked and threw her napkin over her face, an unconscious borrowing of her mother's way with her kitchen apron when she really let loose.

Wick and O'Dell quickly hoisted Vinny to her feet, Bristol with sound instinct whisked the Morris chair from across the hall, and in a trice she was sitting enthroned against its propped back as if she had never rested on a foundation of lesser permanence. Nobody thought of apologizing for what suddenly seemed a delightful caprice; if they had, Vinny was laughing too hard to hear. Tears ran down her face, she leaned first to Wick on one side and then across the table to Lorena. Did you ever see such a funny woman? she seemed to say, though only gurgles came out of her throat. The laughter of the table beat on the air with the sound of applause.

Lorena was suddenly on top of the world. She rightly evaluated the narrow margin and the superb stroke by which Vinny had turned a disaster into a personal triumph. Besides, she liked these people and they liked her—or so she assumed; never being one to dissemble her feelings, she had no picture of their reasons for making themselves agreeable. She doted on her father-in-law. Mr. Redcliff was a real gentleman, and he had such lovely manners ... he certainly seemed stuck on her . . . the way he kept leaning across the table with that tuft of hair standing up on his forehead and that look on his face . . . and what a cinch it had been to bring it there. He seemed to think her line was a scream . . . he kept filling her glass and saying, "Well, tell me some more about yourself. . . ."

"If you give me any more of this claret wine I'll tell you my middle name or anything else you want to hear." They laughed and clinked their glasses.

Lorena confessed to thirty, though the baptismal record at Sacred Heart Church made her nearer thirty-five; but actually both these figures were irrelevant. In experience with the cross grain of life, she was old as a sibyl; in her mental and emotional responses she had not passed beyond adolescence. Events had rushed at her—marriage, desertion, love, money, lean times—and she accepted them all with the frightening simplicity of the young.

As Bristol passed the bowl of peach icecream, she exclaimed, "Ooo-eee! Here goes my downfall—" and heaped her plate, then glancing sidewise at Lucian under her lashes, "Five pounds on my rumpus-bumpus."

Lucian muttered something about being willing to take measurements, but she let his freshness pass and settled down to eat with conscious care; she had gotten on fine so far, she had come out right with the forks and spoons, and she didn't want to spoil it. She wanted terribly to do Tat credit—sweet old Tat. She looked down the table and finding his eyes on her, she blew him a kiss. How nice he looked in that white suit, with his hair brushed. Why, he looked like the other Redcliffs. It would be fun to keep his clothes nice for him now, he needed a wife to jack him up about his looks. I'll get me some good-looking clothes, too, with Poppa's check . . . Mrs. Tatten Redcliff. . . .

She thought of Fen, not knowing why . . . not knowing it was her ardent wish to appear well in his eyes that first made her want to be a lady. Fen would think less of her, she had imagined, if she didn't know how to act. And this supposed expectation of his had called up an answering desire from somewhere down inside her. . . . The blood poured into her face as it came over her that she was in the top row now, Fen's very own row. . . . Then it ran coolly away and left her with a hollow feeling because Fen wasn't there to see. She went on eating icecream as if it could fill the void.

But there was Tat sitting by his mother. "Pass the cake, Bristol," Etta said with just a slight nod, and Lorena took note. People who paraded their natural skins gave her a pain—as if there was any percentage in that scrubbed, unpowdered look. But even without make-up, if you said "Pass the cake" in a certain way, it was done; you got results with 'most anybody.

Mrs. Redcliff was being just lovely to Tat and herself; look at all the trouble she had gone to about this party. "Mrs. Redcliff, this icecream is super," she called down the table. "You must of known peach is my favorite kind."

Etta gave her a friendly smile. "Is it? I'm delighted; I'll have to remember that." Lorena thought she could get on all right with Mrs. Redcliff—and that would please Tat. She had discovered that he was crazy about his mother. He made fun of all the rest of the family, but not her, and that was right. Sometimes he'd say she was very reactionary, but when Lorena had said, "I guess so—she looks like she would be," he hadn't liked it.

If Lorena had heard her mother's silent query a while ago as to how she felt about Tat, she wouldn't have been able to answer. She might have approached it roundabout . . . not the way I felt about Eleck . . . not the way I felt about Fen. . . . But she couldn't have explained how she felt about Fen, except that he had an easy way, a sense of fun, an instinct for taking the cash and letting the credit go that she responded to. Their few brief love-passages had lifted her for a while out of the backyard landscape she knew as life and into the cypress walks of a forbidden garden. From them she looked into Fen's world and found it desirable. This was not altogether snobbery on her part, unless the desire for the romantic, unless the hope that life will let up on its ruthless veracity, is snobbish. But she sought a pleasanter world naïvely—in a name, in a street address, in a way of holding a fork. No, Lorena couldn't have explained to Vinny why she had been beglamored by Fen—she who had always had her feet on the ground—nor why with Tat she had refused to take the path supposedly bordered with primroses, of all unlikely flowers, and held out for marriage. She had balanced the values with too instinctive a bookkeeping to know.

Well, Tat had upset that balancing a little. Marriage with him had had its surprises. Fen had been her only experience with a gentleman, and she had assumed that all gentlemen would be alike in certain respects. But Fen and Tat weren't a bit alike. Tat was tentative with her, he didn't seem to have that feel for what a woman wants . . . he talked an awful lot about love but she couldn't seem to get what he was driving at. Lorena thought she knew what love was; it was what Eleck had given her, for instance. Eleck was certainly a man . . . she had cried a lot when she heard he was dead, because he had been a good egg and she had been crazy about him, even if another woman had claimed she was his wife. But Uncle Harry had hired a smart lawyer who had gotten the pension for Lorena, so she didn't hold it against Eleck, not after all these years, that he had left her.

But Tat wanted something else, it appeared; and it made her uncomfortable. Well, Tat was a bachelor yet—a little green. After all, she had been married before and so had Fen . . . as to Eleck, no Marine was ever green. There were a lot of little things she could teach Tat with time and patience.

Her friends would all consider her mighty lucky, she thought with satisfaction. With the possible exception of her sister Annie. Annie came next to Lorena and was her intimate in the family. She was stout and quiet-looking, but she had been the sly one when they were younger; even Lorena didn't know all that Annie had been up to. She was now happily married to Big Bill Hahn, who was dumber than all hell, Lorena thought, but he gave Annie what she wanted most—love and money. Annie's sensuality was as solid and thick as a cake of brown soap, it was almost wholesome in its simplicity, and looking sidewise at Tat, at his steel-rimmed spectacles, his thin, seeker's face, Lorena was afraid Annie would pronounce him inadequate. Well, she was different from Annie. Tat had class, and she liked class. Also he treated her like a lady; she was grateful to him for that. And while he was impractical about money, she felt proud of this attribute; it showed he was no common clay. She could manage the budget all right.

A new family argument had started at the other end of the table. Judith was reproving the older generation about their eating habits . . . "rice and sweet potatoes and macaroni for dinner—it's enough to kill you. But Bekah makes the best chocolate cake in the world. I wish you'd give me the recipe."

Aunt Quince had helped herself bountifully to all the starches without regard for her figure, so at this she looked grumpy.

"When did you begin to say 'recipe'? I thought you always said 'receipt.'"

"Well—yes; I did," Judith owned. "But I changed when I found it was wrong. The dictionary says 'receipt' is obsolescent."

"Dictionaries!" said Aunt Quince. "They're full of twaddle. I don't see why you should give up your own pronunciation for a dictionary. A word can't be obsolescent as long as people use it."

"If you don't go by a dictionary, may I ask what Holy Writ you do go by?" Tat's voice sank into the bass clef with the heavy weight of his sarcasm. Lorena could tell how much he wanted to hang something on the old girl.

"I speak the way I was brought up to speak, boy."

Etta put her hand over Tat's. "I'm afraid he has no such arbitrary rules to go by, Aunt Quince. I've always encouraged him to think for himself. If I hounded him about his pronunciation the way you do Lucian, he'd never speak to me again." She smiled at Tat.

Aunt Quince looped them both in a wiry glance. "I think that might be vewy westful."

Lucian broke in hastily in the interest of family unity. "Being able to live without a dictionary is a sign of either extreme literacy or the extreme opposite, and the longer I live with my mother the less I know which extreme she belongs to. The truth is," he turned back to Lorena and smiled confidentially, "Mother is like Humpty Dumpty, which makes her difficult to argue with."

Lorena was finding Lucian more and more amusing. She giggled and said, "She is sort of roly-poly."

"It's not my mother's contours I'm referring to," Lucian answered severely, "it's her arrogant attitude toward words."

Lorena pondered the phrase. But what was the old girl's attitude toward *her*? She'd give a lot to know. That gritting of the fan against the cotton voile bosom was getting on her nerves. How much had Aunt Quince caught on to that summer evening three years ago when she and Fen had slipped into the house and found the old lady there? Nosey—that was what Lorena thought, though she claimed she had come to ask Fen to Sunday dinner, being as his family was all away. It scared Lorena a little to think about it, her conscience began to hurt her about the bad things she had done; besides, the old girl might tattle and get her in wrong with Tat's family. Well, you just had to take your chances with this kind of thing, and if you were born lucky and kept on going, you generally got by, in her experience. Uncle Harry seemed to have wound the old lady round his finger; maybe he'd keep her in a good humor. Lorena relaxed; she took a small genteel pull on her claret glass and sat back in her chair, hoping she wasn't high. But what did they expect, giving people all that whisky on an empty stomach? Momma and Poppa had gotten hungry around twelve-thirty and ate a little lunch, but she had gone off with Uncle Harry too excited to eat. They had had one with some friends who wanted to drink her health—and God knew she needed a shot in the arm before coming here to meet Tat's family. She got by with the julep all right, but she hadn't expected this claret wine—at home they drank lots of beer and some rye whisky. Eitalians drank claret wine. Lorena had a feeling her green straw sailor was skidding about on her short curls—or was it? Not being sure, she kept pushing it back and then forward, trying to feel for the right angle . . . pushed back, a sailor made you look younger. . . .

The green nimbus did indeed bring a young, an irresponsible, look to her high-colored face. Lucian was giving Janie a little belated attention, Mr. Redcliff was still locked in the endless family argument—words about words. Lorena and Vinny exchanged slightly superior smiles across the tumult. What ailed these people —didn't they have anything to talk about except the way you pronounced words? With another swoop of her feelings, the O'Dells went up and the Redcliffs declined. Look at Uncle Harry holding his own with the best; he could charm the birds outa the trees, that man, but he never took his eye off the ball.

Her gush of family sentiment slopped over to include August, having himself a time with the icecream. He loved food and drink and making a noise; his big family bewildered him but he was kind of cute the way he was proud of being able to support them. You've sure been a wonderful father to me, she wanted to say to him. But he was talking to Mrs. Redcliff. "I always remember the sweet smell of the bread in the early morning," he was saying. "We lived over the bakery, and before day the smell would begin to come upstairs."

"How pleasant that sounds."

"Yes, ma'am, it was mighty pleasant. Only the flour used to sift in too, and Momma complained about she couldn't keep the place clean. She was always after that white film with her feather duster. . . ."

August's simplicity embarrassed Lorena. Why didn't he tell them about how he had built up his wholesale business? But that was Poppa, he wouldn't put his best foot forward.

August washed his food down with a long drink of wine and wiped his thick lips. "But I can't do anything with my children," he said amiably, "they're a law unto themselves. Excep' I won't stand for loose talk round the house—that's one thing I put my foot down. . . ."

That was better, Lorena thought; that was right to tell these people they never had any loose talk at their house. Even though it was an empty boast on August's part, because plenty went on behind his back—but what else could you expect with a lot of rough boys? Loose talk didn't shock Lorena, only blasphemy against the Church shocked her, and Eleck had hardened her even to that. Eleck came of a family of Freemasons and he had tried to talk her out of her religion, he had even snatched off the gold cross and chain she wore round her neck and thrown them down the toilet. It made him hopping mad because she wouldn't change. Men were generally bad about religion, in her observation. Her father didn't go to church much, but Protestants were different, of course. The rest of the family went to mass in big groups, leaving him in the yard with his chair tilted back against the wall and the Sunday paper all round him; though sometimes he went to the Lutheran church by himself, neatly dressed and walking slowly. His square, retreating back looked sort of lonely . . . but then, he should go to Sacred Heart with her mother, Lorena thought.

A frond of asparagus fern descending in a long curve from the epergne set Judith off, from Lorena's angle at the opposite corner of the table, in a garlanded frame.

Brushing me off her sleeve like that. Judith wasn't high—oh no, not that fine lady. From this distance she looked serious and self-composed. Under the close-fitting cap with the proud-looking wings, her hair came out full and dark. This hot, damp weather

[225]

nad taken all the wave out of it . . . why don't she break down and get a perm . . . she was talking to Uncle Harry in a perfectly pleasant way, though, like she had forgotten all about that fight in the office Thursday. Well, it had been kind of silly for Judith and herself to be fighting about Fen, because Fen was dead, and today was another day. It had just gotten her back up to have Judith talk as if she owned the Redcliffs, when, if she only knew. . . .

Judith turned to Tat, and Lorena heard her asking, "Have you decided where you are going to live, or haven't you had time to make any plans?"

Lorena hadn't made any plans. She seldom thought about the future, today was always so full. They could live with her family until something turned up, then they'd move.

"I hope they'll stay here with us," said Mrs. Redcliff. "We have plenty of room—too much, in fact. Wick and I will be lost in this house."

There you were. Why fuss about plans when it was as easy as that?

But Tat was saying, "Thanks, Mother, that's swell of you, but we want a place of our own. We'll get a furnished apartment, at least for the present—" He smiled at her to ease the refusal.

"But furnished apartments are so awful." The thin skin of Etta's nose wrinkled with distaste. "I don't see why, when you can live in your own house. You and Lorena could have your own sitting room."

Suddenly Lorena felt happy, hearing the house spoken of as hers and Tat's. Just like that.

Naturally, Tat was answering, they'd rather build a house of their own than live in a rented one and sometime they would maybe . . . in a new part of town where things were happening and real estate was going up . . . a modern house . . . they had a way now you could electrify the walls for heat . . . everything functional ("one of these modernistic horrors with plumbing pipes draped all over the front, I suppose," Etta put in). . . . Well, why not? . . . there was nothing sacred about Georgian, and he'd had a bellyful of it, anyway. . . .

Through Lorena's cloudy detachment the contentions shuttled back and forth. She didn't care what kind of house they lived in;

she could make any place homey. And the rented apartment George Belchers had gotten for her was fine; she had been cosy and independent there. He had treated her swell . . . until that sourpuss he was married to busted it up. . . . But it would be nice to live here too.

Mr. Redcliff waded into the fight now, talking kind of sharp. "Don't throw yourself at their heads, Etta—or rather, don't throw the house at them. We'll live in it as long as we last, and then it will have to take its chances."

"All I mean is, nobody wants to live in a house like this nowadays." Feeling himself put in the wrong, Tat raised his voice several pitches. "It's too big and drafty, and that Chippendale number in the basement just wastes coal—as you're the first to say when the bills come in—"

"The furnace tempers the house delightfully. You spoiled young creatures don't remember the days before the furnace when the pipes burst, and when you banked the sitting-room fire and ran through the icy halls undressing as you went and jumped into bed."

Mr. Redcliff was smiling but Lorena could tell from the way he talked that his feelings were hurt by Tat's cracks about the house. He went on. "But as I say, it will last out our time and then you young people can sell it or let it fall down, as you like."

"Don't you worry," she hastened to reassure him, "we won't let it fall down. Or sell it either. We're gonna live here some day."

"On *what?*" Tat cut in.

"Never you mind. We can take roomers, if we have to. We can turn it into apartments. Lots of things you can do."

Lorena thought she felt a thud on the air like a far-off explosion. They were all looking at her kind of stupidly. Even Tat. Well, Tat didn't understand, maybe, but she had walked round and round this house all her life . . . and now she was in it. Fen had let her in the back door, and now Tat had let her in the front door, and she was going to live here—for a while at least. Momma got fifteen dollars a week for rooms in that house on Calhoun Street, and this place was handsomer. People would pay good money to live in the Redcliff house.

"Well, I want to live in a dymaxion house," said Tat harshly, "hung on a pole—that's the right idea," and he began fighting the battle of modern architecture again, supported now by Judith, while August entered the lists on Etta's side. Tat had big ideas, and that was O.K. Lorena had a wistful envy of big ideas. So if Tat wanted to live in a modernistic house, that was all right by her, even though it seemed simple and sensible to live here in these fine rooms and to be where she could run over home every day like the other married daughters did. And they had their children to think about . . . because she intended to start in on a family now, like Momma said. Their children had a right to live here and grow up . . . even little Red. They could make the house pay all right, and someday Tat would have his father's money and then they'd be fixed. . . . A warm current flowed around her at the thought of the children. . . . What a cute little feller Red was. She called him that because it was the nearest she dared come to Fen's name—and his hair was reddish, sort of. His little hands had been perfect when he was born, she remembered. Tat would love him, she was sure she could fix it somehow to give him his right name, now that she was really Mrs. Redcliff. In fancy she had thought of herself that way for three years—since the first time Fen had taken her hand on the Mall and brought her into this house. But the children she would have now would be Tat's children . . . not Fen's. From somewhere outside cold rain seemed to dash in her face, breaking up the claret-colored mist . . . the table, the people came into focus close around her yet stranger-distant, as if she had waked up in an unknown room.

It was funny, but at first she hadn't thought of Red as a child, a being taking shape. She had thought of him as an accident, and she had felt sick and humiliated at getting caught. . . . Fen had been wild when she told him, and said they must do something right off . . . even Momma had been rattled, she was scared of Poppa in some ways, and she said he'd blame it on her for not bringing the girls up stricter. But she put her foot down about Rena's going to that woman, Anna Shadd; there were some things, she said, that were so against the Church that you couldn't get off by prayers or penances.

Mary pity women . . . what we have to go through! Men don't know what it's like. Well, Momma had been fine, she had fixed for Rena to go to Aunt Sue's in Detroit for a year and never grudged what it cost her. And Fen had been kind as could be.

But he was different after that, serious and not fun any more; he blamed himself terribly, said he had been selfish and begged her to forgive him. But she didn't want to forgive him . . . and she didn't see why he said this would have to end everything. He sent her money to pay for the hospital . . . the lonely white walls of the ward closed round her again, sending the table farther and farther away . . . they made her feel sickish the way she felt from the ether, and the way she felt later from guilt and grief and despair because Fen was dead and she'd never see him again.

She let out a long, tremulous breath, and the table came back. Why had Fen married a girl like Judith? Cold and serious—she couldn't have given him much fun. Long baffled by this question, Lorena gazed at her rival through the loophole in the centerpiece. But so much of Fen's life was a mystery to her, a blank, his thoughts unknown. A few talks on the Mall, a few meetings in his house were all she knew of Fen. . . . Her feelings took another wide swing, as if lights went on in the room. In this queer clarity she saw she didn't know Judith either, her picture of the lucky wife of Fen Redcliff didn't fit the girl over there with the dark, unhappy face. After all, Judith had no children . . . no husband . . . she'd probably get married again and be out from under soon. There was no way in which she threatened Lorena as the mother of future Redcliffs. Confidence flowed back into Lorena's body, she felt kindly toward all the world; and as for the old jealousy, well, that belonged in the past, now, buried with Fen and already half-covered with leaves.

The feathery frond meticulously arranged by his mother cut off Tat's view of Lorena so that he had to crane this way and that to see her—a refreshment he needed often during the meal. Events came at him stepped up to twice their natural size: his still-improbable marriage, his family's opposition, self-doubt, a half-shamed yet irrepressible enjoyment of this dinner, this incense to his bridegroom's nostrils . . . he had to steady himself every now and then at the bubbling spring of Lorena's superb assurance. The situation bristled with surprises; his father's capitulation to Lorena filled him with a savage justification, yet he found it disturbing also; Dad was overdoing it. Then he had feared Lorena would think his family was stuffy as all hell and say so, in her outspoken way; instead of which she seemed to like them all right. She showed none of his jealous watchfulness for slights to the Hessenwinkles.

For the time being he had pushed aside the thought that he had compromised his principles in marrying, though he hated compromise. It was only by standing out against a moss-backed morality that you broke it down. Yet you had to come to compromise, it seemed, when another person's happiness was involved. Like his going to church that morning. It was a sham, because he hated organized religion, and as for putting up a good front about his marriage, he didn't give a damn what people thought. Not really. But his mother. . . . A sickening distress surged again in his vitals, repeating absurdly—now that it was all over—the fear and revulsion of this morning when he had come over from the Hessenwinkles to face the music. At first it hadn't been bad; though his father and mother had both been upset, embarrassed, they had taken it all right. But when his mother had led him up to her room for a private talk (the place where she used to take him for a going-over after some youthful delinquency), she had broken down and reproached him dreadfully for not letting her know that he was planning to get married. But he couldn't tell her . . . he didn't know why . . . that when he left the house on Thursday he hadn't expected to get married. Or exactly why he had, so complicated were the pressures and so little was he able to weigh them justly. When he had gone to see Lorena the night before to tell her he was going up to Myrtle Beach on business, she had just said, "How about takin' me with you?"

When things like that happened, you couldn't believe it or understand it at first. Nor could he remember at what stage of the journey she had won him to her point of view. Suddenly it seemed they'd better get married after all.

No, he couldn't tell his mother all this as she reproached him there in the bedroom. He sat on his spine, his chin sunk in his collar, his legs spraddled out, and let her shower him with red hot particles, while he doggedly withheld the healing words.

So he had consented when she asked him, almost timidly, to go to church with them—when he saw how much putting a good face on the marriage meant to her. It eased him in a way for the grievous hurt he had done her. Besides, Lorena had jarred him a little this morning when she put on her hat and went to mass with her family as a matter of course; it seemed to him that on this of all days she might have consulted his feelings. She hadn't meant to irritate him; she simply hadn't thought about it one way or another . . . and he didn't know whether this made it worse or better. So a thin finger of resentment had helped to push him along to his own church with his own tribe. Not that any church was his own. . . .

Well, they would find a place to live as soon as they could, get away from both families and work out their own lives. He discovered with a start that the Hessenwinkles, whom he had sought out because they were real people, because they had none of the stuffiness of his own kind, had suffered a translation in his view. It was the business of religion, mostly. Lorena was so swell, herself . . . get her out of that smothering atmosphere and she'd see lots of things differently; for instance, this war in Spain that no one would take seriously enough, though it kept him in a state of gloom . . . he knew Lorena would be for the Loyalists, if they hadn't gone and murdered a few priests . . . but they *had* to do it (he went over the arguments for the twentieth time), those priests were fighting alongside the Falangists, they *had* to break the corrupt power of the Church. . . .

It would take a while to persuade her, he admitted; these deep-seated prejudices changed slowly.

He had done some changing himself in the past three days.

He leaned forward on one elbow which put him in a better position to see Lorena. She was turned his way, listening to a boring story of Lucian's about the Joneses; she didn't seem to see what a smart aleck Lucian was. . . .

"I know a Mrs. Jones lives on the Battery," she was saying. "You any kin to her?"

"No; she belongs to the Hampton Joneses. We are the Holy-Joneses, a quite different tribe."

"The Holy-Joneses?" she repeated doubtfully.

"Yes, you'll learn in time to distinguish us on sight from others of the name. They say that sometimes we exhibit rudimentary haloes. If you keep your eyes peeled—"

"Is that right?"

It exasperated Tat to have Lucian taking Lorena for a ride.

[2 3 1]

"Don't pay any attention to that dope, Rena," he called down the table. "You don't have to take on the whole damn connection. You married me."

"Do you say so?" teased O'Dell. "Well, I'm glad to have it from the horse's mouth. I thought she might be trying to put something over on us. But you're the man to know. Though I may say, it took me a lot of believing."

"Not you, but me!" exclaimed Lorena. "You should of seen me when he popped the question! The dye 'most fell off my hair."

At this a good gale of spontaneous laughter swept the table, and carried away Tat's megrims. That was the Lorena he loved . . . natural as the day is long. His ardor surged up again, justified. She was a little high, he could tell; she'd better lay off the claret. But liquor just made her funnier, completely uninhibited. He wanted to see her cut loose and tell Lucian off.

Judith had been silent for some time, and looking sidewise at her he said, "Isn't she something! I hope you and Rena are going to be good friends, Judith. I know you'll get along like a house afire, once you know each other."

But the heat or something had taken the starch out of Judith; her hair, her dress, her mouth drooped. It came to him suddenly that this party was awful for her. Overwhelmed, he squeezed her hand and said, "I wish old Fen was here."

She returned his look gratefully with eyes that were brown, familiar, yet estranged by a grief he couldn't wholly share, though the tragedy of Fen's absence hurt him too. Fen would have had himself a time at this party, he'd have pulled the factions together and made the whole thing go. For Fen would have understood better than anyone his pride in making Lorena love him. God, but I miss him, he wanted to cry to Judith, nothing seems the same when Fen isn't in on it. . . .

He felt he ought to cheer Judith up somehow, but for the moment he could think of nothing to say. She sat adrift, one brown hand playing with the stem of her wine glass. O'Dell, on her other side, might help; he had the gift of gab—he could talk to a lamppost. But he was leaning toward Aunt Quince; his half-turned back presented a blank expanse of turquoise blue pinched in with a Norfolk jacket effect. In a rich, smooth murmur, flatteringly exclusive, he was telling her about his fighting cocks. And her eyes, under her little black beetle of a hat, were round with wonder and unashamed enjoyment. A fine pair! Tat loathed cockfighting, bull-fighting, the cruelty of setting animals on each other. . . .

Beyond them he could see Mrs. Hessenwinkle against the straight back of the Morris chair, as if all hell couldn't throw her down. Tat could scarcely believe in the fiasco of half an hour ago. Her sharp gaze was traveling again, up the fluted pilasters of the mantel, along the rosettes and garlands of the cornices. . . . His father was saying, "We think this part of the house is newer . . . Greek revival . . . our bedroom, which used to be the drawing room, has earlier woodwork. . . ."

Vinny's eyes came down and rested on him briefly. "The trouble is, this class of property is hard to handle. I was only thinking if you ever *did* want to turn it into apartments—" Her gaze shifted to Lorena as someone who spoke a common language. "These large rooms don't cut up so good—too much waste space." She measured the ceiling height again with an exact eye.

Oh God, couldn't she keep off that! But Rena came to the rescue.

"Quit worrying, Momma; that's a long time off. And for my money, this house is swell. Besides you could always make enough taking roomers to carry the place if you—if anybody didn't want to change it."

"I don't know—" Vinny thrust her head as far forward as her short neck would allow, not liking her judgment questioned in this her own field.

"Well, I do." Lorena and her mother argued a lot, Tat had discovered; now they both flushed up. "If you wanted to live here you got plenty of rooms to bring in rent, even if they are large."

"Luckily we don't have to consider that problem just now," Etta said. "Suppose we talk of something else."

But mother and daughter were too far away to feel the sting of hail, or else their hot contentions melted the ice as it struck. "You got three bedrooms on the second floor, Momma—four if you count the sewing room."

Tat looked from his wife to his mother and struggled to break in on this nightmare argument, but his divided loyalties tore his thoughts apart and left him only fragments of words.

"The sewing room's kind of small and dark," Lorena persisted, "but it's the coolest room in the house in summer."

This homely detail fell stonily into the pool of the table; the rim of faces swung like sunflowers toward Lorena, then turned irresistibly on him. Tat drew a quivering breath. What the hell . . . Rena!

"Course you'd have to evict Miss Jinny. You'd have to heave out the deadheads and get in some paying guests." She laughed a delighted, shallow laugh.

At the mention of Miss Jinny's name Aunt Quince held up the constant beat of her fan. Then her voice came out in a kind of spurt. "You seem to know the house pretty well."

Tat felt his mother's eyes on him, asking with outrage, what does this mean? Did you bring this girl here . . . ? The blood flew to his ears, he knew he looked twenty times guilty of all he hadn't committed. He took off his spectacles and rubbed them on his sleeve, as if his near-sightedness could shield him.

"Sure I know it," Lorena said self-consciously. "Anyway, it ain't so different from any other house; it's got bedrooms and halls, ain't it, like any other house. . . ." Her slipping grammar showed she was flustered a little.

But it wasn't like any other house. The ill-shaped, cluttered sewing room . . . his mother didn't like people to go into it; except that Fen, whose room got the afternoon sun, often slept there because it was the coolest room in the house in summer . . . Fen! Tat looked at Lorena with dumb anguish, imploring her not to go on, not to thrust it at him . . . after all, I've flouted my family, cast in my lot with yours, staked my future on your worth. . . .

But Lorena didn't understand his entreaty. Aunt Quince's stare which gave her no quarter, the implacable fan, seemed to have some power to overthrow her sturdy self-possession. The table crouched in ravening expectancy through which Lorena's voice sounded large and shrill as she tried to recover her footing.

"Well, we don't have to start out looking for roomers yet, like Mis' Redcliff says. I got a general idea what this house is like." She lowered her voice and added negligently, "Tat took me around it once—on a kind of a rubber-neck tour. . . ."

The green frond hid her as she said it, so he couldn't tell whether she wondered what he'd think; maybe the wine had dulled her quick wits a little. He sat and let the lie burn his bosom. Through the smoke that seemed to rise from his flesh his father was smiling at him with a dreadful comprehension . . . forget that lecture of mine, the smile seemed to say; now that I've seen your temptress . . . after all, you're flesh and blood . . . an understandable impatience. . . . Then he pulled himself together and got the situation in hand, covering up for his son. He began to pour the Madeira and pass it down the table informally to create a diversion.

"Well," he said, "it's quite natural that Tat should show his prospective wife what she was getting into. She's taking on not only the Redcliffs and their eccentricities but the closets with their skeletons—after all she had to meet Miss Jinny sometime. But since it's all had a happy ending, let's drink the bride's health. This, my dear, is the last of the Madeira bought for our wedding."

He rose and bowed fulsomely toward Lorena, his cheeks pink, his cowlick ruffled by the tempestuous air. "To the daring and charming bride—" he bent and kissed her hand, "don't blame us if we Redcliffs find her irresistible."

Tat shoved his chair back as if the fire burned under it instead of under his breastbone. As he jumped up his glasses fell with a light clash and skittered along the waxed floor. "I say we cut out the toasts," he said raucously, "we might as well just skip the whole damn farce. We don't any of us seem to know what we're getting into—what we've all got to do is find out where we stand, so for Christ's sake stop the acting. Let her alone . . . let me alone . . . and let's get this party over with."

He backed out of the circle of ossified, upturned faces and tramped into the hall without knowing that he ground his glasses excruciatingly under his feet.

Judith got up impulsively and followed him. She put a comforting hand on his shoulder. "Keep your hair on, Tat. We suspected, or some of us did, about you and Lorena. It doesn't really matter—"

But he turned on her such a face of pity and anger that her hand slid off again. He shook his head without speaking, then he went slowly upstairs, leaving her to stand in the hall and look after him in bewilderment.

[2 3 5]

Behind her the diners were rising and scuffling among the flattened debris of the structure they had built up so elaborately. "Tat! *Really*—" "What on *earth* got into him?" "I declare—he's vewy tempwamental!" "Don't take this outburst too seriously," —this was Etta—"he's over-excited today, naturally. We'll have coffee in the sitting room."

Isolated by the door, Judith watched them stream across the hall, filling the vacant air with a rummage of words.

Lorena sat on at the table. That dazed, tremulous look was wholly unexpected on a face so shaped to buoyancy. Uncle Wick stayed with her, trying to smooth things over. Judith was furious with both. He *had* deserted to the enemy, in spite of all he had said at her house that day. . . . Even now, after this display of callousness, he was ready to excuse Lorena. Of course, Tat had gone off the deep end, he needn't have taken it so hard . . . but that was the way he was, thin-skinned, always getting in a stew about little things. It was a wife's job to protect him. . . .

Bekah stood by the opposite door, with the long dark face of fate. As Lucian passed she gave him a look of guarded triumph. Lucian avoided Judith's glance; he hurried by, propelling his mother before him with a tight grasp on her shoulder, and driving her into a corner, he stood over her like a jailer.

The bleak feeling assailed Judith of being alone in a crowd; she went restlessly into the sitting room. The Hessenwinkles and O'Dell were lumped together on the sofa for mutual defense. They carried on a private argument in low tones, the nature of which Judith could not guess. O'Dell, who had been pouring out words, paused as she came in and wiped his wet face and hands with a blue-bordered handkerchief. He drew a long breath, as much as to say, my pump's sucked. Etta and Janie passed around coffee cups and conversation, the one as brittle as the other.

Vinny, it became apparent, wanted to go home but didn't know how or when to make the move. Judith had a nightmarish vision of them all hardening there through eternity, like a frieze of concrete figures. When Etta at length inquired, with significant nods and becks, if the ladies would like to go up to her room, she could scarcely believe they still had the use of their limbs.

In the hall upstairs Judith escaped the others and went to the company room where she was used to staying when she and Fen had visited the family. She took down her hair and combed it back from her face, abandoning with infinite relief her attempt to look smart. Then she went rigid with her comb in the air, like a person who feels a cat in the room.

Lorena came straight up to her. "Judith, I been wanting to say something . . . what do you say we call it quits? I guess I been kind of crumby—but it's no need for us to keep on fighting—"

Judith spun round and stared at Lorena, too stupefied to perceive that this was a different mien, simple and sentimental.

"I figure we just as well forget the past and be frien's like Tat says," the voice went on, still subdued. "It's no use for us to fight about Fen anyway. He's—" she made a little deprecating gesture —"well, he's dead now—and out of the picture for good."

It seemed to Judith that Lorena had laid rough hands on her and dragged her bodily to a brink whose sheer drop she had spent these two years denying. Out of reason she hated, not reality, but its agent who forced on her the knowledge of life and death.

"I'm afraid it's too late," she said thickly, squeezing the words from a closed throat. "I don't see any use in our pretending—let's just say we're different and let it go at that. As to quarreling about Fen, there's really nothing for us to quarrel about, so suppose we drop the subject . . . let's not discuss Fen again, if you don't mind."

An unpleasant red patched Lorena's face where the make-up had rubbed off. "Oh. So that's it—snobbish, eh? Well, my fine lady, we ain't so different as you might think."

Useless, Judith thought, to explain that she hadn't meant it that way . . . or had she? In any case, it was useless to explain in the noise of the torrent on which they seemed to be rushing along together at this wilful speed. . . .

For an instant the sharp knock on the door seemed part of the torrential noise, then they both turned, giving each other the quick, consulting glance of duelists surprised in the wood. Before they could fend off the interruption, the door opened and Tat pushed slowly past the edge. Seeing them both transfixed before him, he came in, closed the door and leaned his back against it. He had found himself another pair of spectacles; his mouth was tight and determined. When he spoke, his voice sounded academic against the volume of their female clash.

"I guess we'll have to have this out, Rena, and it might as well be now. We can't go on till we know where we stand."

Like a ball player Lorena made a little rush from her base and back to it. "O.K. I'm kind of short-patienced myself, and all this screaming about nothing is getting my stummick upset. If it's the truth you all want, you'll get it—but jus' remember you asked for it."

The shapeless pain Judith felt settled in her hand. Looking down, she unclenched her fingers slowly and let the comb fall. Across her palm ran the deep red marks of teeth.

Lorena walked over to the bed and sat down on the edge, making them wait while she lighted a cigarette. She leaned back on one arm and blew a long puff into the air. To eyes less blinded than those watching, her parade of nonchalance was forced and tinny, but she had beglamored both her spectators too successfully for them to see her plainly now.

"It was Fen I was here with, and that's how I got to see the house, if you must know. Fen was crazy about me—"

"That's a lie," said Judith, parroting Lorena's flat tone.

"Oh, no, it's not. You think I'm not good enough, hey? You think Fen wouldn't bother with me? Well, Fen was in love with me, I tell you—"

"Oh, stop all this rot about not being good enough! I just don't believe you. That's all."

"I got witnesses. You can ask your grandmother, Tat. She came here one evening. She looks to me like she'd love to tattle."

Judith couldn't feel her knees under her any more. She leaned hard on the marble slab of the bureau. Tat walked over and stood by the bed. "Come along home, Lorena; you're talking too much —you've had too much to drink."

"Drunk, is it?" Lorena jumped up, jerked off the green sailor and threw it on the bed. Hatpins and hairpins showered the matting. "I'm not makin' this up—not by a long shot!" Seeing Judith's blank face she suddenly shouted, "You might as well know—I got in a jam that summer—I went to Detroit and had a baby—"

Tat put his hand over her mouth and cried in a drowning voice, "You're drunk!" but she tore away from his gripping fingers. "You let me go!" She backed off against the bed, the fingermarks mottling her face gave her rage a touch of fantasy. "You don't think

[238]

Fen would love me, huh? Well, lemme tell you—you don't neither of you know what love is—"

Like a sleepwalker Tat lifted his arm and hit her in the face. It was not a hard blow and she fell back on the bed more from surprise than from its force. She lay across the white counterpane for a moment, then raised her head and looked along her body at Tat standing thunderstruck at her knees. She opened her mouth once or twice before anything came out. "You hit me," she said incredulously. "You're just a fake gentleman. You're all a bunch of fakes."

To Judith the scene had the dreadful improbability of a happening in hell. Lorena's spotted face, foreshortened by her position, came queerly out of her shoulders. Tat's glasses masked his eyes; the light flashed on them with an inhuman glare. She herself was vitrified beyond feeling, her flesh had neither blood nor substance . . . were they really human beings . . . could the death of love be so ignoble? She covered her face with her hands and ran from the room as if it had burst into flames behind her.

She rushed across the hall and nearly overset Lucian who had just arrived at the top of the staircase. On tenterhooks to know what was brewing abovestairs, he had approached step by step, looking up and listening while he hunted for a pretext to intrude on the women's domain. As Judith ran past he fell back a step or two and guiltily pretended to be going down, but she didn't even see him; she made for an empty bedroom and slammed the door behind her, so he turned and came quietly up again. Her halting rush, the abandoned swinging of her long hair filled him with foreboding. He stood uncertainly in the hall, hearing voices in the company room; it was not necessary to eavesdrop because the angry epithets were all too audible. He could think of no excuse to intervene between husband and wife, for even Lucian's curiosity had its brakes, but the dilemma was almost instantly resolved. "Get the hell out of here!" Lorena's voice cut through the solid wood, and on the instant the door flew open; Tat dashed by him and ran downstairs, his soles rattling like a machine gun on the uncarpeted treads.

Through the open door Lucian saw Lorena sitting on the edge of the bed, her legs straight in front of her, her skirts in disarray.

Catching sight of him, she leaned forward, her hands on her knees as if making ready to spring. "You get the hell out of here too. I don't want to look at any of you."

Lucian strolled in, sat down in an armchair and pulled up his trousers at the knees before he answered. "Whose house do you think this is, anyway? Firing people out right and left."

"I'll show you whose house it is."

"You don't have to. I'm quite aware that it's my brother's house."

Lorena stared at him as if she had forgotten this circumstance. "Well, it's more my house than *hers*." She nodded toward the hall.

"Come, now—you two haven't been fighting over a house that doesn't belong to either of you. Women are too realistic for that. Give me the real low-down."

"We were fighting about Fen, nosey—if you really want to know."

This brought Lucian to the edge of his chair. "Good God! You told her . . . ?"

"I sure did."

Hurried footsteps broke in on these revelations. They turned and saw Wick at the door. The large oval face of Mrs. Hessenwinkle hung in the gloom of the hall behind him.

"What's up?" As he came in Lorena pulled down her skirt and began to smooth her hair with a purely reflex coquetry. "Tat rushed out of the house as if the devil was after him."

Vinny followed him into the room. "You all right, Rena?"

"Oh, Momma!" cried Lorena, running and throwing herself on the bosom of that stubborn favoritism. "Tell 'em Fen was crazy about me. They won't believe it! They think I'm not good enough. . . ."

Swiftly Vinny slipped the handle of the pink bag over her arm to safety and clasped Lorena to her. "Well, you certainly are . . . he certainly was. . . ." She looked at the Redcliffs first round one side of her sobbing daughter, then round the other. "Fen thought the world of my child. I guess you just don' know, Mr. Redcliff. If these walls could talk—"

Lorena's head came up, she looked with streaming eyes into her mother's face. "I told them it was me Fen loved!" She cried out for corroboration. "Even when I told them about the baby they didn't wanta believe me."

"Baby!" exclaimed Wick and Lucian together.

Lorena shook herself free and turned on them. "Yes—a baby. You don't think because *she* didn't have no children it was Fen's fault!"

Wick walked up and put his hands on her shoulders. "Calm down, Lorena, and tell me the truth. What is this about a baby?"

His tallness and whiteness seemed to cow her. She dropped her arms and stood sullen under the rough grip of his hands. "I had a baby—that same year Fen died. I brought him back from Detroit afterwards. My cousin is raising him for me, in Christ Church Parish. You can go and see him if you want to."

Wick let his hands fall and walked away. "This is shocking," he said. "When did all this begin—between you and Fen?"

" 'Most a year before he died, the summer before, I guess."

"It was three years ago," Vinny said. "I know because it was the same summer August had gallstones. Holy Mother, what a time that was!"

"*She* was sick and went to the mountains, remember? And Fen lived here all that summer. It was that fall I found out about the baby and—" Lorena paused and her color changed again. She turned on her mother with some of Vinny's own sharpness. "*You* sent me away to have that baby! I wish to God I hadn't of gone. I wish to God I'd stayed right here and let everybody know about it! Then they couldn't laugh it off."

"Nobody wants to laugh it off," said Wick. "If you both tell me this is true, I'll accept your word for it."

"I swear to God," said mother and daughter, solemn-eyed.

Lucian, facing the massive Victorian bureau, watched them in its long central mirror. On the wall directly opposite stood a wardrobe with another long mirror and the two, he suddenly noticed, mockingly reduplicated the room and its group of tense figures. This monstrous clash of Redcliff against Hessenwinkle, repeated into infinity, became absurd—one of the sharp little jests of God. Even though he was a part of it, Lucian saw that it was funny, he couldn't in his heart blame God for relishing His joke. . . .

Wick was standing with his hands in his coat pockets and speaking earnestly to the two women. "We must talk together about the child later; I shall of course do something about its support. All I ask is that you give me your word never to speak of it again. It must never come to my daughter-in-law's ears."

The rapid shift in his manner toward Lorena from admiration to severity seemed to flick her pride—understandably, Lucian thought.

"Too late," she said. Going over to the bureau and picking up the comb Judith had dropped, she combed up her hair defiantly. "I told her already—her and Tat."

All three stared at her in the mirror. Their multiplied, accusing faces hemmed her in. She swung around and met them again . . . thus beleaguered, her flippancy broke down, her full lips quivered. From beneath the well-filled plaid taffeta, from beneath even the garment of ripe flesh, Lucian thought he saw a girl come half out, a dryad shape, unaging. But this youth-in-maturity was not, somehow, attractive; the discrepancy had a touch of the grotesque about it. It was against nature, which ruthlessly exacts harmony. Lorena's hardness of heart, Lucian saw, was literally that—not meanness, but the green burr unbursten, not the desire to wound, but the careless infliction of a pain she was too resilient to learn about.

Wick turned his back on this phenomenon and headed for the door, saying, "Where did Judith go?"

"I don' know—across the hall, I guess."

"Sweet Jesus, Rena! What did you go telling Tat for? You sure must of got outa the wrong side of bed this morning. I'm gonna find Poppa." Mrs. Hessenwinkle went off purposefully, swinging her long arms, paddling herself on the thick air.

Lucian followed her a few steps, torn in three parts. Then he closed the door and came back, feeling he had better stay with the sweet sinner of the Borough in case she decided to break up the Redcliff furniture literally as well as figuratively. He unbuttoned his coat and held it open to cool his superheated blood; he went over to the window and seated himself in the deep embrasure. Voices in the hall told him that the ladies, his mother, Etta, and Janie, had refreshed themselves and were starting downstairs again.

Lorena had gone down on all fours, skimming the matting for her hairpins. She returned to the bureau, and having the glass all

[242]

to herself now, she meticulously combed up the stray hairs and pinned them in place. She wiped her face and put rouge and powder on it with esoteric circular motions. Giving Lucian a sulky look, she went and sat in the window next to his, her back toward him. They were silent for a few minutes.

Judith . . . Lucian's thin skin wrinkled over the flat planes of his face and he looked quickly out of the window, unable to face her distressful image. The garden, it astonished him to observe, floated there in silvery peace; pools of water gleamed in the walks between the patterned beds, late sunlight and wet leaves played tricks of innocence and grace . . . but Judith shouldn't be so damned vulnerable . . . she shouldn't give her heart to the hawks that way, people ought to toughen up, as he had, as everybody must. . . . He grew unnecessarily angry thinking about it.

With a sort of amateur clairvoyance, Lorena suddenly spoke to his thought. "What's eating her anyway? All these people are crazy. I didn't come here to raise hell, I swear I didn't, but you've got sense—" She turned round and appealed to him, "You tell me —what did she expect? Did she think she could hold him that tight, that he was never gonna cut his eye at another woman, like he was a monk? Well, marriage ain't no monastery—you can't shut a man up in it for keeps. Not a feller like Fen. He had too much life in him."

"Wives can't seem to see why what you euphemistically call 'life' has to be scattered around the lot. But even if you're right, you didn't have to rub it in. You were damn brutal just now. You might have remembered that Judith is a widow—"

"Well, so was I a widow; but I didn't expect Eleck Thompson to be no angel, and lucky for me I didn't. She's got to learn the facks of life sometime."

"So she has," Lucian conceded, "and maybe you're a blessing in disguise. A gorgeous disguise—nobody'd ever pick you for a blessing."

"What I can't figure out is why Tat got all worked up—pasting me like that." She spoke without resentment. "He acted like I'd been cheating on him. But I wasn't studying my head about Tat in those days, so he hasn't got any grouch that I can see."

Lucian searched for words to convey to her the hurt it would do Tat to learn that even in the field of love Fen had been there before him. But he was finding it astonishingly difficult to give this sinner a conviction of sin; her angle of vision simply didn't include the values that made her acts sinful. And unfortunately his angle of vision included hers among many others—he quite saw her point, wives did expect too much; and still he hated her for hurting Judith. The tip of his nose grew fiery red from being pushed around in the stress of his problem.

"Where do you suppose Tat's gone?"

"I don' know. He'll just go charging around a while till he feels some better, then he'll come back."

Her careless reassurance provoked Lucian to say crossly, "Hasn't anybody ever left you flat? Seems to me I've heard—"

"They may have left me, honey, but never flat."

Heavy footsteps and sharp voices in the hall warned them of the approach of the Hessenwinkles. Tact forbade Lucian's staying to witness the interview between father and daughter; besides he was much too tired. Bystander as he was, he had suffered vicariously with all the personages of the piece and felt worn by a multiple fatigue. Swinging his legs down from the window seat, he smiled on Lorena with acid benignity. "Good luck with the old man," he purred, and skipped through the bathroom door.

He crossed into the darkened room beyond and turning to close the door behind him, ran head on into Miss Jinny. She gave him quite a turn, looming up in the long cambric nightgown. "Damn!" he muttered and groped his way fretfully to the window, "What do you mean—scaring the liver and lights out of people like that." As he raised the shade the blue-cold north light streamed over the carved woodwork, the sewing machine, the scrapbag bulging from its hook on the door. He tipped an imaginary hat to the dress form. "I'll say—you've been a miracle of reticence!"

He threw himself down on the box-lounge for a moment and coddled his weary muscles with neurasthenic tenderness. How tiring all these people were; their over-active emotions sucked you in and wore you to a nub. Then he sat up suddenly and rubbed the prickling nerve ends at the back of his neck because of an immediate sense of Fen that hung about the sewing room—Fen's narrow body, always on the move, his dark hair burnished as if with firelight, his young man's hopeful urgency, his impatience with any hindrance to the rapid flow of his life. And he had been there today at table, like a cheerful ghost, hidden in everyone's thinking; without an uttered word he had changed the course of three lives. Yet you couldn't blame Fen altogether for the destruction. He had simply been himself; it wasn't his fault that people envied, loved, or tried to possess him.

A door closed softly in the hall and Lucian moved gladly toward the living sound. Opening the door of the sewing room a little, he saw Wick standing in deep dejection, his face as painfully crumpled as his linen suit. "Ssst—" Lucian signaled, and when his brother came in, he closed the door behind him and asked, "Judith—?"

"Poor child, she's devastated. She'll be a long time getting over this—if she ever does. She takes things so hard."

They sat down and stared at each other. "What does she say about it?"

"Nothing . . . nothing. At least she won't talk to me. She feels I've taken Lorena's side. It seems I made a spectacle of myself at table just now."

"Oh, well . . . King David danced naked before the Ark . . . it comes over the best of men now and then. You weren't that bad."

Wick collapsed groaning into the big mending basket on the chest beside him. "God Almighty. I don't know how it happened! It didn't mean anything, actually—the girl just stirred up a vague something in me that I thought was dead, that ought to be dead, of course. Well, it's cost me Judith's affection and I wouldn't have had that happen for the world."

"Oh, that'll work itself out. Her worst problem is going to be how to live here in the town with Lorena and have to see her all the time."

"Maybe Etta and I could take her away somewhere; we were talking the other day about going to California to see the girls. I'll have to borrow the money. I suppose that rain has floated the cotton clean out of the fields. Look here—what in God's name are we going to do about the child?"

"The usual thing, I believe, is to put it on the payroll and leave it to the distaff side to bring up."

"I'd willingly leave it to August, but the thought of Vinny gives me pause. Poor little wretch. What sort of future has it?"

[2 4 5]

"A child does have a future, worse luck, and that's what hangs it about our necks."

They stared at the floor for a while.

Lucian crossed the room and applied his ear fleetingly to the door into the bathroom. "The battle of the Titans is still going on. They're shut up in the company room, the three of them."

Wick glued himself together and got up out of the mending basket. "Come on downstairs and help me get the rest of them out. I can't stand this any longer. I wonder where Tat took himself off to . . . he'd better come back and stay here with us for a while, I should think, until things have time to shake down. But God give me strength to keep out of that argument and let them settle their own lives. The harder I try to help my children with their problems, the more of a mess I make." They went downstairs side by side.

The group in the parlor was sitting in a mortuary silence. None of them, Lucian realized—not Etta, nor his mother, nor O'Dell, nor Janie—knew exactly what had happened, but there was a tightness in the air that made O'Dell twist his neck this way and that, and run his finger round his collar. Etta looked at Wick in anguished questioning.

"I'm afraid the bride and groom have had a—er—little falling out," he said. "Of course such things are to be expected, though it's rather early in the game. The only thing to do is to forget about it—in time we'll straighten it out."

Lucian caught the sparkle in his mother's eye. "I declare, it's most unfortunate," she murmured.

He took her by the arm and drew her into the dining room. "Let's break this up, Mother; you go home with Janie and get her and those brats out of the house."

"I prefer to go home as I came, with you and Judith."

"Judith—isn't ready yet. I'll wait and take her home. In the meantime you can clear the Catesbys out. Besides, you've made enough mischief here today to suit even your insatiable appetite."

The antennae in her little black hat quivered. "There's no reason for you to be disagreeable, Lucian. I only asked the girl a simple question—"

"And thoroughly messed up two marriages. That's a good bag, even for you."

[246]

"*Two* marriages?"

"What's happened is you've—" But a second thought flickered in his green eyes. "What happened is something you'll never know. Right here, under the same roof with you, things have gone on that would make the angels weep. But I never speak ill of the dead—as you taught me. Nor of the living. I'd cut my tongue out first."

She questioned him with a look, between curiosity and suspicion that this might be just more of his moonshine. "You'll never know that either," he said aloud and picked his way over to Janie.

"See here," he whispered sitting down behind her chair, "let's break up the obsequies and let poor Etta and Wick get some rest. Take Mother home with you, for God's sake, and get her out of here. I'll stay and run the others off."

"Of course," said Janie, susceptible to the flattery of being in his confidence. But she would only co-operate at a price, he saw. The single pale blue eye in her profile held out for some reward.

"I can't tell you the straight of it." Lucian spoke obscurely between half-closed lips. "Maybe they aren't married at all, maybe this has been a feast to honor adulterers. Then there's a suspicion Tat took the filling station payroll to go off on his honeymooner, that is—his hayride. And they do say she's got another husband in Detroit. But you and Mother can talk it all over on the way home," he added, and rising, pushed Janie toward the door.

As they gathered in the hall over their bleak farewells, footfalls thundered on the stairs. The Hessenwinkles came down with an imposing effect of solidarity. August rolled an anguished eye over the group below and was dumb in the clutch of circumstance. Vinny's black glance darted here and there on its private searching—perhaps for concealed weapons. Only Lorena was smiling. The green sailor was riding high.

"I swear, it's a shame we had to go and break up the crockery like this and spoil your lovely party," she told Etta with cheerful frankness.

Catching Wick's eye, August took a step forward. "Mr. Redcliff, I didn't know anything—" Finding himself ringed round with strange faces, silent mouths, he fell back a step.

Lorena ignored his interruption. "Well, I guess we all understand each other better now, and that's a good thing. If Tat comes back here, tell him I'm over home—"

Not a Redcliff had spoken. Lorena's bland front and the laws of hospitality double-locked their jaws. Fully aware of the ice that had formed in the hall, she used it daringly to skate toward the door. "Good-by, Mrs. Redcliff; thank you for a lovely dinner. Good-by . . . good-by . . ." Vinny closed in behind. "Glad to have met you-all. . . ." August followed in silence, his head low. Unable to be rude and unwilling to be cordial, Wick and Etta answered with silence.

Lucian recovered himself first. "I'll see them out . . . come along, Mother, Janie. . . ." He marshaled them out of the front door and down the steps. The three Hessenwinkles had already turned their backs on the big iron gate when he reached it. They walked along the sidewalk at a leisurely pace—a family group, dressed in their best, going home at the end of a Sunday afternoon.

Lucian packed his own group into Janie's automobile and sent them off to chew over the hash of fact and fiction he had mixed for them. Turning back, he took a moment in the flagged entrance to stretch his back and shoulders, stiff from tension. The high house was silent in the sad-colored evening. As he went up the steps he saw O'Dell, forgotten in the good-bys, come tiptoe into the hall. Etta and Wick had disappeared. Slipping closer, Lucian watched through one of the narrow window glasses that flanked the front door. O'Dell picked up his hat, and finding himself alone, came softly down the hall again, examining the house, the rooms, the furniture, with utter detachment on his long face, as if it were an empty set just cleared of a drawing room comedy. He tiptoed over to a table, helped himself to a cigar, smelt it, and put it into his breast pocket. Putting on the tan straw hat with the Persian band, he ducked out of the front door and nearly ran Lucian down.

"Oh . . . hello! I was just about to blow the joint. I guess there's nothing *I* can do. . . ."

Lucian wagged his head in a solemn negative.

"Well, I'll be seeing you." In his haste to be gone, O'Dell crossed the piazza in three strides. At the top of the steps, however, he halted and looked back. "By the way, tell your brother . . . about that timber deal I spoke of, we better just skip it." He gave Lucian a quick grin, the grin of a good loser, and ran jauntily down the marble flight.

Lucian came into the hall and, examining the house himself, discovered an odd look of otherness about it. The known wearing the strange . . . but the two not steadily co-existent, for in his keyed up state the look of strangeness and the look of familiarity chopped and changed, like images in water. Light, created next after God, pierced the prisms of the lamp which stood immutably on the hall table, and struck out new, quick colors; the sitting room in which he had sat and talked to Etta and Wick three days ago was surely another room, oriented toward a different future. How fast the future changed! And our directions, perforce, with it. . . . It was damnably unsettling.

The ponderous silence was broken by the sound of somebody blowing his nose. Lucian followed the clue upstairs and found Wick before Judith's door, afraid to go in. "Poor child!" he said to Lucian. "Somebody ought to be with her—she's so alone in the world; there should be some womankind to go to her now."

"Where's Etta?"

"Gone out to hunt for Tat. She'll never find him, of course."

"No," Lucian agreed, seeing Etta running about the town hatless and on foot; but it disposed of her for the present, and that was something. "Any signs of life?" he nodded toward the door.

Wick shook his head dolefully and sat down on the top step. His sense of guilt left his bones like macaroni. "Fen seemed so happy with Judith," he said. "I never suspected anything like this."

"Of course he was happy with her. He just wanted a little more than the law allows—even as you and I." Lucian grinned at his brother. Disturbed as he was, he couldn't help enjoying the discomfiture of his elder and mentor. "But woman's intelligence is curiously limited in these matters. Suppose I see what I can do with her. In any case, I'll take her home—if she wants to go."

He opened the door a crack, and hearing no protest, went in.

Book VII

SHE felt no interest in the opening of the door so she did not turn her head but went on looking from her armchair into the nearly dark garden.

"Judith, my dear—"

So it was Lucian. He switched on the light then switched it off again, hastily re-covering the nakedness of the moment with furry dusk. She heard him approach and stop near her chair, and the silence swelled and swelled until the walls seemed ready to burst apart. He had nothing to say, the clever, the glib Lucian. Well, she had nothing to say, either; the raging words that filled her head were for her dead husband, words she couldn't say to any man living.

Why did this have to happen? Why did Fen do this to her? His loving her now became the grossest deception. His tenderness through the last winter of his life . . . guilt! For he knew all that time about the child. She dashed the thought away as she had a dozen times in the past hour . . . once she drank the cup, once the knowledge took hold, it would finish her, she thought. And from within something strong and blind and witless fought the destroying reality back. If she had a child of her own she could have borne this better, but. . . .

At first she and Fen couldn't afford to have a baby; besides, in those days the exciting and perilous role of a young wife had absorbed her consciousness. Setting up a new home, adapting herself to the habits and tastes of another person had been enough; her mind and heart, she now remembered with astonishment, had been quite as virginal as her body. It was hard to believe she had ever felt strange with Fen. Then, as the first months of their marriage passed, Fen taught her to take pride in the natural warmth of her nature; certain impulses that had dismayed her in her youth were really assets in marriage, she discovered, and first fearfully then confidently she gave herself up to the headlong happiness of a relationship that satisfied all the complex of her demands and provoked new demands as it satisfied her.

It was during this period that the desire for a child began to play like a little horn through the concert of her happy emotions. She had even started a special bank account in her own name and felt quite solemn and maternal when she put money in it. How absurd we are . . . imagine a child, a being of immortal substance, beginning in a bank account, this act of creation preceding the seed in the womb. But she and Fen had not been entirely solemn about it, she remembered, they had joked about it in bed. "We have enough now for an arm . . . or a leg . . ." they had said, giggling together over this, their own most private affair. But just as Fen had been promised a promotion and the way seemed clear, she had had that illness. She who had always been perfectly healthy had picked up the virus somehow. It had been a mild case but a long one, with consequent worry, heavy expense, their love-life interrupted . . . how she begrudged that lost year! When she got well again her desire became more insistent; the bank account wasn't necessary, she told Fen—that had been a silly idea, they would get along perfectly well. So they had decided, feeling serious and important, to have a child . . . but nothing had happened. The doctor said not to worry, he could find nothing wrong with Judith. She should build up her health, get plenty of rest, gain ten or fifteen pounds. . . . And then Fen had died.

Lucian still stood there beside her like a gate-post. Now he said timidly, "Do you want to go home, Judith? My car is here—"

She stirred and stretched her stiff legs, frowning. "I suppose I have to go somewhere." But how to face the decision, when there was nowhere to go that wasn't dreadful. Stark walls shut her in. She blinked into the gray murk about her, thinking, this is the color of pain—why should I have to see it again? What have I done wrong?

Lucian erupted in a great gust of urgency. He fell on his knees by her chair and took her hand in both of his. "Judith! I'm sure Fen loved you. Don't doubt it!"

"Oh, Lucian—if you could only give that feeling back to me!"

"I'm sure of it," he repeated. "You must believe me. And yet—"

He turned away and gnawed his lip. "I don't want to give it back. I don't know that I *ought* to give it back. You've got to come out of that cocoon you've wrapped yourself in. Horrible as all this is, someday something had to tear it open. You see, Judith, it's morbid to cling to anything, even love."

"But love . . . is wonderful . . . and so rare. Why should you let it go? It's shallow and unworthy just to let yourself forget." She pushed him away, got up and walked about the room. But Fen didn't really love me, she was thinking; I never really had it. . . .

"Don't ask me why Nature is so ruthless." Lucian sat back on his heels. "But she doesn't mean us to keep anything for long. Mausoleums and mementoes are futile—clothes go out of style, photographs curl and get fly-specked. We are slugged on to make something new—bad things or good things, it doesn't matter. We have to make new lives all the time." How pointless. The slightly pedagogical turn of his thought was characteristic of Lucian, her critic and mentor, but he looked odd kneeling there in the halflight, unsure, in some way vulnerable . . . as she was. Everybody seemed different in the disorientation she was suffering. Watching him she thought with astonishment, this catastrophe has touched him . . . some experience I know nothing of makes him understand. . . . She pulled him to his feet and put her arm around him, thinking that she was being different, too, leaping over the natural reticence that made her shy about touching people.

He responded with a light pressure, gentle and comforting. Then she said, "Where is Tat? I'd like to see him."

"God knows. He went out somewhere. Poor devil. I can't imagine what he'll do now."

"Poor Tat." Her fierce preoccupation cracked for a moment. "How will he ever get over it?"

"Well, it will either make or break him. Either he'll grow up or. . . ."

There he went, talking all round the point again. "Don't you see, Lucian, what it's going to mean to him?" She turned her back and leaned against the chair. Couldn't he see what it meant to *her?* Fen had been a father with all the stirred deeps that state implied. He had had all those profound and transforming emotions and she, his wife, his partner, his other self, had been excluded. She and Tat. She said in a strangling voice, "Can't you see? They had a child!"

"So what, for God's sake!" Lucian sounded fed up. "They didn't *want* the child. They wanted a little fun—that was all. The child was the unwelcome consequence, poor brat. Fen never even saw it."

Judith spun round. "How do you know?"

"Lorena told us about it. It was born in Detroit about the time of Fen's death. She brought it home afterward."

A fierce satisfaction went through Judith. Then she bowed her head on the high back of the chair—how shameful to feel that way, how humiliating. What a horror life is—the awfulness, the triviality, the failure, the desire for a futile revenge!

After a while she straightened up and said, "We'd better go." She went over to the mirror, combed out her messy hair. Hairpins . . . ? Lost long ago, it seemed, in a faraway room where everything else had been lost. As she braided it into a long plait Lucian went into the next room and came back in a moment with two large bone hairpins filched from Etta's bureau.

"These are all I could find."

He handed them to her and she wound the braid around her head and pinned it on each side. "You look more archaic Greek than ever," he said, with a tentative smile.

She frowned at him; but he had found his tongue again. "A primitive, I should say; one of the charming place-deities you see in Attic sculpture. . . ."

You couldn't do anything with Lucian. Once his allusive mind got to spinning— She opened the door violently to cut him short.

Across the hall the door to the sewing room stood open. In the glare of the bright ceiling light a portly, long-hemmed figure dominated the small apartment, the cool room where Fen and Lorena had slept in summer. Miss Jinny appeared to have taken it back again after playing a doubtful hand in their lives. She had become a dress form once more.

Uncle Wick appeared from within and blotted out the view that had stopped Judith in her tracks. He looked at her, dumb, utterly reduced.

But Judith shed his silent appeal. He was no longer the Uncle

[253]

Wick she had loved and trusted. She had lost that wise counselor along with her husband and her hairpins. The warmth that had been his special virtue had betrayed him into mere susceptibility and flirtatiousness. She turned without a word and went down the stairs, holding carefully to the rail to steady her shaky step.

Lucian filled in the conversational gap. "I'm going to take Judith home." He lowered his voice. "Don't worry . . . I'll stay with her. . . ." As Judith reached the landing and turned, she saw Uncle Wick leaning out, his arms spread on the banisters, and watching her down the stair-well. His small rosy face and foreshortened arms hung against the ceiling like a fresco of a chastened cherub.

The lower floor was dark. Lucian caught up and hurried her through the forbidding hall, down the front steps and into his coupé. Beneath her perception of streets, a town, a world grown suddenly dull and harsh, she listened to his make-talk about the storm that had passed, the little breeze springing up, the sharp fragment of moon just cutting through the tree-tops. Her flesh felt stiff and painful, as if she had been in an accident.

Lucian, she had to admit, was rather touching. In front of her house he said, "Is Sarah here?" and when she answered, "No, it's Sunday," he seized her handbag and scrabbled through it for her latch-key. "I'll open the door," he said over his shoulder, speeding to get there first; he turned on the lights everywhere, he rushed about opening the windows and ran to let Rags out of the kitchen enclosure. The house as she went in glittered with speed and light.

"Let's have an old-fashioned. I'll fix it—you go upstairs and get to bed." Lucian sprinted off to the pantry, and in a moment she heard the cheerful racket of water rushing and ice rattling into the ice-tub. The idea of bed suddenly had a dragging appeal, but at the foot of the steps vertigo seized her; she leaned against the newel, helpless with mental and physical fatigue. Presently the dizziness passed; she pulled herself together and started up. For a while the intense effort of this step by step rise absorbed her mind and obliterated mercifully the cause of her distress.

The windows of her bedroom had been closed since morning against the threat of more rain. She crossed the floor to her bedside lamp, asking herself if this was to be her natural gait, to stumble through smothering blackness with her hands out before her. She turned on the light and fell across the bed and lay there, perspiration soaking the sheer white dress with the hand-made ruffles.

Presently Lucian came up, muffling his step as though he walked on bath towels. He set something heavy down on a table and went round the room raising the windows and throwing the shutters wide.

In a moment she heard his voice above her. "Here—sit up, Judith." He pulled her to a sitting position, dabbed at her face with his handkerchief. He brought her dressing gown and a damp washcloth and helped her to undress with the grave unself-consciousness of an old family servant.

When he had propped her against the pillows he held a glass to her lips. "Take a sip—"

The iced whisky stung as it slipped down, and with the curious power of alcohol to restore the ego, it gradually pulled her together again. Her eyes focused on the smooth planes of his famil-iar face, and beyond him she saw the supper tray he had set with the best china.

"Lucian, you're an angel to do all this."

Lucian bowed from the waist. "It's a great pleasure, ma'am." Now that she had come to herself, he began to cover his solicitude with a role. He set the tray on her lap, he flourished a napkin, he became the perfect stage butler. They both picked at the tray and gradually they passed into a kind of philosophic melancholy, in-duced by the food and drink.

"Why does pain go deeper, and last longer than pleasure? We pay so much for so little, somehow. . . ."

"Yes . . . that's why I'm always in debt. Even our second-rate pleasures come damned high."

"Yet we seem to want to go on living . . . millions and millions of people have always wanted to go on living in the face of hide-ous catastrophes and disappointments."

"Well, we never really want to die, however we may kid our-selves. The dregs of some sort of mildewed hope stick at the bot-tom of the bitterest drink. Which reminds me to have another small one. Will you?"

She shook her head. "I'm feeling better already. Thanks to you."

"What's the state of your guest room? I'm going to stay here tonight, in case you want anything."

"Oh, you mustn't do that—" But he overbore her protests, and she didn't care, really.

Lucian took the tray downstairs and washed the dishes. On his way back he stopped to telephone in the hall below. "Is that you, Mother? I called to tell you not to leave the lights on for me, I'm not coming home tonight. . . . Never you mind where. . . . It would certainly surprise you if you knew. . . ."

She got up to complete her preparations for the night and found that her legs were steady again. She went out for a moment on the second floor piazza and walked to the corner where it pointed toward High Battery. The harbor lay calm and self-sufficient, its surface glossy under the milky blue light of the half moon, but a raw little wind was springing somewhere and lifting her hair along her back. A terrifying sense of space upward seized her—an apocalyptic glimpse of her dwarfish place in the scheme of things. She, Judith Redcliff, was not the fortunate beloved, the beneficiary of miracles; she was one of innumerable wives dealing with the infidelities of innumerable husbands. She felt herself being rushed forward at immense speed . . . but how do you come out of an old thinking into a new one? You have to have something to live for; how do you find a new desire?

She had to rush on without the answer to this question, for the future blew hard in her face, past her ears, her hair streamed out in its cold gust.

"Are you all right?" Lucian asked anxiously from the door.

"Yes." She turned back reluctantly. "But—Lucian, there's something I've been wanting to ask you." It would be easier here in this half light. "Where is it?"

"Where is what?"

"The baby."

"Oh. It's farmed out with some relative. Over in Christ Church, I believe."

"Christ Church!"

"I think that's what Lorena said. Doubtless it's being raised a good little O'Dell."

"Good night," she said breathlessly, and closing the door in his face she went over and lay down on the bed.

It seemed to her that she didn't sleep all night but lay awash in black misery. When the light at last began to flow upward from the harbor's rim, she dressed and sat by the window until she heard the cook come in the gate. Then she went into the hall and was startled to see light streaming through the half-open door of the guest room. With her sandals in her hand she went noiselessly and looked in. Lucian had pulled a comfortable chair and a table near the door to hear her more readily if she called. He was fully dressed except for his coat, and an open book lay across his knees. His profile was turned to her, his mouth was ever so slightly open; he looked so himself, to the life, spouting a quatrain from *The Greek Anthology*, that it took Judith a moment to realize that he had fallen asleep. That was Lucian, she thought—the anthologist, the collector of curios of literature and humanity, the gourmet of sensation—sitting up all night to be with her if she needed him. Yet his being there in her guest room, with the lamplight and sunlight crossing, was part of the oddness over the house, of the macabre air in which he was holding a wake over a departed relative. Well, there had been a death in the family. Fen, she now knew, was dead.

Fiercely she drove back her fresh grief and went downstairs; she couldn't give up to it until she had finished what she felt impelled to do. She drank some coffee standing up in the kitchen, but she felt no need of food. "Mr. Lucian spent last night here," she told Sarah. "Give him some breakfast when he wakes up." Ignoring Sarah's astonished glance she added, "Tell him I had to go out early, to see a lady." That was rather mean, after all his sweetness to her; it would tease his imagination worse than he had teased Aunt Quince's. But it couldn't be helped. "Tell him I feel better this morning, and I'll call him later at the office." She went out and got into the car.

It was just eight o'clock when she stopped before the Fuel and Welfare office. Judith went through the gate and found the key in its accustomed place behind the morning-glory that bespattered the wall with its dark blue discs. Their royal color suddenly made a serene and positive declaration that heartened her in a world discolored by death.

She unlocked the office door and went straight to the case-file. Martin, Mims, Mozingo, Maguire . . . Mrs. Mary Maguire, Remley's Road, Christ Church Parish. She stared at the card in her hand as if it were hard to memorize; the stuffiness sang in her ears with a high mosquito whine. She put the card back in place, and going to her desk, took out a sheet of paper and wrote to Mrs. MacNab. . . . She wouldn't be at the office for a day or two . . . a bad cold coming on . . . she would be back as soon as she felt well enough.

From the store-closet she pilfered a can of powdered milk. Then she gave a searching glance about, but no tracks of her presence showed on the powdery silence of the room. She went outside, locked the door and put the note underneath. Then she returned the key to its flowered closet and got into the car.

She made a wide swing to avoid the Borough and turned east over the bridge that crossed the mouth of the river. The trains along the bank screamed self-importantly, a sailing ship with a foreign flag was easing out into the channel. At the top of the high span a breeze right out of the sun engulfed the car; Judith's body drank it in with a thousand parched mouths, and she made a sudden physical recovery that undid her resolution. I'm just being hysterical . . . what would I say to her anyway? It was a fantastic idea to trace down a passing resemblance. . . . There was no turning on the long bridge, so she slowly covered the last half, letting the wind cool her nerve-ends.

On the other side she felt self-conscious about turning back under the very eye of the toll-gate keeper and she drove a little farther. It was a delicious morning after the storm, and the country lay wide and sweet in its healing green. Then, unexpectedly soon, she came to the road sign. She threw out the clutch, the car rolled a little and stopped, the motor idling. She thought sensibly, now that I'm here, I'd better go on; not to know whether I've really seen it will be worse. . . .

She went along the sandy country road reading the letter-boxes.

That was the house, there. The white filigree of the porch looked reassuringly like a valentine between the green bouquets of two umbrella trees. But Judith sat on in the car, paralyzed with self-consciousness; all the excuses she had thought up for this visit now became the most transparent inventions. Her shyness swelled to huge proportions and clutched her by the throat. After a little the cruel hand seemed to relax; with a sort of spurt she got out of the car and went up the path between the candy-pink rows of phlox and verbena.

The slam of the gate brought Mrs. Maguire out on the small front piazza. She peered nearsightedly at the visitor. Judith said faintly, "Good morning, Mrs. Maguire."

"Why, if it ain't Mis' Redcliff! This is mighty early to be seein' you over here."

"Yes—I had to come over here anyway—and I just thought I'd stop in." Judith forced herself to go on and up the steps. "In summer I try to do my visits early before the sun gets too hot."

To her surprise this sounded all right and went down with her hostess. "Why, sure, that's sensible. Come right in and sit down, Mis' Redcliff, and lemme get you a cool glass of water. You look like the sun had blistered you some a'ready."

"Oh, that would be wonderful—" Judith flopped into a rocking chair on the piazza, grateful for the enveloping kindness and also for a moment to be alone. "It *is* hot."

Mrs. Maguire disappeared inside. From what Judith could see through the open door, the valentine effect stopped there. The room looked dark brown and smelt of kerosene oil. "Fine cotton weather," she heard herself saying politely.

"Fine cotton weather!" cried Mrs. Maguire in dudgeon. "I just wish you could a' seen our fiel's in that rain we had Sat'day. Them rows was running like Suannee River." She came back with the glass, and giving it to Judith, pulled up another chair. "Wasn't that a rain, eh? I never see sich a thing. . . ."

Judith laughed. "I'd forgotten about the storm for a moment. I do hope your crops weren't badly hurt." Something about this large, kindly countrywoman made her feel at ease.

While they talked about the storm, Judith wondered what Mrs. Maguire knew of the events of yesterday. Presently she hazarded, "You know the Hessenwinkles, don't you? What did you think of Lorena's marriage?"

"Holy Mary! You could a' knocked me over with a brickbat! I knew she was going with young Mr. Redcliff, but I never looked for this! I never thought to see the day that Vinny Hessenwinkle would get to eat dinner at Mis' Redcliff's!"

Her naïve delight was refreshing, and Judith said, "Mr. Hessen-winkle is such a nice man. My father-in-law admires him very much."

"Sure, August is fine. And good to his folks. He's made a God's plenty of money, too; but they're all born lucky, that family. Look at Rena, now—they're all gifted for landing on their feet."

The quarrel had not been reported then. Judith longed to ask what Rena was like but couldn't bring herself to discuss her. Besides, she now heard indoors the temperish cry of a child—a sign she had been waiting for ever since she had come. She made a supreme effort to speak naturally.

"Mrs. Maguire, how's the youngster you brought into the Welfare the other day? He was such a cute little boy."

"Jus' fine. He's a smart little dickens, but talk about *mean*—Lemme tell you what he did yesterday. . . ." She embarked on a long tale of infantile ruthlessness which she seemed to find vastly amusing, while Judith tried to school her dismay. Fen's child trying to kill a hound-puppy!

She managed to cut off the end of the story. "He didn't look so fine to me the other day; his skin isn't a very good color. Can't I see him, Mrs. Maguire?"

"Lordy, I ain't had time to get him dressed yet, Mis' Redcliff. I wasn't expectin' nobody this early."

"It doesn't matter about his being dressed. I brought him some powdered milk from the Welfare—he looked to me as if he ought to have more milk in his diet." Professional, but constrained, this sounded.

"You don't need to worry 'bout him gettin' enough to eat." Mrs. Maguire hesitated. Then she looked at the container in Judith's hand and appeared to think she ought to repay a favor with a favor. "Willie!" she called. "Bring the baby out here."

During the moment or two of waiting Judith's nerves screwed themselves up to such a pitch that the appearance of the child in the door was like a blow in her face. It stood there for a moment, its slightly bowed legs coming out of an absurd baggy diaper, and regarded her with sharp suspicion. Holding it by the hand was a wizened boy of sixteen or so, also bow-legged, who also searched her with small, curious eyes.

Judith's stagnant blood began to rush through her body again.

This *was* a wild goose chase. . . . Fool that I am. I had no reason to think that *this* was the child. For there was nothing especially familiar about the comical little fellow standing there. His coloring, his stocky shape, even the funny old-wise look on his plump face made no allusions to her life.

"He'yo, darlin'. Come to aunty." Mrs. Maguire stretched out a powerful maternal arm. The child considered her offer cautiously, then decided to exchange the wizened Willie for that stout bar of flesh. He took two or three steps over.

Mrs. Maguire drew him in front of her. "See—he's covered right good." She displayed his arms and legs. " 'Specially about the face. His people provide for him all right; you don't need to worry 'bout him."

"Still, his legs—" Judith had recovered her tongue, but the presence of Willie, who had obviously suffered from Mrs. Maguire's ignorance of the properties of cod-liver oil, shut off the lecture she wanted to give.

The baby, as if annoyed by these personal remarks, sat down suddenly on the floor and put his thumb in his mouth.

"Get up there, son—" Mrs. Maguire dragged him up by both arms. "You'll get your didy all soiled." As she let go with one hand to dust his rear, he went limp and sat down again and returned his thumb to his mouth. "You little devil." Good-naturedly Mrs. Maguire pulled him to his feet. "Stan' up like a nice boy and say howd'y do to the lady."

But he slipped through her large hands like a rubber hose. Never was such determined limpness.

"Aw, baby! Act nice now. Look at the lady come to see you."

The sound of spontaneous laughter was coming, Judith found with amazement, from her own lips. The innocent-scheming look on that little muffin face untied strings somewhere inside her. She felt suddenly weak with the release from strain.

The baby looked at her, and thoroughly affronted now, he let out a frightening roar.

"Sh-h-h! Ain't you *'shamed?*" cried Mrs. Maguire, dragging him up on her lap. But he wasn't ashamed; he screamed with redoubled energy and threw himself around. "Willie! Bring him a sugar-tit, quick!"

Judith hastily offered him a substitute, the container of milk; but

[261]

she knew the gesture was ineffectual as she made it. He slapped the can away between distracting screams and struggled to slide down the sloping lap on which he was pinned. So she made no protest when Willie came back with a well-used little bag and slipped it into the child's mouth.

As the sugary taste began to soothe, the screams stopped abruptly. The last two tears rolled down, his eyes opened round and blue. A ponderous and innocent merriment overspread his plump, pear-shaped face, startlingly familiar. The child, Judith saw, was the image of August Hessenwinkle.

"What's the matter, Mis' Redcliff? You look awful pale!" cried Mrs. Maguire. "Don't you feel good?"

"I feel all right—at least, I feel the heat, I guess," Judith stammered. "I didn't have much breakfast this morning, starting out so early. . . ."

"Well, why didn' you say so before! Lemme get you something right off. I always keep a pot of coffee on the stove."

"Oh, that would be fine—just a cup of coffee—it's so kind of you."

Mrs. Maguire hurried indoors, pushing Willie before her, and Judith was left alone with her discovery. A cold dew had settled on her body; she dried her face and arms with shaking fingers.

The child quickly forgot her presence. He looked about, sucking the sugar-tit with soft gluttonous noises. Having got his way about sitting on the floor, he forgot that too and began to pull himself up precariously by Mrs. Maguire's chair.

"You'll fall—" said Judith in a tight whisper. She leaned forward but she couldn't bring herself to touch his bare arm.

The child lumbered to his feet and began to run about the piazza, his diaper slipping further and further down over his rear. When he turned back in her direction the Hessenwinkle look had vanished from his face.

Judith lay back in her chair. Had she imagined it? Was this sheer hysteria? She looked hard at the child and thought she saw it again, but fainter now. The harder she looked, the less she saw it. And Mary Bonneau had said that day the child came to the office that babies at a certain jowly stage looked like old men.

Mrs. Maguire came back with the coffee and a plate heaped with cornbread and country butter. Food, Judith found, was what she needed; the coffee was like lye and boosted her immediately. She made a business of eating and drinking to recover her poise.

After a while she said, "What's the baby's name, Mrs. Maguire?"

"Michael Astor," said Mrs. Maguire without a trace of humor, "but we call him Red. That's his pet name."

The straight sandy hair showed scarcely enough color to suggest the nickname. Red. . . .

"Did you say it was your niece's child?"

"Well, no; but his mother is kin to me." An uneasy look came over Mrs. Maguire's simple, high-colored face—and this was not imagination. "His father was from off; but he's dead and his mother ain't fixed so she can keep him right now. So I'm takin' care of him for her till she can take him herself."

"He must be about two, isn't he?"

"Two years old this June." Mrs. Maguire spoke up promptly, feeling herself on surer ground with this simple inquiry.

Judith finished her coffee and said, "I understand he was born in Detroit."

"Yes'm; but I had him ever since he was two months old."

Mrs. Maguire looked away from the conversation. I'm distressing her uselessly, Judith thought, and she's so kind and simple. She let her glance rest on the child hanging on to the arm of Mrs. Maguire's chair and found that the shock of seeing him had weakened with repetition.

Suddenly Mrs. Maguire spoke. "I'll tell you how it is, Mis' Redcliff, I give this child a good home and I mind my own business. I don' know too much about him—to tell you the truth, I don' know exactly who his father was, but I think he was a feller from Detroit. Anyway, he's dead now and I don' ask no questions about what ain't my business."

It helped that Mrs. Maguire didn't know who the father was. Lorena had, decently, protected Fen.

She put the coffee cup down and smiled reassuringly. "Don't misunderstand, Mrs. Maguire; I'm not going to interfere in Red's affairs, or do anything about him at all. I only came by this morning because I wanted to see him and find out if he's getting the right food."

"Oh, he gets plenty of food, Mis' Redcliff; he eats everything—that child's got a stomach like a tin can."

[263]

"But he ought not to have everything; he ought to have more milk and lots of cod-liver oil. We've got to make those legs grow straight. Now, do fix this milk I brought and give it to him."

"All right, jus' as you say, but I'm tellin' you, he don't like milk, and if he don't like somethin' he ain't gonna fool with it."

"But you have to *make* him fool with it, you have to just keep at him until he learns to drink it."

"You never raised no children of your own, Mis' Redcliff, or you wouldn't talk like that."

Judith fell back; any allusion to her childlessness was apt to carry, in her mind, a hint of reproach. She said without conviction, "Well, I've had a lot to do with babies through my work at the Welfare—I love them—"

"This little devil is so cute you ain't got the heart to be hard on him. And then some children is jus' naturally mean and you can't do nothing with them."

"Well, don't give him fried foods anyway," Judith implored, getting up to go. "Thanks ever so much for the nice breakfast—it was a life-saver."

Mrs. Maguire picked Red up and came to the steps with her. "Don't you fret about Red, he'll be all right. I guess his folks will be sendin' for him soon now, eh, precious? Jus' as soon as they're fixed. . . ."

At the foot of the steps Judith turned and waved good-by. Riding high on Mrs. Maguire's full bosom, the child gave her a mature, triumphant smile as if he had personally put her to rout.

Judith got into her car and drove back to town.

As Judith drove back over the bridge Lorena was just waking up. Vinny came into her room for a moment in one of the shirtwaist-and-skirt models she wore when she was going out on business. Her hair was skinned up tight on her head. "You poor child—you mus' be dog-tired after all that ruckus yesterday. Well, you jus' sleep right on an' get your rest. I sent the children out, and Poppa's gone to the office."

"O.K., Momma." They exchanged smiles of deep alliance. A mutual partisanship no ruckus could shake.

"I'm goin' out awhile. I'm goin' to Mr. de la Marr's to see what

I can find out. An' lemme tell you, I'm jus' fit to give him a piece of my mind—"

"O.K. See if it's anything he thinks we can do."

When Vinny had gone Lorena sat up in bed, elbows on knees, and buried her head in her hands. It was hot already; after the front door had banged behind Vinny the stillness of the house was like a liquid. The events of yesterday trickled into her head again, and she tugged at her thick hair as if to shake them out. Loudest in her ears was August's voice last night. When they got home from the Redcliffs' he had given her a talking to; he had described her conduct to her in unvarnished terms. She was just a bad girl; she had brought disgrace on her family; she had shamed them before the Redcliffs—before Fen's people. August's honesty could be brutal.

But even that wasn't the worst. After supper he had sent all the children, including Lorena, upstairs, and started to work on Vinny. From her bedroom overhead Lorena could hear the mumbling sound—August's voice falling, falling, and never letting up. She had a confused instinct that his being a Lutheran made him like a soft hammer. Vinny's voice came sharp at first, then slower all the time. And at last a terrible sound—the worst she ever remembered. Vinny was weeping. This went on for a long time.

All through her trouble Vinny had been her stay. More, Vinny fostered the illusion that the baby had been an accident, the result of mysterious conjunctions in the untouchable heavens, and that her, Lorena's, responsibility was therefore negligible. August's indictment brought home to his daughter for the first time a conviction of sin.

Well, no use sitting round moping. Lorena got up. In the half-dark room she stumbled over Tat's suitcase, and its sharp corner stabbed her with a thrust that was more than physical. Funny how quickly she had gotten used to waking with him in the room. Why hadn't he come home sometime during the night? A bride of three days, deserted. . . . Her lip puckered childishly.

She dressed, made her face up listlessly and went downstairs. On the dining room table Vinny's Almanac and Astrological Tables lay open; she must have been checking up to be ready for Mr. de la Marr. Lorena left sidereal calculations pretty much to

Vinny, relying more on hunches herself, but suddenly she put out a panicky hand and seized the book. Calling to the servant to bring her some breakfast, she sat down at the table and leafed through it.

Sometimes the book read your character and sometimes it gave you good advice. She turned to the horoscopes for June and looked for today. *Unexpected journeys.* . . . But she had just got back from an unexpected journey, her wedding trip. If it had said that last week, now. She turned the pages and looked up her birthday. She didn't know what most of the stuff meant but one line she understood: *You are a loving and sacrificing parent.* She loved Red all right, but it was kind of hard, when he lived across the river and she hardly dared to go there for fear of being seen. So this wasn't much help either. If she had only been born the day before she would have drawn *Good fortune and happiness.* Oh, God—the scary thing was her luck might have changed! It was that fear that made her snatch at the Almanac. Or even if she had been born the day after; there it said, *Will acquire wealth.* It's better to be born lucky than rich, Momma always said. Still, if you couldn't be lucky it would sure help to be rich. She pushed the book aside and ate her cornbread, which had a gritty taste of failure and guilt.

The Almanac had reminded her of something she had entirely lost track of in all the excitement—the day of the week. Monday. . . . I might jus' as well wash out my underwear. She got up and hunted about energetically for her own soap-flakes which she kept hidden from the depredations of her sisters; but when she had found the box and shaken the flakes into the basin with the pink froth of rayon and lace, she began to feel blue again—she had expected to be giving these underclothes away to her younger sisters. Uncle Harry said she could take off a little longer from the office, he was so tickled about the marriage, and she had thought she would go this very day and get herself some cute things with Poppa's check. Now she superstitiously tried to un-think the plan. She rubbed the clothes in the suds, wrung them out, and went downstairs.

She went out under the shed in the back and set up the ironing-board there where it was cooler. The smooth to-ing and fro-ing of the iron, the gentle steam that rose began to take the kinks out of her a little. From time to time she looked uneasily across the backyard toward the irregular patch of brick that showed high up between the screening trees. She'd give her eyeteeth to know what was being said and done behind the Redcliff walls. Was Tat right there now, or had he gone off somewhere? He was good and sore, she knew; she wished he would come on home and give her hell and get it over with. She made up her mind not to talk back. Momma always said when a husband was good and sore it was just like they were some other times—they had somp'n they had to get rid of and you jus' as well let them, 'cause you couldn't go on with anything till that was settled. Well, her nerves couldn't stand this sort of thing either; let him come on home and get his soreness off his chest. Then they'd cool off an' settle down, like Momma and Poppa did.

When she had finished her ironing she put the clean clothes in her bureau drawer, moving with exaggerated indifference, with even a faintly martyred air, presumably for the effect on herself, since no other eye observed her. Then she put smoothzum on her hands and did her fingernails. The quiet of the house grew more oppressive. Never one to court solitude, she craved sheer noise in her present mood. She decided to dress and go out on the Mall where there would be something doing. Anyone going to or from the Redcliffs' would have to pass by. . . .

She took the short cut across the yard and went through the back gate which gave on the side street running along the Hessenwinkle and Redcliff properties. From the pavement she got a view of the two places standing back to back, with the Redcliffs' back gate—conveniently, it used to seem—near her own. A few steps brought her abreast of it; the garden within looked dappled and mysterious, as it used to in her childhood before she had learned her way through it. A fig tree sprawled near the gate; she went in a little way and stood shielded by the protective pattern of its ornate leaves. Garden and house were still as judgment day. It felt sort of funny to be at the back gate again, looking in like this. "Why do you want to live in a rented house when you have a house of your own . . . you and Lorena could have your own sitting room. . . ." For a moment she thought Etta's voice had rippled down from the high, silent windows, but it was yesterday that she had said that. And Lorena had felt secure and happy. She supposed Mr. and Mrs. Redcliff hated her now. The house routed up impregnable again.

Had her luck changed? Gooseflesh came out on her bare arms. Or had she brought this on herself by being bad? The daughter of August and Vinny stood in the broken shade, dizzy with double vision. A girl who was no 'count, like Poppa said, and a girl who was pretty lucky, and not too bad . . . the images joined, parted, overlapped, now one on top and now the other. . . .

She stood so fast in the clutch of conscience that she heard nothing until the hot breath of the car throbbed on her neck. She spun round to see Tat coming through the back gate. He went into low gear and roared by not three feet from her, giving her a hard astounded look through the window. He drove into the garage and shut off the motor; after a minute or two he came out and shoving his hands into his pockets, he walked rapidly up the brick path to the house, without a word or a look in her direction.

Surprise and mortification flamed in Lorena's face. She made for the street and hurried back to her own gate, her ankles turning on her high heels, in a blind instinct to feel her own base under her again. But the gray stucco walls of her house looked blankly at her, and she stopped short, remembering how she had just fled their hateful stillness.

As she stood uncertainly in the driveway she heard Tat's step on the sidewalk. In a moment he turned in the gate and came up to her.

"I was just going home to write you a letter." His voice sounded queer with the tight brake he was putting on his feelings. "I was going to let Bristol bring it over and get my bag. But since you're here, I guess I might as well say it."

Lorena opened her mouth to shout at him to get the hell out of her sight, but something in his appearance cut the ground from under her. The white suit of yesterday was anguished by wrinkles and stains; the strain and despair that lined his face gave it, unexpectedly, a boyish droop.

"O.K. We might as well have it out. Come on over here where we can sit down." She led the way to the far side of the fountain, where the solid bulk of the swan and the fleshy cannas made a hedge between them and the possible prying of the cook, and settled herself on a little promontory of cement.

Tat found a clear space on the comfortable curving rim. "I guess there's no point in our arguing—" he began, crumbling off small bits of August's handiwork. "But what I can't understand is—" He suddenly began to hurl reproaches down on her where she sat a little below him: "Why didn't you tell me all this? Why didn't you tell me the truth? That's what I can't forgive!"

"I didn't tell you any lies. If you wanted to think I was different than what I am, could I help that?"

"You didn't tell them, but you acted them—"

"Look-a-here, who did all the talkin' 'bout morals bein' silly? Who kep' on ravin' 'bout how dumb it is to be conventional?"

"That's not the same thing."

"Well, it looks the same to me."

"It's not your having an affair with—it's not the sex part I'm crabbing about; it's your deceiving me—your pretending to love me and hiding the truth—that you had had a baby—"

"When I had that baby you wasn't anything to me. I didn't cheat on anybody."

"Still, you could have told me."

"I was gonna tell you," Lorena admitted. "But I can't ever figure out how you're gonna take things—you're funny that way. So I thought I'd better wait till you came down out the clouds, sort of. Then you see, I had the baby to think of, an' I kind of thought it would be easier—that you wouldn't mind my bringin' him home, if it was your own kin. It seems to me you'd be glad to have your own brother's child—" She looked at him with honest inquiry.

But Tat, she saw, couldn't answer this simple argument. The muscles of his face were stiff; whatever violent refusals churned in his mind, he couldn't utter them. By main force he broke off a chunk of cement and hurled it into the dry bowl of the fountain where it ricocheted in a furious bombardment.

"We just think differently," he said after a while. "We never could get together, I guess, so the best thing is to just skip the arguments and get the parting over with as soon as possible."

The words fell, dry and final, like the stone in the fountain. What surprised her was she didn't feel surprise. "Yeah—I guess we never could make a deal."

"I'm going away somewhere as fast as I can, and find a job. I

[269]

won't have much money, of course, but whatever I make, I'll divide it with you until you can get on your feet. That is, if you care to take it."

As always Tat's clean contempt for money impressed her. Last night Vinny had let fall a remark, throwing out an anchor; no matter what happened, she had said, Tat would have to pay Lorena's support. It was the law.

She said thoughtfully, "Never mind. You don't need to worry 'bout me. I got a job. I can always get along." (She could never explain this decision to Momma.) "I didn't marry you for money, God knows."

"That's right. You didn't. But why did you? You don't love me; admit it."

The word love in Tat's mouth baffled her as always. She thought it over for a moment. "I know you're a decent fellow, Tat; your heart's as big as a house. But I don' know exactly why I married you, and that's the truth. It was partly I let Judith talk me into it, I guess—it burnt me up to have her goin' on like she owned the Redcliff family, when I knew you and Fen both . . . an' her havin' the name an' all."

This explanation sounded foolish as she said it because something was missing from its basis—her anger of yesterday against Judith. Now that she had told Judith everything, now that she was even, her anger had trickled out, she had forgotten it in the press of other grievances.

"So that's why you had that complex about Judith!"

"I guess I did have a complex. But it's funny—I don't hate her now. You kep' on sayin' we'd get along O.K. if we knew each other, an' it looks like you were right. Well, it's too late now; she hates me like poison ivy." It was sad, she thought; the breaks were just bad. With the best will in the world you couldn't change them. She went on, "But that wasn't the only reason I married you. I'm awful fond of you, Tat, honest I am, and women just set more store by bein' married than men—you know that. Then I wanted to get Red back. I'm crazy about him an' I thought I could work him in—I don' know how; but if you wait long enough you generally get the chance you're lookin' for."

"Yeah, it sounds like a perfect marriage—for everybody but me."

"Well, I don't expec' being married to be a picnic like you seem to. I've tried it before, you see."

"Being married to the woman you love isn't a picnic—it's heaven. I've tried it too—for three days."

They stared at each other speechless. Tat threw himself on her and began to kiss her; his lips seemed to sting her face and neck with his passion and despair. As if a shade rolled up in her mind, she saw a little what he meant by love, and what she saw shook her with panic. Because she couldn't give back this love that was demands and hunger and desperation—not to him, anyway. A sense of the tragedy, the misconceptions, the futility of human desires bore her down like the weight of his body.

She braced herself on the stone and held him maternally until the gust blew itself out.

"Oh, Rena . . . you don't know how it hurts to lose you!"

Lorena disengaged herself affectionately and wiped his face with her handkerchief. "You ain't losin' me, honey, you losin' somebody you dreamed up, an' I ain't her, if you know what I mean. The truth is we never would of made it, not in a hundred years. So le's jus' forget it."

"Forget it!"

"You'll forget it; you'd be surprised how fast you kin forget."

Tat got up. "So that's all it means to you. Well, I'll get my bag and be going." He walked angrily toward the house.

She let him go. It was better for him this way. It's easier if you are mad at somebody. Besides, she was busy giving up some things herself not easy to lose. Because Tat was a sweet boy, and lovable, a fellow with big ideas. And she wanted to be married, sure enough. And then there was the house. And the being a Redcliff. But rented apartments were nice, too; at least hers had been, with the good-looking stuff George Belchers had given her from the store. Then being a Redcliff seemed something different to what she had thought yesterday; in fact, she didn't exactly know what a Redcliff was . . . and in the end you'd best just be yourself.

Tat came back carrying his bag. "I'm going off somewhere," he said, "as soon as I can fix it up at the filling station. There are a lot of things I've got to get straightened out in my mind. I've made some mistakes—I suppose I was dreaming as usual—but you've got to dream to lift society out of the muck. I believe in dreaming—" he rested the bag on the fountain's rim and squared his shoulders a little—"and I'm not going to let all this shake my faith in a democratic world. I'm going to go right on working for it, but maybe in a different way."

Lorena didn't crack down as she usually did when he got talky. She didn't want to. She just said, "That's right."

"Well, good-by."

"So long, honey."

He went stiffly through the gate, carrying in the bag all traces of his presence in her life.

Lorena sat on by the fountain, her hair flaming among the canna lilies. The dribble of water from the swan's beak made a tiny sound in the quiet. For the moment she had nowhere to go. Neither today nor tomorrow offered anything. And what about Red? What could she do about him now? Cousin Mary Maguire was all right; but. . . .

Dinner was a glum affair. August's lectures last night seemed to have used up all the words he knew, and, to Lorena's relief, he didn't refer to her moral turpitude again. Vinny gloomed and glowered at her end of the table. Mr. de la Marr hadn't been a piece of help; and from her own account of the way she tore into him, Lorena wasn't surprised. Besides, she had decided that all that star stuff was the bunk, and she told Vinny so. The evidence against her beliefs being strong, Vinny resented this, so she gloomed and glowered.

When August got up from the dinner table he put on his coat and said, "I'm going over to have a talk with Mr. Redcliff and see how we can fix up this mess you-all have got us into."

Vinny accepted silently her partnership in guilt, but Rena answered up. "I've fixed up part of it a'ready and saved you some trouble. Tat was here a while ago, and we decided to split."

"You did!" The blue and the black eyes turned on her.

"I guess it's just as well you left, ruther than being asked out," said August.

"She's his lawful wife, August; he'll have to give her support."

"I don't want to take any of Tat's money, Momma. I can work and support myself."

"That's right, Rena," August said. "That's good sense. I don't want my daughter beholden to the Redcliffs. We can take care of ourselves. Well, I'm going over to see Mr. Redcliff anyway."

When he had gone, Lorena went to the telephone and called up Uncle Harry and told him she'd be back at work in the morning. She could tell he was doubled up with curiosity, but she put him off until she could get her story lined up. "Don't ask me no questions and I'll tell you no lies. And look-a-here—I want a raise."

This threw him back on his haunches. He sputtered and protested, but after a lot of back-talk, he said, well, maybe—he'd see. Whatever you could say about Uncle Harry, he wasn't mean.

This partial success made Lorena feel better right off. You could always pick up and go on if you set your mind to it. She went out under the shed and lay down awhile on the settee.

She must have been dozing when the telephone roused her. Vinny came to the door, with round eyes. "It's for you; an' I think it's Lucian Redcliff, I'm sure I reco'nized that scrawny voice of his."

Lorena took up the receiver. "Hel-lo?" she drawled, to let him know she wasn't taking anything off him.

"That you, Lorena? I'm over here next door, and we're holding a sort of parliament of all the best minds in the Borough to consider the problem in hand. Since the problem is mostly you, we thought you had better come over and give us your views—with your customary pith and picturesqueness."

"What the hell are you talkin' about?"

"Your father says, get the hell on over here."

"Well, why didn' you say so before? I'll be there toreckly."

She put down the receiver with a tingling in her feet and stomach. As she changed her dress and re-did her face, her fingers were all thumbs. Anyway, something was beginning to happen.

She didn't take the short cut this time but paced solemnly around by the side street and entered the Redcliff house by the front door.

Lucian came out and escorted her across the threshold. He looked as if he was having a swell time—at her expense—so she gave him back her special drawl with a little snarl in it. "Hel-lo, sweetheart. Who asked you to the hangin'?"

Lucian grinned appreciatively. "They always ring me up first thing—hadn't you noticed that? It's my invaluable detachment."

[273]

What gave the conclave a solemn look was that they were sitting widely spaced about the dining table. As Lorena came through the door Tat and Mr. Redcliff got up; Mr. Redcliff said, "Howd'y do—" very formally. Poppa had his notebook out; he gave her a nod and got ready to write something down. Mrs. Redcliff wasn't there; Mr. Redcliff explained she had a bad headache and was lying down, but this didn't take Lorena in.

She sat down on the chair pulled out for her before she realized that it was the same one . . . it gave her a creepy feeling, she hadn't counted on sitting where she had sat yesterday, but with everything so different. The white tablecloth was gone; the shiny patches, the somber depths of the wood looked tricky, nothing solid you could lean on; as she put her elbows on the edge she half expected them to go through.

The surface of the moment was tricky too; they all skated fast not to go through to the black ooze of the truth. "Cigarette?" "Thanks." "Anybody got a match?" Much clapping of coat pockets, then two were held out toward her, their flames slipping like fox-fires through the lightless depths of the table.

Wick gave a deep sigh and went at it. "We were sitting here talking about what could be done to straighten out the situation. It's tragic and complicated for everybody—for you and your parents, as well as for all of us. But we must try to arrive at some solution which will be endurable for everyone. Have you anything to suggest?" He looked directly at her with a sort of hope and appeal.

The look unnerved Lorena. The situation rose up threatening, it towered over everybody, she hadn't thought of it just that way before. She felt her ears and neck growing red as she sat there silent under Mr. Redcliff's gaze. He went on.

"My son says you have agreed to separate. Are you both sure that is what you want?"

Lorena looked at Tat. He sat sidewise with one elbow on the table and his chin in his hand.

"Yes," he said obscurely through his fingers. "It's the only way."

Lorena nodded and said, "Yes." When she had said it she felt a kind of relief.

"Well, does that mean you want a legal separation? It isn't a very

[274]

satisfactory arrangement, but perhaps the best that can be made."

Lorena began to feel as if she were in a courtroom. She looked at August but his full, smooth face gave her no help. His pencil hovered—he was going to get everything down in writing.

"For God's sake . . . I don' know!" she burst out. "Don't you-all rush me."

"Nobody's trying to rush you, Lorena," Mr. Redcliff said patiently. "We're only trying to find out what you want. You should take ample time to think it over before you decide."

She wished he wouldn't be so patient. So kind and polite. She'd get on better with these folks if they'd bust right out and say things, instead of being so damn kind.

August tucked his pencil behind his ear, and Lucian spoke up. "While you're thinking that one over there's another question that's rushing *us*. What are we going to tell the dear public? They won't wait."

Tat made a convulsive movement. "It's none of their damn business—"

"So it isn't; but you've got to tell them something, and we'd better get together on the story."

"Besides us five," said August, counting on his thickset fingers, "only Mrs. Hessenwinkle, Mrs. Redcliff, and Miss Judith know the facks. Now we all got a good reason for keeping our mouths shut, so the secret ought to be safe—safe as any secret, that is. But what you gonna tell people was the cause of the split?"

"Well, we can say we fell out over religion. That's true in a way; Tat and I never could agree about religion."

"It's hard," August said, his full face sagging a little, "when you start off with a different religion. Mrs. Hessenwinkle and I, we made it somehow; but it makes a difference in more ways than you'd think."

Lorena stared at him. Certain tensions, certain hardnesses, certain family quarrels, she began to realize, had all been part of the same quarrel, the bedrock Lutheran-ness of August in conflict with the lush Catholic-ness of Vinny. It had gone on and on in the house. . . . Poppa was a sort of sad man. They were all looking at him as if they saw way back into his sad life.

Lucian, as usual, covered over the awkward moment. "Well, we can say it was religious differences, or incompatibility, or a divergence of taste in breakfast foods. The more explanations we give, the more they'll be confused and miss the real one."

"It's all mighty funny to you, isn't it?" Tat turned on him with scalding bitterness. "You're going to have the hell of a good time out of this."

For once he put Lucian to rout. "I didn't mean anything," he expostulated. "I only meant—that is—people are going to garble whatever we tell them, so we might as well have the pleasure of garbling it ourselves." But he said this to the air because Tat had rushed out on to the piazza.

"Come back, Tat," his father called, his voice edgy with parental irritation; "let's try to get somewhere while we're all here together. You and Lucian can settle your vendetta some other time."

But August smiled sympathetically and said, "Leave him go out and cool his head off. He'll come back presen'ly."

"He's always slamming out of the door," said Lucian crossly. "It seems to relieve his mind."

"Well, while he's out we might take the opportunity of talking about the child." Mr. Redcliff sat back, folded his arms and blinked at the ceiling. He looked like a white owl, Lorena thought, wanting to giggle. "What sort of person is Mrs. Maguire?"

"She's loyal to us, all right," Lorena assured him. "She won't spill any beans."

"I meant—is she a good person to bring up a child? We have to consider the baby's future; that's perhaps the most important thing we have to decide."

"They're kind of shif'less," August said.

"I suppose you can't keep him with you, Lorena, though that would be the most desirable thing, of course."

"Not without people would find out about him," said August. "And you don't want your dead son's name bandied about. Besides, it's no fair for Rena to get all the blame."

"Certainly not," Wick agreed hastily. "Some arrangement will have to be made that protects her. I'll assume his support, of course, in Fen's place. Whoever takes him, I'll make him an allowance—"

August wet his pencil and got ready to write. "How much would you think of giving him?"

"I hardly know what it will take—" Wick glanced uncertainly at Lorena. "Have you any idea—?"

Lorena wished for Vinny, she'd have an idea, and quick. "I don' know exactly, I'll have to find out."

August put the pencil back behind his ear.

"It'll depend a little on how he's brought up," Lucian observed, "on the style to which he's going to become accustomed."

"I say bring him up plain. No use to put notions in his head. He's gonna have his way to make."

Lorena frowned at August to shut up. She didn't want Red brought up too plain. After all, he was half Redcliff, and he might as well cash in on his assets. He was gonna have a tough time, poor kid, as it was.

"I'd ruther have him somewhere different than Cousin Mary's, if I could. We jus' put him there because it was the bes' place we could find." Where Poppa'd never see him, the truth was.

"If we could only find some good family to adopt him legally, that would be the best solution, probably. Perhaps Judith can find one through the Welfare."

"Of course I'm neither a mother nor an injured wife," said Wick, "but to me the best solution is for Judith to adopt him."

"Not if I know it!" Panic seized Lorena . . . they were fixing to take Red from her somehow, she could see that.

Wick ignored her outburst. "She could do it so easily through the Welfare—without any scandal. Judith needs something to interest her the worst way in the world. And the child could have his true inheritance."

"It's too reasonable," August sighed. "Women just couldn't do anything so sensible."

"Sensible, hell! Lemme tell you-all something: this child's got a mother even if he ain't got any father. Jus' gimme a little time —I'll take care of the both of us. And in case you think I can't do it, I'll tell you something else. I jus' got a raise in my salary. Half an hour ago."

It wasn't quite true, maybe, but it made her feel good to say it. And it brought looks of surprised admiration to their faces. Then August said, not unkindly, "How you expec' to make your way with a kid you can't explain hanging round your neck?"

[2 7 7]

Her heady emotions took one of their wide swoops. She covered the descent with bravado.

"Never you mind. I'll be moving soon to a little place of my own. An' you can all go lay an egg."

"That's right, Rena." Tat had come quietly in from the piazza. "Now you see what I mean when I talk about keeping your independence. It's the most important thing. And all this just goes to show how silly this marriage business is. If we hadn't gone to that priest, we could just part and let it go at that. Of course—if you'd go to Reno, it would still be fairly simple."

"Not so simple," said Wick, "because her church wouldn't sanction it. A civil divorce would free you without freeing her, which is hardly fair."

"You don't have to tell me that. We're messed up in a wretched marriage by a moss-backed code, religious and legal. I'm just saying that it's crazy we can't get clean away, since we both want it."

No one had an answer to this "theory" of his, and he took advantage of the silence to go on. "Well, it doesn't matter to me, actually; I'll never stick my neck in the noose again, that's a safe bet. I'm going away—I'm going to get out of this atmosphere of conventions based on materialism. I should think you'd want to clear out too, Rena, and get away from the mob and their crawling curiosity, the prying questions—"

A note had crept into his voice that made Lorena feel edgy. "Where's the mob? I don't see so many people that give a damn what happens to me."

"You're tougher than I am. I can't take it."

"I sure am, baby. Why don't you toughen up a little?"

Mr. Redcliff said, "I'm sorry Tat feels he has to go away. Going away never settles your problems; you have to stay with them and work them out. He has responsibilities here, to his partner in the filling station; and his mother and I—with all our other children gone—" He looked dolefully at Tat; it surprised Lorena to see how much he minded Tat's wanting to leave them. He sighed and went on. "But of course I can see how difficult you'll find it, living so close to each other. It will be embarrassing for all of us—to have to meet all the time."

This possibility hadn't bothered Lorena. Jeepers creepers—these people must really think she was poison ivy! Her chair screeched over the bare floor as she jumped up. "If this is all you got me over here for, I'll be goin' along. I had about all the talk I need for today."

Mr. Redcliff got up hurriedly. "You mustn't feel that way, Lorena. I only thought we ought to try to get some picture of the situation—"

August put up his unused notebook and pencil with a gesture that expressed their common frustration. "We got a picture of the situation; too much yeast in it somewheres—" he looked somberly at his daughter. "It's just like you sometimes turn out a batch of sour bread."

He dusted his hands softly together to brush off the remembered flour.

The two people who should have drawn closer together after the debacle unfortunately couldn't bring themselves to meet. They could not have spoken of their common disaster, nor could they have ignored it. Tat sent Judith an affectionate message to call on him if he could do anything for her, and she sent back a grateful reply saying there was nothing at present.

The elder Redcliffs telephoned daily, but tactfully kept away. To casual friends and to Mrs. MacNab she maintained the fiction of a bad cold and sore throat which secured her privacy for the time being. Yet her solitude was hideous to her. Some days she stayed in bed because the muscles of her game leg locked, as if to afflict her with the illness she feigned. She talked incessantly to herself, or rather to Fen's shade, heaping reproaches on him for the wound he had dealt her. . . . Faithless! she cried, in this whispering speech. You were faithless to me, and what is worse, to love. You betrayed the one-ness that we built up through those years—that's what I can't forgive! And all the time the knowledge shamed her that grievances are ugly and repellent; even had Fen been alive, reproaches would have been futile. But reason blew about like a feather in the tropical gust of her bitterness.

The shade of Fen, she noticed, was curiously damaged. Without the over-ripe color her dreams had supplied, he hung about bleached and a little shamefaced. This deflation gave her a wicked satisfaction. Her own passion seemed to her now a murky, female absorption, humiliating to remember.

[279]

The only person she saw was Lucian, who came often to sit by her bed and tell her the news of the town, which seemed to be going on with its trifling existence. The making and breaking of the marriage had rocked the parlors from High Battery to the Borough; Lucian was making a collection of the rumors and theories the catastrophe bred. Aunt Quince had a new idea for breakfast every morning; they grew more fantastic as the days passed. Ignorant of Judith's part in the drama, she accepted the story of the sore throat and sent custards and jellied soup to keep her favorite's strength up. Stuff a cold and starve a fever, she wrote, via Lucian, scorning his reminders that doctors had long since abandoned that adage. Doctors, she said, only gave you theories nowadays, but no doctor earned his fee unless he gave you physic to make you better. And she added some lozenges and a bottle of Dr. Pizo's Pine Tar Syrup to the tray.

Judith ate the jellies and passed the physic on to Bekah who shared Aunt Quince's faith in pills and potions. Actually, Lucian's nonsense did her more good: High Battery had it, he told her, that Tat had discovered on his wedding night that Lorena's first husband was still alive. On the Mall it was bruited that Old Lady Redcliff (meaning Aunt Quince) had threatened to cut them all off from the Redcliff money if Tat and Lorena didn't break up pretty quick. Manya Turner was awfully disappointed about it; she couldn't help telling Lucian she felt sure the Redcliffs (meaning Wick and Etta) were at the bottom of it; if they had just let Tat and Lorena alone, everything would have worked out. Lucian couldn't help replying, with a deep inscrutable smile, that she was right as always; the Redcliffs *were* at the bottom of it—six or seven of them. What he was still trying to figure out was, who had come out on top? Judith listened, diverted in spite of herself; when he had left, the solitary hours to which she saw herself condemned fell on her like great round stones.

One morning Mr. Redcliff called her on the telephone. "How are you today, Judith? Do you feel well enough to see me for a few minutes?"

Judith couldn't command her voice to assent at once. Meeting the reproach in her silence, he explained, "I've had a letter which really concerns you, and I don't feel that I should answer without your seeing it."

"A letter?" she said faintly. "Who—?"

"We can't very well discuss it over the telephone. I'll have to bring it to you."

"Yes, of course; come . . . whenever you like."

She got up and tried to dress. A frenzy of agitation seized her, her game leg refused to hold her weight. The thought of having to speak of her humiliation utterly disorganized her, and yet . . . a letter about her . . . written and read . . . without her knowing. . . . She called Sarah to help her into a dressing gown and onto the sofa.

Uncle Wick took his time to come—or so it seemed. Following his ring, his step sounded on the stairs—reluctant, delaying. When he came into her room they met with mutual shock, like friends parted for long who find each other distressingly different. He came over and kissed her in silence, then walked about the room for a minute, playing with his Panama.

"I hate to disturb you, my dear—I would rather have waited until you felt like sending for me—but time presses and I must answer this letter." He pulled up a chair and sat down by her. Hesitantly he took an envelope out of his pocket. "It's from Lorena."

She held it for a moment in her hand. Tan note paper with a brown border. A slanting back-hand with looped capitals.

Dear Mr. Redcliff,

Since the other day I have been thinking a lot about the matter, and I guess God just doesn't mean me to have Red. So I've changed my mind, I had to. If Judith will take him, I'll give him to her. Cousin Mary says she already went there to see him. I want him to have a good raising like Fen had. Otherwise will you please pay the money to Cousin Mary to keep him, like you said.

Because I am going back to Detroit to live with my aunt, then Tat won't need to leave his business just when it's going good. I'm sorry I made all that trouble, but I didn't know when I started it was going to be so bad. I guess Judith will be good to poor little Red—Lord knows he isn't to blame. She's got everything she wants, she can afford to let him have some.

Yours,
Lorena Redcliff

Judith put the paper quickly back into his hand as if it might stick to her somehow. "I couldn't possibly do it, Uncle Wick, it's out of the question—"

"I didn't for a moment imagine you would," he agreed, too hastily.

"You know I couldn't have that child here in the house! Staring me in the face every day—"

"Of course not. But I couldn't undertake to refuse without consulting you. And in fairness to Lorena I should add this: it was my idea, not hers. Last Monday we all got together and had a talk, Lorena, her father, and ourselves, about what to do with the child, and it seemed a good solution—both for you and for him. But Lorena didn't want to give him up then; and anyway, nobody takes my schemes seriously."

"Lorena apparently did."

"Well, I expect Lorena has done some hard thinking since, poor child. She's got her way to make in Detroit, and being a realist, she's seen the handwriting on the wall. I must admit it would be a wonderful solution for us if she would move away. Tat oughtn't to drop his business just as they were planning to expand it, and he's beginning to see that for himself. Tat's coming out of this all right. He's ripening."

"I hope he'll stay."

"But my God, how will we all go on living here—in a town of this size? It's damn decent of Lorena to offer to be the goat."

With a violent effort, Judith said, "Yes, it is—damn decent."

Uncle Wick leaned over and pressed her hand. "However, that leaves Red more than ever in our laps. We can't just do away with him—rub him out, is the new word, I believe—"

"Oh, no!"

He laughed at her serious face, and suddenly it was like old times again, her being literal and his laughing at her about it. She colored and smiled. "I mean—he's got to be taken good care of."

"Exactly. He's going to grow up into something, *what* seems to depend on us. It's a responsibility that Fen has unwittingly thrust upon us." He looked at her from under his eyebrows. "I'm not satisfied to leave him with that Mrs. Maguire. He ought to have a better home—"

"Oh, he should, Uncle Wick! I know he's not being given the right food, his skin looks sallow and he's getting bow-legged—it's terrible."

"Would you mind telling me how you happened to go to see him?"

It was easier to speak of it now. Judith said, "I'd seen him coming to the Welfare with Mrs. Maguire, and when I found out about—about him, I put some things together and got a hunch he might be the child." Uncle Wick nodded to show he was following her. "Once the idea came into my head, it began to haunt me. I had to know—if it was really Fen's child that I had seen. Uncle Wick, he's like Mr. Hessenwinkle. That helped a lot—that he isn't like Fen."

Uncle Wick smiled and patted her knee. "That does help. And he could do much worse than be like August Hessenwinkle. In fact, if he's going to take after either of his grandfathers, he made a good, hard-headed choice."

But Judith wasn't listening. She snatched up the letter and read it again, searching its implications. "What does she mean—I've got everything? When she took it from me!"

"Well—not everything. Not Fen's name. Not his home—"

"But he wanted her! And that's what matters."

"From the outside looking in, my dear, it doubtless seems that the wife has all the grappling irons. The whole business of living ties a man to his wife; even dividing his income with her, paradoxically, fastens him tighter. And what did Lorena get from Fen? A little passion? A rope of sand! The most unpredictable of qualities—"

"Oh, yes, I know— Well, spare me the rhetoric, if you don't mind. And you're a fine one to talk about unpredictable qualities."

"Yes—exactly. I am a fine one to talk. I can tell you a lot about them." He smoothed his cowlick self-consciously but his lips turned up slightly at the corners, giving him an air that was both pious and puckish, an imp in good standing. "But then, everybody says I talk too much. Even you. Well, I'll be going along. Think over the problem of the boy and tell me what we ought to do. Lorena has faced it with courage and generosity. She's got nerve —that girl." He flung out his hand in a gesture of farewell that oddly suggested the throwing down of a glove.

[2 8 3]

Judith seized his outstretched arm and buried her face in his coat-sleeve. "Uncle Wick—don't go away!" A fear of being alone took hold of her that was violent and childish; she saw herself so reduced, so vain and purposeless that her self-love revolted.

He disengaged himself. "I have to go sometime. But I'll come back—"

The open door swallowed him and she was left with the tearing conflict he had loosed in her.

After a while she went to the telephone and called Lucian. Lucian was out, Aunt Quince said; running about town as usual. "Of course he never lets *me* know what he's up to, but he's out a great deal. And how are you feeling, darling?" Judith cut her short and tried his office, but only the unhopeful periodicity of an answerless ring came to her ears.

It struck her with unpleasant surprise that Lucian had a life of his own, friends, women perhaps, who occupied his time. An obvious fact—one of those things you seem to know until one day you find you don't. Whatever his interests were, she resented them; they took him away from her and left her to walk up and down her piazza all evening to face alone the thing that Uncle Wick had called Reality. What mysterious forces about us keep throwing us on the spear-points? She was not far at this moment from Vinny and her faith in the meddlesome ways of the zodiac.

The next morning she called Lucian again. It was noon when he got to the house, bringing a bright, hot whiff from the streets in with him. He'd been out showing houses to a client who didn't know what she wanted and had run him ragged while she found out. Women exhausted him, he said, and went into the kitchen, from which he emerged presently with two cups of coffee. "May I—?" He took off his coat and hung it on the back of a chair.

She couldn't seem to break in on his solid preoccupation with the everyday; her anguish of the night before was in another mode, it would sound shrill in the morning of Lucian's thoughts, he would find it artistically bad. And she was feeling a reaction today, she didn't especially want to be stirred up again, she found; so she only told him, without comment, about her visit to Mrs. Maguire's and Lorena's letter.

Lucian's eyebrows went up. "I thought that was a rash idea of

[2 8 4]

Wick's." He considered it thoughtfully for a few minutes. "Well, I feel sorry as hell for Lorena, but there's really nothing she can do except give Red to somebody. And we do owe him a hand up, after all—but for Pete's sake, Judith, don't take this on from any love of self-sacrifice. I know you—you'll get into a dither of mothersome sentiment when you ought to be looking at the thing sanely. From what you tell me he's got personality, and that means he's going to be a handful to bring up. You've got to think about that."

His realism affronted Judith, but she couldn't help laughing. Beyond this he wouldn't advise her—he didn't want to discuss it, she saw, and he went back to talking about his business, which with him was intensely personal . . . people and houses. Presently her mind went between his commentaries to wonder if he was good at his job, what really occupied his thoughts, if he had been in love with Amy Matthewson, as Etta suspected. Then she lost even this thread . . . her cigarette tasted good with the coffee; the cups on the lacquer table made two perfect and comforting circles; the sun came in the window and begat a little sun in the bowl of the silver spoon. The noontide seemed to sweep through the house, slow and lulling.

Lucian was grooming Rags whom he accused her of neglecting grossly. "I take much better care of Joseph, but you dog lovers are the fanciest breed of all. . . ." Closing with the usual aspersions on Rags' ancestry, he got up to go.

Judith stretched lazily and swallowed a yawn. "You were an angel to come, Lucian. It did something for me, just to have you sitting around—" She got up, too. "I wish you didn't have to go. There should be some way you could have a man you're fond of live in the house."

"There is. In fact, most women do, one way or another." He took her in his arms. "I could arrange it," he said, and kissed her.

When she got over her surprise she saw that Lucian looked a little startled himself.

"Idiot! I wasn't thinking of marriage. I've heard of that, too."

"I didn't say anything about marriage. How you jump down a man's throat!"

"Oh, so it's that kind of proposal—"

"Well, I'll settle for marriage, if you insist. You're the kind that holds out for it."

She pulled away from his detaining hand. "Lucian, you're a darling—but I couldn't. I'll never love anybody but Fen and there's no use pretending."

"But Fen—" He halted.

"Yes, that's true—Fen didn't feel that way, apparently." She sat on the arm of the sofa and looked down at her sandals. "Still— I'm that way and I don't want to change; I don't want to give up my love. Maybe I'm being a fool . . . maybe it's just that I don't want to give up my grief—" She glanced up at him in dismay.

Lucian's face, she saw, didn't deny the allegation. She thought it over in a long silence. Then she said, "Lucian, it won't do— about us, I mean. Whatever the reason may be, I could never love anybody the way I loved Fen."

"Good God! I don't want to be loved *that* way. It would scare the daylights out of me!"

"You're simply infuriating! There's only one way to love."

"Oh yes? Well, you'd be surprised, ducky. There's a lot I could teach you. . . ." He leaned over, took her face in his hand and held it up to his intent gaze.

The significance in his words sent a trouble surging through her that was smothering and yet, as it passed, faintly ingratiating. She pushed him away. "Honestly, Lucian—it won't do. I'm sorry."

Her embarrassment infected him for a moment. He said sulkily, "You're probably right." He looked so unlike himself, so dashed, that she leaned over and kissed his cheek lightly. "And don't kiss me in that maternal way." He rubbed it off. "It doesn't do a thing for me—at least it doesn't do what you think, what you'd consider legal. Well, I must admit my timing wasn't very good; I should have waited a while. Timing is important whatever you're trying to sell. The truth is I need some time on this myself; your suggestion of marriage is a new idea to me. I'll have to consider it sanely—from every angle. . . ." He went away, covering his dismissal with verbiage which he carried above and apart from his person like an umbrella.

Judith stood in the middle of the room and closed her eyes. Everything that happened these days was incredible.

She opened her eyes again. In their immediate line of vision

Lucian's coat hung on the back of the chair. More than any words the coat revealed the extent to which he had been moved. Imagine Lucian—dashing coatless into the street!

She waited a few moments for him to come back and get it, but self-consciousness prevented, apparently. She took it on her arm and went upstairs smiling.

As she got ready for her midday dinner she glanced occasionally at the coat where she had thrown it across the bed. It gave a sort of look to the room, a new decor. Before the mirror she frowned at the image there; her hair was a sight and she combed it out, wishing she'd fixed it before Lucian came. She twisted it into a neater knot, then she changed her mind and made two long braids which she wound about her head; she leaned toward the mirror, turning this way and that, trying out the archaic Greek effect.

Ten days of blistering heat followed Lucian's visit. Everybody cursed the thermometer except Uncle Wick, who perspired fluently in maintaining that this was a splendid summer climate . . . right on the sea . . . and anyway it was fine weather for cotton, the crops were recovering from the storm, the outlook was most promising. Then the wind shifted, and for two or three days everybody talked even more incessantly about its changing cool, they were nearly blown out of their beds. . . .

Judith came hurriedly down into her living room and bowed the shutters; a strong east wind flattened them against the outside wall and she had scarcely enough force to haul them in. Her lame leg, which had limbered up miraculously in the last few days, felt weak again, she could scarcely brace herself to pull the heavy blind. But it was just nervousness, she realized; actually both legs felt weak tonight, her knees went to water at the prospect of having to face Lorena.

She turned on the lights to hurry away the last strays of daylight, for they wouldn't come until darkness protected them from curious eyes. The adoption papers lay on her desk, signed by her at the lawyer's office. But at the last minute Lorena had refused to go to the lawyer's to sign, apparently regretting her bargain; and Judith, having brought herself step by step to the acceptance of the child, now drove to and fro in a frenzy of nerves at the thought that he might be snatched from her.

"Snatched from her" was the phrase she used as she straightened the room to prepare for the visitors—as if Red were her child already and threatened with kidnaping by unlawful persons. Lorena had, to be sure, consented to come here tonight and sign the papers. Luckily the hot spell had hastened the Turners' departure for their summer vacation and the house was as fine and private a place as the grave for the meeting. Wick and August had gone huffing and puffing between the two principals like a pair of old-time switching engines, arranging the details. But what did these two know of the unprompted pull, the ache for possession, the knife-blade rivalry. . . . In spite of the crib upstairs, the extra milk in the refrigerator, the closet of toys (provided by Aunt Quince) Judith walked the floor with a dread in her heart that wholly obliterated from memory her first horrors and retreats from this very step. . . .

The sharp *ting* of the door bell stung her flesh. Wildly she wished she'd asked Lucian to come—he'd know how to talk to everybody—even Red! Now she'd have to face them alone, and serve her right. The first voice she heard, however, gave her reassurance; Mrs. MacNab was shepherding them along the piazza with eager, kindly clucks.

They had had to let Mrs. MacNab into the secret, at least to the extent of telling her that Lorena was the child's mother. "I always knew you were a fine girl, Judith," she had said glowingly. "It's like you to take responsibility—to take this poor little thing and give him a home." Her solemn approval embarrassed Judith, who couldn't possibly have told by this time whether her motives were good or bad; but Mrs. MacNab and the Welfare made a front for the adoption, and this was all that mattered.

Her ample person, topped by the inevitable toque, filled the living-room door. The ox-eyed Ceres, Lucian called her—and today she came bringing plenty (or so Judith fervently hoped) to this house. Actually it was Mrs. Maguire, behind Mrs. MacNab and Lorena, who brought the child over the threshold.

"Good evening . . . won't you come in?" Not all Judith's pride could stiffen her quavering voice.

Mrs. MacNab came right up and pressed her hand. Lorena, to her relief, merely nodded and said, "Hello," then took the baby from Mrs. Maguire, and finding herself a chair, she sat down and settled him in her lap. He looked doubtfully about the strange room.

Well, she'd brought him anyway. . . . Judith found her tongue and hospitably bustled Mrs. Maguire and Mrs. MacNab into comfortable seats. For a moment they all fixed their attention on the child, twittering the inanities that people imagine a baby comprehends.

"Hello there, little one, how are you doing?" *Anything* you say sounds inane, Judith thought frantically. She stopped at Lorena's chair and laid her hand timidly on the child's arm.

His flesh felt cool and exquisitely soft. She longed to pick him up, but there, close to her hand, she saw Lorena's full arms wound tightly around the square little body . . . for a dizzy moment she felt that, secretly, they both had hold of him and were about to pull him apart. . . . She swung back from the hysterical image and straightened up.

"He feels hateful, that's how he feels," Lorena was saying in her smiling, downright manner. "He raised Cain all the way down. Looked like he had his head set against coming here."

Judith felt the thrust and colored, but she clung to her resolve to say nothing that might jeopardize the outcome. She took a moment lighting a cigarette, then said quite steadily, "I've already signed the papers, Lorena. They are there on the desk, when you want to sign them."

Lorena did not move. Still holding Red securely against her body, she was frankly examining the room. Judith could not see her averted face—whether it was critical, envious, or just curious. Mrs. MacNab said, "You'd better look those papers over; you can't leave it to a lawyer, in my experience. There are all sorts of things men would never think of, though that's what you pay a lawyer for. . . ." She took out her pince-nez, set them briskly on her nose and crossed to the desk. Standing beside it, she began a close perusal of the papers.

Lorena was all dressed up, Judith observed, easily interpreting the feminine idiom of her clothes. The plaid taffeta was out again, and she had borrowed Vinny's pink kid bag to complete the ensemble. Whom had she dressed up for? Not Mrs. MacNab, not Mrs. Maguire. . . . For Judith then? Surely her boundless self-confidence didn't need such armor. She had dressed the baby up, too; the cotton cloth of his suit glistened with newness, she must have spent a lot on it—all those pearl buttons and rows of white braid. This pride, this lawful exhibitionism touched Judith, but she couldn't let herself be unstrung by it—not yet.

She forced herself to say something, for the silence was becoming more and more awkward. Lorena was still withdrawn, gazing now through the open door into the dining room. Mrs. Maguire sat wordless on the sofa, holding her handbag upright with both hands and looking as if she were going to cry.

"What a swell new suit the baby has on!"

Mrs. Maguire smiled tearily. "Ain't it, though; he sure looks cute when he's dressed up. I got his clo'es here—" She produced a bundle and unrolled it on the sofa beside her. Some shirts, some faded sun-suits and one or two shapeless sweaters. . . . Judith was unprepared for the poor little bundle.

Her face must have shown her dismay for Mrs. Maguire said hurriedly, "He ain't got so much now 'cause it's summer, a child don't need so much clo'es in summer."

"Of course not! The fewer clothes the better—he needs lots of sunlight on those arms and legs. Did you give him the cod-liver oil?"

Mrs. Maguire drew in her mouth to a tiny pucker and wagged her head from side to side. "I tol' you Red wasn't gonna take no oil."

"But he'll *have* to take it—he needs it."

"You don' know Red, Mis' Redcliff. He's got his likes, and he'll eat all right if he gets what he wants. He likes plenty bread an' cake."

The baker of the Borough . . . coming up from the floury past! Judith held on to herself and said, "Well, we'll see. . . ."

Mrs. MacNab rustled the papers and looked round. "These seem to be in order except for one thing. I don't see that you're protected from the child's father; you've got to remember that the father's family may make some claim to him. . . ."

The words jerked Lorena out of her abstraction. She and Judith exchanged an agitated glance. "The father's family—I don't expect any trouble from them," Lorena said after a pause.

"But you'll have to protect Mrs. Redcliff," Mrs. MacNab persisted. She took off her glasses and moved forward. "That paper has a hole in it, as I suspected."

Lorena looked Mrs. MacNab up and down. Visibly, it seemed to Judith, she put on her old manner, her canned but superb confidence. For the first time she let go her clutch on the child, and spread her arms languidly on the arms of the chair. "My Dad helped fix up these papers, an' if he says they're O.K., they're O.K. So don't you wear out your brains on them, ma'am."

Mrs. MacNab tilted backward as if she felt a light blast in her face. In addition to everything else she especially disliked the vulgarism O.K., Judith knew.

"This adoption is being arranged through the Welfare Society, and it's my responsibility to see that the child is placed in a good home and that the foster parent is protected—"

Lorena set the child down on the matting and stood up. The sharp movement disclosed the tension that had kept her unnaturally silent. She took several quick, driving steps. "Sure— Judith's got to be protected. That's fine. But who's gonna protec' me? I don't see anybody worrying 'bout me. I have to look out for myself, and I guess she'll have to do the same."

"I'm perfectly satisfied with the papers," Judith exclaimed. "There's no reason to delay any longer. If you are satisfied, Lorena, please sign them and let's settle it now."

"That's what I say—le's get this over with." Lorena changed the direction of her pacing and made a rush for the desk.

A dreadful fascination dragged Judith over to her side. Lorena sat down and looked at the papers, but Judith saw she wasn't reading the words before her. Her bodily fullness, which was so knit with her assurance, seemed to dwindle very slowly like a leaking balloon.

"Where am I 'sposed to write?"

Judith pointed to the line.

Lorena looked up at her. "Does this mean—for good?"

Suffocation closed Judith's throat. No—this is too cruel! she wanted to cry. I can't shut you off from him forever! But another voice said, It has to be so. The terms must be clear. Otherwise you are only laying up trouble.

She looked down at Lorena. "Yes . . . I'm afraid it does. Do you want to change your mind?"

A startling sound broke out behind them. Mrs. Maguire was bawling, unabashed, "Oh, me . . . oh, me . . . don' give away the pore little thing, Rena . . . a mother's got a right. . . ."

Lorena spun around. "What kin I do?" she cried. "I can't raise him decent where I'm goin'. I want him to have a good home like —like he's got a right to!"

"I tell you, you kin leave him with me!" Mrs. Maguire wailed. "I'll give him a Christian home till you kin sen' for him."

Lorena answered with a long stare, seeing the Christian home of Mrs. Maguire. She turned back to the desk and signed.

Judith looked hard at the back-slanting characters with their flourishing capitals. So it was done. A surge of vertigo overtook her . . . from thankfulness or dismay? She went off a step or two.

Mrs. MacNab came up and laid her hand on Lorena's shoulder. "Don't think, my dear," she said with genuine feeling, "that I don't know how much it means to you to give up your child. It's a terrible choice, but I'm sure you've done wisely—that you're thinking of him and not of yourself."

Lorena slipped out from under the burden of Mrs. MacNab's sympathy. Finding Judith in her path she halted, and for a moment they teetered on the brink of a dizzy fall—into unbridled emotion, into tears, into each other's arms. But long rivalry and pride made a counterweight; so they teetered, between centrifugal and centripetal forces, and remained standing a foot or so apart.

Mrs. MacNab made a tactful diversion. "Come along, Mrs. Maguire; we have to witness the signature." She mopped at Mrs. Maguire's copious eyes, bustled her over to the desk and found the place for her.

"Shall we all have something cool to drink?" Judith asked.

Lorena drew an uneven breath; it made a queer noise there beside Judith. "I sure could use one."

"All right—would you like to come and help me—" She nodded toward the other room, offering a refuge.

In the pantry the business of glasses and ice and bottle openers covered the dangerous chasm. Judith had a silly feeling that they *had* gone over, that they had all been walking and talking upside down like people in Australia, and were just swinging back. But there was still something she felt she had to say before they returned to the perpendicular.

"Lorena, I give you my word that I'm going to do everything I can for—for Red; you must think of him as being loved and wanted. I never had a child of my own, so I'm going to love having him—"

But Lorena had that abstracted air again, and her silence gave Judith a twinge of the old hateful feeling she had had long ago at The Hangover, when she found herself ignored and excluded. Lorena continued her deliberate appraisal of the linoleum and the china-cupboards.

"You got a nice place here," she said slowly. "I always wished I could see what kind of home Fen had, but of course I never could get to see it."

The white pantry bulbs searched out her look as she turned— the look of a child with its face pressed against the plate glass window of a bakery. Judith found herself, astonishingly, inside among the bright lights, looking through the clear glass at Lorena, not so young, really, under her make-up, and starting out now for the third time. . . .

"Lorena! What are you going to do? Have you got friends in Detroit—who can help you? If there's any way I can help—"

Lorena shouldered off the naked emotion in Judith's voice as she had shaken off Mrs. MacNab. She smiled, poured out a drink, and lifting the glass, measured it with a practiced eye. "Don't you worry 'bout me, honey. Sure, I got good frien's in Detroit, I can always get a job; it jus' takes a little know-how. . . ." She rolled her eyes and took her drink in a long gulp.

Judith could never learn to gauge the O'Dell manner, either its sincerity or its effrontery. She gave it up and said, "Let's take something in to the others."

In the living room Mrs. MacNab and Mrs. Maguire were amicably discussing the Welfare. Mrs. MacNab refused the whisky Judith poured and took ginger ale. "In my position I don't feel that I should take intoxicants," she explained, "though I have no personal objection." Mrs. Maguire looked longingly at the whisky but fearfully at Mrs. MacNab, and declined also in favor of ginger ale.

Judith set the tray down on the sofa and turned to Lorena. "There are so many things I wanted to ask you about the baby, and now they've all flown out of my head. By the way, I hope you don't mind my changing his name."

Lorena looked surprised. "You don' like Red? I think it's sort of cute—it kind of suits him."

"Well—I don't mind the 'Red' so much; it was the Astor I was thinking of."

Lorena flashed one of her broad smiles. "Oh, that! I guess you might as well change that now. I had to jus' pick a name, and I thought Astor might help him sometime—you never know what might happen—and it sure looked like he was gonna need all the help he could get. But, Red, ol' boy—I guess Redcliff is pretty near as good as Astor, hey? Though it don't have such a rich crunch.

"Well, what do you say we get a move on, Mrs. MacNab? I'm gettin' ready to blow the town tomorrow and I got a lot of important business to wind up. Goo'by, sonny—" She stooped over Red where he was playing on the matting and kissed him with no display of emotion.

Judith had a toy ready for this moment. She took it from the mantel, a giraffe made of wooden blocks. Red looked at it in amazement and was instantly diverted from the grown-ups.

"Good-by, Judith," said Lorena, but she was looking at Red. "Don't spoil him too rotten, hear?"

"Good-by, Lorena, and good luck!" The plaid taffeta fluttered in the doorway and disappeared.

Mrs. MacNab settled her toque before the mirror and bade Judith an affectionate good-by. Mrs. Maguire heaved herself out of the sofa; the highball had somehow vanished from the glass beside her. "Oh, Mis' Redcliff! For the love of God be good to the pore little motherless . . . the pore little fatherless. . . ." Red's status was too much for her anguished tongue.

"I will—I will, Mrs. Maguire. . . ." From the hall door Judith watched them clattering along the piazza and out into the street.

Red tore the neck off the giraffe and joyfully beat it on the matting.

Judith lingered in the door, absorbed in Lorena, in her new pity, in the break-down of the legend she herself had invented.

She gave a little gasp and went back to the living room. This was the moment she had been really dreading.

Red still sat on the floor, bemused with the severed members of the giraffe. It seemed incredible that he hadn't seen the lightning that had been playing above his head. His profile was turned to her; his straight hair had been ruffled by Lorena's parting embrace, a wisp stood up on his forehead like a wicked little horn. His mouth was drawn in with fanatical absorption in his toy, like Fen when he was mending his tackle or taking a fish off his hook.

"God . . . I can't go through with this! Lorena! Wait—" Forgetting her lameness, Judith flung across the room. But before she had reached the window she knew it was an act of desperation; they would be half-way down the block by this time.

Her movement startled Red. His head came up, he looked about and found himself alone with her. His outcry tore the room apart.

Cursing herself for frightening him, Judith hurried back. "There, there, darling—everything's going to be all right. . . ." But her quaver was thrust back into her throat by the volume of his roar.

She picked him up and began to walk, making placating noises in his ear. He threw himself about with such a lunge of his strong back that she barely got him to the sofa before she dropped him.

"Good Lord!" Judith took a deep breath and snatched up the legs of the giraffe. "Here, baby—look at these lovely legs. . . ."

At this outrage to common sense, Red settled down to scream in good earnest. With his constitution he could probably keep up this din all night. Judith sprang up in a cold panic . . . but how do you stop them? . . . how do you stop them? . . . there must be *some* way!

There was only one way, to shout louder. "Shut up, you little fiend!" Judith threw herself on the sofa and shook him. "I don't like you any more than you like me! But I've got to learn . . . you've got to learn . . . we've just *got* to learn to get along; nobody can help us now. . . ."

She found a queer sort of excitement in the thought. Her passage into the future was still breakneck, but even as she skidded along she felt her life between her hands again. The child's crying lost its piercing quality. She took him on her lap and held him loosely, letting him squirm, struggle, and tire himself. He still cried, but formally now, saving face, testing his ability to bully her with his lung power. No doubt he wanted the sugar-tit. "You won't get it," she said, flushing with the argument beginning at once between them. Suppose he turned out badly, or suppose he never learned to love her! A frightening experience—being born into motherhood. She suddenly remembered the first time she had seen Red at the Welfare. "Maybe he's a changeling," she had said to Mary Bonneau . . . with arrow-like intuition, it appeared. For so he was, a changeling at her hearth, far different from the smiling child of her wish-dreams. But far crisper and more provocative. . . . The lights in the room seemed to go up a little as if from some hidden source of candle-power; the yellow and gray chintz, she noticed in this challenging clarity, had worn out its time; it would have to go, the new furniture covers would have to be practical, planned (like everything else in her life) to withstand marauding hands and feet. Red made himself comfortable against her and his demand set up a flow from her body to his as warm and direct as milk.